MARKED BY THE GODS

Finding Sanctuary Book Two

Natasha Madden

Magic Mist Publishing

To all those readers out there who love living in a fantasy world… Who want a touch of magic with their morning coffee..

CHAPTER ONE

Oh, shit!!

The room goes deathly quiet. My lips part in shock as I turn my head, peering up at Lukas. His expression mirrors mine. Through our bond, I can sense his concern and wariness. Nerves flutter wildly as I look back to the god in front of us and raise an eyebrow in disbelief.

"Hades?" I question, surprised by how steady my voice is.

"Yes," he replies, inclining his head ever so slightly. He never breaks eye contact, not even to blink. It's incredibly intimidating and unnerving.

"As in Hades, god of the underworld? That Hades?" I ask again.

I need clear confirmation here that the damn god of the underworld is standing in front of us.

"The one and only," he smirks, and oh, man. He is gorgeous. Like drop dead, set your panties on fire gorgeous. Just what you'd expect of a god. He's taller than Lukas, but not by much. Also, somehow leaner. Though Lukas certainly has more muscle. Hades's dark onyx hair is short and styled messy, and he carries himself with confidence. And, while his posture and outward appearance is relaxed, his sharp golden eyes are hard.

"You look just like your sister," he observes, his deep voice filling the silence, jerking me out of my dazed state.

"I'm sorry, what?" My words tumble out at once.

Worry tightens my stomach. How does Hades know my sister? My hands tighten into fists at my sides. The pain from my nails digging into my palms is helping me stay focused. I really don't want to adult anymore today. I just want to curl up with a big bowl of ice cream and worry about everything tomorrow. My eyes narrow on the god standing in our entryway, preventing me from having a pleasant night.

"You have a delightful home," he says, continuing on as if he didn't hear my question.

Lukas bows his head at the statement and my brows creep up my forehead as I stare at Hades in confusion.

"You're speaking about Leila? Where is she? What have you done with her?"

"I've done nothing with her," he replies, nonplussed, placing both his hands in the pockets of his black dress pants. The black-on-black ensemble suits him. It strikes me that he looks more like a billionaire CEO who might be featured on the cover of a romance novel than an ancient god.

"Tell me where she is, then. It's been a long fucking week, and I'm tired," I half whine, half growl.

Lukas's arm bands around my waist, drawing me back to his side and holding me in place.

'Don't challenge a god, Nesrin. I realize that you want answers, but we have to be smart about this.'

Hades mouth quirks and his eyes glimmer with amusement at my outburst. "You understand it's only Tuesday, right? Your week is going to be much longer at this rate," he smirks.

I blink in surprise. Is he teasing me?

Lukas clears his throat, squeezing my waist. "Let's just hear him out."

"You should listen to him, you know," Hades points out, laughter coating his words.

I shoot him a dark look, completely confused right now. I want to know what he has done with my sister. Then Kaida's words come back to me. *There was another who wanted Blanchette—a god.* Was it him? Hades?

"I thought you guys were a myth?" Asena blurts from somewhere behind me.

Hades's smile stretches as he regards everybody in the entryway, as if noticing them for the first time, but we know he had everyone pinned the moment he appeared.

"Considering you have a legacy as a luna, I'm surprised you think that. We most certainly exist. Everything you've heard about us is real." His golden eyes light with laughter as he shrugs his shoulders casually. "Mostly exaggerated, though. There are many gods, deities, creatures, and monsters from legend that do actually exist."

I gawk at him, speechless. Is he serious? They all exist? I mean, I have seen creatures and magical beings from all mythologies, but I haven't really thought about it. As a witch—I mean legacy—I have to stop thinking some creatures are simply myths or legends.

Hades's piercing gaze swings back to me, pinning me to the spot, my body locking up in anticipation of what might come out of his mouth next.

"You, Nesrin, come from Greek roots, but your time growing up in Ireland, however short, has given you a . . . How would you say it?" He seems to mull over his words before continuing. "You've become a beacon of light for the magical beings there; the banshee, the puca, the kelpies. Even the fairies and sprites are sticking close to you."

An unintelligible sound climbs up my throat, and I blink rapidly as my thoughts jumble. "Beacon of light?"

"Yes, my dear. You signify change to come. They gravitate toward you for many reasons, each varying, but mostly because you offer protection whether or not you realize it."

Zee stalks forward, his ears pinned back, a menacing growl rumbling from his throat. He moves past me, brushing my legs. I reach a hand down and grip his fur in warning.

'*No, Zee.*'

'*He has Leila,*' he growls back.

'*We don't know that yet,*' Lukas interrupts our silent exchange.

"You realize it's rude to have a conversation between yourselves when you have company." Hades's eyes flash in annoyance and Zee growls again. The god's jaw hardens as he rocks back on his heels.

Letting out a soft sigh, he shakes his head. "I'm only here for my dog, nothing else. It seems someone left the gates to the underworld open and lured poor Cerberus here, among other things."

As if hearing his name, the hellhound howls, three sounds mingling together. The sound is haunting and eerie. A loud crack of splintering wood sounds from outside, followed by the thundering of paws. "There goes the barn door," Lukas sighs, letting go of my waist to rub his forehead. My hand moves to his arm in a comforting gesture. I just keep causing trouble for him and his pack. Well, it's technically our pack now, but still. We can't seem to catch a break, and it's all my fault.

I turn back to Hades, planting my hands on my hips. His smile is unsettling. I press my lips together as my frustration mounts. After a moment of silence, I gesture at the door behind him.

"Well, he isn't in the house." Exasperation coats my clipped words.

Lukas's body stiffens in response to my tone.

Hades's smile evaporates, golden eyes flashing in warning. "You'd do well to remember who it is you're speaking to," he cautions, causing the hairs on my arms to stand on end.

Heat flares in my cheeks, and I open my mouth to reply, but Lukas steps in front of me. I bite down hard on my bottom lip to keep from saying something else and cross my arms. It wouldn't be good to get into an argument with Hades right now. *Maybe another time.*

Lukas's amusement floats down the bond as he moves toward the front door, brushing past the god, and opens the door, motioning him outside, his face set firm.

"Very well," Hades says, turning and strolling out the door. I follow behind him and we all make our way onto the porch, Hades walking straight down the stairs toward a very excited Cerberus. The hellhound is jumping and dancing circles around his master.

"Okay, boy. Calm down," his silky voice is soft, but edged with command, and Cerberus stills and sits. Hades rubs each of the three heads, murmuring too low for me to hear. It's clear to see that he loves his hellhound. I don't know why that surprises me so much.

My eyes flicker to Lukas, his glare aimed at the god of the underworld.

"What do we do?" I whisper.

Before Lukas can reply, I hear the others gasp. I glance to Finan in question, but it's Zee who responds.

'Incoming.' His growl is practically a groan, his long sharp fangs glinting in the moonlight.

My gaze whirls back to Hades, only to see Cerberus charging toward us. "It's okay, he won't hurt us," I say, though uncertainty flickers through me.

The others withdraw a step, but Lukas and I hold our ground as the beast skids to a stop in front of us, giving us a few wet licks across the face.

"Okay, okay. Stop, Cerberus," I groan, covering my face with my arms. Lukas laughs and steps behind me, his hands gripping my hips as he holds me there.

I glance at him over my shoulder. "Really, using me as your shield?" I try to feign outrage, but I can't hold back my smile.

"Against a slobbering dog, yes."

"He likes you," Hades's voice cuts through our mirth. We both glance over, and I'm startled by the predatory look on his face, even though his stance is casual.

"He doesn't like anyone but me and my kin," he replies curiously, tilting his head at us.

Lukas moves back to my side, my hand immediately reaching for him in search of something to ground myself. Lukas glances down at me and the expression he gives me has my stomach flip flopping. It's pure sin.

"I appreciate you looking after him, but I'll be on my way now. Cerberus." A portal begins to form behind him, all the shadows seeming to converge on him like he is gathering them to him the way Leila did earlier.

I step forward. "Wait."

"Yes?"

"My sister, where is she?" I ask with a bravado I don't really feel.

Hades stares at me for several seconds, unblinking, those golden eyes burning into mine.

"She is in Hades at this present moment, recovering from her run in with the wraith that was hunting the children earlier by the river. Then, I believe she will return to the Order to continue her job."

Huh? I'm stunned into silence. I open my mouth several times to speak, but nothing comes out. I narrow my eyes and Hades grins.

"Ah, I see. You thought she was my prisoner," he claims, a smirk taking over his handsome face.

"I'm so confused," I respond, my heart accelerating. My brain is struggling to sift through everything I've learned, which isn't much at this point.

"I can see that," Hades smirks.

"Why would my sister go to Hades to recover?" I ask.

"I rescued your sister from my brother's vendetta when her own family abandoned her. Leila is my kin, my ward, and she is safe with me."

My breathing falters. "What?" I whisper, moving closer to Hades. "I didn't even know I had a sister until a month ago."

Hades's expression darkens. "Your parents elected to forget one of their children. To hide the fact that one of their triplets ever existed.

They assumed she died along with her grandparents that night and erased her from all of your lives. Though, I suppose that you're not to blame for that."

My world tilts, and I sway as my legs buckle. Lukas's arms shoot out, wrapping around me. Without his powerful arms holding me up, I'm sure I'd be crumpled on the floor. I try to concentrate on his firm, warm body against mine to keep myself from spiraling, but my emotions well up.

I was never a twin at all. I'm a triplet?

My parents abandoned her, made Niamh and I forget about our sister. We never even got to mourn or remember her. *I don't remember her.*

A strangled sound escapes me as my chest cracks in half. *What must she have thought of us?*

My body heats as my emotions spill over, a glow is emanating from me, a white haze dotting my vision again.

'Breathe, sweetheart.' Lukas's voice resonates through the fog as he tries to communicate with me through our bond.

What happened to her? Why did my parents lie to us? I have so many questions. Questions no one can answer.

'It's okay. We will figure it out,' Lukas replies in my head, and I realize I must be projecting my thoughts.

"Leila informed me of the breach. The monsters who have escaped are yours to deal with, but I have contained the situation at my end. I expect you can handle it." I don't understand how Hades's voice reaches me through the roar of blood pounding through me.

Lukas glares at Hades. It's such an imposing glare that even I want to hide. "We will be fine," he clips out, clearly pissed off with the god of the underworld.

I can barely see through the white haze coating my vision. It is a struggle to contain my magic. It slips through my fingers, and I grasp for it with my mind, trying to draw it all back into me. The need to release it is overpowering. I've never had this amount of magic build up before, and certainly not this quickly. The flow is too much. But I don't know what would happen if I just let it go. I double over with the effort to keep it in my grasp. Panic and desperation rise swiftly, and Lukas holds me close to his body, his strong arms banding around me.

"It's okay, Nesrin. Let it go. I got you, I swear."

I must have made a noise, some kind of distressed whimper, because Lukas's hand grasps my chin firmly, tilting my head up to his.

"I thought I couldn't love you more than I already do, but sweetheart, I know for a fact I'm going to love you more tomorrow and the next day and the next," Lukas whispers to me.

My whole body sags at his words, the white haze receding. I see Hades turn toward the portal, beckoning Cerberus to follow. He doesn't seem the least bit fazed or even surprised by my meltdown. His golden eyes lock on mine.

"You should listen to Althaea and put that pendant on. It will help you control it." Then he's wrapped in shadows, Cerberus at his side as they both disappear.

Shit, that asshole just left. I have questions!!

"Hey, sweetheart, look at me." Lukas lightly cups my cheek. I turn my head, and the moment his stormy green gaze meets mine, magic stops pouring in, the proverbial bucket stops filling. His eyes soften. "You with me?"

"Yeah," I croak, and instead of bursting out of me, my magic slowly begins to drain out. It seeps from me into the ground at my feet. I watch in awe as the ground soaks up the magic, lighting up as it does. I wonder if the others can see what I see. I feel Lukas through the bond, his love, warmth, and unwavering loyalty—it fills my heart. The surrounding ground glows with magic, slowly spreading outward. As the magic disappears, it's replaced with sprouts. I watch speechlessly, as meadowfoam flowers rise and bloom from the ground where my magic soaked in, like a carpet of white and gold.

"What the fuck?" someone says from behind us.

Lukas's arms release me and together we turn in a slow circle. The flowers surround us. A circle of them grows, reaching about to my waist. I reach out and tentatively touch one, reveling in the soft texture of the petals.

"Wow," I breathe.

How is this possible? I've never had my magic overflow before, and I have most definitely never seen it grow things.

My mother's voice resounds in my head, her soothing voice ringing clearly. *Meadowfoam blooms where the tears of gods fall . . .*

That doesn't make sense. My mind drifts back to Leila and my heart thumps painfully in my chest. I need to see my sister.

The sound of shifting hits my ears before Zee bellows, "Seriously, what the fuck, Nesrin?"

Lukas's responding growl holds authority behind it. His power rolls over the ground, silencing everyone as he spins on his beta. Ignoring Zee's outburst, I reach down, running my fingers across the flowers again. How am I ever going to control these powers if doing so means unlocking more? No one can tell me exactly how much magic I should expect to be dealing with. I glance up and see Lukas standing there, concern lining his eyes. Zee seems pissed off, and everybody else just looks stunned. The last ten minutes have been hectic, chaotic, and eye opening, to say the least.

Finan moves toward me, his bright blue eyes full of worry. "Are you okay?" he asks in a soft voice one might use with a wounded animal.

I shake my head and turn away, wiping at the tears on my cheek.

CHAPTER TWO

I gnoring everyone, I race inside and up the stairs, bursting into our bedroom. I go straight for the suitcase in the corner that I still haven't unpacked, falling to my knees before it. Ripping the zipper open, I push aside the clothes that are still in there, my hands shaking uncontrollably.

"Where is it? Where is it?"

Butterfly wings flutter along my mind as I sense Lukas coming up the stairs, his worry bleeding down our bond. He probably wishes he had a normal mate, one who isn't so much trouble. My shoulders droop at the thought. I am nothing but trouble. The last few months prove it.

Strong arms wrap around me from behind, and I'm lifted from the floor as if I were no more than a child. Lukas takes a few steps back and sits on the bed, placing me across his lap.

"You are my perfect match. You are a strong, smart woman who takes care of everyone around her. I wouldn't have any other," he whispers into my neck before laying a tender kiss on our mating mark.

My heart flutters in response, my mark stirring along my skin.

I bite the inside of my cheek to stave off the tears burning my eyes. "Are you sure, because I am–"

"Beautiful. Irresistible. Mine," he growls, cutting me off. "You found your way to me. Through all the odds, you found me, and damn if I let anything take you away from me, even yourself. Everything that has guided you here was for this, for us. You were meant to be here. And no matter what happens, we will always find our way back to each other. Always."

Our gazes catch and hold. My heart thumps loudly in my chest at his words, at his unwavering confidence in us. I am lost for words. What can I even say to match that? I drape my arms around his shoulders, and using our bond, I send my feelings out to him. Lukas's green eyes flare, squeezing me tighter as he gets right in my face, our noses touching. I swallow over the ball of emotions sitting in my throat as I look back at him. His scent wraps around me like silk, brushing against my skin. Between his scent, his voice, and his nearness, my body is overheating with need.

"Nesrin, my love for you is the one thing you will never have to doubt."

The tender expression on his face contradicts the hardness of his voice.

My eyes drift shut, and I lean into him, my chest filling with warmth.

"I love you," I whisper, resting my head on his shoulder. I breathe in his scent as we sit there in silence for a few minutes.

Pulling back, he brushes the hair from my face. "Are you okay?"

I know he's asking about what Hades said about Leila. Am I okay? No, I don't think I am. They hid my sister from me; my parents, Hades. But why? Why did my parents never mention her? They never talked about my grandparents, either. When we came to America, it was literally a new start, a clean slate. And we got by in peace for ten years until their murder. I wish Leila—or Emerson, as she goes by now—had stuck around, but instead she disappeared into a swarm of shadows.

"I honestly don't know. But what I do know is we are going to need to talk to my sister. And most definitely Marcus to see what he knows. If she has been undercover in the covens . . ."

Lukas's groan interrupts me, and he rests his head against mine.

I can't stop the small smile spreading across my face.

"You will have to learn to get along," I say, placing a soft kiss on his lips.

"Do we?"

"Yes."

"For you, I will try."

"That's all I ask," I reply.

Lukas pecks me on the lips before looking over at my suitcase. "You were looking for the pendant?"

"Yes, I figured I should, maybe consider putting it on."

"You don't sound so sure."

I untangle myself from his lap and stand to pace the room, my hands twisting my hair as I walk.

"I'm not. I don't know what will happen. Grace hinted that it unlocks some sort of power. Hades said it will help me balance the flow of magic. And Althaea . . . "

I let out a heavy breath and run my fingers through my messy hair, gripping it. "Althaea said I have to accept my fate, be willing to unlock my power and restore balance. Whatever that's supposed to mean."

Dropping my hands, I face Lukas. Frustration builds in my chest, tears stinging my eyes, but I refuse to let them fall.

"Lukas, I'm afraid. I don't understand anything anymore." I gesture to the window. "We had the god of the underworld here not ten minutes ago to collect his dog. Seriously, this is our life now?"

Lukas stands, walking over to me, and places his hands on my shoulders. Bending, he brings his eyes level with mine, his stormy green eyes soothing me somewhat.

"Breathe, freckles. It's okay, everything is going to be fine. We are in it together, remember? If this is our life now, then I'll happily take it, as long as it means I get you."

I bite my lip. "Why do you have to say the sweetest things when all I want to do is have an epic meltdown?" I mumble, disgruntled.

Lukas chuckles, rubbing my arms.

I sigh, nodding over at the suitcase. "Can you find the pendant for me?"

"Sure can, sweetheart."

Lukas captures my face with his palms. He leans down and brushes his lips over mine in a tender kiss, his hands circling around my waist, pulling me hard against his body. His lips leave mine, trailing a path across my jaw to my ear.

"You are extremely hot when you go all glowy."

Laughing, I pull back, looking up into his sparkling green eyes. "All glowy?"

Nuzzling my neck, he hums "Mmmhmm . . . "

Lukas's hands slip under my shirt, pulling it up and sliding it off my body.

"We should get downstairs and have a meeting about what happened tonight," I whisper, finding it really hard to concentrate with his lips and tongue moving over my skin.

"They can wait. My mate needs me more." He pulls the cup of my bra down, sucking my nipple into his mouth. I arch my back and sink my hands into his hair, a moan falling from my lips.

"Lukas . . . " I breathe, and just like that, the whirlwind of emotions brought on by today's events disappears, leaving me consumed with desire.

"Yes?" he answers, moving over to my other breast.

But I don't have any words. I tug at his hair, bringing our mouths together again in a desperate kiss. Our hands work quickly to shed our clothes. Lifting me into his arms, Lukas turns, placing me on the bed, and slides inside of me like he can't wait another minute. One of his hands moves up my back and fists my hair, making my back arch. Lukas's lips and teeth lavish my neck and mouth. I am lost. Completely swept up in what he's doing to me.

My pace is slow as I make my way back downstairs, Lukas close behind me. I will my face not to heat with embarrassment. The fact our friends were in our house while we were upstairs makes me flush. A light smack lands on my ass, and my eyes widen. I spin around to face Lukas.

"W– what the hell?" I stammer, heat rising to my cheeks.

"You have nothing to be embarrassed about," he says, winking at me as he strolls past me into the living room where we can make out the murmurs of the others. I let out a low growl and follow him into the room. Gabe and Asena are standing by the door. Merve, Finan, Kate, Alex, and Roan are seated on the other chairs around the room. Zee paces by the window. With everything that's been thrown at us tonight, I hope he's okay.

'Always thinking about others,' Lukas's deep voice says in my mind.

The wingback chair closest to the fire is free, and Lukas takes a seat there, patting his leg. I arch an eyebrow at him and walk over, planning to sit on the floor. Lukas must have read my intentions because he snatches my wrist, tugging me down onto his lap. I snuggle back into him as I face the others.

Finan looks angry and worried all at once. I don't blame him. Everyone seems to be waiting for me to speak, but I don't have a clue what to say.

I twist my fingers together and give them a weak smile. "Crazy night, eh?"

"Oh, do you mean the new dragon you acquired? The hellhound? Or maybe it was the vampire running to your rescue? Oh, no, wait. The god of the fucking underworld showing up. That is the crazy part, right?" Zee goes off, his voice rising with each new point he throws my way.

I cringe at his harsh tone and a little hurt creeps into my chest. I resist the urge to cry. I am their luna. I won't let them see me break. Lukas's growl vibrates through my body. I squeeze his leg, letting him know I can handle this.

I draw in a deep breath and steel myself. "Look, Zee. I know it's been a lot to take in." Before I can continue, he barks out a humorless laugh.

Pain and anger mingle in my chest, but I push on, determined to not let him get to me. He is hurt and irritable.

"It's not like I invited them here. I didn't know this would happen, and I'm sorry I'm bringing it all to your doorstep. But after a good night's sleep, everything will look better in the morning. I have to find Leila and talk to Marcus. They have to know more about this order. And yes, we have a new pack member in the form of a dragon, but we are a pack of misfits. What's another, right?" I smile, hoping to lighten the mood.

Asena leans forward in her seat. "Watching you light up like a firefly was amazing, and then the magic just fell down your body like water into the ground." Her eyes are wide as she stares at me.

"You saw that?" I ask, tension spreading through my body.

Everyone nods, curiosity evident on their faces. "We've seen your hands and eyes light up before, but not your whole body," Gabe says, reclining back in his chair.

"It was a little unnerving, if you ask me," Roan says, rubbing the back of his neck.

"Sorry?" My voice is uncertain, causing Alex to laugh.

"Why? You were a light show. That was a massive amount of magic you showed back there. You just let your emotions control you. That is something we can work on," Gabe says with ease.

"I could live without seeing Hades or Cerberus again, that's for sure. They both have creepy stares that seem to creep into your soul," Alex adds with a visible shudder. Roan looks down at her and frowns, wrapping a gigantic arm around her. The hulking redhead is very protective of her.

I recall those intense golden eyes, the way they seemed to track everybody's movement. I run a hand through my hair and sigh. "He was pretty intimidating. Those eyes were absolutely unsettling."

"And what's with the flowers?" Merve mentions, speaking for the first time since I entered the room.

I peer over at him and shrug. "I don't know. That has never happened before. Any of it."

Finan paces, his biceps flexing as his fists clench and unclench. "Nesrin, I don't think I can leave with so much going on."

I sigh, my shoulders dropping a fraction. "This isn't your fight, Finan."

His eyes whip to mine and flash yellow. "Like fuck it's not."

"Watch your mouth when you're speaking to my mate!" Lukas snarls.

Finan drops his head. "Sorry. It's just . . . I don't like leaving when everything is up in the air."

Kate stands and moves to her brother's side. "Finan, you need to go back. Lukas and Nesrin can handle this, and they aren't alone." She places a hand on his arm, and he looks at her. So much emotion clouds his eyes. My heart throbs in response. I haven't thought of this from his point of view.

"I already lost a brother, and now I just found my sister and niece. Forgive me if I have a hard time leaving you all behind. I feel like I'm running from battle. Leaving you all, it feels wrong." His voice is hoarse, and I want to go to him and hug that big caring mountain of a man. So, I do.

Finan's arms wrap around me and hold me tight. His cheek rests on top of my head and I sense him deflate as he concedes, "Please call me if you need anything."

"We will, I promise."

We reluctantly break away from each other, and I return to my spot on Lukas's lap. His eyes are like pools of warmth that envelope me as he pulls me back down to him. As his strong arms wrap around me, I'm filled with contentment, my heart bursting with love.

Gabe talks about upping training, and Zee agrees. Lukas absently strokes my arm, and every so often his fingers thread through my hair, gliding through the curls. I fight to stay awake, utterly exhausted. They move on to patrols and new recruits. Alex and Roan are the first to leave. I murmur goodbye, unable to do more than raise my head. Lukas's body shakes with laughter.

'Go to bed, sweetheart,' he whispers in my mind.

I mumble something and admit defeat just before my eyelids droop. I must have fallen asleep, because the next time I stir, Lukas is carrying me up the stairs.

CHAPTER THREE

I am so tired I can barely keep my eyes open as I make my way down the stairs. Astraea sees me first and runs for me. I scoop her up in my arms and hug her tightly to me.

"Morning, sweet girl," I hum, breathing in her scent.

Her tiny hands reach for my hair on either side of my face, and she holds me close, our foreheads touching. I love the way she does this. It's always been like this since she was a baby.

"*Missed you,*" she says into my mind.

"I missed you, too. Did you see our new family member?" I ask, remembering that I put Malachite in her room last night before Hades showed up.

She nods her head eagerly, her excitement chasing away my exhaustion.

"She made us breakfast as well," comes Lukas's voice from the kitchen.

Frowning, I make my way down the hall toward him, really hoping there is going to be coffee in my near future. I draw to a halt in the doorway. The sight that greets me sends laughter bubbling up in my throat. I widen my eyes as I look at Lukas, who is standing with his hands on his hips, surveying the mess around him. His dark hair is all tousled from running his hand through it, no doubt.

I notice Malachite on the table, curled up in the fruit bowl. How he finds that comfortable, I do not know.

I bite my lip and turn my head, looking into Astraea's wide, innocent blue eyes, her expression one of hope. "You made us breakfast?" I ask her, pushing the laughter down.

She nods her head enthusiastically. '*Uh huh! Buts I spills a little bits milk.*'

I grin at her thoughts on *little* and face Lukas, who has turned his back to us, his shoulders shaking with laughter, and my cheeks hurt from holding back my own. I glance around the kitchen and see a trail of milk that leads from the fridge to the table, where more milk is pooled. The empty milk carton sits in the middle of it. There is cereal scattered across the table in what looks like an attempt to get it in two bowls. The loaf of bread looks completely squashed, as if she used it to stand on.

A tug at my hair has me meeting a set of now worried blue eyes. '*Is you mad with me?*'

"What? No," I assure her, hugging her close.

Lukas moves over to us, kissing her on the head, then placing a soft peck on my forehead.

"Of course we aren't mad at you, little star," he says, ruffling her hair, and I realize she is speaking to both of us together telepathically.

Giggling, she wiggles in my arms, and I put her on her feet. She runs for the table, climbing up and sitting next to the bowl of fruit with a side of baby dragon. Her tiny hand reaches out, stroking him, and the dragon leans into her touch, lapping up the affection.

Lukas wraps his arms around my waist, drawing me back into his chest. "So fucking adorable," he murmurs in my ear as we watch Astraea and Malachite.

The dragon stretches his legs out, then darts forward and up Astraea's body, nestling under her mass of blonde curls, his tail wrapped loosely around her neck for support. Astraea squirms and giggles.

'*Tickles,*' her voice echoes in my head.

She has been wanting a pet, one that we could have with a pack of shifters, and although Malachite isn't a pet—he's a family member—he is perfect for my girl.

"Let's get out of here," Lukas says. "Will you go on a date with me tonight?"

I spin in his arms, my hands landing on his chest, excitement bubbling up. "Really?"

Lukas tips his head back, laughing at my eager response. "Yes, sweetheart."

"Hell yes!" I exclaim, bouncing on my toes.

With everything that's happened since we met, we haven't actually had a chance to go on a date yet. I can hardly contain my excitement as I push on my toes and kiss the man of my dreams. Lukas's arms pull me tighter against him, my fingers running over the planes of his chest and around his neck. I feel loved and protected in his arms. I can't imagine being anywhere else.

Guilt rushes in a moment later. "What about all the monsters and creatures that got loose? Shouldn't that be our priority?"

"Sweetheart, you are my priority. And I have organized patrols. If anything happens, we will know. But I haven't taken my mate out on a date, and I really, really want to. Finan and his pack leave today, so we will see them off, and then tonight I'm taking you out for a nice meal. Just the two of us."

I melt, an enormous smile breaking across my face, making my body feel lighter than it has in months.

"Okay," I whisper.

I reach up, placing my hands on either side of his face, drinking in the gorgeous sight of him. Standing on my tiptoes, I pull his head down. Our lips touch softly, leisurely. Lukas's hands roaming my back and waist as he pulls me in closer, until we hear Astraea squealing and break apart to see Malachite sliding around the table in the puddle of milk.

Sweat drips down my back as I adjust the dagger in my grip. "This is a stupid, dumb idea," I grumble, dodging the hit Gabe throws my way. We circle each other, my bare feet slipping on the grass. But a shirtless Gabe is a bonus.

Gabe raises an eyebrow, his almond eyes widening in amusement. "You do realize you just said that in my head, right?"

My cheeks heat, and I make a face. "No, I didn't."

"Yep."

"You're just trying to distract me," I say, stepping forward and lunging out with the dagger. Gabe deflects my blow easily and smirks.

"A shirtless Gabe . . . " he sings, his eyes flashing with laughter.

"Okay, shut up!" I blurt, embarrassment flooding through me, making me accidentally drop my dagger in the grass. "So, what if I did?" I snap, bending to retrieve it.

He drops, swinging his leg out, taking my legs out from under me. I land on my side in the grass and scowl up at him. "Seriously?"

He holds out a hand, and I take it. He easily pulls me to my feet. I brush the dirt off my clothes, trying not to make eye contact.

Gabe laughs. "You randomly blurt your thoughts out all the time, so it's probably a given you will do it telepathically as well. But if you do it with your telepathy when you don't mean to," he shrugs, "then you may get yourself into uncomfortable situations. That is all I'm saying."

"Oh."

I know I have to work on my connections with everyone. The pack links have finally settled in. After I was able to connect to Zee that night in the forest, the others all just sort of fell into place. Now it's a matter of sorting it all out in my mind. But I didn't realize before that stray thoughts have been leaking out that way as well.

"Will you help me control it?" I ask Gabe, cringing because this is the last thing he probably wants to do.

"Of course I will." He claps me on the shoulder. "We can make it part of our training. You should be training to fortify your mind anyway, after what you went through with the coven."

I groan. "Oh, goodie."

Gabe laughs. "Don't sound so happy."

"Why do I even need to train?"

"You know why."

Gabe lifts his hands, taking up a fighting stance. Smirking, I toss my dagger into the air, catching it before moving into position. We aren't allowed to use magic or shift. This training is all about defense and offense. I need to be able to fight without my magic, and I can, but not well enough, apparently.

Gabe moves fast, his hand gripping my shoulder. I allow instinct to take over. Twisting around, I kick out. Surprise flashes across his face, and he drops his hand just in time to leap out of the way.

"Nice," he praises.

Bouncing on my toes, I adjust the dagger in my grasp. "Thanks."

Before the word has even finished forming on my tongue, Gabe is on me again. I barely have time to block the blow he's aimed at my face. He's pushing me back step after step, blow after blow. The hum of magic dances just beneath the surface, begging to be used as I can sense my anger building with each hit. I push it down, not giving in to my impulses. I trip over my feet as I take a step back, and Gabe kicks out, his foot connecting with my chest, sending me sprawling across the dirt.

Straightening, Gabe looks down at me.

"You can do better than that, Nesrin."

He turns away, walking back toward where we started, and anger burns hot through my veins, clouding my judgment. I jump to my feet and launch myself at him, using my speed. Sensing my movement, Gabe spins and catches my hand, swinging me around so I face away from him. My arms are pinned to my sides for a second before he pushes me away, my dagger falling uselessly to the ground again. My breathing is harsh and choppy as I spin around. Without thinking, I wrap my magic around him, binding his arms to his sides.

His eyes flicker with surprise, but he recovers quickly, a smirk pinching at his lips. "Magic?"

Frustration wells up inside of me, and I lift him from the ground, tossing him a few feet into a pile of leaves.

Gabe stands with a grace I envy. A few leaves cling to his hair as he walks toward me. "Feel better?"

I groan, tipping my head to the sky. "I'm sorry."

"Tantrum over with?"

I glare at him, and he laughs.

"Yes."

"Good. I think we can stop for lunch, and then we can work on the telepathy after."

I reach down, collecting my dagger, then walk over to Gabe. He slings his arm over my shoulder. "You know, you're different from most girls."

"I'll take that as a compliment."

Chuckling, Gabe drops his arm. "You should. And by the way, you have a little dirt here," he says, pointing to his cheek.

I frown, rubbing at my face, making Gabe's smile widen.

"Did I get it?" I ask.

"Not even close." He chuckles before turning and walking away.

CHAPTER FOUR

Sliding my foot into my black boots, I pull the zipper up and stand in front of the mirror. The boots are a favorite of mine, black suede with the top lined with fur. I've paired them with burgundy jeans that are fitted perfectly to my ass. I don't really have any nice tops, so Asena lent me a deep v-neck strappy tank made of black silk. It feels like cream against my skin, pure, unadulterated luxury. And, of course, I throw my usual black leather jacket on over the top.

Asena heard about the date and came over to help with my hair and makeup. I haven't had someone help me get ready for a date since Niamh, and it felt so nice to have that again. Asena did an amazing job, I have never felt so beautiful before. My long auburn hair falls down to my waist in a cascade of curls. The makeup she did is light and natural, but makes my amber eyes shine like jewels. It's as if I am a different person. My stomach clenches in anticipation. I am so ready for this date.

Finan left before lunch, leaving Kate and Roan here with us to help us fight for whatever is coming our way. I could tell he really didn't want to leave us here. He has become the brother in my life I've always longed for. But as much as I may want him here, and as much as he may want to stay, he is the alpha of his own pack and they need him back. I'm not selfish. I have plenty of people here to help me. Everything will be fine. I refuse to believe anything else. My Viking brother-in-law will just have to deal.

My eyes drift over to the wooden box on the dresser, to my crescent moon pendant I know will complete the outfit. Lukas found it among my clothes and placed it there this morning. Every time I enter the bedroom, the wooden box seems to vibrate with energy. Calling to me, to my magic. Bringing my hand to my mouth, I bite my thumbnail as I take small steps toward the dresser. I stop in front of the box and slowly reach out, my fingers tracing the patterns etched into its surface. Taking a breath, I click it open, staring down at the pendant. I gently run a finger over the star hanging from the top point of the moon. The hum of magic coming from it is so strong it sends a pulse of warmth through my finger and up my arm. I draw in a sharp breath, feeling my eyes widen and snap it closed just as Lukas walks in. He halts in the doorway, his gaze drifting from the box in my hands to my eyes, then slowly tracking down my body, pausing on my cleavage boldly on display. As he catches sight of my boots, a grin tugs at his lips.

"Cute boots," he says.

The heat from his gaze temporarily fries my brain and I forget how to speak. Lukas stalks over to me slowly, his eyes never straying from mine. Reaching up, he tugs my bottom lip free from my teeth, running the pad of his thumb over it.

His voice is rough when he speaks. "You look beautiful, Nesrin."

"Thank you," I breathe.

The way he is looking at me with such intensity steals my breath and makes my pulse kick up. I feel like a schoolgirl swooning over a hot guy right now, as butterflies take flight in my stomach. This man always turns me into mush with one look, one hitch of his lips. It isn't fair.

Lukas brings his mouth to mine, moving his thumb as our lips meet, the kiss warm and soft. He kisses me as if we have all the time in the world; slow and sweet, exploring every inch of my mouth. I am completely breathless when he breaks the kiss, his lips lingering an inch from mine.

"I can't wait to undress you."

"Well, you promised me a night out first." I laugh before coming to my senses and stepping back.

"That I did. You ready?" Lukas chuckles, the sound warming my insides. Desire floods my body and the mate bond, turning Lukas's eyes dark with hunger, a growl rumbling up his throat. Knowing that if I don't break free of this moment we won't be leaving, I turn and place the box back on the dresser. I hesitate.

Stop being such a baby. Just put it on. What's the worst that could happen? That's right, I have no idea. No one knows.

Lukas steps closer, boxing me in against the dresser. I stare up into his bright green eyes, noting the worry in them. He leans down, getting in my face. "Put it on, sweetheart."

"What?"

"Put it on. I'm here with you. I won't let anything happen to you."

"I'm scared."

"I know, but I'm here," he replies, wrapping a curl around his finger and giving it a gentle tug before letting it go.

I blow out a breath. He's right. It is time.

"Okay," I groan, and with shaky hands, I reach for the box and open it. Lukas reaches inside and plucks the chain up, unclasping it. Our eyes lock, as I pull my hair over one shoulder, then his hands go around my neck and fasten the necklace. His fingers follow the chain down to the pendant that is now sitting between my breasts. I give him a weak smile and slowly release the air from my lungs.

Lukas seems to hold his breath, waiting. My chest warms as magic pulses from the pendant. It glows lightly as I absorb its energy, causing everything to tighten and tingle. Then a popping sensation, like a release of pressure. I reach up, putting my hands on Lukas's chest to keep myself grounded. The glowing recedes, and the humming dies down as the pendant settles against my skin.

"Are you okay?" Lukas asks, his eyes darting between mine, trying to read me. I seem fine, I think. I am less tired, lighter somehow.

"I think so," I say, blowing out a deep breath.

We wait in silence for a few moments, and I can't help but grumble, "Well, that was anticlimactic."

Lukas barks out a laugh, "Don't sound so disappointed. I, for one, am grateful the light show was minimal. Now I think we could use some downtime, don't you?"

He captures my hand and leads me down the stairs and out the door. I see Lukas's motorcycle parked at the base of the steps, and a giddy squeal leaves my lips as I spin to him. "Tell me we're taking your bike," I say, clasping my hands under my chin.

Lukas smirks, making his way to the bike, and grabbing the helmet. "Yes, we are taking the bike. I want you close to me. Now come here and get this helmet on."

I bound over, unable to hide my excitement. I've only ridden on it once, and at the time I was too worried about Astraea to really enjoy it. Lukas places the helmet on my head, fastening the strap. '*You good?*' he asks.

'*Yes.*'

He winks and turns, getting on the bike. I throw my leg over, climbing on behind him, then wrap my arms around his middle, but obviously not tight enough. Lukas grabs my wrists gently, pulling me closer, flush against his back.

'*Hold on, sweetheart*' is all the warning I get before Lukas takes off, dirt and gravel flying everywhere as we speed down the driveway. My heart hammers in exhilaration, and I tighten my grip around Lukas's middle. Laughter bubbles up my throat in excitement as we take the windy forest road into Portland.

CHAPTER FIVE

"**A**nything else I can get you?" The young blonde server's voice is sweet and silky.

She hasn't addressed me once during our time here. Her eyes have been trained on Lukas all night. Honestly, I can't even be mad. Lukas is hot. Especially in his black button-up shirt with the sleeves rolled up to his elbows, showing off his muscular forearms. I lightly trace over the tattoos on his left arm while he politely converses with the flirty server. He remains courteous, and doesn't look below her neck the entire time, not once. Even when, to my utter annoyance, she unfastens a few buttons to show off the edges of her lacy black bra.

Lukas's green eyes ignite as he looks at me. "Did you want dessert?" I don't miss the innuendo in his tone.

Leaning on the table, I rest my chin in my hand and smile. "Sure."

My cheeks hurt from how much I've been smiling tonight. This has been amazing, and with Grace and Merve taking Astraea tonight, we can really relax. I'm still a little shocked by that development. That for once I'm able to push all my worries aside for a night. Of course, they'll all still be there in the morning, but I need this. I need a night of normalcy with my mate.

Lukas hands the server the menus and orders the chocolate cake and ice cream to share. She flashes him a smile and touches her blonde hair. I roll my eyes and chuckle. Lukas's eyes find mine again. "What's so funny?"

"If you don't know. I'm not cluing you in." I grin.

Lukas reaches over the table and tugs on a curl. "You are stunning, especially when you're smiling."

I can't help the flutter in my chest and the heat that rises to my cheeks. I lean in closer and bat my lashes at him. "You aren't too bad yourself."

Lukas's eyes darken with desire, but before he can respond, his not-so-subtle admirer returns with our cake. Placing it on the table, she stands there for a moment, twisting her apron. I can't bite my tongue this time.

"That will be all, thanks," I say, beaming at her.

For what feels like the first time, she looks at me and blinks. "Oh, yes. Okay." Embarrassed, she scuttles away. Lukas tips his head down, his hand covering his mouth, the small fork hanging from his fingers.

"What?" I ask.

"I love you."

I melt in my chair. "You better."

Lukas's grin widens and my breath stalls. *Damn, he's hot.* Especially with that dimple showing.

His head tips back, and he laughs. Dammit all, I said that out loud. Oh well, it was worth it. He has the best laugh. I press my lips together, trying to hold back my own laughter. I pick up a spoon and dig into the cake, smiling around a mouthful of chocolatey goodness.

Lukas's laughter tapers off, and he smiles at me, the dimple still on display. I love him with his short beard, but I also love being able to see his dimples.

We finish the cake in a few bites, a perfect ending to our meal. I grab a napkin and wipe my mouth before scrunching it up and tossing it on the plate. Looking up, I spot the server spying on Lukas from her workstation and roll my eyes. We'd better go before I really go all possessive and ruin the night by making her cry.

"Ready?" I ask sweetly.

Chuckling, Lukas stands, pulling out some money and throwing enough to cover our meal and a tip on the table. Then he holds out his hand for me to take and helps me stand.

"After you, freckles."

Spinning on my heels, I lead the way out of the restaurant, his hand warming my lower back the whole way. When we're outside, Lukas's hands grip my waist, spinning me around to face him. His fingers slip under my jacket, caressing the silk top. Goosebumps scatter across my skin, and I fight back a shiver. His green eyes are ablaze with desire, making my pulse kick up. When he looks at me like this, it's like an electrical current going through me. I can feel it down to my bones.

"You're perfect," he says, dipping his head.

When his lips meet mine, a sense of belonging hits me square in the chest. This man is everything to me.

"No one's perfect," I reply when we pull apart.

"Well, you're perfect for me, then."

I can't help the giant grin that takes over my face. We make our way down the street, his large hand swallowing mine. I feel happy and content, a sense of peace that has been missing from my life since Niamh died. My cheeks ache a little from the smile I can't seem to wipe off my face. Flirty waitress and all, this has been the best night ever.

'Even better than our mating?' Lukas asks. I glance at him in surprise. "You're so happy that you're not filtering your thoughts; you're shouting them at me. I love seeing you this happy."

I open my mouth to reply when the pendant pulses. An icy cold touch blooms in my chest. I reach up, gripping the pendant tightly in my palm as I try to sort through what I'm feeling.

"Are you okay?" Lukas asks, sensing my discomfort.

The weird sensation in my chest increases, taking my breath with it. We round the corner, and Lukas pulls me in close to avoid a man coming the other way. I drop the pendant as my hands grab hold of Lukas, the cool weight of it settling on my chest. The man looks up, his bloodshot eyes staring at me. He looks down at my pendant, his eyes widening in surprise before lifting to mine. I watch as he takes a step back, raising his hands in front of him as if to warn me off. A second later, he spins, running back the way he came, his long coat billowing behind him. He doesn't spare me a second glance before he is around the next corner, my pendant lying normally against my chest again, the icy sensation dissipating. What was that?

"That was weird."

"Very," Lukas agrees. He crowds me against the wall, and I tilt my head back, looking up into his handsome face.

"What did you feel?" he asks.

I think about it for a second, trying to put my feelings into words.

"It was strange. My pendant pulsed, and my chest felt like it was cold. So cold it took my breath away."

"And your eyes started glowing."

I jerk against his hold. "What?"

Shit, that can't be good, especially out in public. I glance around, but Lukas is blocking my view of the street.

"That vampire took one look at you and ran the other way," he chuckles lightly. "He didn't even spare me a glance."

My eyes widen and my mouth drops open in surprise. "That was a *vampire?*"

Lukas nods, a thoughtful expression crossing his face. "Let's go. I want to test something out." He steps away, grabbing my hand again.

"Okay. Want to clue me in?" I ask.

"Nope."

We make it a few blocks in comfortable silence, both of us in our own thoughts. Music hits my ears and I gaze up at Lukas with curiosity. "A club?"

He grins down at me and winks. "Yep."

"Man of many words," I joke.

He smirks down at me, and my heart skips a beat. Lukas's grip on my hand tightens, and he tugs me past the line of people to the front, where a massive bouncer is blocking the entrance. Seeing Lukas, he nods and moves aside to open the door. The line of people behind us groans, and I smile. I have never had the luxury of skipping the line before. I catch the eye of the bouncer as we pass and notice the glamor surrounding him, his horns standing out clear as day for me. *Holy crap,* I wonder if Lukas realizes the bouncer is a demon.

Lukas pulls me through the door into the dimly lit club. My mouth drops open as I look around, seeing so many mythical creatures. The sweet smell of magic hits me, making me dizzy. There are a countless number of spells spinning around me, mostly glamor spells, hiding the true natures of the creatures here. I've never been able to identify them so easily before. Unless they're using a spell or glamor to hide their true appearance, I'm not usually able to tell. Like Grace and Blue, neither uses glamor to hide what they are, so I never knew.

"How do you feel?" Lukas inquires, his gaze zeroing in on me with an intensity that makes me pause.

I think before answering.

"Fine, I would–"

I don't finish my sentence, my words cut off by the blast of cold that hits me in the chest. Icy fingers wrap around my heart, squeezing almost painfully. I draw in a sharp breath, and I stare out at the crowded dance floor. The cold sensation seems to be urging me forward. A soft light emerges from my chest and glides around the bodies of dancers until it reaches the private tables in the back.

"Do you see that?" I yell over the music, then remember Lukas has exceptional hearing.

Leaning down, he talks in my ear. "What do you see, freckles?"

"I think my pendant unlocked something in here," I tap a finger to my chest. "The light is guiding me to something."

Lukas straightens and scans the area. Looking back at me, he shakes his head. Okay, so just me, then. The feeling in my chest grows desperate, tugging me forward again. I move through the dancers, getting a few odd looks as I go, but then they spot Lukas at my back and step away. My light disappears behind the curtain of one of the private areas.

Tensing, I point it out to Lukas, "There's a vampire in there. That's where I have to go," I whisper, knowing Lukas will hear me. I don't know how I know it's a vampire, but I do.

I move, needing to follow my instinct, until I'm standing in the darkened alcove to the secluded dining area. As my hand lifts to the curtain, my phone dings with an incoming message. I pull it from my pocket and see it's Grace.

'Nesrin, are you okay?'

I frown down at my phone and quickly type out a reply before pocketing my phone. I take a deep breath, and my hand slides across the smooth texture of the sheer fabric. Gripping it tightly in my hand, I tug it aside and step into the alcove. I halt mid step as a chill runs down my spine, making goosebumps scatter across my skin. I focus my eyes on the back of a tall man, who has a pretty blonde girl held against the wall. His large hand covers her mouth, and he looks to be drinking from her neck. The girl notices me, and as our eyes lock I feel her desperate plea for help radiating from her hazel eyes. Vampires can make the feeding pleasurable or painful for their victims. This one doesn't seem to be doing either.

Lukas's warm hands land on my waist as he moves us further into the alcove. *'I've got you, sweetheart.'*

Lukas gives my waist a gentle reassuring squeeze, letting me know he's there and he won't let anything bad happen. I take a deep, shaky breath as the curtain falls shut, concealing us away from the rest of the club. I take comfort in Lukas's presence and focus my attention fully on the vampire in front of us. Lukas clears his throat, the sound echoing off the walls of the room.

If not for the slight tightening in the vampire's shoulders, I would think he doesn't hear us. He continues to feed, and that icy sensation explodes outward, causing me to gasp in panic.

"It's rude to ignore people," I snarl, shocking myself with the harshness of my voice.

"It's rude to interrupt one's meal," the vampire replies, straightening up and ever so slowly turning around. His tongue darts out, licking the blood from his lips, his canines gleaming in the low light. When his eyes fall on me, he freezes, looking taken aback. It doesn't take him long to gather himself though, totally ignoring Lukas's presence behind me.

"Well, hello. Aren't you a gorgeous creature?" he says, looking me up and down.

Lukas's fingers spasm on my waist. I can tell he wants to throw me behind him. Protect me. But he also knows I can take care of myself. I love him even more for letting me take control of the situation. Plus, through our bond I can feel his curiosity about this new development in my magic.

I roll my eyes at the vampire's words and take in his appearance for myself. His features are sharp, angular. His head of thick blonde hair is cropped short, styled artfully. The red is slowly bleeding away from his eyes, leaving their original color of cerulean ringed in silver. I flick my gaze to the girl who is now sagging against the wall, looking dazed and confused.

"Why don't you run along?" Lukas says, motioning to the girl. She nods, taking the escape while she can. She brushes past me, whispering her thanks.

As the pendant pulses in warning, I feel my magic surge through me. It's as if the pendant is sending me a warning of impending danger. I blink, my mouth falling open slightly on a inhale as sudden clarity washes over me. I almost felt it the moment whatever has been waiting dormant inside me is unlocked. I can sense the darkness emanating from others, my inner light instinctively responding to it. And suddenly it occurs to me that Lukas brought me here to test exactly what it is that I was sensing on the street earlier. Why the vampire felt the need to run away from me. My light expands, a subtle hum reverberating around me. I feel a strong desire to wrap the vampire in my embrace and let my light surround him. I feel the chill of adrenaline in my veins and a bead of sweat forms on my forehead as my eyes lock with the vampire.

His elegant face morphs into one of shock as he takes me in properly, realizing I'm not here to play.

Suddenly, my vision shifts, and the world takes on a different hue. I tilt my head slowly, as the darkness within him becomes visible to me. I study the black inkiness swirling inside of him, how it's overtaking what little light he has left. Like a ball of chaos pulsing in his chest. Out of instinct, I take a step forward, reaching my hand out to touch his chest.

Startled, he jerks back. "What are you doing?"

I take comfort in having Lukas at my back, a solid wall of protection, backup should things go sideways. Another tug in my chest pulls at me and then another. It's all so overwhelming that I sway on my feet, and Lukas's arm wraps around my middle to hold me steady.

"Your eyes are glowing again, sweetheart," he whispers against my ear, his hot breath sending shivers over my body. But my focus remains on the vampire, his unique eyes studying me with disdain.

The vampire scowls at me, making a noise of disapproval, and it's as if he can somehow read my intentions before I know what they are myself. He steps back and I move without thinking, lunging for him, the insistent pull in my chest giving me the strength to break Lukas's hold. My hands grip his face, my eyes locking on his, as my fingers sink into his thick blond hair, and I close my eyes.

This vampire is full of darkness; so much hate, anger, and loathing. Whether at himself or the world, I'm not sure. As a witch, I've been taught that dark and light need to exist together to balance each other out, and this vampire doesn't have much light left. I can't stop myself from doing what comes next as warmth flows from my body, encasing him, my light reaching out and wrapping around his darkness. It doesn't engulf it so much as it balances it. My magic dances with his darkness, the two tugging and pulling at each other until they reach a true harmony. An act of embracing darkness and light, perfect duality. A sense of peace washes over me, and I realize it's his feelings. I have healed his darkness. It doesn't seem so thick anymore.

When the balancing is complete, we break apart, panting. The vampire stands there, eyes closed. Lukas moves in front of me, putting his back to the vampire. I know he isn't at risk, but does Lukas know that? He bends, his face coming within inches of me, his green gaze searching mine.

I swallow hard, my voice coming out croaky. "What?"

"Are you okay?" he asks, his tone serious.

"I think so?"

"Rose sauvage, I hope you have a good explanation for what just happened?" Stephan's silky voice floats in from behind me. I turn as Lukas steps between Stephan and me, but I can feel through the bond that he's unsure where to place himself with me and two vampires.

The vampire I confronted stumbles forward, falling to his knees at my feet. "What did you do?"

I gulp and freeze. "I uh . . . "

"I have never felt such peace. Thank you." His face is filled with wonder as he looks at me in awe. "What can I do to repay you?"

Startled, I try to take a step back, but his hands grip mine, holding me in place. Lukas's growl reverberates the air around us. The small alcove only offers so much privacy.

"There is no need for that," I say, trying to pry myself free. The vampire leans forward, resting his head on my hands. I look to Lukas and Stephan for help, but both wear perplexed looks and seem to want to see how this plays out.

My chest tightens, and I can sense something settling there. Closing my eyes, I follow the feeling. I can see the threads of magic, the pack. But . . . Oh no. That can't be good. I see the threads in my mind, the bonded links I have with Zee, Gabe, and the other members of the pack. Since accepting my position as luna of the pack, I have had a connection with each of them. They are my pack, I am their luna. I am bonded to them. Not like my mate bond with Lukas, but similar. And there, next to those threads, a new bond is forming. I follow that thread, and it leads me to the vampire on his knees before me.

My eyes fly open as I gasp. "No way," I whisper.

"Nesrin?" Lukas asks, moving closer.

I can sense his confusion and concern as if it were my own.

Shit, I am in so much trouble.

"Quite possibly," Stephan agrees, his voice dropping a few octaves.

The blonde vampire at my feet looks up, his cerulean eyes ringed with red. "I pledge my allegiance to you, ma reine. I am yours now."

At his words, the new thread settles in my chest and seems to send a ripple down the other links. Lukas's eyes widen, and he appears, dare I say, horrified.

"Did you just make him pack?" His voice is calm, too calm.

"What? No?" I look at each of them. "Did I?"

Stephan tilts his head, regarding me carefully. "My office. Now." The words come out clipped and harsh before he turns and walks away. I stare after him, then back to Lukas. A mask has fallen over his features. I try to get a sense of what he's feeling down the bond, but he seems to be muffling it.

Yep, so much trouble. I tip my head back, gazing up at the ceiling and taking a few deep breaths. Lukas steps up to me, his chest against mine. His hands rub my arms as he tilts his head down to meet my eyes. "I don't know what you just did, but we are in this together, remember?"

I feel the wind leave my sails, so to speak, and I sag against him.

"So, you're not mad?" I ask.

"Oh, I'm mad."

"Oh." I swallow over the lump in my throat.

"Come on. We better see what the master of the city has to say about you stealing one of his vampires."

I startle, taking a step back. "Master?"

"Yes. I didn't want to tell you before and have you freak out, but now it seems like important information."

"You think!" I screech.

"He won't hurt you, ma reine," the vampire behind me says in an accent that sounds like he may be French.

I spin and look at him. He's standing again and I realize how tall he actually is. His lean form is dressed in an impeccable suit.

"What's your name?" I ask, reaching for Lukas's hand. Love floats down the bond to me as his fingers link with mine, sending a sense of calm washing over me.

'*Together*' is whispered softly in my mind.

The vampire smiles affectionately at me, and I can't help but shuffle on my feet. Having him stare at me in such a relaxed and intimate way makes me nervous.

"I am Nikolas," he introduces himself, walking toward us. He reaches for my other hand, and Lukas's chest rumbles with his growl. Even so, the vampire lifts my hand to his mouth, kissing it. "We must not keep him waiting."

The vampire, Nikolas, drops my hand then simply walks out of the alcove and into the club, Lukas's fiery gaze following him. As soon as we step out of the alcove, the music comes roaring back to my ears. I guess I was able to somehow block it out back there.

"You sealed the alcove with your magic," Lukas whispers in my ear.

I jerk back, frowning. *I don't remember doing that.*

"Well, you did."

"But Stephan?"

"You can't stop a master with a simple spell in his own establishment, freckles."

Lukas leads me through the club toward the back, where Nikolas is patiently waiting for us by a door marked: Staff Only. He holds open the door, allowing us to pass through before him.

We come to a halt in front of a plain black door and Lukas knocks twice.

"Come in."

As the door swings open and we start to walk in, my mouth falls open. The room is huge, the furnishings luxurious. Stephan is standing at a small bar in the corner of what appears to be an elaborate office, pouring himself a drink. Without turning, he offers, "Care for one?"

"Make it a double. No—triple," Lukas says, walking over and sitting on one of the lounges.

Surprised, I cross my arms and raise an eyebrow at him.

"What? I think I deserve it," he says, his eyes following the blonde vampire as he enters the room behind me.

Stephan takes his time, his movements slow as opposed to the rushed movements I would expect from someone who is angry. I wish I knew what he's thinking. I shift on my feet, getting antsy with nervous energy.

"Come sit down," Lukas says, patting the seat next to him.

I swing my head his way and bite my nail. I'm not sure I can. Lukas gives me a soft look as he relaxes back in the chair. Releasing a soft huff, I relent and walk over, plonking down next to him. His hand lands on my thigh and squeezes gently in reassurance.

"So," Stephan starts, turning with three drinks in his hands. He hands one to Lukas, the other to Nikolas. "What exactly did you do to break the blood bond between me and my vampire?"

My mouth opens and closes. "I'm . . . not sure."

"Try explaining it to us," Lukas coaxes.

"There was a tug in my chest. It was cold. Different from my usual healing magic—that's warm. The coldness grew the closer I got to Nikolas. It was like it led me to him. My light reacted to the darkness in him. I needed to balance it, heal it. Make them coexist equally. It's hard to explain."

Stephan eyes the other vampire with interest. "How do you feel, Nikolas?"

"The lightest I've felt in centuries," he replies.

Lukas's phone rings, but he ignores it. It goes to voicemail, and immediately rings again. Sighing, he pulls it out of his pocket and answers without seeing who it is. "Yes?"

"We will talk about it when we are back." He hangs up.

Stephan's expression turns to amusement. "Your pack felt it, too?"

Lukas purses his lips, nodding, and my stomach drops.

"They know what I did?" I whisper.

"Yes, but it will be fine," he says, patting my leg. I bite my nails as I glance around the room. Shit. I am far out of my depths right now.

"Can you both guarantee Nikolas's safety?" Stephan asks abruptly.

Fiery anger surges through me at the implication in his words. "Of course!" I snap, then turn to Lukas. "Right?"

Lukas sits up, resting his elbows on his knees as he eyes Nikolas. "Are you going to be a problem?"

Nikolas looks affronted. "No."

"Since you're a part of our pack now, you are allowed on pack land, but there will be rules, and of course, I'll ask that you wait until I have a chance to . . . " Lukas seems to consider his next words " . . . smooth things over. This was unexpected."

Nikolas bows his head in acknowledgment. "I understand."

"Good."

"I will remain in the city. I will be here whenever you have need of me. Night hours, of course."

I turn to Stephan, finding his gaze unreadable as he sits back in his chair. He looks so intimidating, those magnetic eyes staring directly into mine, unblinking.

"You have no idea what you've done, do you, rose sauvage?" his deep voice drawls.

Goosebumps scatter across my body, and I suppress my shiver. He really doesn't sound happy.

After a shaky breath, I answer. "This is new to me. My power has always leaned toward healing, but . . . " I trail off. I still don't understand what happened. My light had sought out the darkness, picking who needed saving. Then I brought the dark and light into balance within Nikolas. He has duality now, a conscious choice on how to act.

"This is new. I usually only heal physical wounds. This is the first time I've ever healed someone of the darkness tainting their soul," I repeat, as I let a quick breath out in astonishment, gazing at Nikolas.

"And I thank you for it." He smiles softly at me and bows at the waist.

Stephan stands from his chair. "You have taken someone from my line, someone I care for. Someone who has been with me for a long time." A hint of a growl sounds from the back of his throat. His eyes flash magenta and Lukas stiffens next to me. Nikolas casually moves across the room, standing in front of Stephan.

"My friend, nothing changes. You have known I needed help for a long time, and despite your attempts, nothing you've done has helped me. I understand you feel you've lost me, but I will always be here."

Stephan's eyes dim just slightly, and he gives Nikolas a curt nod. "I apologize."

Nikolas shrugs, the act so human it catches me off guard. "At least now you won't have to put me down. I fear I was extremely close to losing all of my humanity."

"I would never do that!" Stephan snaps incredulously, his eyes flashing again. Like the thought of killing his friend is unbearable.

"You would have had to, and you know it."

Stephan's jaw clenches, and he looks away. Nikolas lays a hand on his shoulder, giving it a squeeze, before turning and taking Lukas and me in. "I shall wait to hear from you. Thank you again, ma reine." He gives us a small smile.

"Wait! What does *ma reine* mean?" I ask, the words sounding nothing like the way he pronounced it as my native tongue butchers the French accent.

Stephan chuckles and moves back to the bar. Nikolas grins and continues toward the door. Before he closes it behind him, he whispers, "My queen."

CHAPTER SIX

When Lukas and I pull the motorbike to a stop in front of the house, I can sense the group of pack members waiting inside. Zee is angrily pacing the front porch, talking animatedly to Gabe, who is leaning back against the railing. I can't see his face, but I can feel his amusement from here. I take a long, deep breath as I swing my leg over the bike, Lukas following. My fingers shake as I reach for the strap on the helmet. Lukas's fingers brush mine aside and he unclips it. Then he slowly slides it off my head and runs his fingers through my hair, smoothing down the wild strands. The ride back was spent in silence, both of us lost in our own thoughts. Stephan isn't happy I've taken one of his vampires. Apparently the feeling is a painful one, on Stephan's side, and for that I do feel badly. I didn't mean for any of this to happen.

"Everything will be fine, freckles."

I chew my lip, looking toward the house at a fuming Zee, and I cast a quick glance to Gabe. I'm surprised when I see his smile and the wink he sends me before slapping Zee on the back and hauling him inside.

Lukas's hand cups my face, his thumb tugging my lip free from my teeth. He bends down so his eyes meet mine. "Together."

I nod, squaring my shoulders. "Together."

I don't have time to draw in a breath before his lips capture mine and his arm sweeps around my waist, yanking me against his hard body. My arms slip around his neck, fingers sinking into his hair and running through the thick strands, making him growl and nip at my lips. Liquid fire heats my veins at the sound, and I want nothing more than for him to carry me upstairs and do extremely naughty things to me, but the pack's irritation leaks through my lust-filled haze, bringing me back to earth.

We part on a sigh. "You ready?" he asks.

"No."

Lukas grins and holds out his palm. Hand in hand, we walk up the stairs and into the house. My first assessment is correct. The house is indeed packed full of shifters, each in various states of concern. Lukas leads me into the main room, making his way to the fireplace and turning us to address everybody.

Everyone is talking over each other. It is loud and chaotic. I peer up at my mate with troubled eyes. I can tell his irritation level is rising only because I can feel it. His face is a blank mask of indifference. I would love to know how he keeps all feelings from showing on his face.

"Tonight, we discovered something new."

He lets the pause linger as he glances around the room. "My mate, your luna, is an extraordinary healer. I know you all sensed a new member enter our pack tonight."

Voices rise all around, making it difficult to pick out what's being said. My panic rises, swift and nauseating. Shit. I knew they wouldn't be happy. I've made a mess of things again. My stomach clenches in anticipation and I swallow back the bile threatening its way up my throat as I draw my shoulders back. All I have to do is show them everything will be okay.

"ENOUGH!" Lukas bellows, all hints of softness vanishing from his voice. This is the voice of an alpha. His stormy green eyes flicker with hints of yellow as he takes in the room. Reminding me of a lightning storm raging over the ocean. "She is your luna, my mate, and she has earned the right to be respected."

My eyes find Gabe in the crowded room, and his gentle smile has my shoulders relaxing slightly. He, for one, doesn't seem to be worried about the anger rolling from Lukas, who is extremely pissed off right now. My gaze then shifts to Zee, who is standing next to him, arms crossed, a heavy frown on his face.

Lukas continues, his voice firm, "Her gifts are to be respected. Tonight, she healed a vampire of his darkness, and yes, that vampire was brought into this pack. We did not know this was possible, but Nesrin just likes to keep me on my toes," he says, tilting his head a little, his eyes meeting mine.

My heart gives a hard thump, and I am flooded with a mixture of tenderness, love, and amusement all balled up together. I stand there, dumbstruck, and his smile grows. I blink in surprise when his dimple appears, my face heating. Holy cow, this man is a weapon all on his own.

Lukas turns his attention back to the room. "By now, you should all know that, when faced with a hard choice, Nesrin always comes out on top. Not because she chooses the easy option, but because she never gives up. She will always fight for the underdog, not basing her choices on whether it will be difficult, but whether it is *right*. You all know this. Tonight was no different. She had a choice to make, and she chose compassion. For that, I'm grateful. Grateful for a mate who has a heart of gold. Nesrin does not discriminate, and we, as a pack, shouldn't judge her for that."

"He's right," Jameson speaks up, rising from his chair. "Nesrin has done nothing but have our backs. It's only right that we have hers."

Jameson's hazel eyes burn into mine, his mouth twisting into a grin. "She is our luna. She deserves the benefit of the doubt."

I smile at the young shifter. His boyish looks remind me of a young Brad Pitt.

"But she made a vampire pack," someone yells from the back, and I cringe a little at the anger in their tone.

Lukas bristles, but I quickly step forward, grabbing Lukas's arm to halt his words.

"I did. And I know you all have a lot of questions, but I'm unsure of how exactly I did it. I thought at the time that I was balancing his darkness with my healing light. But somehow, during that process, a link formed between us. I haven't had a chance to talk with Lukas about it yet, and once I do, maybe we will have more information for you."

"Will he be staying here?" Zee asks, stepping forward. I look toward him, feeling down the bond we share. Other than Lukas, my connection to Zee is the strongest in the pack. All I sense from him now is wariness and confusion. To be fair, his feelings mirror my own.

"No. Nikolas will remain in the city. He is pack, and he will be treated as such, but we have made it clear that he maintains his distance until we can arrange a gathering. A formal introduction to the pack," Lukas responds, wrapping an arm around my middle and tugging me into his warm chest. My arms go around his waist and I stare up at him as he speaks.

"Things are changing. We as a pack will change. If this is something you are not happy with, step forward now and I will help you make arrangements to leave. I will not force anyone to stay. I won't ever be that sort of leader. But just know, if you stay, you stay with Nesrin as your luna," Lukas declares.

Silence reigns throughout the room and hallway, only broken by the occasional creak of the floorboards. My heart sinks, making me feel nauseous at the idea of anyone leaving because of something I've done.

Jameson stands again, and I lock down my feelings. I really like this kid. Please don't let him leave because of me. Lukas must sense my anxiety because the arm around my waist flexes slightly, a gentle squeeze of comfort. Jameson steps forward, his face a mask of seriousness, and kneels on one knee in front of us, his fist raised over his heart.

"I pledge my loyalty to you, Alpha Lukas and Luna Nesrin, now and forever."

Everyone else in the room raises their fists and covers their hearts, repeating the words that send a pins and needle sensation over my body. Tears of relief sting my eyes but I blink rapidly trying to clear them. Gabe catches my eye and winks at me, the gesture allowing me to finally relax and smile.

CHAPTER SEVEN

I wake to Lukas's warm body pressed against my back, his arm draped over me, fingers lazily drawing patterns over my stomach. I squirm, pushing into him, his deep chuckle sounds from behind me. His hand moves lower, causing my breath to catch and my body to tense. He traces the line of my underwear, slipping his fingers under the material, his fingers graze my center.

"Nesrin."

That one word is filled with so much desire, it sends heat coursing through my body. My breathing picks up and my heart races as I grip the pillow under my head tighter. He circles my clit slowly, applying just the right amount of pressure to have me craving more. Lukas knows exactly how to touch me. Who am I kidding? Just a hint of his smirk, and I'm ready to go, my body aching for his touch like a drug addict. I don't think I am ever going to grow tired of him, of this.

He keeps going, and I rock into his palm, which causes my ass to stroke against the hard cock currently pressed firmly to my backside.

"Fuck," he mutters gruffly before removing his hand and freeing himself from his boxers. Wasting no time, he drags my panties to the side, sliding inside of me in one stroke. My breath catches in my throat and my mouth drops open as sparks of pleasure move through me. His palm travels up over the swells of my body, lightly gripping the base of my neck, holding me more firmly against him, rocking lazily into me and pulling out just as slowly. Lukas groans, nipping and sucking my shoulder. The pace is tortuously languid. I turn my head, needing his mouth on mine, and as if reading my thoughts, his mouth captures mine in a kiss filled with the desperation of pent-up desire. His fingers pinch my nipple hard, making me jerk against him, my muscles tightening around his cock. I reluctantly break the kiss, the soft moan that escapes my lips filling the air between us. Lukas reaches down, and I feel his arm wrap around my leg, securely lifting it as he drives in deeper.

The shift in angle allows him to hit all the right spots. It sends a tingling sensation racing across my skin, like static electricity.

Needing to hold onto something, I reach my hand back, and sink my fingers into his hair, tugging at the long strands. He groans into my neck and increases his pace.

"Sweetheart, you feel so fucking good," his voice vibrates through me, causing my heart to skip a beat or three at his words. A trail of kisses is laid along my shoulder and up my neck. I tilt my head to the side, giving him better access, loving the sensation of his lips on me. My breathing picks up as we move together a little more desperately. Lukas's hand slides up my neck and he grips my chin, turning my face toward his as he takes my mouth in a savage kiss, our tongues dueling and sliding against each other's, making me clench around his cock. A couple strokes later and we both climax simultaneously, his mouth swallowing my cries. Lukas slows his thrusts, drawing out the sparks of pleasure. We lay there for a long-time, hands tracing each other. Lukas sighs, kissing my shoulder, then rolling onto his back. I feel the loss of his warmth immediately and roll toward him.

"I need to get up."

I smile lazily. "Yeah, we should get moving. I need to pick Astraea up from Grace's."

Lukas sits up and tenderly brushes his lips against mine, the kiss lingering sweetly. He pulls back an inch, no more than a breath away.

"I love you," he whispers, sending love and longing down the mate bond, filling me with a sense of peace.

I grin, sending all my love back to him. *"I love you more."*

"Not possible. Now get that beautiful ass up and in the shower," he says, giving me a quick kiss on the tip of my nose before getting up and walking into the bathroom, his muscled back and ass on full display. I lie there a moment longer, a giant grin on my face.

Showered and dressed, I make my way downstairs, braiding my wet hair over my shoulder as I go. My cheeks ache from the wide smile on my face, which seems to be immovable. Thankfully, Grace offered to drop Astraea off, so I was able to take my time getting ready. The comforting smell of coffee catches my attention, and my smile spreads even wider as I head for the kitchen. Nothing could break through this good mood–

"Fuck you, Marcus!" Zee yells, startling me.

My smile vanishes in an instant as I walk into the kitchen.

"Zee!!" My hands go to my hips as I glare at my usually easy-going friend.

Looking around, I take in the group. Thank the goddess Astraea isn't here yet. If she were, I'd have to rip his balls off.

'Calm down, sweetheart,' Lukas says, walking into the room behind me and placing a gentle kiss on the top of my head.

Marcus is standing to one side of the kitchen table, arms leaning on it, while Zee is on the other side, glaring daggers at him. Leila or Emerson—whatever she wishes to be called—is leaning back against the door frame on the other side of the room, a blank expression on her face. My heart gives a painful thud at the sight of her. I haven't seen her since the river, since I discovered who she is. I want to run to her, but I also don't know her. Ugh, this is all so fucked.

"What's going on?" I demand of anyone.

No one makes eye contact, and my irritation rises swiftly. "Fine. If you don't want to tell me, you can all leave. The door is that way." My arm flies out, pointing towards the door.

Zee spins to face me. His incredulous look says it all. "What?" he bites out.

I widen my eyes in challenge, and realizing I'm serious, Zee huffs, his hand running through his blonde hair. "Fine. Whatever." Turning, he storms from the room and out of the house.

I wince as the front door slams shut behind him, then turn my eyes over to the rest of them. My shoulders sag as I make my way over to the espresso machine. I thought it would be a good day. I don't blame Zee for being pissed. If I was him, I'd be pissed too. Leila lied to him. She captured his heart and disappeared. I don't know the whole story, but it can wait.

"Marcus, I can see you still like to make early house calls," I say over my shoulder.

A low growl sounds from behind me, and I turn, arching an eyebrow at Lukas as I lean against the bench, crossing my arms.

"Really. You as well?"

Lukas smirks, and I feel my heart flutter in my chest. He runs a hand through his still wet hair and saunters toward me. Goddess, he is sexy as sin, and all mine. Lukas comes to a halt right in front of me, causing me to stand up straight and tilt my head back to keep our gazes locked. I can sense his mild irritation aimed at Marcus—likely amplified by the fact that the mage has made early morning house calls in the past. Lukas softly pulled me closer to him and his arm wrapped around my waist, providing a comforting embrace. Dropping his head, he takes my mouth in a tender kiss, his scent wrapping around me, rain and sandalwood cocooning me in its comforting warmth. Lukas lifts his head, and my stomach tightens at the intense look in his green eyes.

"Yes. Me, too," he states.

'You're mine,' echoes down the bond.

Rolling my eyes, I lightly pinch his side. *'Of course I am.'*

'I'm yours, too.'

I can't help but grin at him.

Marcus clears his throat. "Nesrin, we need to talk to you about the gates of Tartarus being open, and what my father is planning."

I groan, the tattered remains of my good mood vanishing in an instant. Lukas gives me a kiss on the mate mark, sending tingles all over my body.

'Don't lose that smile, sweetheart. We got this.'

I raise my gaze to Lukas, a blush working its way over my cheeks when Marcus bangs a hand on the table, making me jump.

"I can't believe you went out *on a date* last night with everything that's happening," his voice is dripping with displeasure.

Lukas stiffens and slowly turns back to our visitors. "What we do is none of your concern, mage."

Marcus snorts. "When she doesn't have a bunch of beasts out hunting her and a coven hell bent on sending her to the underworld, then sure, go out on as many dates as you want. But last night was reckless." He stares at me. "You have to know that."

My arms cross over my chest. "What I know is I needed a night of normalcy. I craved a moment of solitude with my mate, time to soothe my soul, recharge," I explain.

Dropping my arms, I spin around and start on the coffee machine. I need caffeine if I am going to deal with this shit storm.

"I understand that. But Nesrin, there is a whole damn coven out to get you. They are just *waiting* for the moment you let your guard down."

"I was fine." I flick my hand over my shoulder, dismissing his concern. "Plus, we discovered something."

'Do you think it's wise to tell him?' Lukas warns.

'Half the vampires in the city probably know by now,' I point out.

Turning around to lean back against the bench, I take a sip of my coffee, the rich flavor of the roasted beans lingering on my tongue as the warmth soothes me. I feel myself relax almost instantly.

"You're wearing the sanans sidus lucis?" Leila inquires, speaking for the first time since I came in.

My gaze swings to her, and I see her staring at the necklace sitting against my chest. I wrap my hand around it and feel it hum in response. Leila pushes off the wall and steps closer. She must have in contacts, because her eyes are green today.

"How do you know about the pendant?" I ask, curiosity eating at me. How much does she know?

"I handed it over to Grace to pass on to you. Our Grandmother gave it to me with strict instructions to get it to you. Grace offered to hold on to it in trust for you. It marks you as the fated legacy born. The one who is chosen to receive Althaea's powers. The star of light. The healer."

My pulse quickens and my stomach lurches uneasily. Grace was aware of my sister's existence. I wonder why she didn't tell me about her before? It seems like Leila was aware I existed, but she didn't make any effort to find me. She deliberately concealed herself from us, but why?

"Why?" the words spill from my mouth.

Leila jerks her gaze from the pendant grasped in my hand to my face. Her mouth opens, but no sound comes out.

"Why didn't you find me? Tell me who you were? Why are you with the council?"

"It's complicated," she replies, her eyes pleading with me to drop it. But I won't, not this time. I am over everyone keeping me in the dark. I place my mug on the counter behind me and take a step toward her.

"What about it is complicated, Leila?" I snap.

Marcus steps between us, his arms out as if to keep us apart, his face clouded with confusion. "Leila?"

"Oh, you didn't know?" I laugh without humor, throwing my hands in the air before I spin around in a circle, then point an accusatory finger at her.

"Emerson is actually Leila . . . " I pause as I stare into her eyes. "My sister."

Marcus's coal-black eyes widen in shock as he stares between us. Leila sighs and reaches up, plucking out one of her colored contacts, revealing her whiskey-hued eye.

Marcus shakes his head. "How did I not see the resemblance before?" he mutters to himself in disbelief.

"You see what you want to see. I don't technically exist, so it was never an option for you or anyone else," Leila tells him.

"You exist! You just chose to stay hidden!" I yell, my emotions getting the better of me. I rarely get riled up so quickly, but this is my sister, my family, and she has been here the whole time. Lukas's palm lands on my back, the warmth soaking through my light sweater.

'Take it easy, sweetheart. That famous Irish temper and stubbornness is coming out' A growl rumbles from my throat, and Lukas chuckles. 'I'm sure she had her reasons.' Leaning down, he plants a kiss on my head and motions for Marcus to follow him. Marcus looks back at my sister and me as he exits the room, hesitating a moment before following Lukas from the room.

"Why didn't you tell me who you were?" I demand.

"I was undercover. It was too dangerous."

"You could have found me before."

"And you would have believed me?"

"Yes!"

We both stare at each other. Confusion and hurt line her eyes, mirroring my own.

"It was you helping me in that room, when I was healing Alex. Wasn't it? I felt you."

She reaches up, tucking some hair behind her ear as she nods her head. "You were draining yourself. Any more and you would have slipped into a coma."

I remember her cool hands on my face, her shadows and the magic that flowed into me. Leila was there for me when I needed it. She even helped me escape the coven. But she also tortured me. Manipulated my mind and thoughts. She is a phantom caster, she can manipulate and control the shadows. As if reading where my thoughts have turned, she takes another step toward me.

"I didn't have a choice. I had to do it, but I gave you hints so you could break through the visions," she whispers ever so softly, as if the words are painful for her to speak.

My throat goes dry as tears form in my eyes. "I spent weeks thinking I was in another hallucination. That every time I woke up, I was going to be back there."

Leila's eyes fill with tears as she hangs her head. When she looks up, a tear slides down her cheek. "I'm sorry."

"I know," I murmur, hating that we're in this position.

"I hated doing it every minute. But Marcus and I formed a plan to get you out. It was a half-assed plan, but I couldn't let you stay there another minute."

When I don't speak, she continues on.

"Claudia helped. She created the storm to push you in the direction you needed to go and to confuse the other witches and mages on which way you went. But when you were caught a second time, I realized I couldn't wait for help. They were going to kill you."

"Why?" my voice breaks on that one word. My heart aches just looking at her. She must understand my meaning, because she looks away, as if thinking over her words before she faces me again. This time, resolve fills her eyes.

"That fire. It was supposed to kill *me*. It killed our grandparents. Grace was there. She tried to get us out, but it was no use. The containment spell was too strong."

She lets out a shuddering breath before proceeding. "We were in the living room. The fire was so hot. I remember crying, and my tears seemed to evaporate straight away. Suddenly, Hades stepped out of the flames. I was so scared. Grandpa slowly stood up and stepped in front of us. Their raised voices filled the air, and I could feel the anger, though I couldn't make out what was being said. Grandpa kept shaking his head at the god and then motioning to me, his hands trembling in the air.

"Hades nodded, and suddenly our grandparents were embracing me and murmuring words of love and urgency. Grandma took off the necklace, thrusting it into my hands before pushing me to Hades's waiting arms. He scooped me up, and we disappeared from the house into darkness so thick, I couldn't even see my hand in front of my face. I was terrified. I had no clue what was happening."

I stand numbly, listening as my sister recalls her terrifying last moments with our grandparents. My heart breaks for that little girl and a wave of sadness washes over me.

"Hades took me to his palace. At first, I refused food and water. Not until I was able to see my family. Finally, he relented and portalled me home, but there was no sign of you. Only Grace. She told us what had happened. That my parents had fled to America. I didn't believe her. Why would they leave me? I was their daughter. Hades may have saved my life that night, but I'd lost so much."

A sob rips from her throat and hot tears drip down my face. I crave to reach for her, to take her in my arms, but I'm not certain it would be welcomed.

"Hades took me back and ordered Grace to find my parents. I spent weeks, months waiting, barely living. When Grace finally got in touch, she informed me they had wiped their memory of me. That they couldn't deal with the pain of losing me, so they made it as if I had never existed."

My heart cracks open for what she must have felt. "I'm sorry," the words stick in my throat. But she just goes on.

"I wanted to see for myself that they had moved on. So, I learned to portal. I practiced every day until I could do it. Took me months to get it right. I remember the day clearly. You and Niamh were baking with Mom, and Dad was on the deck cleaning his fishing gear. It was sunny, with a light breeze in the air. You and Niamh had come running outside yelling at Dad to taste your cake. I can still see the way his eyes lit up as he took the two of you in. The love in his eyes made me take a step toward you all. Then, as if sensing me watching Dad's eyes looked up and locked with mine, and there was no recognition there. None. I had been left behind, forgotten. I had never experienced a pain so deep, I couldn't breathe through the tears. It was true. You had all moved on. I was scared if I made myself known, it would happen again, and I couldn't go through it and lose you all over again, so I stayed away."

This time, I don't stop myself. I rush forward and wrap my arms tightly around her. If she doesn't want it, well then, she can tell me to go to hell. But to my surprise, her arms embrace me, hugging me back just as tightly.

"I'm so sorry. I–" I choke on my emotions.

Our pain seems to flow freely between us, intertwining our souls. It feels as if our past is scratching its way up from the depths.

"I realize it doesn't mean much. Goddess, what could even begin to– Anyway, it's just when I found out you were alive, that I had a sister out there, I was so torn up. So angry at our parents. Angry doesn't even begin to cover it. You deserved better."

"I mean, I guess it turned out okay. Hades did right by me. Sure, I was numb, broken after what happened, but he pulled me up, gave me a purpose. If it weren't for him and Milinoe, I am positive I would have spiraled into nothingness. He gets a bad rap because of the whole god of the underworld thing," she says as if she were discussing a run of the mill celebrity, pulling away and wiping her face, "but he is the best of all of them. I've never met someone as honest, loyal, and stubborn as Hades." She shrugs and makes her way over to the sink, splashing some water on her face. Her eye roll might as well be audible as she adds, "Zeus and Hera are the worst of them all."

I suppose when you gather the myths about the brothers, Zeus and Poseidon both are guilty of hurting mortals and gods alike on a much larger scale than Hades. When I really think about it, though, what is it about Hades that makes us all think he is dark, and bad, exactly? Is it the fact that he rules the dead? Certainly not. Which probably makes it the most likely reason. Freaking gods.

"When compared to some of the atrocities committed by other gods, Hades does seem to be one of the fairest and just gods," I agree.

"Hades thinks Zeus is behind all of it. The Order of Tartarus. He thinks that Blanchette embarrassed Zeus, and he needed revenge."

"But Zeus wouldn't stick to something like this, not for this long. It's not that I don't know how petty he's known to be, but from everything I've read about him, facts would suggest that he tends to get bored quickly, moves on to new things almost immediately."

"He does seem to do that a lot," Leila muses.

I jerk my eyes to hers. "Wait, have you met him?"

"No. Hades kept me in his palace. I didn't leave until I was fully trained. No one realized who I was, not even his children. Only he and Persephone knew. But if Zeus is behind this, we need to find a way to stop him. Or maybe we could strike a bargain."

My head is spinning. My sister was raised by Hades. In the underworld, as his kin. I shove my hands into my hair as I walk over to the table and drop down on a chair.

Just then, Zee storms in through the back door. He gives us both a look and I know he is studying the tear-stricken faces of two sisters in desperate need of time to reconnect.

"Everything okay here?" he asks carefully, his voice almost gruff. His gaze is fixed on Leila, standing at the sink, her fingers intertwined and knotted.

"We're fine, Zee. Could you get Lukas and Marcus? I need to discuss the thing that happened last night."

Zee casts one last look at Leila before nodding and walking through the house.

Turning, I face my sister first. "You hurt him," I whisper. She knows exactly who I'm talking about.

To her credit, Leila doesn't break eye contact. "I know."

Leila excuses herself to the bathroom to wash her face, so here I am clearing the dishes from the table and waiting for Zee to get back with the others. Awareness creeps along my skin and my head jerks up, my gaze locking on a tall figure standing on the other side of the table. His baby blue eyes twinkle with mischief. What the fuck?

"Who are you?" I gasp, an octave too high.

A smirk appears on his face as he takes me in. "I can't say."

I scan the room, as if it holds any of the answers I require. "Where'd you come from?"

The stranger runs a hand through his blonde hair, his white linen shirt unbuttoned to show off his chiseled chest. "I really can't say."

"What–"

"I still can't say."

"I just want–"

"When I say, *I can't say*, what do you hear exactly? Coffee?" he laughs, and it's all I can do not to scream in exasperation.

Who the hell is this guy?

"There's coffee?" I deadpan.

His eyes widen as if he isn't sure if I'm being serious or not. "Uh . . . "

"Infuriating, isn't it?" I snap. "This is my house, so tell me what the fuck you're doing in it!"

Leila comes to an erupt stop in the doorway, confusion written all over her face. "Hermes, what are you doing here?"

My eyes go wide. "Hermes?!"

Leila moves to take a chair at the table. She looks uncomfortable. I'm not sure if it's being around me or that Hermes just showed up in my kitchen.

"The one and only," the light-haired god says, winking at me. Huh. He's shorter than I'd expect a god to be, and his choice of clothing is odd.

"You look like you're dressed to go sailing," I point out.

Hermes peers down at his clothes, and smiles, wiggling his eyebrows. "I know. Dashing right?"

Bemused, I glance at Leila. "Is he always like this?"

Shrugging, she picks up a bread roll and throws it at him. "What do you want, Hermes?"

He catches it with ease and takes a bite. "Is that any way to talk to the messenger?"

Leila lets out a soft growl. "Yes. Now, why are you here?"

"Your father wishes to see you."

"And he couldn't tell me this himself?" she fires back.

"He is rather occupied at the moment, trying to figure out who opened the gates and let those monsters and daemons out," Hermes argues.

We both straighten. "Does he have any leads?" I demand.

Twisting around, Hermes looks around the room and spots the fridge. "Do you have any juice?"

Startled, I blink at him, "Yes." I grab a glass and make quick work of pouring some juice. Hermes smiles and holds out a hand as I approach, but I keep hold of the glass.

"Answer my question."

"Really? You're going to withhold my juice?"

"Yes."

Hermes rolls his eyes. "Fine. Hades has a lead, but I don't know who. He wants to speak to Leila, and I'm sure she will fill you in on what he says afterward."

I pass him the glass as Astraea and Nissa come bounding into the room. Nissa draws up short, her eyes narrowing on Hermes, her wings beating furiously in agitation. Astraea just skips right past the god as if he weren't even there, her curls bouncing around her face.

'Grace outside,' she says, pointing out the kitchen window.

'Thanks, sweet girl. Did you have fun?'

She nods her head enthusiastically, wide indigo eyes sparkling with a level of joy and energy only attainable in childhood. I've noticed the slight change in her eye color lately, the blue fading into something deeper, the purple more prominent.

'*See Cerberus gain?*' she asks excitedly, and I squat down in front of her, pushing her hair off her face.

'*I don't know,*' I reply with a gentle smile.

"Who is this sweet child?" Hermes interrupts.

I glance at him and straighten up. Astraea maneuvers behind my legs and slips under the hem of my long sweater, as Nissa lands on my shoulder, a menacing look on her face that has my eyebrows lifting in question. I stare back at Hermes and cross my arms with a shrug.

"She is none of your concern," I answer smoothly.

Hermes laughs, raising his palm. "Okay. I get it. Stranger danger." He looks at Leila, who is also glaring daggers at him. "She's feisty like you."

We both snort at the same time, our eyes darting to each other, and Hermes huffs before pinning Leila with a stern look. "Hades," is all he says before turning and strolling out of the kitchen.

Where is he going? I start forward, but Leila's voice stops me. "He's gone."

"I don't trust him," Nissa growls, her voice reverberating through the air like tiny bells.

"Me neither," I counter.

Astraea sticks her head out from under my sweater and peers around the room. Satisfied Hermes is gone, she peeks over at Leila.

"Hi," Leila says, getting on her knees on the floor. She beams at Astra, tears misting her eyes again.

Astraea peeps up at me, and I run a hand over her hair. "It's okay. This is Leila, your Aunty."

Astraea moves closer, stopping about a foot from her, and stares into Leila's whiskey-colored eyes. She must've taken out her contacts.

"I've waited a long time to see you," she says to Astraea, who glances back at me for reassurance.

I smile, nodding my head. "Go ahead."

Leila holds her arms out, hope lining her face. I put my hand behind my back and crossed my fingers. Astraea doesn't disappoint; she slowly moves into Leila's waiting arms, the embrace simple and sweet. They stay like that for a few moments before they pull back.

I clear my throat and glance out the window. "So, Hades?"

"What about him?" Leila asks, arranging Astraea on her lap.

"He's your father now?"

"Well, yes. He raised me."

My chest aches. She has a family, but she should have been with us. I swallow my feelings. Now isn't the time to start spiraling.

CHAPTER EIGHT

Lukas strolls through the doorway, and his eyes lock with mine in an instant. Our bond is filled with uncertainty and confusion as he lifts his head, his nostrils flaring as he tries to make sense of the scent in the air. When his gaze falls back down to mine, his eyes are glowing a vibrant yellow.

"Who was here?" he demands.

"Hermes." I shrug, not knowing what else to say.

Lukas frowns and walks over to me, wrapping an arm around me and kissing my head.

"Everything okay?" he murmurs, his lips brushing over my skin.

I nod my head even as I become overwhelmed by the events of this morning, my anxiety at a whole new level. I feel a tug in my heart to go outside and reconnect with nature, to ground myself.

Lukas slowly pivots and fixes his gaze on the floor, where Leila and Astraea are still seated. Malachite dashes into the kitchen, his paws scratching against the wooden floors as he slides across the room and collides with Lukas's legs. I stifle a giggle as Astraea launches herself excitedly toward the small dragon. Lukas intercepts her and gathers us up in a single, tight hug, and I'm filled with a sense of peace and warmth as I'm surrounded by my favorite people.

"Did you have a good night, little star?" Lukas asks her. Astraea squishes his cheeks with both of her tiny hands and nods.

My mood deflates as Zee and Marcus storm in next, Zee taking a place at the table, and Marcus leaning against the wall. Leila pauses before choosing a seat next to Zee. I see him stiffen in response to the proximity. Merve and Grace trail in a minute later and I smile. I watch carefully as Grace's gaze moves around the room, and the moment she sees Leila, her expression turns to one of shock. Her eyes find mine next, remorse reflecting in her clear light blue eyes.

"Okay. Now that we're all here, and the air has been cleared, Nesrin can tell you what happened last night," Lukas says, placing Astraea on the floor, and she hurries after the dragon, Nissa flying close behind her.

I turn to my sister. "Do you know what the pendant does?"

Frowning, she looks down at where it rests on my chest. "I was told the Moirai chose you at birth to harness the true powers of our ancestors. That your goddess powers were locked away at birth, and once you accepted your role and donned the pendant, your true power would be unlocked. You are the fated legacy; half fae, half goddess. You have the Sanans Sidus Lucis, the star of light."

I gape at her, speechless. That's more than I thought she would know. More than I knew, for sure. Lukas's voice sounds in my head, his warmth and love flowing down the bond. '*You got this.*'

I take a deep breath. "I healed a vampire last night."

"Vampires don't need to be healed. They practically heal immediately," Marcus retorts.

Lukas flashes his teeth. "Let her finish, Mage."

Marcus raises his palms in surrender. "Sorry."

"It wasn't an injury I healed, but the darkness consuming him. It had almost overrun his light. If that had happened, he would have lost his humanity completely."

Lukas speaks up, "Last thing we need is a feral vampire on the loose in Portland."

Marcus shakes his head. "That we can agree on."

"My magic drew me to him, and somehow flipped a switch inside of me making it possible for me to see his darkness. I think the pendant," I look to Leila, "Sanans Sidus Lucis?" I question, and she nods. "Made it possible. My light reacted to it. Wanting to balance the two halves. He still has darkness within him, of course. We can't all be just light or just dark. There has to be duality. But by doing this, I somehow bought him into the pack. I'm now linked to the vampire, as if he were any other member of the pack."

Leila makes a wheezing sound of distress, her eyes wide in shock. Or maybe that's horror. Maybe both? I'm not even sure.

Marcus pushes off the wall, mouth agape as he steps forward. "You *what?*"

"Healed a vampire and made him pack," I recap cautiously.

"Are you fucking crazy?!" Marcus shouts.

Lukas growls, his voice deliberately low when he speaks. "Watch your tone with my mate, Mage."

Marcus's brows lower as he regards us both. "This doesn't trouble you?" he asks Lukas, incredulous.

Lukas shrugs. "She enjoys collecting strays. I will not stop her."

Zee laughs, rubbing his chin. "She really does, doesn't she?"

Marcus pins him with a look. "What about you? Doesn't this bother you?"

"Nesrin does what she has to do. We will back her a hundred percent," Zee replies.

My spirits lift at the praise, and I beam at Lukas and Zee. They're the best, and I am beyond lucky to have them in my life. If this new power of mine seeks out those struggling to find duality, I need to work out how to heal them without linking them to the pack.

Marcus exhales slowly. "Okay, well, I honestly don't know what to do with that information."

My attention moves to Grace, who has been standing by Merve, silently watching everything unfold. "Why did you message me last night? Did you sense something?"

"Oh, no. Astraea here demanded I check on you."

I glance down at Astraea and she grins up at me. I ruffle her hair and look around the room. Leila is still in shock as she sits there, eyes fixed on me.

"Are you okay?" I inquire softly.

Shaking her head, she looks at me, baffled. "Yes, sorry. I was just thinking. That is a powerful healing ability."

"I realize that. I just need to figure out how to heal without adding everyone to the pack."

I laugh nervously and Lukas reaches over, taking my hand as he assures, "You will."

"I hope so." I glance around and see Astraea is back, but no Malachite. "Hey, Astra, where's Malachite?" Astraea looks up at the name and points outside. "Is he still at the river?" I ask her. She nods.

Shit. Okay, I better go check on him.

"Leila mentioned Hades suspects Zeus is behind all this mess with my family. I will let her fill you in while I check on Malachite," I inform the others, jogging from the room.

Nissa trails after me, and I hear Astraea's tiny feet following behind. We make our way down to the river and I see Malachite laying curled up on a rock, taking in the morning sunshine. Several sprites surround him. A grin overtakes my face and I let out a breath of relief just as Nissa lands on my shoulder.

"I wouldn't have left him unprotected," she tells me, nudging my neck affectionately with her shoulder.

"Thank you. I can't let anything happen to him. I promised his mother I would take care of him."

"I know. You're doing a great job, Nesrin, and you have plenty of us around to help."

I sit down next to the rock and Astra sits on my lap. I should get back, but I instead decide to join them and soak up some sunshine. The other sprites shyly flying off at my approach.

Nissa sits on the rock next to Malachite, drawing her knees to her chest. The sprite has been a constant in our life and it strikes me that I still haven't figured out why. "Nissa, why do you trust me?"

The tiny sprite looks out over the water, and for a moment, I don't think she's going to respond. Then she turns her head my way, her violet eyes blazing, "You are the daughter of light. And though you've lost much in your life, you step up and help others without question, you treat us all as equals. You don't have an agenda behind it; you're just trying to do what's right. The trials ahead will be hard. You need friends and allies."

Her gaze is unwavering as it turns to the water, and I'm left speechless. I take in the sounds of nature, the birds chirping and leaves rustling. My fingers gently comb through Astraea's silky hair. I must have been dozing off, because the next thing I know, I feel Kyra's gentle hand shaking my shoulder, her kind brown eyes fixed on me.

"Oh, good. You're alive," she jokes as I sit up, blinking.

"What time is it?"

"After noon. Around two, I think."

"Shit."

I rub my hands over my face, and Kyra laughs, her soft voice like sweet chimes.

"Are Leila and Marcus still here?"

"No, they left a couple of hours ago."

I stand up, running a hand through my hair and spot at least a dozen sprites watching me from the water's edge. I peer around, frowning, "Where did the others go off to?" I ask.

"They took off for the house with Liam and Noah." She holds out a hand and helps me to my feet. "You realize it's really not safe to be falling asleep out here like that?"

Sighing, I reply, "I know."

"Come on, let's go make you some lunch and see what the rascals are up to." She grins, tossing her corkscrew curls off her face.

"Sounds wonderful," I reply, linking my arm through hers.

CHAPTER NINE

"You're crazy, you know that, right?" Zee tosses one of my sofa cushions at me.

Catching it, I shrug. "So I've been told."

"How did you even get this in here?" Kyra says, scratching her head. She frowns as she attempts to gather her tightly coiled curls into a ponytail.

"Magic." I answer with a wink.

Both huff out a laugh.

"Well, is that how you plan on getting it out of here? 'Cause I can tell you now, that monster of a sofa will not fit through that door," Zee replies, pointing at my sofa like it has surely committed a serious crime.

"It'll be fine." I roll my eyes and wave off his concern, laughing.

"Have you not seen that episode of Friends?" Kyra laughs.

"Pivot!" Zee and I both say at the same time in Ross's voice.

We all erupt in laughter, making me feel like a weight has been lifted off my chest.

"Well, we only need to worry about the small stuff today. Lukas said he would handle the furniture tomorrow."

"Thank god." Kyra laughs, picking up a packing box. "Where do you want me to start?"

"Wherever," I reply.

"Okay, I'll start in the kitchen."

I cringe because I don't exactly put stuff away the way an adult probably should. I tend to shove objects into the cupboard and quickly close the door, listening for the telltale thud of something falling. I stack plates and cups alright, but the pots, pans, and containers . . . *Eek* . . .

"I'll help you," I say, following her. I don't want an avalanche of containers taking her out.

"And me?" Zee asks.

"Could you pack my books?" I point at the shelves that line the far wall.

"No problem."

"And, Zee. Be careful."

Zee frowns over his shoulder. "Okay."

"I mean it."

Shaking his head, he chuckles under his breath. "Damn bookworms."

I bring up my playlist and it automatically connects to the bluetooth speaker. Zee jumps when Katy Perry's voice comes blaring through the speakers. I chuckle, feeling my face heat and mouth *sorry* before turning it down to a more suitable volume for the present company.

"So, how are you handling everything?" Kyra asks as she pulls glasses from the cupboard above the counter and begins wrapping them in newspaper.

I give a slight shrug. "There has been . . . a lot to take in lately."

"How are things with Leila?"

Out of the corner of my vision, I notice Zee become tense at the sound of her name, and a pang of regret hits me in my chest that I think might be coming from Zee.

"Alright. We've talked things over, but it will take a while to become familiar with one another. Though we share the same blood, we are still strangers," I admit quietly.

"It's a start. Once the Order is taken care of, you will have all the time in the world to reconnect with your sister." Kyra smiles, nudging my shoulder.

I return her smile and open the cupboard under the stove, immediately wishing I hadn't as an array of containers and lids spill onto the kitchen floor.

As Kyra chuckles, her eyes seem to twinkle with mirth. "Is that why you raced in here after me?"

"Guilty," I laugh.

Zee strolls in a moment later. "All the books are done, honey. I'm going to start on Astraea's room. You girls can do your room, don't need the alpha pissed at me cause I saw your lingerie or vibrator."

My jaw drops open and I stand there, speechless, as Kyra's laughter reverberates through the room.

"I can see it now. Lukas would train his ass hard for weeks."

I slowly shake my head in disbelief and plop down on the hard wooden floor in the center of my chaotic mess. After hastily weaving my wayward hair into a braid over my shoulder, I finally get to work packing my things. I underestimated how long it would take to pack up all the rooms. It's taking much longer than I thought.

"Only one room left," I say, stretching my arms over my head. *Lukas is so giving me a massage tonight.*

"We don't need to know what you make Lukas do in the bedroom." Zee smirks as he walks by. My face and neck grow hot with embarrassment. My damn mouth.

Kyra snorts, trying to contain her laugher. "It's just the bathroom left, right?" she says, reaching for her water bottle.

I respond with a nod just as Kyra's phone buzzes with a message. Pulling it out of her back pocket, she cringes. "I have to head back. Are you ready to go? The kids are starting to get a bit much for Kate."

Zee maneuvers the box labeled Astraea down the hallway, the weight of it straining his arms. "I've still got to run an errand for Lukas."

Looking to me, he places the box on the floor in the living area. "Can Suzy drive us back?"

"What errand?"

"Nothing you need to worry about."

"Why didn't he ask me?"

Zee shrugs. "Don't know but I'll go now."

Before I could ask anymore questions, he was gone, the front door closing behind him. I cast a questioning glance at Kyra, but her furrowed brow shows she is just as lost as I am.

"I'll message Suzy," I reply and whip out my phone, sending off a quick message.

Suzy responds immediately with a '*Hell yes.*'

"Suzy will take us home."

Kyra pulls me into a bone-crushing hug. "I'll see you tonight for dinner!"

Suzy taps her fingers on the steering wheel, an easy smile on her face while we sit in her compact car parked on a small side street while we wait for Zee. He has been gone nearly an hour, and despite my messages he won't tell me where. I have a sneaking suspicion he and Lukas are scheming something. I don't appreciate being kept in the dark, especially now with all that has taken place. It only makes me more anxious. Two days have gone by since Leila and Marcus dropped by the house, and let's not forget Hermes. I feel a tad overwhelmed, struggling to take in everything that has happened. The coven, the gods, the gates to the underworld being opened, having a sister, bringing a vampire into the pack. I can feel the pendant sitting quietly against my chest, its weight comforting.

"Ugh, where the hell is he? Suzy, I'm so sorry you have to wait on Zee after agreeing to pick us up."

"That's okay. I have a lot of spare time now that the bookstore's gone." As she turns toward me, a smile forms on her face. With her loose purple hair held back by a stylish pair of large-framed sunglasses resting on her head, she looks so vibrant it's nearly impossible not to smile in return. Still, the mention of my bookstore causes a pang of emotion to surge through my chest. To divert my thoughts, I reach into my bag and quickly retrieve my phone to send Zee a message.

Nesrin: Where are you?

The reply is immediate.

Zee: Two minutes away.
Nesrin: You said that ten minutes ago.
Zee: Two minutes. Don't get your panties in a bunch.

I bark out a laugh and show Suzy the message.
"Seriously?" she giggles, and I type a quick response.

Nesrin: Really Zee? Panties in a bunch?
Zee: Leave me be, woman. I'm multitasking.

"He is multi-tasking," I tell Suzy, and she rolls her eyes. Her fingers are still drumming away on the steering wheel to the beat on the radio. I glance down at my phone.

Nesrin: Shit, my bad.
Zee: See it doesn't happen again.
Nesrin: You love me.
Zee: I tolerate you.
Nesrin: You'd be lost without me.

"How are classes going?" I ask, dropping my hands into my lap.

Suzy releases a deep, resigned sigh and sinks back into her chair. "They're . . . okay."

"Doesn't sound okay. What happened?"

"I don't want to talk about it," she replies, running her teeth over her bottom lip.

I reach over and place my hand gently on her arm. "What's up?"

Suzy swallows hard and looks out her window before glancing over at me. "Do you think I'm a failure?"

I jerk my head back, my eyes going wide. "What? NO! Why would you say that?"

She shrugs. "My brother's in pre-med and he will be a doctor. A *doctor*, Nesrin, and what am I doing? Art major. What good is that in the real world? I shouldn't be wasting my time studying something–"

"That makes you happy?" I say, cutting her off. "Suzy, when you talk to me about your lessons, you light up. You have a passion for this. No one expects you to be anyone but who you are. Some people are meant to be doctors, others dancers. Whatever you decide to do, do it for you, because it feeds your soul and makes you happy. Screw what anyone else thinks."

A broad smile breaks across her face and I see a mist of tears line her eyes as she looks at me. "Thanks, Nesrin. Jessie just said–"

"Jessie's a bitch and a fake ass Barbie doll," I snap, feeling my anger toward her roommate flare.

That girl has been green with envy of Suzy since the day they were introduced. I can't stand the way she rubs her money and status in Suzy's face, making her feel inferior. I've had to bite my tongue on far too many occasions when she stopped by the bookstore.

"So, do you want to make this a weekly thing?" I ask, waggling my brow in a suggestive manner in my best attempt to change the subject.

Suzy giggles and I'm happy to see her smiling again. "Dinner or me picking you up?"

"Dinner."

"It's a date. Plus, Lukas always cooks a feast." Her stomach rumbles as if even the thought of food is too much for her hungry belly.

"You're drooling," I tease.

A loud bang on my window makes me jump. A shriek falls from my lips and my phone tumbles to the floor of the car. I glower out my window at Zee, who's just standing there, smirking mischievously.

I flip him off as he jumps into the back of Suzy's car.

"Ladies."

"Zee," we reply in unison.

"Hey, you know, Zee, women wear an array of underwear now, not just panties. That saying went out the window a decade ago," Suzy says, grinning at him in the rear-view mirror.

"Good god, not you, too," Zee groans.

Laughing, I turn in my seat to study him. "What happened to you?"

"Nothing."

Arching an eyebrow, I pin him with a look. *'I'll zap you.'*

I've recently realized I can get Zee to fall into line quicker if I just zap his furry butt with a little bit of magic.

"I don't want to talk about it," he answers, struggling to get comfortable in the back of Suzy's compact car. I bite my lip to contain my laughter as I watch him fumble.

"You look like shit," I point out and Suzy chokes on her laugh as she pulls into traffic.

"Thanks," Zee replies sarcastically.

"No, seriously. Did you fight ten people and run a mile to get here? What took you so long?"

"It was four men and five miles, actually."

I jerk my head back, and even Suzy swerves the car at the seriousness in his voice. I turn back around in my seat and give Suzy a small smile.

'What happened, Zee?' I ask down our link.

'I had a run in with some bloody high fae.'

I do my best to keep my reaction contained. The fae never come to this world. They live in Faerie. I didn't even think the gates between worlds still worked. The high fae generally resemble humans, although their pointed ears do stand out, and they are apparently remarkably beautiful. I don't know for sure though, as I've never seen any myself. I've heard there are two separate courts in Faerie, each striving for power and dominance. The Seelie Queen reigns over the light fae creatures. The Unseelie Queen commands the dark fae creatures. From my understanding, Nissa and Merve are Seelie, but Grace, Joseph, and Sophie are Unseelie.

'Is it taken care of?' I ask.

'Of course,'

'Okay. Hey, Zee?'

'Yeah?'

'I'm glad you're okay. But next time, call for help.'

I'm on edge, my knee bouncing the entire drive as I bite at my nails. An inexplicable feeling of alarm washes over me when I think about the fae being here. And I must not be doing a very good job of keeping my unease locked down. Suzy's casting me questioning looks and Lukas's worry seems to radiate through the bond, almost like a physical force in response to my emotions. Whenever I'm stressed, I find it more difficult to filter my emotions and thoughts. And, though we can't communicate over long distances, we still feel each other's emotions.

I don't know how he does it, but Lukas is a master at masking his feelings, while I always seem to be more transparent. I express my love and assurance through the bond, feeling it reverberate in my chest. My way of letting him know I'm okay and not in any danger.

Something catches my attention on the radio, and I lean forward to turn it up: "Breaking news. Update on missing hiker Everly Baker. Search and rescue teams have suspended their search for the missing hiker due to increasingly bad weather. The twenty-five-year-old hiker has been missing for over forty-eight hours–"

Suzy reaches over, turning it back down. "What do you think happened to her?"

"I don't know. It seems a little odd."

"Right? Like, she was familiar with the area, and she was with her friends. How does someone just disappear into thin air like that?"

"Aliens?" Zee pipes up from the backseat, and Suzy and I share a look, both rolling our eyes.

"Right. Aliens," Suzy scoffs, turning the music back up.

I gaze out the window, my mind drifting back to the fae. Really, fae is the general word we use for them, like calling us all humans. Under the fae umbrella, there is a diverse array of races and species: fairies with their delicate wings, shapeshifters capable of altering their form, sprites with their mischievous charm, demons with their sinister nature, gnomes with their ancient knowledge, and trolls with their intimidating presence. The list stretches on, with no end in sight. But to have the high fae roaming the streets of Portland, what does that mean? It can't be anything good.

At the mere thought of having them here, my chest tightens and my palms grow slick with sweat. The majority of the high fae went back to their realm in the midst of World War One. Despite the heavy concentration of iron and other metals in our realm, they are able to manage life here quite well. Merve, Nissa, and the shifters are among the other lesser fae that settled here and adapted to their surroundings. But the fae are condescending, manipulative, and arrogant. They think our world to be distasteful and polluted.

Before I know it, Suzy is pulling onto the dirt road leading to my house.

"That was quick," I say.

"You were zoned out the entire drive," Suzy chuckles.

"Yeah, you didn't even respond when I asked Suzy about her hair."

"What about her hair?" I look over at Suzy and she blushes furiously. "Zee. What did you say to her? Suzy never blushes like that." I laugh.

"I just want to know if the carpet matches the drapes." His voice is so innocent and sweet that I roll my eyes.

"You did not! You're a real shithead, Zee."

Suzy just giggles and pulls to a stop in front of the house. As the three of us make our way to the door, Zee steps around Suzy and me to get there first, holding it open for us and bowing with a flourish. "Miladies," he says with a wink.

"Why, thank you, good sir," Suzy responds with a chuckle.

I let out a chuckle, shaking my head in amused disbelief at these two fast friends and following her inside. I make it two steps in before the shouting starts.

"Oh, you're a deceiving, cheating piece of shit," Alex's voice booms from the living room.

My eyes widen as I whip my head toward Zee, who simply shrugs.

"Oh yeah? You're the one who thinks you can get away with everything. Just bat those eyelashes and get what you want!"

Alex's voice is smug when she fires back, "Welcome to the real world."

"I think we should call it quits," Kate says, amusement lighting her words.

"NO!" two angry voices yell at the same time.

Zee and I venture into the living room to find Gabe, Alex, Kate, and Roan seated around the coffee table playing Monopoly.

"Uh oh," I groan. I have an intense dislike for this game. It is literally a friendship destroyer. I remember once Niamh and I played with some friends in seventh grade and two of our friends got so mad at each other they didn't speak for the rest of the year. I have refused to play since.

"Hey, guys," I drawl.

Kate and Roan look up at me, and I can see their eyes twinkling with amusement. Gabe and Alex are locked in a mutual stare-down, the tension thick in the air. I fight the urge to laugh, feeling the corners of my mouth twitching. Suzy has no such qualms and her laughter rings out, the sound echoing off the walls of the room.

"Oh. My. God. Whose dumb idea was this?" she cackles.

All eyes turn her way, Alex's eyes flashing in warning. With a swiftness that's meant to be discreet, I step in front of Suzy, my warning look toward Alex unmistakable.

"Suzy's staying for dinner. I think it's time for the game to end before someone ends a friendship."

Zee saunters past and stares down at the board. "Looks like Gabe is gonna win."

Alex abruptly stands and points her finger at Zee, then at Gabe, before she growls loudly and storms from the room. The crash of the back door reverberates off the walls as it slams shut.

Kate stands, and a light, airy giggle escapes her lips. "Thank god you showed up when you did. I think they were about to trade blows."

Roan follows, running his hand over his red hair. "I better make sure she doesn't destroy anything."

"Good luck!" I call out to him as he follows after her.

Spending more time with Alex has given me a glimpse of her competitive nature and fiery temper. Roan will be good for her. The redhead is calm and patient.

Suzy moves around me into the room, placing her bag down on an armchair in the corner.

"I will never get over how beautiful this house is," she says, smiling at me.

"I know, right? Lukas did all the renovations himself." I grin.

"Hey!" Zee exclaims, his face set in a mask of faux offense. "He had help."

I snort with laughter as Zee puffs out his chest, a smirk lighting up his features. "Sorry. I didn't mean to offend you. Did I damage your manly ego?"

"Psh," Zee says, waving me off.

Smiling, I turn and start helping Gabe pack up the game. "I thought you'd know better than to play any kind of game with Alex."

A sparkle of amusement lights up his almond eyes as he looks up at me from the floor. "It's fun to wind her up."

I slowly shake my head, unable to contain my grin, and snap the lid shut on the box. "This game is going in the bin," I declare.

"What?!" Zee objects, halting his steps into the kitchen, making Kate bump into him.

"This is not staying here."

"But–"

"No." I shake my head. I move past him and Kate into the kitchen, placing the board game in the cupboard next to the bin. With a firm push, I close the door and brush my hands together.

"So, where is Lukas?" I ask.

"He's down at the barn getting the meat ready. I was planning to go and help him after the game," Gabe pipes up as he and Suzy follow us into the kitchen. Suzy settles onto the bar stool at the breakfast bar, Kate joining her with a friendly smile.

Zee slaps a hand on Gabe's back. "Let's go help Lukas."

Gabe nods and gives Suzy and Kate a genuine smile before walking out the door. Suzy's eyes widen with surprise when Zee walks over and places a kiss on each of our heads before striding out the back door.

I cover my mouth to stifle my laugh.

"So smooth," Kate says, making Suzy blush and giggle.

Her giggles are contagious, and I can't help but join in with a hearty laugh.

"I can't believe they still sell that game. It caused so many fights between me and my brother growing up," Suzy admits.

"How old is your brother?" Kate asks.

"Jared's two years older than me. He's studying to become a doctor. The brains of the family. I'm the artistic one." She gets up and does a little twirl, emphasizing her words, her ruffled layered maxi skirt flaring out with the movement. I swear this girl just never feels the cold.

I grin at her. "Want a coffee?"

"Yes, please," Suzy answers.

I put the milk on the counter and reach for two glasses.

"Kate, did you want a coffee?"

"Is that a trick question?" she jokes.

I shake my head, a wide grin spreading across my face, and the sound of the espresso machine starting fills the room as I make us some drinks.

"Do you miss home?" I hear Suzy ask Kate.

"Kind of, but I'm happy to be here and getting to know Nesrin and Astraea."

"I'm sorry about the death of your brother," Suzy whispers.

When I turn my head to peek over my shoulder, I notice Kate's slight shrug, her body language speaking volumes. "Thanks. He was the baby in the family, always up to something he shouldn't be."

Suzy stands and moves closer, wrapping Kate in a gentle hug, and Kate releases a weak, trembling laugh, freezing for a moment before her body melts into Suzy's comforting hug.

"Seems we have all lost someone close to us," Suzy says before taking her seat again.

"Yeah," Kate sighs.

We shift the conversation to something more cheerful before heading down to the barn, the smell of dinner wafting through the air.

"Hey, girls! What crawled up Alex's butt and died?" Asena asks as she comes to stand next to me.

I snort, choking on my water, then erupt into a full belly laugh, doubling over and gasping for breath. Asena's pale blue eyes hold mirth as she looks between us all. Kate smacks me on the back, doing her best not to laugh. Suzy and Kyra have no such trouble containing their laughter. It rings out around us.

"We tried to have a civil game of Monopoly today," Kate responds in amusement.

Asena cringes, pulling her silky brown hair over her shoulder. "Damn. That game is never civilized."

"Right?" Suzy agrees, snickering.

Suzy seems to be fitting in nicely with the girls, I just worry about her finding out about us. I don't think it's something I can keep from her for much longer, but I also have no idea how she'll take it. Then I mentally slap myself as it dawns on me that this is Suzy. She'll be fine about it. But, as usual, I'm still dragging my feet.

I sense Lukas's presence the moment he arrives, peering over my shoulder as he makes his way toward me, the fading light from the sunset lighting his eyes.

They just had a meeting about what happened in the city. Having the high fae roaming the streets doesn't bode well for any of us. They are a whole different kettle of fish.

'Stop worrying, freckles.'

His voice is low, his deep green eyes boring into mine.

'It's hard not to.'

He gazes down at me, a tender expression on his face, though I can see concern in the depths of his eyes.

'I don't want you to worry about it.' His eyes search mine, making time stand still. My body heats, and my pulse speeds up. Then his mouth descends on mine, forestalling my response. He takes his time, his tongue sliding against mine in a slow, sensual glide. When he draws back, his teeth catch on my bottom lip, gently tugging before he releases it. I let out a sigh of contentment and feel the strength of his arms around me, as my forehead rests against his chest.

I turn my head and feel his strong, steady heartbeat against my cheek, and the low hum of my friends' conversation is comforting. We're safe for now. Marcus mentioned the coven is lying low, and we haven't come across any more monsters, daemons, or beasts—whatever you want to call them. Leila hasn't returned or mentioned anything about who Hades suspects opened the gates. So, at the moment, we're all just waiting. I can't bear the waiting. The energy in the air tells me the reprieve won't last. And, despite my usual patience, I'm beginning to feel my nerves fraying as I give people a chance to prove themselves. I suck in deep, soothing breaths, trying my hardest to remain calm.

CHAPTER TEN

The following morning, I stomp angrily down the stairs and storm into the kitchen where I find Zee and Gabe at the coffee machine talking, and my irritation ignites.

"What the hell is wrong with you?" I growl.

Both men abruptly turn toward me, each pointing a thumb at themselves in question.

My gaze zeroes in on Zee. "You!"

Zee takes a sip of his coffee before answering, "Okay, wow. I realize you're not a morning person—like, at all—but you could at least say good morning."

I cross my arms over my chest, thrusting my hip out to the side as aggravation wholly takes control, and let out a huff. "Good morning. Now, what the hell is wrong with you?" I ask again.

"You're going to have to be more specific."

"Yeah, there is a lot wrong with him," Gabe quips, walking over and handing me a mug of coffee, the smell warming my body and making my mouth water.

Bringing it to my mouth, I take a sip and sigh, already starting to feel better as the caffeine works its way through my body, providing comfort and warmth. My frayed edges suddenly smooth and I relax as the coffee works its magic on me.

"Thank you."

With a slight nod, Gabe's eyes crinkle in warmth before he ambles over to the table and takes a seat.

"Well?" Zee asks, arching an eyebrow, waiting for me to explain my outburst.

"Your mom arrived yesterday, and you didn't tell me. Being that I'm the new luna, I should have welcomed her back!" I exclaim, my anger rising again.

I don't know why I'm so worked up about this. Usually, I would brush my feelings aside and move on, but today the weight of everything seems a little extra. Lukas only informed me ten minutes ago that Blue's wife Nadia has returned from Russia. I was shocked at first that no one even bothered to mention anything last night. Then I bypassed my feelings of upset entirely and was quickly overcome with anger.

He thought my reaction was amusing, so I left him to shower on his own. Zee must have thought it was entertaining as well, judging by the way he's currently trying to hide his obnoxious smirk behind his coffee mug.

I stomp my foot, throwing my fists down by my sides in a move that reminds me very much of Astraea when she doesn't get her way, which only makes my mood more sour. "Zee, it's not funny! I've been waiting forever to meet your mom, and I haven't seen Blue in ages. Astraea and I would have loved to know she was home."

Zee's eyes soften, and he twists, putting his coffee down before walking over to me. He crosses his arm over his waist and bows, grinning up at me. His long blonde hair is unbound and hanging over his face. "I'm so sorry for my grave mistake, milady. I shall remedy it immediately," he says teasingly.

Playing along because, shit, now I feel stupid, I take a sip of my coffee, mustering as much authority as I can in my tone, replying, "See that you do."

Gabe's laugh echoes through the kitchen, and I lose my battle to keep a straight face. Zee chuckles and turns back for his coffee as Lukas walks in behind me. Wrapping his arms around my waist, he kisses the top of my head. "Sorted?" he murmurs.

"Yes. Zee is fixing his mistake," I tell him.

Lukas laughs, moving past me for the coffee machine. "I'm glad. You will love Nadia. I'm sure she's already baked her favorite chicken casserole and apple pie for you," he promises, and I can practically hear the longing in his voice.

Zee chuckles. He seems lighter today, and I wonder if it's because his mom is finally home after spending months visiting family in Russia.

I rub my hands together, bouncing on my toes. "Great. When are we leaving?"

"Calm down, tiger. Mom invited us for dinner, and we have training today," Zee bursts right through my bubble.

I drop my hands and stop bouncing, almost whining. "Really?" All three guys laugh.

"Can you hear her excitement?" Gabe chuckles.

"Hey, the disappointment is real," I pout. With Nadia coming back, I was definitely hoping to use that to be able to get out of training. I point at Zee. "You said you'd fix your mistake immediately."

Zee shrugs as he moves toward me. "I did. We're going for dinner. AFTER training."

Lukas brushes past me, dropping a kiss to the top of my head. "Get your sneakers on. We have a five-mile run in twenty minutes."

"Five miles!" I actually do whine this time. I'm about to bring up Astraea, but Lukas beats me to it.

"And Kate has Astraea. So, no excuse," he shouts over his shoulder, striding out the back door with Zee and Gabe.

I let out a loud groan, tilting my head back in frustration as I contemplate the five miles I have to run. Just the thought of it exhausts me. I know there's a reason why we're doing it. Lukas wants to make sure I'm familiar with his territory and borders. Things would be a lot easier if I were able to shift into my wolf again. My senses would be enhanced, and I wouldn't tire as easily. Unfortunately, I haven't had the courage to shift again since that first time, and I'm ashamed to admit that I'm too scared to try.

I'm out of breath and dripping with sweat when we reach the top of the hill behind the barn. I slowly bend at the waist, my hands landing on my knees. Tilting my head back, I look up and take in the sight of Zee, Gabe and Lukas, who are somehow able to speak with no sign of breathlessness.

"That's totally unfair," I whine, waving my hand at them.

There's a mischievous glint in Lukas's eyes as he approaches me with a smirk. Standing up, my hands go to my hips as I pull in a few more deep breaths. I can feel the sweat cooling on my skin, my tank top soaked. Lukas's warm hands slide around my waist and pull me into him. I instinctively put my hands on his biceps for support.

"Lukas, I'm all sweaty and gross."

His head dips and his mouth is on my neck, his hands moving to my hips as he holds me close to his hard body. He bites down on my neck, making my skin erupt in goosebumps and a needy moan escapes my lips. Lukas's mouth moves to mine, his tongue sliding over my bottom lip before claiming my mouth in a hot kiss. I dig my fingers into his arms as he makes me pant for a whole new reason.

When Lukas pulls back, his eyes are blazing with desire. "You taste divine, freckles," he murmurs.

Suddenly, we are hit with an icy blast of water, soaking us within seconds. Coughing, I duck my face into his chest, trying to hide. A deep rumbling comes from Lukas's chest, and I feel him shaking as the onslaught stops. I raise my eyes and see that he's laughing.

"Glad you're enjoying yourself," I grumble, as I glare at Gabe, who simply shrugs in innocence.

"Immensely." Lukas grins, looking me up and down.

Zee claps Gabe on the back, "That's one way to cool them down. Good job," he chuckles.

"So are we sparring?" Gabe asks.

Startled, I glance around at them. "Sparring?"

"Yes." Zee smiles broadly.

I shake my head. "Nope. No. Not happening."

"Come on." Gabe chuckles, taunting, "Don't be a baby."

My jaw drops and I grit my teeth. "Fine."

Lukas walks past me, slapping me on the ass. My eyes flare wide as my face heats. What is going on right now? Are they trying to wind me up?

Gabe steps forward, shaking his head. "I'll pair with Nesrin."

Lukas looks like he wants to object, but Zee slaps him on the back. "Save it for the bedroom, brother."

I'm absolutely mortified. I turn away from them and walk toward the river, waiting for Gabe. When he reaches me, I take a deep breath.

"Right, you ready?" Gabe asks.

I bob my head in agreement and bounce up and down on the balls of my feet to make sure I'm ready to move.

Gabe steps forward, throwing a punch toward my face. Spinning around, I grip his forearm as I duck and twist, pulling his arm behind his back. I try to push Gabe off balance by kicking the back of his knees, but he manages to stay upright and escape my hold.

He faces me, sending a few more blows my way, which I easily counter. His next hit, instead of deflecting, I grab his arm again. Only this time, I use his body weight as an anchor as I lean back, planting my left leg and bringing my right knee up to connect with his midsection.

Gabe lets out a rare grunt, his eyes wide with surprise. Straightening up, he spins, somehow taking my legs out from under me. I land flat on my back with a loud thud. Gabe's hand is suddenly in my face, and I feel the warmth of his palm as I reach up and grab it to pull myself to my feet.

"You're getting better," he says.

I narrow my eyes in his direction.

"What? You are."

"Thanks."

We go at it for another ten minutes before I flop down onto the grassy hill exhausted, gazing up at the sky. "I'm done."

Gabe's face hovers over mine, and he chuckles. "Okay."

I hear him make his way over to the others and sigh in relief. Thank the goddess that's over. I sit up with a groan, my gaze landing on the river. It's not long before I see Astraea come skipping over to sit on my lap. My arms wrap around her as I pull her close, breathing in her scent.

This girl is everything

I sense Lukas approach, butterflies taking flight in my stomach as the bond brushes against my mental shields. Lukas's warm body fits in behind mine, his arms wrapping around me, pulling me back to lean against his chest. Astraea's head lifts, her indigo eyes locking with Lukas's and a gentle smile playing on her lips before she nestles closer to my chest. We sit in silence, feeling the coolness of the evening air as the sun sets on the horizon. Shades of oranges, red, pinks, and purples streak across the sky.

"We should get ready for dinner," Lukas murmurs.

"Yeah," I whisper back.

CHAPTER ELEVEN

Nerves fill my stomach as Blue opens the front door, his warm, friendly face and bright eyes greeting us. A blonde lady around Blue's age pushes past him and grabs my hands, pulling me toward her. Her startling blue eyes, only a shade darker than Blue and Zee's, soften as she regards me. "Oh. Look at you, you're gorgeous," Nadia beams, then she looks at Lukas. "Dear boy, you've done well." She winks at him, and I swear I see his cheeks flush.

Astraea's small body wriggles in his arms as she tries to get a better glimpse of the stranger.

"And who is this sweet thing?!" Nadia exclaims, pushing her blonde hair behind her ears as she steps closer to Astraea.

Blue comes to stand next to his wife, and directly in Astraea's line of sight. Letting out a barely audible giggle, she basically leaps from Lukas's arms to his, Blue easily catching her and bringing her to his chest.

"Oh, she is adorable," Nadia gushes.

I can practically see little hearts in her eyes as she takes in Blue and Astraea. Her gaze moves over the four of us, and she fixes Zee with a stare.

"Not now, mom," Zee groans.

Nadia waves him away. "What? Is it too much to ask for some grandchildren?"

I smother my laugh and Zee grunts. Blue comes to the rescue at Zee's pleading look.

"Leave the boy be, Nadia. We can't rush these things." Blue chuckles, wrapping an arm around his wife's shoulders.

Nissa comes drifting in at that moment, settling on my shoulder. Nadia looks at the sprite and again at me. Her eyes are filled with questions, but she holds back. Giving me a warm smile, she motions for us to follow her through the house and outside to a closed-in entertainment area. A small fireplace is nestled in the corner, and a large wooden table is set in the middle of the room, wooden chairs situated around it. Zee's hand lands on my shoulder, giving it a gentle squeeze as he moves past me to the table where food is already waiting. I grin, shaking my head. This man is always hungry.

A knock sounds from the door a moment before Gabe walks in. His long, dark hair is down for a change, seeming to soften his sharp features. His features often make him appear strong and silent, especially when his hair is pulled back. But when he lets his hair down, his true personality shines through. Gabe is caring, loyal, and selfless, but he's also fun and gives everyone the benefit of the doubt. Lukas and I both know that Gabe is the only one, other than the two of us, who has attempted to get to know our newest pack member over the last couple of days.

I open my mouth to say *hi,* when another figure walks in behind him. A genuine smile lights my face as I watch Nikolas follow Gabe through the house, uncertainty lining his face.

"We didn't miss the food, did we?" Gabe asks, sending me a wink.

"Not at all, Gabe," Nadia says, kissing him on the cheek. Her eyes move past Gabe and a snarl forms on her lips. My stomach bottoms out, and before I even realize I've moved, I am in front of Nikolas.

"He is family," I state quickly.

Everyone goes deadly quiet. I can feel Nissa's tight grip on my hair, but I don't take my eyes off Nadia's. Nikolas can take care of himself, but I won't risk it. I promised Stephan. Nikolas is pack, and mine to defend as such.

Nadia is standing stock still. Surprise shines in her eyes as they move from me to the vampire and then the sprite. Astraea moves through the group and walks over to me. Her tiny hand reaches up and takes my hand before she reaches behind me, grabbing Nikolas's.

"Lukas, what exactly is going on here?" Nadia asks.

Blue walks over to his wife's side and smiles down at her, grabbing her hands in his. His expression is tender and understanding.

"It's okay, love. I told you we had a lot to discuss. Lukas can explain everything. And, though Nesrin is different, she is also a beautiful soul. She would never put us in harm's way. I trust her." Warmth flows through me at the compliment. Still, I can see concern lining Nadia's face.

Her voice is shaky. "We have a vampire in our house, Blue."

Gabe speaks up. "I'm sorry. I didn't really think about it. I ran into Nikolas in town, and asked him to join us. Sorry. I should have asked first."

I can sense his unease and open my mouth to reassure him. But Nikolas's hand squeezes my arm as he moves around me, Astraea's hand still clasped in his.

"I mean no harm. Nesrin is my master, and I would do nothing to endanger her or this pack. Lukas and Nesrin have my full loyalty."

Lukas has been watching the entire scene play out with Zee a few feet away. He nods his head at Nikolas in acceptance.

Nadia merely shakes her head in what looks like resignation. "Okay, then let's eat."

"I don't like the word master, by the way," I whisper, poking Nikolas in the side as I move past him and make my way over to Lukas, who pulls out a chair for me, and we take our seats.

"It is what you are. It's another title like luna. But if you prefer, I will stick with ma reine."

I roll my eyes, holding back a smile. Nikolas is really quite charming, and not at all what I expected of a vampire. Lukas and Zee are slowly warming up to him. But Astraea is basically in love with the man, and I trust her judgment on these things. She always seems to know who to trust and who not to.

A scratching noise comes from the door behind Blue that leads into the back yard.

"Do you hear that?" I cock my head, trying to make out the noise.

"Honey, we are shifters. Of course, we hear that," Zee laughs, shaking his head at me. I immediately poke my tongue out as Lukas pats my leg under the table.

"It's Malachite," he says with a grin, his dimple on full display.

Blue stands and opens the door. Without delay, a tiny dragon with blue and green scales scurries between his legs, and under the table before quickly ascending Lukas's body to perch on his shoulder. Smiling, I reach over and run a hand over his head. Malachite has taken a liking to Lukas. Whenever Lukas is around, the dragon has to be perched on his shoulder. Malachite's tail wraps around my wrist, holding my hand close so he can nuzzle it. My heart flutters. I love this creature so much already.

"What are you doing here? You should know better," I chide softly at the dragon.

Malachite lets out a small huff, shaking his body, causing his scales to ripple in color. I don't think he enjoyed being left behind. I have no clue how he found us though. We're at least a twenty-minute drive away, and most of the distance between is forest.

Astraea climbs onto the chair next to me and I grin down at her. When I glance up, Nadia is staring at us in bewilderment. She seems lost for words. Zee takes pity on his mom and helps her sit in her chair across from us.

Nissa stays perched on my shoulder. Tonight, her long brown hair is braided in flowers, and she wears a glittery yellow gown. "You look beautiful, Nissa," I whisper. The sprite's eerie violet eyes swung my way, and she preens.

"Thank you," she chimes.

With everybody seated, Lukas leans forward, his elbows resting on the table. My eyes automatically go to his biceps and forearms, the movement flexing the muscles. My face flushes and I glance away. Lukas's amusement floats down our bond and I glare his way. Even though he isn't looking at me, I can see the smile tugging at his lips.

"Nadia, as you can tell, a few things have changed since you've been away."

"I can see that. I have been gone for one year . . . Which, yes, I suppose quite a lot can happen in that amount of time," she replies, rubbing at her temples. I feel a pang of sympathy for her. She wouldn't have been expecting a bunch of changes waiting for her when she arrived home. It's no surprise that she was off balance.

"Yes. In that time, I met Nesrin." This time, he turns my way. A tender expression passes over his face before he turns back to Nadia. "Nesrin is a legacy."

"She also likes to bring home strays," Zee adds, and I scowl at him.

"What? It's true. We have a dragon and a vampire now, and not to mention other creatures that like to hang around," he says, looking pointedly at Nissa.

I try not to laugh as she crosses her tiny arms and raises her chin, glaring back at Zee.

"A legacy?" Nadia asks.

"I'm descended from the goddess Althaea, and part shifter." I peer down at Astraea, running my hand over her head. She tips her head up to look at me. "So is Astraea."

'I love you, sweet girl,' I whisper into her head. Her answering smile lights my soul.

Blue holds his wife's hand. "Nesrin and Astraea moved here not long after you left. They have lost everybody dear to them. Nesrin has the coven after her—well, more specifically, the Order of Tartarus. They are determined to kill her and any remaining family of this goddess."

"She restored Nikolas of his light. Healed two pack members of a hex and Alex from the spell that had left her with third-degree burns to most of her body," Gabe pipes up.

"Delivered a troll baby," Lukas adds.

"Don't forget our friend, Cerberus," Zee says, smirking as he takes a sip of his beer. I shoot him a glare. Is he trying to freak his mom out?

"That was all Astraea. Plus, he was just a big playful puppy dog." I shrug, shifting uncomfortably in my seat.

"Sure, he was," Zee fires back.

"What?" Nadia croaks, placing a hand over her heart.

"Someone released Cerberus and a few other creatures from Tartarus in order to hunt me down, but Astraea here tamed the beast of Hades."

"Who later showed up in your house to retrieve him," Zee adds.

I glare at Zee, wishing he was close enough to kick. He is not helping.

"Nothing bad happened."

"Hades?!" "Nothing bad?!" Nadia and Zee both exclaim at the same time.

Oh my god, the poor woman looks like she's going to faint. Lukas rushes to reassure her.

"Nadia, it's okay. Yes, we have had a few interesting encounters, but I assure you we are handling it. I will do everything in my power to protect you all."

"As will I," I agree.

Nadia blows out a long breath. She looks at her husband and laughs weakly. "I'm a Russian woman and we are born tough." Nodding as if to reassure herself, she glances back at me. "Don't like that the gods have shown so much interest in you, but as Lukas said, it's nothing we can't handle," Nadia says, her blue eyes locked on me. She blinks and takes in the rest of our group. "Well then. I'm happy to have you all here. Let's eat before dinner gets cold."

Blue looks at Nikolas and frowns. "Can you eat?"

Nikolas gives the older man a genuine smile. "No sir, I cannot. But I'm just happy to be here." His eyes are more silver than blue tonight and I wonder if his eye color reflects his mood.

Nissa lifts from my shoulder with a flutter of wings, landing gracefully on the dinner table next to Astraea. I have a sneaking suspicion they're communicating telepathically. Taking my fork, I scoop up some chicken pot pie, then hum in delight as the flavors explode on my tongue.

Lukas was right. Nadia's cooking is amazing!

I hear a chorus of chuckles go around the table and glance up. Everyone's eyes are on me, and I stop chewing, sensing their amusement through the pack bond.

"What?" I mumble, around a mouth full of food.

"Nothing, sweetheart," Lukas responds, squeezing my thigh lightly.

"I spoke out loud, didn't I?"

"Yes."

"I'm pleased everybody appreciates my cooking," Nadia beams.

The rest of dinner passes smoothly, Gabe and Zee keeping the conversation light and fun. I relax back in my chair, smiling contentedly, and ever so grateful for Zee's simple, easy-going nature. Nikolas is quietly observing the group. This is, after all, his first get together with the pack. Malachite is wandering around under the table taking what food he can, shining those gorgeous, adorable golden eyes up at people. He kind of reminds me of a puppy.

CHAPTER TWELVE

Nikolas is the first to leave after dinner, having business to attend to back in Portland. Lukas, Zee, and I decide we'll walk back, so Gabe goes ahead, taking Astraea and Malachite home in his car. Usually the thought of walking that far would make me drag my feet in dismay, but tonight I need the forest. As I step outside, I feel the cool, fresh air on my skin, the sensation soothing my soul and replenishing my magical energy. My magic feels connected to the energy of the world around me, even though I draw on it from within. It's what my mother taught me, to draw on the elements. She didn't realize at the time that I hold my own spark of magic. Now it's a habit I can't break.

I groan, rubbing my stomach as we crunch over the dried leaves on the ground. The three of us are thoroughly full after that feast. Zee seems content, and I'm happy his mom is finally back home. I think she and Grace will probably get along well.

We walk in comfortable silence for around twenty minutes, taking in the sounds and smells of the forest. I can faintly sense the hint of rain in the air. The earthy rich scent around me is calming. I stumble on a rock and manage to stay upright by sheer luck. I felt a strange tingling sensation between my shoulder blades, like the feeling of being watched. Shrugging my shoulders, I roll them around, trying to dispel the feeling that's creeping over my skin. With each step I take toward Lukas and Zee, my anxiety rises, and I feel my palms begin to sweat. An icy chill runs up my spine, making the hairs at the back of my neck stand on end. I stop and take a deep breath, my eyes sweeping the area, looking for anything amidst the stillness of the trees. My body feels a wave of pain radiating outward from my chest and down my arms and legs as the prickling sensations become more intense.

"Guys," I gasp, not able to hide the panic in my voice.

Both stop talking and turn toward me, instantly reading my expression, and go on guard.

"Do you feel that?" I whisper, turning in a slow circle. Warning bells are now ringing loudly in my head. My phone vibrates in my pocket, and I glance down to see who's calling.

Grace.

I answer the call, lifting the phone to my ear.

'Nesrin, something is about to happen. I can't tell what, but–

'I know. Call later.'

I hang up and pocket my phone. Tension is tightening every muscle in my body. I can definitely sense something is out there watching, waiting, and if Grace got the sense something is wrong, it only means possible death.

Lukas's growl fills the air with a low, menacing rumble coming from deep within his chest. He moves in front of me, creating a wall between me and the imminent danger, while Zee moves behind me, enveloping me in a sense of security.

There is something out there. Where is it?

My pulse is thundering in my ears as I glance around Lukas's enormous frame. I can't make out anything as my eyes scan our surroundings. Abruptly, my chest grows cold, sucking the breath from me. Lukas spins, his glowing eyes searching my face.

Clutching my shoulder, he peers down at me. "Deep breaths. What do you feel?"

I close my eyes, taking a breath, concentrating on the awareness building inside me. "Evil. All I can sense is hostility. It is observing us, waiting. Northeast, about half a mile," I breathe.

I don't know how I know that, but I do. Somehow, I can sense its location and its intentions. Both men turn toward the area I indicated. I grip Lukas's arm, his muscles as hard as stone, his body tense and alert.

"Quarter mile," I whisper.

The creature is moving swiftly but silently through the forest.

"Where?" Zee asks, his eyes searching the forest.

Lukas makes a resounding noise in the back of his throat. "I can smell it, but I can't see it."

"It reeks," Zee agrees.

My eyes flash open, my vision tinted with white. My gaze lands on a large tree directly in front of me and I raise my hand, pointing. "There."

They both look to where I point as a large body materializes from behind the tree. Its appearance is almost completely camouflaged within the background.

"Anyone else feel like this is a really bad dream?" Zee questions.

I must make a sound of distress because Lukas's head whips down at me. His eyes are completely yellow now, and glowing brightly. I can sense his worry and protectiveness bleeding through our bond. The creature drifts closer, stepping into the moonlight, and I want to rub my eyes and make sure I'm not seeing things. Lukas reaches down and unsheaths my dagger, placing it in my hand as I stare transfixed at the giant ogre in front of us. Although it's man-like in appearance, its gigantic body and bluish-green skin make clear that it is not human in nature. From here, I can clearly see a lot of muscle that makes up the ogre's size, giving it a sturdy shape. It only wears a pair of pants that are ripped, torn, and completely filthy. A thick layer of hair covers its entire upper body, which is probably where the smell is coming from. I fight the urge to gag, choosing instead to breathe through my mouth. Though, even that's a challenge—the rancid smell is unavoidable. The evil grin it sends our way shows off its sharp yellow teeth. I shiver in repulsion at the creature standing before us. Its overall appearance is at once fearsome and animalistic.

Lukas and Zee shift in an instant, both taking up the space in front of me. Lukas's hackles rise, his lips pulled back to expose long, sharp pearl-white fangs. He stalks toward the ogre, his ears pinned down. Zee stays in front of me, and I take the opportunity to discreetly draw my magic to the surface. My vision shifts, turning white, so I can only assume my goddess powers are making an appearance. I really wish I understood my power more.

My attention stays focused on Lukas as he approaches the ogre. Both pace in a circle, Lukas's tail lashes as he waits for the ogre to make a move. The ogre's body is coiled tight for an attack. It has the advantage of size, but Lukas is fast, and he has fangs.

The sound of the ogre's roar shakes the trees, sending birds scattering through the air before a hush falls over the forest. Zee's hackles rise, and he lets out a long snarl. My hands warm and I peer down to notice them moving, not having realized I was casting. As my hands work the spell, I hum. A bright ball of light floats in front of me as the threads weave together.

Glancing back at the ogre, I watch him lunge at Lukas, and have to bite back my panic. Lukas is a skilled fighter in both forms. He quickly dodges under the massive meaty arm currently swinging at him. The ogre spins around faster than something of his size should be capable of and charges Lukas again. He moves in time, but doesn't escape the backhand, sending him flying into a nearby tree. Zee howls before charging at the ogre.

The ogre's hand snaps out, punching Zee in the side of the head. Zee's limp body falls to the ground, and he doesn't move. Shock has me frozen to the spot, but Lukas's pain shoots through the bond, snapping me out of my panic. His shoulder has been broken, and he's cracked a few ribs. Before I have a chance to react, a black horse comes charging into the clearing, rearing up on its back legs. It kicks out, smacking the ogre in the face. The ogre stumbles, clearly dazed by the kick.

I blink in surprise. The Puca keeps showing up, like it's been sticking close by. Keeping watch over me. Maybe it thinks it owes me after I helped it all those months ago? Its golden eyes catch mine and it trots over to me, nudging me in the back, in the direction of the massively hideous ogre.

The ogre grins wickedly at me, and I realize I've just been standing here holding the spell.

Understanding dawns. The Puca wants me to use my spell. I bring my arms up in front of me, the ball of light sparking between my palms. My arms swing to the side and rotate up around behind my head, the movement drawing in and weaving the magic in the air around me.

As I move my arms around and down, I release the spell, sending it hurling at the ogre. Before he can react, I hurl another as he sidesteps the first spell, but he doesn't detect the second coming. It hits him in the chest, his body erupting in white flames. His screams rip through me, churning my stomach. I have never used that kind of spell before. I've never possessed that kind of power. A vanquishing spell requires lots of practice and certain skill.

I turn to face the Puca, but it's gone. Frowning, I scan the area and see Zee rising on unsteady paws. He shakes his fur as if shaking off water before shifting back into human form.

"Shit, he was built like a goddamn concrete house," Lukas groans, rolling to his feet in his human form once more. He winces, holding his arm against his body. His pain ripples through our bond, making me wince. Both my mate bond and my magic are pulling me toward him, demanding I heal him.

I reach for him. "Let me fix that shoulder."

"No, I'm fine."

I roll my eyes, crossing my arms. Does he always have to act like allowing me to heal him is a sign of weakness?

"No, you're not. I can sense your pain, remember?"

Lukas grunts and keeps walking.

"It's distracting. Let me heal you."

"Yeah, Lukas. Do you want your mate to feel your pain the entire way back to the house?" Zee smirks, obviously enjoying this way more than he should. I'm glad he seems to have gotten over that blow to the head.

Lukas lets out a low, menacing growl, halting his steps. A sigh of relief escapes me as I search for a place to take a seat.

"Over there. Sit down." I point toward a large boulder.

"Fine," Lukas grumbles.

As he sits, I move behind him, my hands going to his left shoulder. Lukas hisses in pain. I see Zee's forehead crease, his eyebrows drawing together.

Shifters generally heal quickly. The fact Lukas is still in pain means something is wrong. Closing my eyes I focus on his shoulder, realizing it's much worse than I realized. The injury has already begun healing, but it's healing the bones all wrong. I'm going to have to re-break it in order to fix it properly. I open my eyes, looking to Zee. "I need you to come here and take my spot."

Walking around to face Lukas, I grip his chin, tilting his head to mine so he can see my face.

"This is going to hurt," I warn.

He nods, his jaw clenched tightly. I place a soft kiss on his lips and straighten, my gaze meeting Zee's.

'Zee, when I say go, I want you to re-break the shoulder.'

Zee's eyes widen comically. *'What?!'*

'You heard me. On the count of three. One.'

'Nesrin. No.'

'Two.'

'I can't.'

'Yes, you can. You have to.'

Zee looks sick. The color drains from his face as he grips Lukas's arm tightly in his hands.

'Three!'

The crack that sounds makes me want to puke, but I've already started working my magic. Eyes closed, I knit the bones and muscles back together properly. Lukas's harsh breaths saw in and out, making my hair flutter around my face. His hand comes up, fisting the hair at the back of my head as I work. My eyes fly open, and I draw in a breath at the desire burning in his glowing green eyes. They are so bright with a mixture of lust and pain; they look like gems.

When the healing is complete, I slowly open my eyes and blink. Lukas's fist tightens almost painfully in my hair, sending a shiver across my skin. Before I can speak, his mouth slams down on mine. A wave of intense desire and hunger sweeps through me when his lips meet mine, making my stomach drop and my core clench.

Lukas suddenly lets go of my hair, and grips my waist with both hands. Spinning us, he pushes me back against the rock, the coolness seeping into my clothes making me gasp. He wastes no time, his tongue sweeping into my mouth, consuming me. His lips are a wildfire, burning a path across my jaw and down my neck. I moan and close my eyes as I melt into the touch, desperate to feel the sensation for as long as possible. My body instantly lights up, my breath coming out in quick sharp pants. His mouth hovers tantalizingly close to my neck, sending shivers down my spine before his lips curve into a smile and he bites down on my mating mark. I groan as heat rushes through me like molten lava, a desperate need coursing through me. Lukas grinds his erection against me, and I open my legs wider.

Somewhere in the back of my mind, I remember Zee is with us. I try to come out of the lust-filled haze that has overtaken me, but Lukas is dragging me down like quicksand. A warm palm glides under my shirt. His hand flattens against my stomach, pushing my t-shirt up. The cool breeze caresses my skin as Lukas lifts my shirt higher. I have enough sense left to search around for Zee, but I can't see him anywhere.

"He has gone ahead," Lukas murmurs, lips grazing my exposed stomach. I tip my head back, closing my eyes, enjoying his touch. The button on my jeans flicks open and so do my eyes.

"Lukas!" I exclaim.

"Yes?" he murmurs against my skin.

"We can't. Not here."

"'Course we can, sweetheart." Lukas tugs my jeans down my legs. His mouth moves lower, and I suck in a breath as his tongue flattens over my panties, sliding over me. My eyes flutter closed, a low moan escaping me. My fingers sink into his hair, and I give up my fight, my legs opening as much as my jeans will allow. Lukas shreds my panties, and before I can protest, his mouth is on me, licking, sucking, consuming me. I can't help but rock my hips into his mouth, shamelessly chasing my release.

Suddenly, Lukas pulls back, ripping my shoes off. My jeans follow close behind. It's now so dark and I can barely see a thing, which only serves to heighten my other senses. Lukas spins me again, this time guiding my hands to the rock. He grips my hips, lifting me to my tiptoes before rubbing the head of his cock along my entrance. I bite my lip to keep from moaning too loudly. Lukas's massive, warm body folds over mine, his teeth scraping my neck and shoulder. Without warning, he bites down on the mate mark at the same time as he sinks into me, sending sparks of pleasure coursing through me. Thank the goddess he has a firm hold on my hips or I would collapse from the sheer force of it.

Lukas's pace is relentless as he pounds into me over and over. I'm sure I'll have bruises from his fingers's tight grip on my hips, as he pulls me into his thrusts.

Hints of my orgasm squeeze him, making him wild. Savagely, he plunges into me, demanding that sweet release. One of his hands releases my hip and reaches up, his fingers sinking into my hair, clutching the back of my head. Lukas groans, his fist pulling my head back, causing me to arch my back as he sinks in deeper. My eyes water at the exquisite pain, my release right there.

Light flares, and energy crackles in the surrounding air. Biting down on my arm, I smother a scream as my orgasm is ripped from depths of my soul. I shatter into a million pieces. I feel all the particles floating in the air, lit with electricity.

"Fuuuuuuuck," Lukas roars. He thrusts a few more times before stilling inside of me.

It takes several minutes for our breathing to calm and reality to seep back in. As we come back to ourselves, Lukas gently turns me around, his palms framing my face, concern shining in his eyes.

"Are you okay?"

"Yes," I hum, a wave of exhaustion sweeping over me.

"I was too rough." His eyes move down my body. "You have bruises." How he can see anything is beyond me.

"What I have is an extraordinary mate, who just gave me the best sex of my life." I push up on my toes and kiss him tenderly on the lips then pull back, smiling. "Now, help me find my clothes, you caveman."

Lukas chuckles and collects my clothes, helping me dress. "Are you sure you're okay?" he asks again.

"I swear I'm fine. I'm more than fine."

"I love you." His hand engulfs mine, and I smile into the darkness as we make our way back home.

"I love you, too."

CHAPTER THIRTEEN

Asena certainly likes to shop. I despise it. My feet are killing me, and my body's sore from my romp in the forest with Lukas last night. Sure, I wanted to spend a day doing normal things after the events of the last few weeks, and I'm thankful that she offered to take me out, but I would have preferred to spend it with lunch and a movie as opposed to finding her a new wardrobe. Of course, I'm terrible at saying no to people, so I've just spent my day doing something I hate just to appease her. I'm honestly not sure I'm going to make a great luna.

Suzy joined us for lunch, which was a bright point, but she had to leave for class after we ate. I miss her already. I got so used to seeing her every day when she worked for me at the bookstore. And now I'm thinking about my poor, burned down bookstore, and feel a pinch in my chest. I'm not confident I have the funds to start over, even with the insurance money. I push those depressing thoughts from my mind and check the time on my phone.

We have been at the mall for *three hours*. Letting out a sigh, I send a message to Asena telling her I'll be waiting outside and to come find me when she's done. Distracted, I toy with the necklace at my throat and make my way outside. All I want is to escape the noise of the people around me. If another sales assistant tries to sell me a new jacket, I will scream. I love my jacket, and I will wear it until it falls apart. And probably even then. Niamh bought me this jacket for our twentieth birthday, knowing how much I wanted to buy it, but that I wouldn't be willing to spend that kind of money on myself.

Finding a bench close to the door, I make my way over. But before I have the chance to sit down, a curvy woman with a fashionable brown bob and beautiful caramel brown eyes appears in front of me.

"Hi, I'm Liv," she says brightly, twisting her hands on the strap of her handbag.

I blink in surprise and glance around, puzzled. "Hi," I reply slowly, unsure of what's happening, or why she's talking to me.

"I like your shoes," she chirps happily, rocking forward on her toes.

I stare down at my suede boots and frown before glancing back at her. My pendant hasn't warned me of danger, but this woman seems . . . off somehow. I wait for the feeling of ice to hit my chest, but nothing. I tilt my head as I study the woman in front of me. She's young—maybe early twenties—and seems a little unhinged, so I'm beginning to feel grateful Astraea had wanted to stay with Noah and Liam today.

"Thanks?"

The woman beams at me, and unease slithers down my spine.

"Well, it was nice to meet you," I say, going to step around her, but she moves with me, her brown eyes widening, an odd smile spreading across her round face.

"Really?"

I don't have to look at my face to know I'm pulling a *What the fuck* look right now. "What?"

"Was it nice meeting me?" she asks in a bubbly tone, but her strained smile is giving away her unease.

When I don't answer, she steps closer. "It was nice meeting you."

"Okay. Well. See you around," I reply, thoroughly confused by this conversation. If that's what you would even call it. She blocks me when I try to go around her, and I fight the urge to groan. I don't want to be rude, but I really need to sit down.

"You will. When?"

What the hell is wrong with this woman? I was just being polite, but she is making it so weird.

"When?" I question.

She seems really eager for my response, but I'm honestly just freaked out at this point, and her bubbliness is putting me on edge.

"When will you see me?" she clarifies, hope shining in her eyes. *For fuck's sake.*

Her eyes widen in surprise at my slip up, and I quickly scan the area for anyone who might be accompanying her, but I can't see anyone lurking nearby.

"I really don't know. Sorry," I stammer. I am beyond bewildered by this woman. This is, without a doubt, the weirdest conversation I've ever had. Which, considering recent events, really is saying something.

"Okay," she says brightly before turning on her heel and walking back through the throng of people. As I watch her walk away, I get the sense that someone else is watching me. I look around, my eyes drifting over the people on the street, but don't find anyone with their attention on me. Not a moment later, I see Asena come strolling out of the shops.

"Pumpkin spice! There you are."

I smother a laugh at the new nickname she has chosen for me. "Here I am," I chuckle.

"Want to get our nails done?" she asks, her light blue eyes filled with happiness. I won't ruin that. She needs this as much as I do.

I take another glance around, not spotting anyone paying us any attention. I smile at her. "Sure."

The impression of being watched follows me, making me edgy and uneasy. Now I just want to go back home.

Katy Perry's *Hot N Cold* is blaring from the car speakers as Asena and I speed down the dark and surprisingly empty forest road toward home. We're singing our hearts outs, my lungs and throat burning with the overuse. Something up ahead catches my attention and I frown, taking my foot off the accelerator. Reaching over, I turn the volume of the music down. Asena glances at me and pouts, but she must read my expression because she goes on alert.

"What's wrong?" she asks in alarm.

Leaning forward in my seat, my hands tighten on the steering wheel. "Do you see that?" I ask, my voice strangely calm as I point ahead. There, walking on the side of the road, is a woman. But, incredibly, that isn't the weird part. It's what she's wearing. The dress is long, white, and clearly very outdated. The bottom is brown from dragging along the ground. As we draw closer, I can see it's filthy from dirt and torn in places. Her gait is slow and unnatural. I put my foot on the brake so I can pull up next to her.

Rolling my window down, I lean out slightly, my heart thumping wildly in my chest.

"Excuse me, miss. Are you okay?" I call out to her.

I swallow hard as I wait, a sense of foreboding filling me. The woman stops walking, but doesn't answer. She doesn't look over at the car. Her long black hair whips around her head, keeping her face concealed. Asena grips my arm, her nails digging into my skin. My pendant chooses that moment to flare to life, and the awful realization hits me as ice seizes my chest, squeezing tightly, making my breath wheeze out of me.

Danger.

I open my mouth to ask again if she's okay when she turns her head. Her eyes connect with mine, and before I can even blink she's only inches from my face. Startled, I jerk back in my seat, and Asena lets out a squeak of surprise. How did she move so fast?

My eyes stay glued to the woman at the window. She looks to be in her teens. Her empty gray eyes are swollen, and red rimmed as if she's been crying for a long, long time. So at odds with her otherwise ashen and lifeless face. My gaze moves from her eyes to her mouth, which is open in a silent scream. Her black teeth are sharpened to points. Asena gasps, her nails cutting into my arm deeply enough that I know I'm going to have crescent-shaped bruises tomorrow.

"Nesrin," she says, unnerved.

Deciding this is not a woman I can help, I start to drive forward, wanting to put as much space between us and whatever this thing is. Suddenly, a sharp keening wail comes from her mouth. It's so loud I have to cover my ears, my own scream rising in my throat. My chest is frozen with fear. I push my foot down on the accelerator, flooring it. The car speeds forward, my hands slamming back down on the steering wheel.

"What the hell was that??" Asena asks, sounding breathless.

Asena twists in her seat, trying to see where the woman went. Looking in the rearview mirror, I see nothing. I shake my head. If not for the icy pain in my chest and the ringing in my ears, I would think I imagined it. We make it to the house in record time. Putting the brakes on, I skid to a stop in front of the house. Asena and I are sitting there panting as if we ran the entire way home. Next thing I know, the car door is being ripped open and Lukas is hauling me out of the car.

I'm smashed against a hard chest as he holds me like I might disappear at any moment. My hands rest on his back. I can feel his body tremble under my palms.

Lukas's arms tighten around me. "I felt your fear. It nearly knocked me over, it was so strong. I was on my way to come find you when I spotted your headlights."

"I'm sorry," I mumble into his chest, soaking up the warmth from his body. All mine seemed to vanish as soon as I met the eyes of that strange woman. Pulling back, he takes in my face, then scans my body from head to toe and back again before his eyes reach mine. His desperation steals my breath.

"Are you hurt?"

"No. I– I'm fine," I stammer.

Asena is out of the car and making her way over to us, her arms wrapped tightly around her waist, her pale blue eyes wide in shock. Even her dark skin looks ghostly white.

Lukas looks at the two of us. "Tell me exactly what happened, and don't say '*nothing.*' You're both pale, your heart rate is elevated, and Asena looks like she's seen a ghost."

I give him a wary look. "Actually, it was something like that. We saw a woman," I admit, reaching up and playing with my pendant.

Lukas's eyes track my movement, and his face hardens. A shiver runs over me and even under my jacket I can feel the hairs on my arm stand on end. Lukas notices, mistaking it for being cold. He grabs my hand, pulling me toward the house behind him. The events of the drive home are fresh in my mind. The image of that woman's face is burned into my brain. Those dead, soulless eyes and sharp black teeth will forever haunt me in my dreams, I'm sure of it.

I recall the moments before we came across the woman and then what happened during our encounter, even how I felt. Asena pipes in, adding her versions of the event. Mostly our tales are the same, except that she never heard the wailing, which is odd because it was ear piercing.

Looking at Lukas, I can see the thunder cloud forming over him. He is furious, his knuckles turning white from the grip he has on the kitchen bench. He stares at me hard for a long moment before pushing off the bench and running a hand through his hair.

"FUCK!" he shouts, turning away from me.

When he turns back around, his eyes have flecks of yellow flashing through them and his body is taut, which tells me he is struggling to keep his anger in check, so I decide not to say a word until he's had a chance to calm down.

'He is acting like a male whose mate was threatened. Just give him a moment,' Zee's voice floats through my mind. I peer over to find him standing behind where Asena is seated at the table. She looks nervous as she tracks Lukas.

"Do you know what it was?" he grinds out. I merely shake my head. I've seen nothing like it before, but . . .

"If I had to guess, I would say a banshee. But Grace is the only banshee I know, and she is *nothing* like that woman. She was a creature made of nightmares, the kind of banshees they tell stories about."

Chills run down my spine, accompanied by a burst of goosebumps. I can't shake that horrible feeling from seeing the woman. The sound of her scream and those lifeless eyes. I shift uncomfortably on my feet, wanting this feeling to just go away. My hands reach for my hair, pulling it over my shoulder as my fingers twist in the strands. Lukas releases a ragged sigh, running a hand through his disheveled hair.

"There's not much to do about it tonight, but I can talk to Grace in the morning," I say, trying to reassure him.

"I sent out a scouting team to see what they can find. If she's still around, which I highly doubt, we'll find her," Lukas replies.

"Okay," I answer softly, sending him a wave of affection down the bond.

Lukas's composure falters, and in two purposeful strides, he is on me, his hands holding my face as his lips descend, devouring mine. He is relentless in his exploration. I could stay like this forever, but the murmurs from Zee and Asena bring me back to the present, and I slowly pull back from Lukas, giving him a reassuring smile.

Asena and Zee say goodnight and make their way outside so Zee can escort her home. I watch them disappear down the hill from my spot at the door, goosebumps scattering across my body. I rub my hands over my arms, trying to wipe away the sense of wrongness that's lingering over me. The temperature in the air drops enough that my breath comes out in puffs of smoke and my teeth chatter. Stepping back, I shut the door quickly and turn the lock. I peer out the small window into the dark yard. *Could she be out there watching?*

'Ma reine. Are you okay? I can sense your worry.'

Startled by Nikolas's voice in my head, I jerk, tugging on the curtain with force enough to nearly make it fall down.

"Are you okay?" Lukas says from behind me.

I startle again, a shriek falling from my lips. My hand goes to my heart, where it pounds against my ribcage. "You scared the shit out of me, Lukas," I grumble.

He closes the distance between us and takes my face in his hands. They are so warm they seem to burn my ice-cold cheeks. Lukas's brow creases. "You're freezing."

"Yeah . . . I got a chill. Come, let's go up to bed," I say, grabbing his hand and pulling him upstairs. I need to get my mind off this sense of impending doom that is slowly creeping its way into my body.

I stop at Astraea's room, pushing the door open. She is curled up on the gigantic bed with Malachite next to her, his head resting on her small body. She's sleeping on her side, her wolf teddy clutched tightly to her chest. Malachite lifts his sleepy head at my appearance and, seeing it's just me, he plops it back down on Astraea's side. Slowly, I walk over to the bed, sitting down gently so as not to wake her. She looks like an angel when she's sleeping, blonde hair scattered around her sweet, innocent face. I stroke my fingers over her head and smile.

Leaning down, I kiss her softly on the head and whisper, "I love you."

Malachite, appearing left out, gives my hand a nudge. A soft chuckle escapes me, and I reach over to run a hand down his back. "I love you, too."

The dragon preens and snuggles back down, closing his golden eyes, a soft purr-like sound leaving his mouth.

'*Ma reine?*'

'*I'm okay, Nikolas. Just had a scare tonight. Everything is fine. Thank you for checking.*'

'*Okay. If you need me, I'm at your disposal.*'

'*Thank you, but we're fine now.*'

I stand, making my way into the hall. I lean on the wall, rubbing my temples. My life just keeps getting weirder. I can't believe Nikolas can mindspeak with me. I honestly thought that was a shifter thing. But maybe it's actually a pack thing, and since Nikolas is technically pack, I suppose it makes sense that he can communicate with me.

CHAPTER FOURTEEN

My feet crunch on the snow as I make my way toward the common building at the bottom of the hill. I love how Lukas set up his land with the pack. The building where the pack hangs out and has meals together is like a large barn with a loft and fireplace; warm, cozy, and welcoming. Each family has their own house here on the property, all spaced out enough that each has some semblance of privacy and then the enormous area in the middle where they all gather. Not everybody eats with the group all the time, obviously. Each has their own family, job, and life, so they join with the group when they choose to.

By now, the pack should all be finished eating dinner. Merve and Grace are here visiting tonight and I'm excited to get to see them. I still can't believe they're dating.

I sigh. It would have been nice for Lukas to be here. I was disappointed when he went out on patrol with Zee. Astraea is asleep with Malachite in her room, and I don't want to be alone in the house when I have the chance to be around friends.

My feet slide on the cold ground and my breath mists in front of me as I walk hastily down the hill. I frown as I approach the building. It's quiet. Too quiet. My steps slow and I glance around as a tingling sensation prickles at my back. I'm being watched; I am sure of it. As I near the double doors to the building, the strange feeling only increases, moving from between my shoulder blades, outward across my body.

"Where is everyone?" I mutter. It's unusual for it to be this quiet, especially if we have visitors.

I reach up and place my hand on the door, dread washing over me. My chest fills with a deep-seated coldness, and I gasp, rubbing at it. I know it means something important, and I frown as I can't recall what exactly that is. The urge to turn and run hits me square in the gut, stealing my breath. I glance over my shoulder, scanning the area surrounding the building. The only sound is the river that flows through the valley. Looking back to the door, I take a deep breath and push it open. I make it two steps inside and jerk to a stop. My hands come up to cover my mouth as an inhuman moan escapes me.

"No, no, no, no, no, no, no, no, no . . ."

Blood is coating everything—the walls, the tables, the chairs. A scream builds in my throat as I look over the limbs scattered about the room. Someone has ripped them from the bodies and they now lie among overturned tables and chairs. I take an unsteady step forward, wavering on rubber legs.

This can't be happening.

Grief strikes me hard and fast at the massacre laid out in front of me. It slices through the haze in my mind, a crack splintering my chest.

"Kyra!! Grace!!" I swing my gaze around the room. "Merve!! Gabe!! Anyone??" I scream, my voice cracking and breaking with each and every name.

I move further into the room, the only light coming from the dying fire in the corner. My arms fly out wide as I slip in something wet and look down at the blood coating the floor. There is just so much blood. Bile rises in my throat, and I clamp a hand over my mouth, panting. My gaze travels along the ground until they collide with a set of dull blue eyes—eyes that always held so much love and warmth. A sob rips from my throat, and tears stream down my face as I rush forward.

I land at Grace's side, my knees sliding in the wet blood.

There is so much blood!!

My hands are shaking as I reach for her, pulling her head onto my legs. I push her long gray hair from her face. It is soaked in blood. Her face is void of color.

"Grace. Grace, please wake up," I choke out on a sob.

"Grace!" I shake her, even though I know she's gone. I can't help it. "Grace," I plead. I glance away from her lifeless eyes only to spot Gabe a few feet away, his chest torn open, gashes covering the majority of his body.

Oh my god, oh my god, oh my god.

I squeeze my eyes shut, rocking back and forth with Grace in my arms. "This isn't happening," I repeat over and over and over, willing this to all be a bad dream. The pack can't be dead. Grace and Merve—they can't all be dead. Tears stream down my face, and I don't bother wiping them away.

A loud bang startles me, drawing me from my downward spiral. My head shoots up, looking around.

"Hello?" I call, my voice hoarse.

A growl rolls through the room, and I suck in a sharp breath before gently laying Grace's head back down on the ground and standing. I reach for my dagger that's strapped to my thigh, noticing my clothes are now soaked in blood, sticking to me. A shadow moves outside as I glance toward the doors. Dark wisps lick at the edges of my vision. The more I try to focus on the shape pacing beyond those doors, the less I can see.

A loud thud has me jumping out of my skin. My vision darkens further. What is happening to me? A scream tears from me as darkness descends, my chest swelling with ice, and I thrash in agony. All I feel is terror and pain so potent it's as if I'm drowning in the River Styx.

I jerk upright as I wake screaming, writhing in the sheet that's now wrapped around me. I am slick with sweat, my damp clothes sticking to my body. Lukas bursts into the room, his eyes already glowing yellow with the change.

"What's wrong?" he demands, stalking toward the bed.

"It was so bad, Lukas," I sob, as he sits next to me on the bed, pushing my damp hair off my face.

"Talk to me, sweetheart." His voice sounds raw and I realize I'm flooding the bond with my own emotions.

Tears spill down my cheeks, and he brushes them away. "I hate seeing you upset."

Covering my face with my hands, I sob, and Lukas gathers me in his arms, rocking me tenderly. "Shhhh, it's okay. It was just a nightmare. You're okay."

"They were all dead," I whimper. All that blood . . .

"It wasn't real."

I pull back, holding onto his arms, and notice Astraea sitting on the other side of the bed, watching me with those strange knowing eyes. How does she always know when I'm having a nightmare? Slowly, she crawls over the bed to me and climbs into my lap.

'It's okay, Mommy. We's are here.'

'I know, sweet girl.'

I take a few deep inhales and bury my head in her hair, before looking up at Lukas.

His fingers brush a few stray tears from my cheek. "Are you okay?"

"No," I reply, my voice cracking along with my heart. All those dead bodies, my heart seizes at the images, horror spiking through me, pulsing in waves that almost cause me to double over in pain.

I hear Zee downstairs and then Leila's voice. My pulse picks up and I gently lift Astraea off me, bolting for the door. My mind goes numb as I race down the stairs, my fight response kicking in. My dream is still running on a loop in my head, churning my stomach as I make it to the bottom of the stairs, and slam into a startled Zee.

"Where is she!" I yell frantically.

Zee grabs my arms, stopping me from moving past him. He looks down at me, frowning, before looking back up the stairs to Lukas. "Who?"

"Leila!" I scream, desperation and the need for a reasonable explanation to what I saw making me lash out. I can't seem to control myself. My magic swells and I struggle to contain it.

"Leila!" I scream again, and this time a burst of magic accompanies it, rattling the windows. Could she have put that in my head? The thought of having my mind manipulated again scares me. Then there's also the fact that I'm clearly feeling a bit unhinged at seeing my friends quite literally torn to pieces. I have the sudden urge to check on all of them right now.

"I'm here," Leila says, coming from the kitchen.

Jerking myself free from Zee's hold, I stalk toward my sister. I stop a foot away, leaning into her space. "Why? Why would you do that?" my voice cracks.

Perplexed, she glances behind me.

Lukas speaks up. "She had a nightmare."

Looking back at me, she takes in my appearance, her eyes widening with some sort of understanding. "Tell me what you saw," she demands urgently.

A couple tears roll down my face. "My dream was so real," I whisper, trying not to choke on the words.

Sympathy shines in her eyes. "Show me."

"What?" Uncertainty rolls through me. How can I show her?

"Show me what you saw," she repeats.

I swallow hard, the tears clogging my throat. "How?"

"Just close your eyes and take me through it. Go to the beginning of your dream," Leila says as she puts her hands on my temples and closes her own eyes. I don't want to see that horror again.

Lukas must sense my panic, because next thing I know he's beside me. *'I got you, sweetheart. I've always got you. You can do this.'*

My chest feels constricted, as though someone were sitting on me, not allowing the air to reach my lungs. I close my eyes and push through the pain. Taking a deep breath, I show her what I saw.

We break apart, panting as we stare at each other. Suddenly, she is dragging me into a fierce hug. "Shit," she breathes into my hair.

"What was it? It seemed so real," I mumble into her shoulder.

"You had a vision. Your powers . . . It seems the goddess also gave you the power of sight."

I pull back, breaking our hold on each other and wiping my face with the sleeve of my jumper. "What do you mean?"

"Your gifts are stronger than most other legacies, as you are the fated. You've been blessed with the abilities of healing, magic sight, and visions."

My stomach drops, and my pulse picks up as fear grows in the pit of my stomach. If that was a vision, does that mean it's going to come true?

"How do we stop it?" I plead. Shaking my hands, desperate to stop them from trembling.

Leila starts pacing in front of me, her head tilted down to the ground. "I don't know, but just because you saw it doesn't mean it will come to pass. Sometimes trying to change fate is what causes it to happen in the first place," she murmurs.

I cross my arms over my chest. "It can't happen, Leila. I can't . . . " I trail off, bringing my thumb nail to my mouth without thinking, biting down on my already damaged nails; a habit I thought I grew out of in high school.

"What are yours?" I ask curiously.

"My what?" she asks, stopping her pacing and turning to me.

"Your gifts, powers."

"Well, when Hades took me as his kin, it overrode Althaea's claim to me. I'm still a legacy, I still have the same blood running through my veins as you. Just, with Hades, my gifts manifested differently. What they are isn't important right now."

I shiver at the memory of her invading my mind while I was captive at the coven's estate.

She continues, oblivious to my unease, her arms gesturing wildly. "This is a vision, something that may come to pass, but the future can change. Grace would warn us if death was coming. Unless . . . " Leila pauses, her voice fading, a frown marring her face.

"What?" I question, her expression doing nothing to ease the dread curling in my stomach.

"I have to go. I need to check something," she blurts out, a note of concern bleeding into her voice.

Before she can move away, I grab her arm. "Tell me," I demand, my voice harsher than it needs to be.

She hesitates. "Whoever is behind the attack, the one in your vision. They don't know you have this gift. That might mean they will try to eliminate the one person who could warn us."

"Grace," I breathe, all the air rushing from my lungs with that one word. Leila nods, and I watch in a daze as shadows gather around her and she simply vanishes.

I turn to Lukas and Zee. "We need to get to Grace's apartment now."

"Okay, and you can fill us in on the way about what just happened," Lukas says, grabbing my hand.

Lukas pushes open the front door, almost taking out Gabe in the process. When his warm almond eyes meet mine, the image of his lifeless body flashes through my mind, and I lunge at him, my arms wrapping around his neck. Gabe catches me easily in his arms, enclosing around my middle as my feet dangle off the ground. I hold on tight, reminding myself he is alive and right here.

"I'm glad you're okay," I whisper into his neck. Gabe squeezes me gently and lowers my feet to the ground. He looks confused as he stares down at me.

"Are you okay, Nesrin?" he asks softly.

"No," I choke out. Then peer at Lukas. "We need to go. Where is Kate?"

"Zee already called her, she's on her way. She'll take Astraea."

I bite my lip, guilt creeping in at having to leave her.

The door swings open and Astraea walks out, Malachite on her heels. I squat down and take her face in my hands. "I've got to go into town. Aunt Kate is coming over to stay with you, okay?"

Astraea nods, but her usual excitement over seeing Kate is dimmed by my current state.

Lukas scoops her up and I rise just as Kate comes jogging up the stairs and holds her arms out for Astraea.

"Go, I've got her."

"Thank you," I reply, and give Astraea a kiss on the head before Lukas passes her over.

I breathe a sigh of relief as we all pile into Lukas's truck and set out for Grace's apartment. I fill everyone in on my vision on the way. They don't interrupt me once. Lukas's hand reaches over and grabs my hand firmly, lifting it to his mouth and pressing a kiss to my knuckles.

"I'm sorry you had to see that, sweetheart."

A knot forms in my throat. "Me, too," I reply, my gaze going out the window.

Gabe and Zee are silent in the back, both absorbing what I just told them.

"Could this be related to what you saw last night?" Zee asks.

I consider that, if what I saw was a banshee, one who is malevolent, then it's entirely possible she is letting me know death is coming. They could have sent her to me, or she could have come to warn me.

CHAPTER FIFTEEN

Pulling up at Grace's, we all jump out. I glance up at the building as I close the door. My lungs draw in a deep, fortifying breath before I move to the door of the apartment building. Lukas takes my hand in silent support, our fingers linking. When we make it up to Grace's floor, my feet are heavy, as if I were walking against a current of water. I grab the key for Grace's apartment and hand it over to Lukas. He takes it out of my outstretched hand and unlocks the door, stepping inside.

Turning quickly, he grabs my shoulders, holding me back.

"Nesrin."

My name is all he says, but I know. I push past him into the apartment, my mind whirling on the impossibility of what I am seeing. Grace is lying on the floor, her gaze fixed and empty.

Leila is hunched over her body, her fist gripped in Grace's sweater. Shadows pulse around her as if they were trying to soothe her. My body trembles, but I can't move. I can't breathe. I just stand there watching, waiting for her to blink. Deep down, I know it will never happen. A tear streaks down my face. Her absence is palpable, that spark of life gone. I can't understand what I'm seeing, unable to process what is happening right in front of me. Grace can't be dead. Reaching up, my hands sink into my hair, tugging at my scalp. I let out a whine before dropping my hands and making my way over to Leila. I fall to my knees on Grace's other side. My hand shakes as I slowly reach out, closing her eyes. She looks so peaceful, as if she were simply sleeping. I sweep her hair back off her face and stare at her.

Something twists deep inside of me, a pain I haven't felt since Niamh and Hunter's deaths. Grief settles around me like an old blanket. I hate it. I take a painful, shuddering breath and close my eyes.

Leila tips her head back as a sob tears from her throat, all her anguish pouring out. The shadows seem to push in closer, comforting her. At my sister's cries, pressure builds in my own chest and behind my eyes. Pain and fury wage war in my body. A white haze creeps over my vision, my muscles seizing and magic flaring with my growing need for retribution.

Our magics swirl around us in complete contrast, my white light blending with her dark shadows. The two powers are not fighting but rather interlacing, merging together. My magic seems to throb against my skin, strengthening as it dances around the room.

Suddenly, there is silence, an unnatural stillness. Then Hades stands with us in the room. It surprises me to note the look of concern on his face. His golden eyes are lined with worry as he looks to my sister. Lukas, Gabe, and Zee move in closer.

"What are you doing here?" Lukas demands, his voice rough, not unaffected by our distress.

Hades's eyes move over to the alpha who stands at my back. The god of the underworld doesn't blink. Not a single movement passes over his face. It's eerie.

"Hermes told me who he just delivered to Charon. I needed to see my daughter to make sure she was okay. As I can see, she is not," Hades sighs.

Moving swiftly, he places a hand on Leila's shoulder. "She will be in Elysium. She will live her afterlife comfortably. You know she is okay, sunflower."

"I want to see her," Leila croaks, her eyes red, swollen with pain. My heart lurches for her. Grace has been a part of her life a lot longer than she has mine.

Hades shakes his head. "You know it is forbidden. I cannot allow it." His voice is gentle but firm. He will not relent on this.

I have gone completely numb, as if I were detached from my body, watching all of this unfold as an outsider.

Hades's piercing gaze meets mine. "I'm sorry this happened."

I swallow over my distress, my heart sinking steadily in my chest. I school my features and watch as Leila stands up. Her shadows retreated when Hades showed up, as if his very presence calmed her somewhat. My own light has dimmed almost completely, as I draw my pain back inside. Letting out a deep breath, I rise as well. Lukas's hand slides around my waist, pulling me back against his firm chest.

Leila's pained gaze meets mine, her expression slowly changing to one of determination. Her shoulders straighten as she speaks.

"We need to find who did this," she declares.

I nod and look past her to the window, gasping at my reflection. My eyes are orbs of white light set in a pale face. I reach up slowly and touch the skin below my eye. They look so eerie. I look eerie. I feel as if I must be having an out of body experience. My mind fogs over and my limbs tingle.

A blur of movement has me jerking against Lukas as Hades moves faster than I thought possible. He grabs my arm, causing an intense jolt of energy to move through me, traveling up and down my limbs. Blood thunders in my ears, and I cry out as strange images flash through my mind at rapid speed. I gasp at the onslaught, Lukas's arm tightening around me as he spins, placing me behind him. My hand instinctively reaches up, touching his back, his muscles as hard as granite. Waves of fury roll off Lukas as he faces Hades, Gabe and Zee stepping to his side, forming a wall of muscle.

"God or not, you will not touch her," Lukas snarls, his voice taking on an inhuman sound.

Hades replies, but his voice sounds far off in the distance, as if I'm standing at the end of a long tunnel. I'm still recovering from whatever the hell Hades just did, unable to fully register what is being said in the room. I hear raised voices around me and sense Lukas's rage and protectiveness through the bond, but my mind is stuck on the image of the young teenage girl, with blonde hair streaming behind her as she runs laughing through the trees, the last image to float through my mind. It was the same one I had when I was with Grace.

Lukas takes a menacing step forward, and my hand drops from his back. It startles me out of my daze, and everything rushes back in with clarity.

"Stand down, wolf," Hades's voice takes on a harsh edge.

My stomach clenches and goosebumps scatter at the sounds. I can feel Hades's power fill the room. It is suffocating. I move forward and grab Lukas's arm. He doesn't look at me though, his focus fully on Hades.

"I'm okay, Lukas," I reassure him.

Lukas's chest heaves as he tries to rein in his temper. When I'm sure he will not launch himself at the god, I move my attention to Hades.

"What was that?"

His golden eyes penetrate mine, making it hard for me to take a breath. We can never forget this man is a god. He could crush us all in an instant if he wished.

"You have been given the gift of sight. This makes you a seer. I wanted to see how powerful." He tilts his head in a predatory manner, and I suppress my shiver.

"And?" I choke out.

"You're able to see the past and the future. So . . . very," he says with a shrug, like it isn't that big a deal.

"And the images I saw when you touched me?"

"Things you've already seen."

"But I have seen none of that," I argue, thinking back to the image of a young woman in a field of long grass, her hand gliding over the top of it, as if skimming her hands through water. I was able to feel her contentment, she was at peace in her surroundings. The woman looked like me, but I don't have this memory. So was it a vision?

"That you can remember."

I frown as I consider his words. Have I always had visions and just not realized it? I don't think so. I have strong intuition, sure, and I even let my instincts guide me. But actual visions? I shake my head.

"Those images that flashed through your mind are from previous visions you have received. You may not have realized what they were, given your magic was locked away. They may have come to you as dreams. You may have been part of them, taking part in each vision, similar to dream walking," he explains, giving me a knowing look. "You have grown stronger, more capable of controlling your gifts. They will manifest in ways we can't predict."

I rub at my face with both hands. A headache is forming behind my eyes and at the base of my head. Why don't these gifts come with a manual? Why does the Order have to be after my family? My friends? I need to contact Marcus and see what he knows. The coven has been too quiet. I don't like it. If they are responsible for this, I will seek retribution. If it was the Order, I want blood. I want to destroy the people responsible for all of this. The thought startles me.

Leila's voice snaps me out of my thoughts. "Dad, take me home."

My head whirls to Leila. "What? You're leaving?"

Wrapping her arms around herself, she nods, letting her long, wavy red hair hide her face. "I need time."

Without another word, Hades is beside her, and they disappear through a portal. I draw in a breath and turn to Lukas. The tears won't come. They're there, but they won't fall. I dread having to tell Astraea, she has already lost so much. And what about Merve?

Merve. Where is he?

Lukas gathers me up in his arms, his palm stroking up and down my back, the movements soothing. My gaze moves back to the window. My eyes were back to normal.

I can hear Gabe and Zee murmuring behind me, but I couldn't care less what they're saying. I just want all of this to be over.

CHAPTER SIXTEEN

Nesrin

*T*he fire is so hot I can barely stand it. Smoke is everywhere, making it hard to breathe. With my throat burning, I gasp, but I can't get enough air to fill my lungs. Flames suddenly burst skyward, running up the walls and across the ceiling. I'm in the hallway outside my room, crawling forward on my hands and knees. I can only stare in shock and horror at the flames as I try moving forward, pain piercing my body with every move.

My eyes blur, and I wipe at them with the back of my hand, and try to take a deep breath, only to choke on smoke. My whole body seems to be shutting down. Everywhere the air touches my skin, it burns, the heat is unbearable. What happened, where are Niamh and Hunter? Did they get out of the house? Is Astraea with them?

Up ahead, I can just make out the sound of a baby crying, and begin pushing aside the pain each movement brings as I crawl forward as quickly as I can. The smoke is growing thicker, my eyes burning with tears I can feel making tracks down my face. Opening my mouth, I try to call out, but no sound comes from my throat. It's like drowning not on water but on smoke. I'm coming up to the baby room. If Astraea's in there, I have to get her out. I'm not sure the crying I heard wasn't just my imagination, but I need to be sure.

I try to cast my magic outward to see if I can find anyone else in the house, but I'm in too much distress, and it just fizzes out. I propel myself forward as fast as I can manage on my hands and knees, trying to keep below the smoke. I reach Astraea's door and push it open, crawling into the room, the smoke and flames biting at my heels.

I quickly shut the door behind me, and smoke starts billowing in through the space under the door. I blindly reach for the towel hanging on the door and throw it down to cover the crack. The fire hasn't reached this room yet, but that won't last. Any minute, the flames will engulf us. I force myself to stand and run over to the crib, cursing my weak legs as I stumble. Astraea's in her crib, staring up at me with her big blue eyes. I reach for her and bundle her in a blanket before running for the window. That's when, for the first time, I notice magic stirring in the air, moving with the fire. It swells, then a surge of power lifts the hair from my shoulders. I drop to the floor as all the windows smash, glass flying everywhere as I curl my body over Astraea's, shielding her with my body as I'm too weak to form a magical one. Tiny cuts are scattered across my body, but I barely feel a thing as I get up and climb onto the ledge of the window. There is a vine on this side of the house I can use to get down if my body will allow it. There's no other choice. I sit on the ledge and slowly lower myself down onto the vine, holding Astraea as tightly as I can with my free arm.

My heart is thumping wildly in my chest to the point of it being painful. I hear sirens in the distance coming closer. Help is coming. But the relief I feel is short-lived. I make it to the ground and stumble onto the lawn, carefully adjusting Astraea in my arms. Looking around, I see a few neighbors out watching the scene unfold from the street, though I can't make out anyone's faces with the tears burning my eyes. Heat from the flames still licks at my skin. My whole body is on fire. I turn and turn, searching for my sister, but I can't see her. Where is she? Icy dread fills my veins as realization hits.

"No, no, no, no, no, Niamh!" I scream, spinning around and running back toward the house. People are now trying to stop me, holding me back, keeping me from reaching my sister. Twisting, I tear free from their hold and run, a choked sob escaping me. I look down to the bundle in my arms as I run,

Astraea—all of eight months old—staring at me, eyes wide with fear. I stop running, my knees slamming to the ground. Pain radiates through my body, another sob working its way up my throat. I gently grasp my niece to my chest, hoping with all my heart Niamh will make it out alive. A heavy hand lands on my shoulder, squeezing painfully.

I jerk my head up, a scream building in my throat. My gaze connects with a set of unique golden eyes. The handsome man stares down at me, regret swelled in his eyes. Darkness envelops us, and I gasp as we appear somewhere else. A woman with long red hair drops to her knees in front of me. She is crying and screaming something at the man. He shakes his head at her, dropping his gaze. The woman cries out in anguish, the sound tearing at my already battered heart.

I can't move or speak. The tears roll down my cheeks, one after another. I feel Astraea squirming in my grip, her cries ringing out around me, mingling with the woman's. So much pain and agony is surrounding us, I'm practically drowning in it.

The woman grabs my face with her hands, brushing away my tears. She looks just like me.

"I'm so sorry," she sobs, but I don't understand what she's sorry for.

"It wasn't your fault. We didn't know they'd found them," the man says from where he stands, towering over us.

The woman closes her eyes, shaking her head. When her gaze meets mine again, there is resolve there. She leans forward and kisses my forehead and then there is darkness.

I sit up in bed, a panting, sweaty mess. I don't wait for my heart to settle before reaching for my phone. Picking it up, I find Leila's number. It rings twice before she answers. "Nesrin, is everything okay?"

"I saw you," I whisper.

Silence greets me, so I go on, "The night of the fire, Hades came and got me and Astraea. He took us to you. You were crying." My voice is rough and hoarse from all my emotions. I haven't had that dream in months. Every time I have that dream, it ends with me waking up before I can see who grabbed me. But it was Hades. Did they wipe my memories?

"I was too late. Hades didn't get there in time to save Niamh. But you had somehow broken the containment spell, and Hades thought it would be best to get you out of there." Her breathing is heavy.

"Did you make me forget seeing you? Did you take my memories?" I ask, afraid of the answer.

There is a long pause before she answers, "Yes."

I pull the phone from my ear and hang up. It rings a moment later, but I silence it. Numbly, I walk over to the empty bed and climb under the covers, burying my head in the blankets. I am *over* all the secrets and lies. My chest hurts and I want to cry, but I can't bring myself to expend the energy. I close my eyes and take several unsteady breaths, then lie there for hours, hoping sleep will find me. But all I can do is concentrate on my pounding heart.

Leila

Stopping in the center of the courtyard, I take in the sound of the water fountain trickling and the wind swaying through the trees and ferns that surround me. I look up at the bright full moon and inhale the earthly scents around me. I love coming here, it's so peaceful. Scooping up my long, thick red hair, I hold it off my neck, relishing in the breeze caressing my bare skin.

It feels heavenly.

I can't believe Grace is dead. They killed her. All my time undercover in the council and I haven't gotten any closer to finding a foothold in the Order. Am I just wasting my time?

I take several deep breaths to calm myself, so I don't start crying again. Hades held me for hours when we returned, trying to soothe my tears.

"Want to talk about it?" he asked softly, opening his arms to me.

I stepped into his embrace, replying, "No," as I relaxed into his chest, letting his arms hold me together.

After a long moment, Hades guided me to the chair and sat down, pulling me down next to him as I soaked his shirt in my tears.

Just like when I was a child—when he held me after the fire, and when I found out my family had wiped their memories of me, and then again when I lost Niamh. He's always been so strong, so loyal, protecting me for years with nothing to gain.

He knew Grace's death would affect me greatly. She was the only link I had to my old life, the only person who remembered me. I visited Grace every month starting as soon as I learned to create shadow portals. She was like a grandmother to me, and I am going to miss her dearly.

My phone ringing draws my attention and I look down, seeing it's Nesrin. My stomach clenches, but I answer the call just in case something is wrong.

"Nesrin, is everything okay?"

"I saw you," she whispers.

I don't answer. I remain silent, hoping it's not what I think it is.

"The night of the fire, Hades came and got me and Astraea. He took us to you. You were crying." Her voice is rough and hoarse.

I can't speak louder than a whisper when I answer her. "I was too late. Hades didn't get there in time to save Niamh. But you had somehow broken the containment spell, and Hades thought it would be best to get you out of there."

"Did you make me forget seeing you? Did you take my memories?" she asks slowly, as if afraid of the answer.

I pause, releasing a heavy sigh. I won't lie, not again. "Yes."

Silence greets me and I pull the phone away to find the screen blank. She hung up.

Fuck.

I dial her number and it goes straight to voicemail. Nesrin must have turned off her phone. She has every right to hate me. I robbed her of her memories and hidden things from her. I thought I was doing it to protect her, but really, it was myself I was protecting. The sound of defeat in her voice stole my own. My vision blurs from the tears that fall down my face. I scream in anger at myself, throwing my phone at the stone wall. My voice grows hoarse and my breath heaves as I pace the small courtyard of one of Hades's properties, noticing as one of the guards rounds the corner, halting when he sees me.

"Are you alright, daughter of Hades?" he asks, his eyes drifting over to my phone, lying smashed on the ground.

I narrow my eyes at the guard, Roland. One of Hades's personal guards, he stands a foot or so taller than me and resembles a sleek black panther. Two horns protrude from his forehead, not glamored or hidden in any way. We are all safe on Hades's properties.

I straighten my shoulders, determination filling me. "Duel me," I demand, pulling my hair up into a bun, having learned the hard way and at a young age that having your hair down during a fight is a massive disadvantage.

Roland looks at me steadily with his golden cat eyes blinking slowly, then nods. He becomes distorted as I blend with shadows, but I have enough clarity before disappearing to watch him pull a dagger from his thigh. As I reappear behind him, he swings the dagger around, but I am ready, stepping into his swing and grabbing his arm with both hands. I pull him into me and slam my knee into his thigh as hard as I can, then quickly let go, dancing away. Roland narrows his eyes on me and charges. I slip a blade from my waistband and block his swing. I count and we dance back and forth, trading blows.

Roland gets in way more hits than I do, which only fuels the fire burning inside me. I lunge forward, ducking under his arm and slice his side. He lets out a small hiss and spins quicker than I anticipate, the tip of his blade slicing across my cheek. I stumble back, relishing in the sting. A feral grin spreads over Roland's face, and I match it with my own. From the corner of my vision I see a swirl of black and my moment of distraction gives Roland an opening.

Roland's foot slams into my chest, sending me sprawling across the stone ground. Pain robs me of my breath as I stare up at the darkened sky. I can feel my energy slipping away and raise my hand. I am done.

I close my eyes and take a fortifying breath. When I look up, Roland is smirking down at me. My answering growl only serves to deepen his grin. I tip my head to the side to see Hades standing at the side of the courtyard, his hand in the pockets of his pants as he watches me climb to my feet. Roland steps forward to help, but I shoot him a glare, which has him raising his hands in surrender and stepping back.

"Got that out of your system, sunflower?" Hades asks.

I wipe the blood from my chin with the back of my hand and slowly walk toward him. My lungs still strain for air. That knock was fucking hard.

I stop in front of him and take the offered water bottle he holds out for me.

"Nesrin knows," I croak.

Hades's golden eyes glow in intensity as he stares back at me. I can feel the thread of concern he has for me. He is worried I'll spiral again.

"She is strong, her powers growing."

"What did you expect? The Moirai chose her."

Hades hums in agreement. "Are you okay?"

"I'm fine."

Hades steps up to me brushing a tear from my cheek. "I hate seeing you like this."

"Then take me to see her."

His hands return to his pockets as he rocks back on his heels, "You know that's not possible."

"Please."

He shakes his head, parts of his black hair falling over his forehead. "There must be balance."

"She was the only part of my old life I had left. She was there for me when I needed!" I yell, my voice cracking with emotion.

Hades's hand squeezes my shoulder. "You have Nesrin. She is your sister."

"She probably *hates* me! I made her forget meeting me, and then I *tortured* her."

"That was to keep your cover within the covens, so you can find a way into the Order."

"I hate them," I seethe. "I despise everything they are, everything they stand for."

"Nesrin will be the start of that change. But she cannot do it without you, Leila."

Dark to balance the light. Light to balance the dark. Together they are stronger.

I roll my eyes and Hades raises an eyebrow. There's a moment of silence before he speaks again, softer this time, "Give her time. She is your sister. There is no way she would turn her back on you. She will forgive you."

CHAPTER SEVENTEEN

I stand in front of the full-length mirror, my hands smoothing over my black dress. My eyes go to Astraea in the reflection. She's lying on my bed, Malachite curled up at her side with one of Grace's old pillows, the fabric still carrying the scent of the woman who was like a grandmother to her. Her fingertips lightly trace the smooth lines of the symbols etched on the front of my grimoire, which lies at her side. She has been hiding in here all morning, adamantly refusing to go downstairs where everyone is gathered. I take a deep, quivering breath, trying to keep my sorrow at bay. Not a single night has passed since Lukas and I informed her of Grace's death, that she has slept in her own room. She's snuggled into my chest with Lukas's arms wrapped around us, and the warmth of Malachite radiating against our feet.

A soft knock sounds at the door just before Suzy pokes her head in. Her purple hair is pinned back, and her blue eyes are lined with sadness. Grace is going to be so missed.

"Hey," she whispers. Her eyes automatically go to Astraea, and I watch as her lip wobbles. I twist my hair into a bun, then turn my back on my reflection and grab my jacket from the bed, tugging it on.

"Hey." Goddess, my throat is tight. I'm not sure I'll actually be capable of talking today.

As I turn my gaze to Malachite snuggled up to Astraea, it occurs to me that I'm glad I thought to cloak him this morning before everyone arrived. Suzy would lose it if she saw a dragon. I know he's tiny and cute, but a human may not think so.

I move over to Astraea and stroke her hair. "You ready, sweet girl?" I whisper.

She just grips the pillow tighter against her chest and my heart breaks. I sit down on the edge of the bed and feel Suzy move further into the room.

"I know it's hard to say goodbye. Grace was family, and it's always hard to say goodbye to family," I murmur.

Malachite lifts his head, his delicate dragon face blinking up at me. I don't think he understands what's going on, only that everyone is sad. He has been stuck to Astraea's side since we broke the news to her. Needless to say, she withdrew from everyone. Her outward silence has been more deafening than ever. I bundle Astraea up in my arms and we make our way out of the room.

I peer back at Malachite. '*You need to stay here, okay?*'

The dragon tilts its head, regarding me carefully. '*I'm going to leave you in here. Just rest, okay, Malachite?*' I say, shutting the door behind me, then mutter a quick spell, locking Malachite in. The last thing we need is for him to come looking for us.

Suzy holds my hand as we make our way down the stairs. Looking up, I see Merve out on the porch and tug Suzy to a stop. "I want to speak to Merve. Can you take her?"

Nodding, Suzy reaches for Astraea, and I pass her over, stroking her blonde curls before moving to the door. I open it gently and slip outside. The air is warmer than usual, and the clouds are dark and ominous. We're due for a storm any day now.

Merve looks handsome, and it's the first time I've ever seen him clean shaven. I can see he's using one of my glamor spells today, making it a bit easier for him to move around in public. He sees me approaching, his eyes red and face pale.

His voice breaks as he pleads, "How do I say goodbye, Ness? How? My heart is still wanting to hold on. It doesn't want to let go." His shoulders shake as he buries his face in his hands. I just step up to him, wrapping my arms around him the best I can.

"I'm sorry, Merve. I really am," I breathe into his chest. His arms wrap around me, holding me tight. We stay like that for a long moment, soaking in each other's pain and comfort. Things will never feel the same without Grace.

I hear the others coming toward us and give Merve one last squeeze, then step back as the front door swings open. Everyone files out, making their way down to their cars, subdued looks on every face. I don't see Astraea, so I quickly walk back inside,

"Astraea?" I call out.

There's no reply, and I frown. Lukas's hand lands on my back, his gaze silently asking me if I'm okay. I nod, but he knows I'm not. How could I be? As I turn, I see Astraea's feet poking out from behind the sofa and walk over. It breaks my heart to see her this way. Her little knees are pulled into her chest, head resting on them. I kneel in front of her, reaching out to stroke her hair.

"Sweet girl, it's time to go."

She doesn't raise her head, just shakes it, refusing to look up at me. Hot tears instantly fill my eyes and sting my nose at her pain. So much loss in her life already. My heart cracks and crumbles when her gaze finally lifts, and I see the pain in her blue eyes that flicker between blue and violet. They appear to be more of a deep indigo these days. It seems as if she understands what's happening around her, and that she's keeping her distance from everyone. Blue arrived earlier, and she came to find me in my room instead of attaching herself to him like she usually would.

"Oh, sweet girl." I reach for her, pulling her into my arms. She comes willingly, wrapping her arms tightly around my neck.

"We will survive today. It's going to be hard, so hard, but we will get through it," I whisper into her golden locks.

"Together, we will survive anything." Lukas's voice is gruff as he speaks behind us. Crouching down, he runs a hand over both our heads. He stands, helping us up, and guides us out of the house. He reaches for Astraea, and she moves to him, her head resting on his strong, broad shoulder. Then he wraps an arm around my waist and plants a lingering kiss to my forehead.

"Ready?"

I nod, letting out a sigh. He leads me down the stairs to the car. The drive passes by quickly, so quickly that I don't remember. I'm so lost in my thoughts, looking out the window the entire time. When the car pulls to a stop, Lukas gets out first, extending his hand to me. I smile weakly up at him and take it. I can't help but admire the way his broad shoulders fill out the suit, making him look even more handsome. Leaving the jeans, motorcycle boots, and fitted t-shirt behind.

The procession goes quickly. By some miracle, I manage to get through my speech without breaking down. Merve tries, but he isn't able to get the words out, so Suzy steps in to read his speech for him. I will forever be grateful for her support these last few days.

I look over my shoulder and spot Leila up on the hill, watching the funeral. Her shadows allow her to blend into the background, but now that I know what I'm seeing, I can spot her easily. A pang echoes in my chest at her decision to wipe my memories of her that night. I focus on her for a moment, letting my magic stretch out toward her. Raw pain and desperation strike me like a knife to the chest and I withdraw, panting slightly.

I turn back and see everyone walking over to Grace's coffin, placing a flower on top. Suzy takes Astraea's hand, leading her over. When I peer back over my shoulder, Leila is gone. It's as if she was never there. Sadness sweeps over me, and I sag, the weight of everything making me feel defeated. Lukas's warm body embraces me, tugging me close and pressing a soft kiss on my head.

I let my eyes drift back to Astraea, my heart was hammering and my soul aching as I watch her. Then a pinprick of awareness tingles along my skin and I stare in confusion as Astraea turns to me, panic clearly visible on her tiny face. Seeing her so terrified morphs my emotions into something fierce, something full of protectiveness.

I hastily take a step forward. Her indigo eyes begin to glow and a white shimmering light pulses around her. I watch in slow motion as a tear rolls down her cheek and a burst of raw magic explodes from her. I put an arm up, covering my face, a glittering blue shield forming around Lukas and myself.

Everyone around us seems to fall unconscious to the ground as waves of anguish pulse from Astraea. Lukas takes a step forward, approaching her, and I follow his lead, keeping the shield in place. The last thing I want is for us to fall unconscious and leave her to cope on her own. When we are close enough, Lukas crouches down in front of her.

"Little star, what's going on?" he asks gently.

As her eyes blink up at him, they are so wide, so lost. I drop to my knees, my shield falling as I reach for her, pulling her tiny frame into me. Lukas's arms wrap around both of us as we huddle together, cocooning Astraea between us.

'*Too much,*' she whispers through our minds, the layers of grief and heartache drenching each word.

'*What is little star?*' Lukas replies.

'*Everyone. Everyone sad.*'

Lukas and I share a look. Astraea has always been intuitive and sensitive. She is great at reading people and seems to know who she can trust. I should have realized how this would affect her.

"I'm so sorry." I let my magic surface and flow into Astraea. I send wave after wave of magic washing over her, soothing and comforting her. I whisper words of reassurance as her tears slow, and she closes her eyes, soft snores coming from her.

I tilt my head back at Lukas. Our eyes connect. '*I'm worried.*'

'*We will get to the bottom of this, freckles.*'

'*What are we going to do? How do we explain this?*' I hold my hand out toward the cemetery full of unconscious people. Lukas wipes a tear from my cheek before standing. He runs a hand through his thick black hair as he looks around.

'What do you think she did?' he asks.

I adjust Astraea in my arms and stand. '*I don't know.*'

Lukas walks over to where Zee, Kate, and Gabe lay and squats down, tapping Zee lightly on the cheek. Zee grunts, turning his head. Suddenly, I hear a flutter of wings and turn down the hill to the forest's edge. I can just make out the glow of hundreds of sprites. I gasp, and Lukas stands abruptly. Surprise tightens the corners of his mouth and his eyes meet mine.

"I'll stay here and deal with this," he says, gesturing to all our unconscious friends. "And you deal with them."

I nod and make my way down the small grassy hill. Nissa is easy to single out in the crowd of sprites. She flutters closer, her eyes drifting down to where Astraea sleeps in my arms.

"Why are you here? And with so many?" I question.

"We all felt her distress," she replies quickly. Before I can clarify, she goes on, "She shares their pain, as much as she shares their happiness," Nissa explains, barely above a sigh, but I hear it clearly.

"What do you mean?"

There is a pause. "Astraea doesn't need words to know what is going on around her. Just by *sense*, she can already pick up the feelings in the room. She is like the gateway of everyone's emotions, absorbing other people's energy. She experiences everyone's emotions as if they were her own. It can be overwhelming for her, which can result in meltdowns. Like today."

Her silence makes more sense now. If she has always been like this, then I need to help her, to shield her from it.

"What happened to everyone?" I ask.

"Astraea couldn't handle all the negative emotions, it created too much pressure. Like a volcano she erupted, causing a wave of her magic surge, hitting everyone nearby."

"I don't understand."

"Astraea is young, but her magic is strong. She is a telepathic empath. Which means she is highly attuned to those around her. Until she can learn to control it, she will become overwhelmed while in groups. It will deplete her energy, especially if that energy is negative."

I swallow roughly, feeling once more the burn of tears, but I push my guilt and sorrow down to the pit of my stomach to deal with later as Nissa continues.

"Astraea will become burned out, overwhelmed, have mood swings. These are all things she will have to deal with, because she will pick up on all the feelings and emotions of every single person in a room. That would be a lot for anybody to deal with, let alone someone so young."

"Is that how she can speak to you and other creatures?"

Nissa inclines her head, her wings fluttering gently. "The same way creatures gravitate to you; they seek comfort from you. You exude safety and offer them healing, and in return they protect you. Astraea has strong fae ties. Her ability to communicate telepathically with any creature or being is because of her fae magic, not so much her legacy powers. With time, she will be able to read minds as easily as she can recognize people's true intentions. This is why Astraea gravitates to animals. They have no hidden agenda. They are pure in their feelings. Her fae side is powerful, and I fear she will go through renascitur. Becoming a high fae, a powerful one at that."

"She will become fae?" I whisper, stunned by this information. Renascitur is Latin for reborn.

"How? Why?" My heart rate sped up. How am I supposed to navigate this? I glance over to where Lukas is helping the others to stand. As if feeling my eyes on him, Lukas looks my way and I feel the flutter of him along the bond.

"I'm not sure how it's possible, but you legacies just keep things interesting."

I groan and try my best not to stamp my foot like a child.

Nissa smiles gently. "Astra will become fae if she goes through renascitur, but it's not something that will happen until she is at least twenty, maybe later. Until then, I can help you guide her, help her shield herself from feeling too much. Learn to have some control over her abilities."

Lukas's eyes meet mine and even from this distance, he can see into my heart and soul. *'Together.'*

The pressure in my chest eases with his words, and I smile. Grace's funeral is still underway, and knowing what I do now, I realize this is not the place for Astraea. Goddess, how I wish Grace were here to help guide us in this. I am going to miss her unwavering love and support. I thank Nissa and turn, heading back over to the others. Lukas must have read me, because he meets me halfway, guiding me toward the car. Opening the door, he helps me settle an exhausted Astra in the backseat. Lukas removes his jacket and drapes it over her. I plant a kiss on her forehead, whispering a spell into her ear. She will sleep for a few hours at least.

The last of the guests have left, and now only Suzy and Kate remain with us in our home. Both have been staying here this week. Kate has a house down the hill, but with what's happened, she wants to be here for Astraea. I can't fault her for that. Since Grace's death, Finan has been calling me nightly, offering solace and support. He wishes he could be here, but the weight of being alpha keeps him from straying too far from his pack.

I have just gotten off the phone with Marcus, who called to express his apologies for not attending the funeral. He explained that he was trying to be mindful of the potential danger of being seen with me. Which I completely understand. Marcus is building his following, poaching members of the coven over to his side. From what he said tonight, a lot of the coven members already know something is wrong.

Lukas strolls over to where I am collecting glasses, grabs them from my hands, and places them back on the coffee table before pulling me down onto his lap. I sigh and melt into him, his hand stroking my hair. Suzy sits across from us, her mind elsewhere as she frowns at her hands.

"Thank you for today," I mumble.

"I'm going to check on Astraea before I turn in," Kate says, coming over and squeezing my shoulder before heading upstairs.

Astraea has slept all afternoon, only waking long enough to eat something before curling up in the middle of her bed with Malachite. The little dragon is her loyal companion.

"What happened today?" Suzy asks, her blue eyes searching mine.

The thump in my chest startles me just as much as her words. I've been afraid people would question what happened. Our quick explanation of a gas leak really isn't plausible.

"What do you mean?" My nerves are frayed, and my voice betrays it. I don't enjoy lying to my friend. Guilt churns heavily in the pit of my stomach as Suzy's eyes raise and meet mine.

"I saw Astraea's eyes. I'm not stupid. Something is different about her. She was glowing before we all passed out."

Lukas's body stiffens under mine and his hand stops moving. I sit up, taking a deep breath and wonder if maybe I should have called Stephan or Nikolas to wipe Suzy's memory, but I know how that feels and I won't do that, ever.

"You're right," I reply, thinking it better to rip off the bandage than to drag it out any further.

Suzy jerks back in surprise at my honest response. Lukas rubs my arms in reassurance. He will back me with whatever I decide to do.

"Astraea is different, I'm different." I won't give the others' secrets away. That is theirs to tell, not mine.

Lukas's warmth and support flow through the bond, giving me the courage to go on.

"I was brought up a witch. But I have recently discovered I'm a descendant of a goddess, more specifically a Greek goddess."

Suzy's eyes are as wide as saucers. Her mouth drops open as she stares at me in shock. A tiny squeak escapes her mouth. "Witch? Goddess?"

Lukas chuckles behind me and I can feel his amusement. "She is special."

"Of course she is," Suzy says, shaking off her initial shock.

"And Astraea, she is like you?"

"Yes. We are legacies."

"Legacies . . . " Suzy speaks the word, as if testing it out on her tongue.

"Astraea is different from me though. I'm unsure how her magic will manifest, but today we found out she's an empath, and with everyone around her so highly emotional she couldn't cope."

Suzy bows her head. "I see."

I build a wall up around my heart as I watch Suzy process what I've told her. I wait for the rejection, the look of disgust or pity. Neither comes as Suzy smiles and stands. "Well, I'll see you in the morning."

I jerk in my seat. "Wait . . . that's it?"

"Yes. It's been a long, draining day for everyone. We should turn in and get some rest. You definitely need it."

With that, she turns and makes her way to the guest room. Stunned, I sit here for a moment, Lukas's arms wrapped around my middle, his chin resting on my shoulder.

"She took that well," he observes.

There is a soft knock on the door and I follow Lukas to the front of the house. Swinging the door open, I look around his shoulder, seeing Stephan standing there, hands in his pant pockets, gaze pointed at the ground.

"Stephan?"

"I've just stopped by to see how you are, my rose sauvage."

When he lifts his head, I see the stress lining his face, how affected he is by Grace's death.

Lukas bends, kissing me on the head. "I'll wait inside."

I step out onto the porch and move over to lean back against the rail. Stephan joins me, his shoulder pressed against mine.

"Are you okay?" I ask.

"I should be asking you that." He sighs, running a hand through his dark hair.

"Yet I'm asking you."

A deep breath. "I didn't think death would affect me anymore, but Grace was special. Like you, you're special, my rose sauvage."

"Why do you call me that? When we first met you said you were–"

"J'ai senti la rose sauvage," Stephan says with a small smile gracing his lips. "Your name means wild rose. You smell different from other witches; sweeter, more pure. That is what I sensed at first, and rose sauvage is simply wild rose in French. *I was looking for the wild rose.*"

"Oh . . . "

"I just wanted to check on you, but I see you're in good hands." With a gentle kiss on my head, Stephan is gone, a blur in the night as he disappears from sight.

CHAPTER EIGHTEEN

Lukas

Yesterday was a big day, and Astraea wiped herself out both physically and emotionally. I have some ideas on ways to help her cope with her empathy. I slip out of bed, pulling the covers over Nesrin's bare shoulders, tucking the blankets around her. My hand lingers and I smooth the curls from her face. She is so small and delicate, so much more than I ever thought I'd deserve, but I won't give her up. I'll fight until my last breath for this woman and the little girl in the room down the hall. I would sacrifice the world if it meant they would live and be happy.

I quietly move and grab my clothes from the chair in the corner and walk into the bathroom, shutting the door behind me. I get dressed and splash some cold water on my face. Looking into the mirror, I stare at myself for a moment. My green eyes seem darker today, the stubble on my face more pronounced. I shrug on my jacket and quietly sneak out of the room and down the hall. I push open the door to Astra's room, stepping inside. A wave of warmth floods my chest as I see she is already awake, her wolf teddy hugged close to her chest. Her eyes light up when she notices me, like she's been waiting for me. She tracks my movements as I walk over to her dresser and pull the drawer open, looking for some warmer clothes. Grabbing a long sleeve pink top and a pair of gray sweatpants, I shut the drawer and move over to her closet to grab a jacket from the hanger, along with her rain boots. I smile when I turn and make my way over to the bed.

'*Hey, little star.*'

Her gaze moves from the clothes in my hands to my face, and she gives me a soft smile.

'*Want to come for a run with me? I want to show you something.*'

Her eyes sparkle like two precious gems as she clambers out of the bed. '*Yes.*'

I kneel down on the floor and help her get dressed.

'*Socks?*' she questions softly. Her words are like a flutter of butterfly wings brushing against my mental walls.

'*Right,*' I reply, standing and opening up some more drawers. I find them tucked under some singlets.

When I turn, Astraea is sitting on the edge of the bed, her tiny legs swinging back and forth as she waits patiently for me. I hold up the socks and grin. '*Found them.*'

In response, she lifts her foot, and I watch her toes wiggle in the air. I shake my head, trying to hide my grin, and pull on her socks and boots, then together we make our way downstairs and out into the yard. The only sound to be heard is the chirping of crickets in the darkness.

I look down at her. '*Ready?*'

She nods, and I shift seamlessly into my wolf. Astra's hand comes up, stroking the fur on my neck. I am a lot bigger than her, and it surprises me that she is so at ease when we are in our animal forms. I bend my head down to hers, her hand reaching up and tugging at my ear. I give her a gentle nudge in return and she grins.

'*Hop on,*' I say, gesturing toward my back as I hunch down. Astra grips my fur and pulls herself up onto my back. Once she is secure, I take off, moving as lightly as I can on my paws and into the woods. We continue on for twenty minutes until I can hear the sound of water. We are close. I have kept my thoughts shielded the entire time, my mind blank and my spirit one with the forest as I ran. As I approach the waterfall, I slow to a trot and crouch down. Before I can say anything, Astra climbs down.

I shift and we walk hand in hand silently to the water's edge. The soft roar from the waterfall is like white noise. We say nothing as we take a seat, kicking off our shoes and place our feet in the cool water. Our breathing mingles with the noises of nature, we soak in the light of the rising sun on our skin, the smell of the forest, the green of the plants, the cool breeze across our skin. That calming wave of nature caresses over us, magically shifting our internal landscape.

We sit there until the sun is high in the sky, the birds and insects creating their own symphony. Our silence is calm as we open our hearts and minds to absorb the peace and wisdom of nature.

It isn't until I hear the grumble of Astra's stomach that I realize we've been out here longer than I intended.

'Ready to go back?' I ask her softly so as not to startle her.

Leaning her head on my arm, she nods. Standing, we collect our things and make our way back home, calmer, minds clear and bodies grounded. It will take time to heal from the loss of Grace, but this will help.

Nesrin

The next morning, I wake to find myself alone in bed. I stretch out my body, wriggling my toes and fingers. Once I feel awareness creep into my muscles, I roll over, reaching for Lukas' pillow. I pull it under me, wrapping my arms around it, and breathe in his woodsy scent, my cheek resting on the pillow as I gaze out the window across the room. The sun is only just rising, casting the sky in an array of reds and oranges. I startle as I feel something move on the bed and relax when I realize it's only Malachite. The baby dragon sleepily walks up the side of my body, curling into my side. I move my arm so I can run my fingers over his soft scales. The vibrations he makes remind me of the contented purr of a cat. I feel a warmth in my chest as my lips curl into a smile. Amid all the chaos, I haven't taken a single moment to just be still and listen, to take time to myself and soak in the silence. I've been so focused on the coven and the gods that I've failed to truly take in the things happening around me. I feel a pang of longing when I realize I am missing out on time with Astraea and Lukas.

A storm of emotions rage inside of me, so many thoughts swirling through my head. I should have protected Grace. My anxiety begins rising steadily and I let out a breath. I do my best to empty my mind and relax. I can't let the what ifs drag me down.

Between Malachite's soft snores and Lukas's scent surrounding me, I drift back off to sleep. The words *dum spiro, spero* repeating in my head.

While I breathe, I hope.

CHAPTER NINETEEN

"Truth or dare?" I ask as we turn down another empty street.

My boots splash down in a puddle. It's been raining a lot lately, which means the sun isn't out as much and neither is the moon. Gray clouds hide everything bright, warm, and wonderful. My mood is down, and I am trying so hard to be positive for Astraea. I'm not one to dwell on things, but losing Grace has hit me hard, as has the deception Leila has shown and the destruction of my bookstore. I just feel lost.

Zee smirks over at me. "Dare."

My finger taps my chin as I think about it, grinning as I glance around. We are alone on the street, and I want to test out the shifter abilities.

"Shift and scale that fire escape," I say, pointing down the alley.

"Piece of cake."

Zee winks and takes off running. His shift is seamless as he runs, never breaking his stride. He leaps for the first landing, his paws touch down silently, and way more gracefully than I thought possible. He keeps climbing, making it to the roof in record time. I gaze up at him as he disappears for a moment before soaring over the edge of the building. A squeal escapes my throat and panic shoots through me, as I watch Zee's form fall. Adrenaline shoots through my veins, replacing my amusement with utter terror. I cover my mouth as Zee lands in front of me, his tongue lolling out.

I double over. "Oh my god, Zee! You almost gave me a heart attack!!" I shriek.

His wolf trots over and brushes up against me. I run my hand over him, my healing magic seeking any injuries. Nothing. I sigh in relief, and then Zee shifts into his cocky human form, grinning down at me.

"Okay, your turn. Truth or dare?"

"Truth," I fire back, not wanting to know what his form of dare is.

"How many hours have you slept this week?"

I stand silently staring at Zee, he folds his arms over his chest, a look on his face daring me to lie. Sneaky bastard. I know what he's doing.

"Dare, I chose dare," I finally answer.

Zee shakes his head. "Go home, Nesrin. Rest, okay? We got this."

"I don't like this game," I grumble, putting my hands in the pocket of my leather jacket. My fingers curl around the clear quartz I have in there. I take a few deep, calming breaths as my thumb glides over the smooth surface.

"No offense, honey, but you look like shit."

A growl slips from my lips as I scowl at him. I know the dark circles around my eyes are more prominent right now and my skin has paled, but it isn't that bad. So what if I've been out on patrol every night this last week? I can't sit at home. I need to be out doing something, anything, to be helping. All this mess is my fault. Between losing Grace and finding out my sister took away my memories, along with my parents taking my memories of her. I need to keep myself busy. I need to give Astraea a break from my turmoil of emotions. I won't be the cause of her pain.

"You're not listening to me."

"I am, Zee. But I'm fine." Zee's worried gaze meets mine. I sense his concern, and I understand it, but I am fine.

"No, you're not. You're going to burn yourself out."

A steady pulsing current of despair moves through me, making itself known as if calling me out on my lies. "I can handle it," I snap.

His voice softens with his next words. "Emotional pain is harder to heal, Nesrin. It takes time. No one will think any less of you if you stay home and rest. We all know you're the most unselfish person I know. You hold more compassion in your little finger than twenty people combined."

I grunt in response, turning and walking back the way we came. I hear Zee sigh and follow behind me.

"Have you talked to Leila?"

The ground seems to give way beneath me. Like I'm sinking into a void. The sensation is so strong I have to look at my feet just to make sure I'm not. I shoot Zee a glare over my shoulder. "No."

"Don't you think–"

"Stop," I growl, spinning on him. "Who even invited you?"

"Ahh . . . you did. I believe your words were. '*Zee, get me out of this damn house,*'" he says, mimicking my voice.

Giving him the stink eye, I cross my arms. "Well, that was stupid of me. Remind me not to do that again."

"Rude." He huffs, scratching his head.

I fight a smile. "Shut up."

"You shut up," he volleys back, instantly causing me to chuckle.

"You love me."

"Are you sure about that?" Zee laughs.

Zee always lightens my moods, even when he's annoying me to no end. My next step falters and I stumble, Zee's hand shooting out to grip my arm as a wave of dizziness swamps me. Closing my eyes, I take a breath and when I open them, I'm standing on a beach, the waves crashing on the shore in front of me. I blink and I'm back in the alley. I look around, confused. What was that?

"Are you okay, honey?"

"Yeah, I think so. Just got dizzy."

"I told you–"

I hold up my hand, silencing him. "Enough, Zee, I'm fine."

A tingle works its way over my body, and I sense Lukas's presence before he turns down the street we're standing on. He strolls toward us, looking like a badass warrior in his dark jeans, black t-shirt and combat boots. The shirt is straining across his chest and arms, and I find it difficult to drag my eyes up to his.

"Like what you see, sweetheart?" His green eyes sparkle with amusement when I meet his gaze.

"Yes."

Lukas chuckles and strolls up to me. I sense Zee moving down the alley, giving us some semblance of privacy. Lukas doesn't stop until his body is touching mine. His hand comes up, wrapping my hair around his fist and tugging my head back. I gasp at the desire that pulses through me, the slight sting on my scalp making my legs tremble. Leaning down, Lukas claims my mouth in a devastating kiss. I feel it all the way to my toes as it scorches a hot path of burning desire through me. The bond surges, and I feel his desire along with my own. I groan into his mouth. The answering growl that rumbles up his throat does nothing to calm the lust burning in my belly. This isn't gentle. This kiss is a claiming. He kisses me like I am the air he needs to breathe. When he slows the kiss, it becomes soft and sweet, like we have all the time in the world to explore each other. I forget there is evil out to get us, that it is constantly snapping at our heels. We break apart, and I settle my ear over his heart.

I sigh as Lukas strokes my back.

"I've missed you," he says sweetly.

I groan, pulling back to look up at him. Hesitantly, I reach up and stroke his face. "I'm sorry."

His eyes peer into mine, darkening with promise. "Nothing to apologize for, freckles."

"I have just been keeping myself busy to avoid everything. I know it's affecting my life more than it should. That I also need to deal with Leila and put things to rest and move forward. But with every movement forward, my heart grows heavier, like I'm leaving everyone I've lost behind. I just . . . it's too much." I sigh and run my fingers over the tattoos peeking out of the neck of his shirt.

"I'm here for you. I will help in whatever way I can."

"I know. I love you."

He smirks before leaning down for another kiss. His lips graze mine a moment before he jerks back. As his green gaze whips around the alley, his fingers go to his lips. I glance around, not hearing anything.

My gaze is drawn to the end of the alley where Zee went. I see one, two, three figures run past, yelling.

'*A little help when you're done, guys,*' Zee grunts down the link.

Shit.

Lukas and I take off down the alley. I burst out into a large courtyard, skidding to a stop as I take in six young trolls, each throwing . . .

My head tilts to the side and I squint, trying to understand what I am seeing. I duck as an object flies toward my face. Lukas's hand snaps up, catching it. I stare up at him and he smirks at me, taking a large bite.

"Mmm, custard filled. My favorite."

He shoots me a wink before popping the rest of the donut into his mouth. I stare at him in shock, then my gaze is dragged to the sugar on his lips. Goddess, I crave to lick it off. I lick my own lips in response. Lukas's eyes track the movement and darken.

"Keep thinking like that, and we won't be able to save Zee from all the donuts," Lukas threatens teasingly.

Something soft hits me in the side of the face and Lukas bursts out laughing. I reach up, swiping my face. It was a powdered sugar donut. There is white powdered sugar all over the side of my face. I hear the trolls laughing their asses off and spin to face them, magic warming my body. I cast a net over the two standing on the fence. Their eyes widen in surprise as they fall to the ground, pinned. Zee has two more subdued on the other side of the courtyard. He is covered in icing, jam, and custard. It's all over his clothes. I try—and fail—to smother my laughter. His gaze swings to me, annoyance lighting his blue eyes. Clearing my throat, I avert my eyes quickly and glance around at the absolute mess the trolls have made here. Lukas makes his way over to Zee and I watch him shake his head in disapproval. No doubt Lukas will have them all scrubbing this place clean in no time.

One troll tries to get past me, and I step in the way. He tries to go left, but I sidestep, blocking his escape again. My eyes widen when he pulls out a knife. I angle my head.

"Well, this took a dark turn," I grumble.

What happened to the donuts? I preferred the donuts.

He growls, lunging at me with the knife. My feet shift instantly to evade the knife, and the troll scowls at me like I've wronged him.

"What did you think, I'd let you stab me?" I glare back.

His sharp, toothy grin sends shivers across my skin. He pounces again, and I feint left, but dive right, zapping the troll with my magic. His face says it all.

"Weren't expecting that, were you?" I taunt, letting my magic flow under my skin. The tingle at my fingertips itching to lash out at him.

The troll spins on me, snapping those sharp pointed teeth at me, then charges me head on. I'm ready, though. I whirl to the side at the last minute, grabbing his arm with the knife and twisting it behind his back. He drops to his knees with a grunt. Lukas taps me on the shoulder.

"We got him." He smiles at me before running a finger over my cheek. It comes away white from all the sugar, and he puts it in his mouth, sucking all the icing off. "Mmm, delicious."

My stomach tumbles and my core clenches at the wicked look in his green eyes.

"Stop flirting, you two!" Zee shouts.

And I giggle. Bloody giggle. Embarrassment flushes my cheeks and my neck and chest heat as well. Lukas drags the troll over to the others. He and Zee keep them rounded up, but I see one slipping away into the shadows.

"I got this one!" I shout, not waiting for an answer as I take after the young troll. Lately, the younger trolls have been causing quite a bit of havoc around Portland, and it has started to draw the attention of the humans.

I've just rounded the edge of the alley when Lukas's voice rings out.

"Nesrin!!" His voice is full of a fury tinged with fear. This is just a troll. I'll be fine. I catch a glimpse of the troll's figure slipping into the storm drain across the road and quickly run after him.

Shit, I should just let him go. I really don't want to go into that drain. I've seen the movie It, and I do *not* want to run into Pennywise.

Come on, Nesrin, don't be a baby.

I shake my hands and blow out a breath, bouncing on my toes. *I got this.* Getting on my stomach, I slide into the drain feet first and land in the stormwater. Thank the goddess, it's only ankle deep here. I glance both ways as I summon an orb of light. As I listen, the sound of someone's footsteps reverberates from the left, so I take off running in that direction. I can feel the cold biting into my fingers, and I have to resist the urge to wrap my arms around myself as the chill spreads through my clothes. The tunnel is freezing cold, and the air is damp, smelling like mildew. I jog lightly in the direction I think the troll went. The sound of my feet echoes off the walls of the long, dark tunnel. I slowly come to a halt as I enter the silent expanse of the cavern.

I peer around and see nothing.

Damn it, I must have lost him.

I look around, feeling disoriented, as I try to gauge how far I've traveled. I take my phone out of my back pocket and notice there's no signal bars.

"Argh, just great," I growl and glance around, searching for a ladder. *Why, oh why, did I decide to come down here?* Now I am starting to get creeped out. A scuffling noise startles me and I turn in a circle.

"Hello?"

Silence greets me. Okay, now I am officially freaking out. I take a deep breath as I push my panic down. My instincts are telling me to run. I turn to go back, when there's a sharp pinch in my arm. My heart drops as I stare down, seeing a dart protruding from my arm. I reach up and pluck it out, frowning. The world abruptly tilts and I'm falling. I don't feel the impact of my body hitting the cold, hard ground. Nor do my eyes register the figures approaching me. I must be hallucinating, because they look to be naked women.

Huh.

CHAPTER TWENTY

I take a moment to study the intricate details of the limestone ceiling above me, feeling the coolness of the stone against my back as I lie on the floor. I sit up slowly, covering my eyes with my arm, the light too bright for my eyes to adjust to. I feel like I'm dreaming, but it also seems like I've been pulled here, like I was months ago when my mom pulled me to her. This must be either a vision or a dreamscape. I'm not sure which.

I blink my eyes several times as I reach down to pinch my arm.

Ouch. Okay, that hurt, and I still don't know.

My gaze darts around the room, my mouth falling open at the luxurious decor and the grandeur of the room. It looks like a palace from centuries ago. Sandstone and limestone walls, which are high with arched windows, surround me. Sheer fabrics hang from the windows, blowing in the wind. A gigantic bed stands in the middle of the room. It's covered in silks and pillows. I spin in a slow circle, taking in the area. It's jaw droppingly beautiful, something out of a fairytale.

The sheer curtains catch my attention as they dance in the breeze, and I make my way out onto the balcony that overlooks the ocean.

"Wow." A gasp falls from my lips at the beauty of it. Crystal blue water stretches as far as the eye can see. Thunder claps in the sky, followed by a streak of lightning, startling me. *What on earth?*

The skies are blue and clear. I take one last look at the gorgeous view then turn, going back into the room. I spot a cabinet in the corner and walk over, wanting to have a look around. Opening the doors to the small wooden cabinet, I note an arrangement of colorful glass bottles. I go to pick one up, but as I do, my hand glides straight through it.

Suddenly the door flings open, banging against the wall, making me jump. My hand goes to my chest, trying to slow my heart. A woman rushes in, a bright smile on her face. She sounds slightly out of breath as she runs into the chamber, closing the double doors behind her. She is stunning. Her skin is dark and her long, thick black hair is flowing freely around her waist. She wears a small gold crown amongst all the hair. Her dark brown eyes seem to sparkle in anticipation as she quickly moves about the chamber. She wears a long, sleeveless, sheer white dress, the bra and panties a turquoise blue underneath. More sheer fabric falls down the shoulders of the dress and trails behind her as she moves about. Another clap of thunder, this time closer, has me jumping.

What the hell? Where did this storm come from?

The woman seems excited as she climbs up on the enormous bed, laying back against the pillows in an innocent yet seductive way. She keeps her eyes on the balcony as a bolt of lightning strikes the balcony with a resounding *crack*. Only, this time, a man appears in the archway. My mouth drops open in awe.

First of all, where did he come from?

And second, he is gorgeous. Like, movie star gorgeous. He's older, but not old. His body is built, with muscles on top of muscles. He only wears a loose pair of white pants and in his hands rests *a thunderbolt*. His blonde hair is on the longer side, his beard neatly trimmed to his face, and his blue eyes shine with appreciation as he looks to the woman on the bed.

"Zeus," the woman says affectionately.

My eyes widen. *This is Zeus?* I mean, I can see it, but still, Zeus? The Zeus. Okay, I might be a little focused on the whole *Zeus* part. But my bloody brain is having a meltdown right now.

"Lamia, you're more beautiful than I recall," his deep tone rumbles through the chamber.

Lamia … Lamia … I try to remember my history, where I've heard her name before. My heart thunders in my ears as my thoughts race. That's right, Lamia was Queen of Libya and one of Zeus's lovers, though in the stories it doesn't end well for her. I want to seize her hand and drag her away before it's too late.

"You'd remember if you visited more," she says, pouting. Zeus frowns, staying where he is.

"You know time moves differently where I live. And you know how busy I am."

"It's been three years," Lamia points out as she moves off the bed gracefully and approaches the god. It's obvious in the way she gazes upon him that she cares for him deeply. I wonder if he feels the same way. I highly doubt it. Zeus is a well known player with a long line of mistresses.

Lamia's hands move to rest on Zeus's chest. His hands run down her back as their lips meet in a passionate kiss. I look away, feeling like I'm totally intruding on their moment. I peek back just as Zeus's palms move down to cup Lamia's ass and squeeze, making her moan into his mouth. Zeus picks her up and swiftly moves to the bed, where he lays her down.

Oh shit. I don't want to watch this. I close my eyes, turning my back to them. *Why am I here? I don't want to listen to these two getting it on. There must be a point to all this, surely.*

There is a steady stream of thunder and lightning. I can still see the flashes of lightning through my closed eyes. The air shifts suddenly, and everything goes quiet. I peek open one of my eyes, noting night has passed and the sun is rising. After a quick glance at the bed, I realize only Lamia lies there asleep.

Thank the goddess.

Unexpectedly, the door swings open, and four children of varying ages—the oldest looks to be eight and the youngest two—come running in and jumping up on the bed. I laugh as I watch them muck about and tease each other while Lamia wakes, a smile stretching across her face. These must be her children. She reaches for her youngest, pulling her into her arms and squeezing. Lamia whispers something into the little girl's ear and she giggles. She wriggles from her mother's arms and runs across the chamber to a chair, grabbing a silk robe and bringing it back to the bed. Lamia gets up, wrapping the robe around her and gives each child a hug and a kiss on the head.

The kids are chasing each other around the chamber, laughing, when a prickling sensation overwhelms me. I pause, glancing about for the source of my unease, and see Lamia freeze looking toward the balcony. She sucks in a sharp breath as her face pales. I spin and see a woman enter the room. Warning bells are ringing in my head as I watch the woman approach. Her long brown hair is pulled back from her face in an elaborate braid. A long white robed gown hangs from her shoulders. Her eyes are intelligent, predatory as she looks around the chamber. An air of importance surrounds her.

Lamia darts forward to grab her youngest daughter and the woman tsks, clicking her fingers. Lamia falls to the ground with a cry, then looks to her legs in distress. Her legs are limp and unmoving. My heart is thundering in my chest painfully as I stare at the scene unfolding in front of me. I hate that I can't do anything to stop it. These dream states or visions I keep getting sucked into are going to do my mental health some serious damage.

"Hera, please," Lamia begs, tears streaming down the queen of Libya's face. I take an involuntary step back at the name Hera.

The Hera. Zeus's Hera. Shit.

A deep-seated fear takes up place in my stomach. Hera, wife of Zeus, is known to be a jealous and vengeful woman. Everyone knows how far she could take things when she thought she'd been wronged in some way. There are plenty of stories in which the queen of the gods takes revenge on her husband's mistresses. She is the embodiment of wickedness and jealousy.

Hera regards the children, her cold blue eyes like ice chips. The children have stopped running around and stand quietly in place, their eyes wide in fear. Hera's eyes come back to Lamia. "Your children have the same eyes as my husband," she says coldly.

Lamia closes her eyes and visibly swallows. I watch as a few tears escape her closed eyes. When she opens them, she has a look of resolve on her face.

"Please don't hurt my children. Do whatever you want to me, but please don't harm them. They shouldn't pay for the sins of a parent."

Hera takes a step forward, a cruel smile on her face. "Oh, I will do what I want with you. You will suffer for an eternity. I will make sure of it. As for your children, they won't suffer. Much."

Lamia gasps and desperately tries to drag herself forward toward her children. My heart aches furiously as I watch on helplessly. My breath is sawing in and out at a rapid pace as Hera approaches the children.

"No!" I wail, shaking my head frantically. I step in her way, only for her to walk straight through me. I try to summon magic, but of course I can't here. Why am I here? I don't want to see this. My heart is already cracking with what is to come.

Hera places her hand on the children's heads, one by one, and they each fall to the ground, not breathing, eyes wide open. Lamia screams and screams, as she tries desperately to reach her babies. Tears cascade down my face at the fate of the children, of the pain and anguish in Lamia's screams. Hera just struck down Lamia's children in front of her without so much as blinking an eye. Pain tears through me so deep and fast I can't catch my breath. How could she be so cruel? Those children were innocent. I can barely see through the tears, but I watch as Hera turns to Lamia and smirks. With a wave of her hand, Lamia's legs fuse together, creating a serpent-like tail. Lamia lets out a piercing wail of agony, her body withering on the floor. When the pain passes, she slides over to her children. Gathering them up in her arms, she squeezes them, placing a kiss on each of their heads, her suffering and despair so strong I can feel it as if it were my own. I crave to go to her, to hold her in my arms. I want to tear Hera apart for her cruel and unfair punishments.

When I glance up, Hera is gone, and Lamia has transformed into a monstrous creature. A half snake, half woman, her eyes deformed. Hera has turned her into a daemon. The guards come crashing through the doors, as if they've been struggling to get through the whole time, skidding to a stop. They regard their queen and the dead children. Lamia looks up, hissing at them, then slithers to the balcony and throws herself over the ledge. I race outside and search below, but I see nothing. She's disappeared.

The world suddenly spins, and I find myself in complete blackness. Slowly, as light filters back in, I realize I'm lying down in something soft. I blink a few times, seeing a darkening blue sky above and the smell of the ocean captures my attention. I sit up, startled, and look around. *Shit, where am I now?*

I fist my hands in the sand before I stand up on shaky legs, brushing the sand from my jeans as I take in my surroundings. I'm at the beach. How on earth did I get here? I try to think of where I was before I was sucked into the vision. I remember being on patrol with Lukas and Zee. There was a run-in with a group of unruly trolls. I chased after one and got separated from the others, then I remember being hit with a dart and my world turning fuzzy as I hit the ground. With how much training I've been doing lately, I'm surprised I was caught off guard. The others are probably losing their damn minds. I can't sense Lukas, so I must be too far away.

I think about my vision—or dream, whatever these things are, it's hard to tell them apart. I have no one to ask, either. My thoughts flitter back to what I just witnessed. My anger at Hera burns so strong, along with my sorrow for Lamia and what she endured. Losing her children drove her mad. It turned her into a monster, one her people feared. I hope she found peace, but I'm not so sure. Hera has never seemed like the kind to allow her victims a reprieve.

Another thought occurs to me: if Hera did this, could she be behind what happened to my family? I've assumed it was Zeus's anger at not getting his way that drove him, but what if it was Hera and her jealousy? Kaida mentioned this was all because of a god's jealousy. What if I've had it all wrong, and I've been looking at the wrong god? Hades assumed Zeus as well, but now I'm not so sure. This makes a lot more sense than our previous theory.

Movement from the water catches my attention. There is a slight change in the rocks. It looks as if the rock is moving as the waves wash around it. I drift closer when I realize there is actually something on the rocks. A pair of slitted eyes blink at me from the spot I am staring at. I stumble back in alarm, my hand gripping the pendant at my chest as I realize what I'm seeing. It was Lamia perched on some rocks, her body camouflaged well. I take a step forward again.

"Please don't come any closer." Though her words come as a hiss, her tone is not one of anger. "I can't promise I won't try to hurt you." Her gaze lowers as if she is ashamed. I take a step closer still, and her head shoots up in warning. I sit cross-legged on the sand.

"You brought me here, showed me what Hera did to you." It isn't a question, but she nods anyway.

I want to help her. I desperately wish I could take her pain away. My heart hurts as I watch her, broken and defeated on those rocks. The fact that no one has put an end to Hera or helped Lamia causes a hurricane of emotion to riot through me.

"Can I help? Tell me what I can do," I ask softly. Surprise has her eyes widening almost comically. "What?" I ask, confused.

Lamia shakes her head in disbelief, her serpent tail wrapping around herself. "No one has ever asked if I wanted or needed help before."

I'm beginning to understand that the gods do nothing unless it benefits them directly. Bunch of useless asses. There is no good or evil when it comes to them. It's simply doing what they want to do in order to achieve their own selfish agendas.

I shake my head and pin Lamia with a serious stare. "It was Hera who cursed my family, who set this in motion. All because Zeus showed interest in Blanchette. And even though Althaea had already gotten her away and hid her in the mortal world, it wasn't enough. Hera had to kill her and hunt her descendants for centuries."

"Yes."

"Thank you for showing me. I know it must have been difficult."

"You had to know who you're dealing with. Everyone involved has likely been bound to the goddess, so they can't speak her name. She forgot about me though. That she never bound me to her like that."

"Short sighted on her part," I say, winking.

Lamia puffs her chest out with the compliment, but then her shoulders sag. "I should go. I just wanted to warn you."

"Thank you."

Lamia nods, then turns to dive into the water.

"Wait." I start forward but stop when panic shoots across Lamia's face. I mentally chastise myself. "Sorry," I whisper, knowing she can hear me. "It's just. Is there anything I can do?"

"Destroy her," Lamia hisses as flames flicker in the depths of her dark eyes. I can feel the static in the air as her long black hair swirls around her face, her eyes never leaving mine. My heart beats painfully in my chest, the wind howling in my ears. Lamia has been cursed for millennia to exist without the possibility of rejoining her children in the afterlife. Condemned to murder, unable to control that desire. And yet she took a risk to break free from her self-imposed confinement to find me, to help me. So I will find a way to help her.

Lamia dives into the waves and disappears under the water. I watch for a long while, hoping to get even a tiny glimpse of the once-beautiful queen of Libya, but she is gone. For a long time, I stand watching the waves roll and crash on the beach, taking comfort in mother nature. My thoughts drift back to the children, and a few tears escape my eyes. They didn't deserve that fate. What Hera did to them . . . It's inexcusable.

I close my eyes, listening to the harmony of the ocean, and breathe in the smell of salt. The familiar scent brings me to the realization that this was what I saw when I was with Zee earlier; it was a vision. I'm not clear how long I've been standing here basking in this feeling, but when I open my eyes again, the sky has darkened substantially. Soon it will be nightfall. I would guess I've been gone almost twenty-four hours, and Lukas is almost definitely beside himself with worry.

Suddenly, the sound of pounding hooves pulls my attention further down the beach. With purpose, a gleaming black horse gallops toward me, its golden eyes glittering like stars. I can't stop the smile that spreads across my face, nor the warmth that flows through me at the sight of him. I am filled with an intense feeling of joy as he draws near. I watch as the Puca circles me, his vibrant eyes sparkling. He seems agitated, nudging me with his head and stamping his front hooves as he stares at me.

"You always seem to show up when I need you," I whisper, running my hand up his nose.

His eyes seem to say, *I was worried about you.*

"I'm okay," I reply.

His nose nudges one more time, before he motions me to climb on. Excitement fills me and I manage to get on him first go. I honestly thought I'd go straight over the top and land on the ground. I shuffle around, getting comfortable, and lean forward.

"I need to give you a name," I say, rubbing his neck. This seems to make him happy, and he dances on the spot, nodding his head. "Okay, let's think on one while we ride." I laugh.

I've barely gotten a grip on his long, black mane when he shoots forward, causing me to yelp in surprise. A thrill of excitement blasts through my soul as the Puca takes off. My grip on his mane tightens as I wrap it around my hands. I brace my thighs on his sides, leaning forward and lifting slightly, moving with him as my heartbeat matches his pounding hooves in the sand. The sound thunders through my body as it hums with adrenaline. A familiar warmth spreads through my chest,

Lukas. He's close. I know the closest shoreline to the pack lands just out of Portland is at least one hour's drive. So how was anyone able to find me this far away?

The ocean is to my left and the woods to my right and rising above the noise of the waves crashing and the pounding of hooves, I can hear his howl. I send up a flare with my magic and flood our bond with love as I ride forward, the wind whipping my hair around my face. Tipping my head back, I relish the wind in my face, breathing in the salty sea air.

Suddenly, two enormous wolves break from the trees and sprint for me. The Puca doesn't break his stride as the wolves flank him. Lukas's midnight black wolf and Zee's gray wolf keep pace with the Puca as he sprints down the shoreline, their massive forms barely half the size of the Puca, but no less impressive.

I am really going to need to name this beautiful horse. He keeps showing up to rescue me. I don't know where he's taking me right now, but I trust him with my life.

'*Are you okay?*' Lukas's voice rings in my head.

Relief and worry both flood the bond, and my heart swells and aches at his presence near me again. I want to have his arms around me, and I will soon enough. Zee is a quiet, formidable presence on my other side. I can sense his worry and irritation, but he is also relieved.

'*Yes, I'm okay. I think I figured out who is behind the order.*'

Surprise bleeds down the bond. '*I thought it was Zeus?*'

'*So did I, but someone helped me see things a little clearer. I'll fill you in when we are back.*'

"*Okay, sweetheart. You had me worried. If I had lost you . . .*" he trails off, but the emotions coming through the bond can't be hidden. He was panicked, angry and desperate when he realized I was gone . . . again. If the roles were reversed, I would have felt the same.

'*You won't lose me. You're stuck with me forever,*' I say with conviction.

CHAPTER TWENTY ONE

"What about Onyx?" I suggest, running the brush over the Puca's side while he eats some horse feed that someone kindly found for me. He seems content here, and I won't send him away. If he wants to stay, he can.

He shakes his head and snorts.

"Okay, that's a no." Hmm . . . "Midnight?"

Another shake and a huff.

"Yeah, too original. I agree."

I move to the other side and continue brushing him down. He leans into my touch, and I rest my forehead on his body. "What about Nero?" I ask gently.

That gets me a nicker and a nudge.

"You like that one? Nero?" I ask.

I pull back, smiling, and he nods, pushing me with his head. "Okay. Nero it is."

I feel movement approaching the barn. A slow purposeful stride, Lukas. I knew I wouldn't get to hide for long. Everyone wants to know where I've been and what happened, but I need time to get my thoughts in order.

"You're still hiding?" Lukas walks over to me, his massive arms wrap around me from behind and his chin rests on my head.

I lean back into him and close my eyes. "I was reflecting."

"Uhm hmm . . . " he murmurs, moving his face into my neck and nuzzling me. As I reach up and run my hand through his soft, thick hair, I can hear him sigh in contentment. Lukas turns me in his arms and takes my mouth in a kiss that has my stomach plunging to my feet and my core throbbing with need. I faintly hear Nero trot away, giving us some privacy.

My hands roam up Lukas's broad chest over all the muscles and into his devilishly messy hair. I stop thinking then. About everything; there is no Hera, no Lamia and her children, no order, nothing. It's just me and him and the love we share together.

Lukas's kiss deepens, his tongue sliding against mine. A groan rumbles from deep in his throat, which sets my blood on fire. A deep burning hunger for this man has my soul lighting up. Even if I wanted to, I couldn't stop myself. I need him. I need him inside me now. My hands move from his shoulders to the belt on his jeans as I fumble to undo the buckle. Lukas breaks the kiss and stares down at me, his eyes darkening with unveiled desire.

Then he makes a noise, a low growl that tears from deep in his chest, a claiming.

Mine, it seems to say, and my heart thunders as I long to show him the same.

I quickly finish with his belt and pop the button before starting on mine. Lukas brushes my hands aside, hooking his thumbs in the belt loops of my jeans, tearing them down my legs. He reaches for my panties and shreds them instantly. If I wasn't already wet, that absolutely would have done the trick.

My eyes lock with his, our gazes hungry and hard breaths mingling as I brace my hands on his shoulders. Lukas grips my ass in both hands, then I jump, wrapping my legs around his waist, my heels pushing his jeans down over his ass. Lukas takes a couple of steps forward into the stall, pinning me to the barn wall, then he pushes inside of me. A gasp falls from my lips, my head tipping back against the wall and fingertips pressing into his shoulders as Lukas buries his face in my neck, groaning. We move together, rocking into each other. I bring one hand up to grip his hair, the other still holding his shoulder. My breathing comes out in heavy pants as I savor the feel of him inside of me. Lukas's arm bands under my ass, his other hand holding the back of my neck, as he drives into me harder. I hold him tight, needing him closer. His tongue swirls up my neck to my ear, biting down gently on my earlobe. I shiver, my nails digging into his shoulder.

'*Lukas . . .*'

I move both my hands into his hair, my fingers sinking into the soft strands and gripping them tightly. Goddess, I am close. Lukas's mouth devours my neck, placing open mouthed kisses everywhere until he gets to the mating mark. He isn't gentle when he bites down on our mark, his teeth sinking into my skin. Sparks ignite inside me, and I cry out, bucking in his arms, the climax ripping through me hard and fast. I relish in the rumble of his chest as he joins me, slowing his movements. Tremors move through his muscled body as he rests his head on my shoulder. Sweat coats both of us as we stand there panting, trying to catch our breath again. He gently kisses my mark before pulling back to stare at me. I am still wrapped around him, and he still has me pinned to the wall with his hips. Lukas groans, dropping his forehead to mine as I clench my walls around him. I lift my hands to grip his cheeks and tilt his face up to mine. Leaning forward, I kiss him, my tongue slipping into his mouth.

I feel Lukas growing hard again when Zee calls through the pack bond, '*You guys done?*'

'*Fuck off,*' Lukas counters.

I let my head fall back with a groan as Lukas trails more kisses up my neck. He takes my mouth in another kiss before lifting me off him and stepping away. His hands still grip my hips tightly, as if he can't bear to let me go yet. I reach up, cupping his cheek as my thumb moves over his jaw, his stubble scratching my hand. "I love you."

"I love you, too, sweetheart."

We right our clothing . . . well, minus my underwear. When I search around the floor for what's left of them, Lukas snatches them up and stuffs them in his pocket. I raise an eyebrow at him, and he simply smirks, grabbing my hand and leading me back toward the house.

"Astraea's having a sleepover at Kyra's. I hope that's okay. I wasn't certain how late we would be out searching for you."

"It's fine, Lukas. I understand. You realize she's yours as well, right?"

His green eyes dart to mine in surprise, and I sense the stutter in his heart as he whispers softly, "I know."

Lukas's hand warms the small of my back as we walk in the front door. I can sense Zee's amusement the second we get inside. I look over and find him sitting on the couch in the sitting room, a shit-eating grin on his face.

I narrow my gaze at him. "Don't start."

He holds his hands up in surrender, the grin firmly in place. "I didn't say a word."

I grab a pillow on my way past the couch and throw it at him. "You didn't have to, its written all over your face."

Zee's laughter fills the room, and I lose my fight to hold back my amusement.

'I love seeing you like this.' Lukas reaches for me and pulls me into his arms. "But don't disappear on me again," he mumbles into my hair, which is still a tangled mess from waking up on the beach and the ride that followed.

"On us. Don't disappear on *us* again, Nesrin," Zee amends, all laughter gone from his tone. I peer up and my eyes lock with his.

A feeling of dismay fills me as I look from Zee to Lukas and back again. "I will do my best to not vanish again. I promise." I hate that I was the cause of such stress for them.

Warmth and affection pulse through the bond as Lukas holds me tighter. I watch Zee get up and move toward us. He grabs for my hand, smoothly plucking me from Lukas's hold to wrap me in his arms. I return the hug, wrapping my arms around his waist and resting my cheek on his chest.

"You scared us, Nesrin," he says, running a hand down my hair, his chin atop my head. Zee gives me one more squeeze and steps back. Tears fill my eyes and I try to smile but fail.

"I'm sorry," I choke.

"Hey, it's okay," Lukas soothes, leading me over to the sofa. I sit down just as Gabe and Asena walk in carrying some hot drinks. Gabe looks tired and Asena won't meet anyone's eyes as she places the drinks on the coffee table.

"Thank you," I say, smiling at Gabe as he hands me a hot chocolate. I read the words on the mug and burst out laughing.

The mug reads: **What (and I can't stress this enough) the fuck, Nesrin!**

When I look up, Gabe gives me a sheepish grin, his dark eyes twinkling with mirth. He has half of his hair pulled back in a man bun, which always makes his features more sharp.

"You made me a personalized mug?" I whisper, my smile wobbling.

Gabe shrugs like he didn't just brighten my mood. "Well, it's something we all think on a pretty regular basis. Seemed fitting."

"Thank you."

"You're welcome." He nods, taking a seat on the single armchair. Asena looks slightly more relaxed as she perches on the arm of Gabe's chair on the opposite side of the room to Zee, which is where she would usually have been before my sister showed up.

There's a knock at the door, and Lukas lifts me off his lap to answer it. Moments later, he comes back with Nikolas following behind. Nikolas's eyes take me in and he moves fast, his arms wrapping around me tightly. I return the hug, a small smile forming on my lips as I take in the vampire's scent. It's not what I'd expect of a vampire. He smells like a dark cocktail with hints of bergamot, rum, and leather.

"Ma reine, you scared us," his voice rumbles. I pull back, giving a weak shrug.

"Maybe one day I'll stop getting knocked out and kidnapped," I attempt to joke, but nobody laughs.

I notice Stephan standing in the doorway, hand in his pants pockets, dressed in his usual dashing suit.

"Stephan?" I say, surprised. I haven't seen him much since the night I made Nikolas a part of the pack. It's like he's avoiding me now. Is he worried I'll make him pack, too? The thought makes me grin.

"You sure know how to keep things interesting, rose sauvage," His deep voice replies, lit with amusement.

"Sorry?"

He chuckles, shaking his head at me. "Half of Portland was looking for you. When the coven found out you were missing, the streets were crawling with witches and mages eager to bring the high priest his prize."

I spin to where Lukas is seated in the chair behind me, his chin propped on his hand. *'Yes, sweetheart. They were out in masses. We were worried they'd find you first.'*

Shit.

Everyone grunts in response, and I realize that, once again, I've spoken my thoughts out loud.

I turn and climb back into Lukas's lap. Guilt rolls through me, making me feel queasy. I hate that I've put everyone through this again. I know it isn't my fault I keep getting kidnapped, but I also know that while nothing bad happened this time, they didn't know that until they found me. I hope we can solve this soon so we can take care of the coven, and I don't have to keep looking over my shoulder all the time.

"How did you know where to find me?"

"Nero," Lukas replies.

Huh. He really is like my guardian angel. But instead of showing up to stop something from happening, he helps me after the fact.

Stephan and Nikolas take a seat in the chairs next to mine and Lukas. Zee looks around expectantly. "Who are we waiting for?" he asks, leaning forward in his chair and rubbing his hands together like he can't wait to dive into this new turn of events.

"I invited Marcus and Leila here." Everyone stiffens at the names, so I explain, "I didn't want to have to repeat myself." I sigh, taking a long sip from my new mug. I hate all the tension. If anyone has something to be sour about, it's me, but I am pushing my own issues aside so I can work on the bigger picture. I will clear the air with Leila soon. My hurt feelings are the least of our problems right now.

CHAPTER TWENTY TWO

"Hera? Are you sure?"

This is coming from Marcus as he paces the living room, clearly agitated by my revelation. His shoulders are tense, and his fingers are rubbing at his forehead as if to soothe a pounding headache.

I furrow my brow and take a deep breath before answering. "Of course I'm sure, Marcus. I wouldn't have brought you all here if I wasn't. Hera couldn't silence everyone. She has made so many enemies that it was only a matter of time before one was able to slip by her. I don't know if Zeus knows what his wife has been up to, but we should probably talk to Hades. This whole time, we've all assumed Zeus is behind it all. Everything points that way. Jealous and entitled god is unable to win the girl, and then she runs off with what he'd consider a lesser being. But Zeus is not a long game kind of guy. His attention is on the next shiny thing. What I don't understand is why Hera would do this if Zeus never had an affair with Blanchette."

It doesn't make any sense. Why would she target Blanchette? And why to this extreme?

"There has to be more to it," Lukas agrees from the chair behind where I sit on the floor between his legs, his fingers gliding through my hair leisurely. It feels so good I have to fight the urge to close my eyes.

Zee whistles low, resting back in his chair. "So, this Queen Lamia paid some young selkies to kidnap you and deliver you to her. Then she shows you a vision of her past, where Hera kills her children and turns her into a half woman, half serpent for having an affair with Zeus."

"Sounds about right," I hum, feeling my eyes droop.

"Shit!!" Marcus's loud curse startles me. I glance up and see him running his hands through his black hair. It's grown quite a bit over the last few months. The untamed look is good on him.

"Why is this so bad?" I ask, rubbing my hands over my face in an attempt to stay awake.

"Yeah. We thought it was Zeus, but now we know it's Hera. She can't be any worse than Zeus, right?" Asena agrees from her spot next to Gabe. She has done her best to avoid looking directly at anyone. I have a suspicion Zee has called things off with her now that Leila's back in the picture.

My mind flashes back to Lamia's children lying dead on the floor, their mother's wails echoing in my head. I have a feeling Hera is the worst of them all. But I'm still trying to figure out why she would go to so much trouble.

"Any worse? No, but she basically made an entire cult dedicated to wiping out Blanchette's bloodline. That's pretty dedicated, even for a god," Stephan's deep voice rings out for the first time since we started, echoing my thoughts. He and Nikolas have both been silent this whole time, which is highly unusual for the vampire master. He always seems to have something to say.

"They all think of you as abominations because of her," Marcus spits. He seems extremely worked up about this, but this is good. We now know who is truly targeting me. Now we just have to figure out where she is. The why could come later.

I can feel the wheels turning in Lukas's mind, as he sifts through everything we have learned over the last few months. Now that we know who's behind the Order, maybe we can finally figure out how to stop them.

"There must be more behind her agenda. Kaida mentioned that Althaea and Hecate got Blanchette out of Greece because she had caught the attention of another higher god. Could it have been Hera they meant and not Zeus?"

Everyone goes quiet, each of us lost in our own thoughts for a time.

"I can speak to Hades and see what he thinks. But whatever Hera's been up to, she has kept it close to her chest," Leila breaks the silence as she stands up.

I nod my head. "Thank you."

"It's up to us to destroy this Order. They need to be stopped," Leila continues, and I nod my head in agreement.

Whatever's going on, we have to get to the bottom of it. Astraea will not carry this burden.

'She won't. Plus, our own children will need a safe world to grow in.'

I balk at that. I hadn't realized I'd conveyed that thought to Lukas. Feeling suddenly very awake, I spin around and stare up at him. A smirk pulls at his lips and there's a twinkle in his eyes that warms my heart. His dark hair falls over his face as he looks down at me. A feeling of contentment pours down the bond and emotions clog my throat. We haven't actually spoken about having kids. Hell, the thought has never really entered my mind with everything that's been going on.

'You want kids?'

'I want everything with you, freckles.'

I want to climb on his lap and kiss the life out of him right now, but with company, it kind of puts a damper on things.

Malachite comes bouncing into the room, zipping through legs until he sees me. He reminds me of a puppy as he bounds around, then darts up my body and into Lukas's lap. Not a second later, Astraea runs in after him, a big smile on her face.

Kyra pokes her head into the room, her eyes finding mine. "I figured you were all back. She couldn't sleep and wanted to come home. I think she knew you were back and wanted to be with you."

"Thank you," I say sincerely.

Kyra has been a lifesaver, taking Astraea and Malachite often while Lukas and I are out. Between her and Kate, Astraea has been well watched over.

"Thank you, Kyra," Lukas adds as well. A blush rises to her tanned cheeks at the praise, and she nods before disappearing out the front door.

Astraea climbs into my lap, taking in everyone in the room. Her eyes catch on Marcus, and she frowns a little. I stare up at Marcus and see him studying Astraea. Lukas notices and reacts before I do. "Care to share with the group, mage?"

Marcus's head snaps up and he glares at Lukas. "What if it does have something to do with Zeus?"

I frown, perplexed. "But Lamia clearly stated it's Hera."

"Yes, but hear me out." Marcus takes a fortifying breath before continuing. "Hera has had to deal with Zeus's copious number of affairs, which has in turn made her into an enraged, jealous, and vengeful bitch with a frightful temper. History shows it caused her to lash out at any who dared to cross her. The easy targets for her anger being Zeus's lovers and his children. She proved it over and over that she was callous and unforgiving. We also knew her to curse his lover's children, so no one ever escaped her ire. She was so jealous of these children, that she was driven to the point of cruelty. Zeus didn't help the matter. He always favored his illegitimate children over those he had with Hera."

"She punished Hercules his whole life. Sent snakes to kill him as a baby and when that didn't work, she kept at him. Made him crazy, causing him to kill his own family," Leila chimes in.

A sense of foreboding hits me, and Astraea senses the shift in the room as all eyes land on us, then slowly move to Leila.

"What are you suggesting exactly? Because it sounds like you think we might be from Zeus's bloodline?" I inquire, doing my best not to choke on the words.

"I think that is exactly what they're saying, and it makes sense," Zee replies before Marcus can.

Marcus sags into a lounge chair, looking extremely tired. "Think about it. Why else would she be so persistent?"

I lock eyes with Leila. "Who was Blanchette's father?"

Shaking her head, she grimaces. "I don't know."

"Well, fuck," I curse, and Lukas grunts from behind me. Malachite nudges the back of my head in response to my mood shift and I reach back, stroking his head softly. Astraea looks up at me, cupping my cheek, her own way of offering reassurance.

'*Sorry, sweet girl.*' I bend down and rub my nose with hers.

"Althaea and Hecate worked so hard to get Blanchette out. Blanchette looks nothing like either of them, so Althaea must have thought she wouldn't be noticed."

"We will figure this out. Either way, this ends. I will not lose anyone else." There's a sharp edge to my words and I know everyone senses my simmering anger.

"Agreed. I will talk to Hades and see if he knows who Blanchette's father was. I don't think he even suspected Hera, to be honest. His rivalry with Zeus has very likely clouded his judgment," Leila replies.

Astraea stands up and holds her tiny hand out for me and I smile, giving it a squeeze as I stand up. I can feel the numbness spread through my legs from sitting on the floor for so long, a pins and needles sensation seizing my feet. I stamp them a little, hoping to ease the discomfort, but as the blood rushes back, it only makes it worse. My legs buckle, but Lukas is there, his arm wrapping around my middle, his body heat soaking into my back.

"I'm getting my girls into bed now. We will continue this tomorrow," he tells the room as his arm tightens around my waist. My heart swells with emotions at the tenderness in his voice when he says *my girls.*

Astraea moves into my legs, and Malachite nudges the back of my head again, from his spot around Lukas's neck. My emotions get the better of me, tears prick my eyes.

Leila moves first, standing and making her way over to me. She hesitates for a second, then ignoring Lukas, she pulls me into a hug. I smile into her shoulder, my heart full. When she pulls back, she has a soft smile on her face. Astraea moves forward and hugs her legs, making her smile fuller.

"Marcus, thank you for coming. If you hear anything from your inside man, let us know," Lukas says, moving toward the front door, effectively telling everyone to leave.

Marcus looks over at me. "We'll figure this out. Whatever's happening is leaking through the covens. I want to be what we were. I hate what we've become. The coven, my sister, they never used to be like this. It's like a sickness spreading through them."

Zee grunts from his spot on the couch and I'm just thankful he kept his mouth shut for a change. Asena and Gabe move toward the door, the former sending us a wave as she heads out the door.

Gabe's eyes connect with mine and soften. *'Get some rest, luna. Try to not disappear in the night.'*

After Lukas, Gabe is the pack member I have the strongest mental connection with. I wonder if it has to do with his abilities as a kitsune.

'I will do my best. Thank you for the coffee mug, Gabe. I love it.' I grin at him, and he chuckles quietly to himself as he follows Asena out the door.

Reaching for Astraea, I lift her into my arms as Nikolas makes his way over and kisses me and Astraea on the head. *'Stay safe, ma reine.'*

'I will. Thank you for coming, Nikolas.'

Stepping back, my eyes lock with Stephan's and he nods at me before making his way out of the room, Nikolas following. He was unusually quiet tonight, like he was only here to observe. He and Zee didn't even trade barbs. It's made me rather uneasy.

Marcus and Leila move for the door next, but Leila stops, turning toward me. "I know we still have things to discuss. Just know that I'm sorry."

My heart thumps hard in my chest as emotions rise in my stomach, making me feel queasy. I nod as she turns, following Marcus out the door. Truth is, after what Lamia showed me, I came to the realization that life is unpredictable and I have my sister back. That's what I should focus on. Everything else is in the past.

Lukas shuts the door, running a hand through his disheveled hair. Zee frowns and sits back in his chair, appearing flustered. "Do we really need the mage?"

I groan, resting my head on Astraea's, "Yes, Zee. He and Leila are working the covens and gathering supporters. Plus, Claudia is our inside spy."

"I don't like him."

Lukas grunts in response, moving around, clearing all the coffee mugs and silently making his way to the kitchen.

"I know, Zee, but he's here helping, and he wants this to end as much as we do."

"He wants in your pants more like it," he snaps in irritation.

I glare over at him as I hear the sound of something breaking in the kitchen, Lukas's displeasure flowing down the bond before he can stop it.

'That better have not been my new mug.'

'It wasn't.'

Zee holds his hands up as he stands, making his way to the door. "I'm just saying his motives aren't clear."

Biting my lip, I contemplate his words. My mind whirls. Can Marcus be trusted? I think so. But if the pack isn't comfortable, maybe I need to rethink things. Before I can stop myself, I cast my senses out toward Zee. I feel resentment, frustration, and heartache.

I don't realize I'm standing here in a daze until Lukas places his hands on my hips, laying a kiss on Astraea's head and mine. "Come on, it's late."

I glance around and notice Zee has left. "I just gotta do something really quick. Here, take Astraea. I'll be right back."

I quickly rush to the front door and push outside. Zee has just gotten to the bottom of the stairs, and is starting across the lawn.

"Wait! Zee!" I call, running down the stairs to follow. He spins so quickly and unexpectedly that I trip, slamming into him hard. Zee's arms come up, steadying me.

"Shit, honey. What's up?"

"Leila," I say. His hands drop and I watch as the light fades from his face. He looks so sad and defeated. I hate it. I'm so used to the upbeat pain in my ass.

"Zee, I know it's hard."

Zee slowly starts back toward the house, taking a seat on the bottom step. I follow and sit next to him. He doesn't respond, so I bump my shoulder against his, shooting him a sad smile.

"Leila totally broke your heart, huh?"

Zee lets out a sigh, running his hands over his face. "I was captivated by her, and when she left, it felt like a punch to the gut."

"Yet you still feel the need to hold on to her with every splintered piece of your heart, as tight as you can. That hurt is real love. Nothing can stand in the way of that. You two have a lot to figure out, but you've got a second chance."

"She doesn't want me."

I chuckle. "I thought you were everyone's type."

Zee huffs, hanging his head. "I fell for the right girl at the wrong time and now I'm paying for it."

I smile and bump his shoulder again. "Are you really going to let a stubborn woman stop you from claiming her heart?"

Zee's blue eyes lift to mine and he smiles, a really genuine Zee grin and ruffles my hair. "Thanks, luna," he says before pushing to his feet.

I push to my feet and climb the stairs, waving to Zee.

"Night!" I call out.

"Night."

I walk inside and quietly shut the door. Lukas's arm goes around my waist, pulling my back against his chest. "Talk some sense into him?"

"I hope so," I whisper.

Lukas turns me in his arms and drops his mouth to mine. Goddess, I could get lost in his kisses. Lukas pulls back and gently guides me up the stairs. Astraea is already sleeping in our bed, so we climb in carefully on either side, the three of us, plus Malachite curled at the end of the bed. My thoughts stop the moment my head hits the pillow, sleep pulling me under instantly.

CHAPTER TWENTY THREE

The next morning, I'm uneasy, feeling anxious about the revelations we had last night. I wish there were a way I could truly hide us. Sure, I'm cloaking our powers and what we are, but it's clearly not enough. What if Hera discovers Astraea? I need to protect her. So far, Hera only knows about me. Leila and Astraea are safe, but if things change, I want to be ready.

I'm extremely twitchy when I follow Astraea and Malachite out the front door, headed for an early breakfast with Kyra and her boys. The thick fog blanketing the valley comes as a shock, and I shiver a little, pulling my jacket tighter around me. Astraea turns back to me as if sensing my anxiety, her big violet blue eyes studying me as she grabs my hand to pull me along. My breath streams from my mouth like smoke as we make our way down the hill. This chill is definitely unusual. It's supposed to be warming up by now.

Malachite is running in circles up ahead, entranced by the mist floating around him. I suddenly remember Kaida's powers. She didn't breathe fire, she was an air dragon, and was responsible for the thick fog when I was captured. Although I doubt this fog is Malachite's doing as he's only a baby, it is something I'll have to keep an eye on. He reminds me of a big playful puppy, the way he bounds about without a worry in the world. He had grown to the length of my arm now, and I was curious to see how big he would get. As we walk, the fog thickens until I can barely see a few feet in front of me.

"What the hell?" I mumble.

I pull Astraea to a stop and turn in a circle. The thick fog is now fully surrounding us. I reach out and watch as it wraps around my hand, gently caressing it, the touch soft and reassuring. A memory floats in my mind of a book I was reading a few months ago about magical mists. *Could this be one of those?* The Tuatha Dé Danann are said to be able to hide themselves with féth fíada, a magic mist they can control and use to their advantage. It hides them from the enemy.

We start walking again, and the mist seems to part for us. I knock twice on the wooden door in front of us, Astraea's excitement apparent as she jumps on the spot, her hand still clutching mine.

Liam opens the door, his cute little face smiling up at us. "You're here!" he shouts, turning and running back through the house. I chuckle, following him in and shutting the door. Astraea tugs on my hand and I glance down at her. "Yes, sweet girl?"

She tugs again and I bend down till we are eye level, then she steps into me, giving me a kiss on the cheek before turning and running after Liam. I stand there a moment, absorbing the sweetness of the gesture. I move toward the kitchen just as Noah runs past, almost knocking my feet from under me, Malachite on his heels.

Kyra is by the sink as I stroll into the kitchen. Her dark curls are pinned back off her face and she looks flushed.

"Everything alright?" I ask.

"Yes, it's just that the boys have been at it all morning."

I frown and check the clock on the wall. "It's eight."

"Yes, well, my day started at 4 a.m." she groans, rolling her head around as if trying to relieve the tension in her shoulders.

I cringe. "That sucks."

Her shoulders deflate, and she leans against the bench. "They miss their father, and I'm struggling to keep up with them."

"Why didn't you say something? You've been helping me so much with Astraea, I could have taken the boys so you could have a break." Guilt eats at me. I have been relying on her too much. I don't know much about Sander, only that he works in a security firm based in Portland, but he's away on an extended business trip at the moment. Despite his busy schedule, he always manages to make time to call his family throughout the day, which is sweet. Most of the pack hold jobs at Lukas's timber yard, only a few have jobs in the city.

"You have enough going on."

"I will always have time for you. If you need me, please ask. I don't mind having the boys over."

Her eyes drop to the floor, and she chews on her lip for a long moment. I can see her internal struggle and I completely understand it. She doesn't want to be a burden. I open my mouth to say more when I sense Lukas is close by. Kyra stops what she's doing, her warm brown eyes swinging to mine. She draws in a sharp breath, and I watch as tears line her eyes.

"What?" I ask gently.

Worry starts twisting my insides at her tears. I hear a car door close outside and feel that familiar tug in my chest. Lukas is here. The side door into the kitchen swings open and a tall military-looking man with short-cropped brown hair strolls in. His light brown eyes warm as he takes in Kyra. Letting out a half laugh, half cry, Kyra takes two steps and launches herself into his arms. This must be her husband and mate, Sander.

I hear the boys come running from the other room, each yelling, "Daddy!"

Pulling away, he kneels, taking the impact of both boys.

My heart fills with joy at seeing the family together again. I tear my eyes away and see Lukas standing in the doorway, his shoulder resting against the frame, watching his friends with a soft smile on his face.

Kyra hits her husband on the arm. "You didn't tell me you were coming home!"

"I wanted to surprise you and the boys," Sander replies easily, a twinkle in his eye as he watches his wife.

"You were in on this, then?" she says, staring at me.

I hold my hands up, grinning. "I didn't know. I swear!"

Sander gets to his feet, ruffling both boys' hair before moving to me.

I smile and hold out my hand. "Hi, I'm–"

Before I can finish, I'm scooped up into a hug. Surprise has me frozen for a hot second before I hug him back. When I'm placed back on my feet, Sander grins at me. The boyish smile matches his sons'. Noah edges closer and grips his dad's hand, smiling up at him. I'm a puddle on the floor right now. The way these boys are looking at their dad is like he is their personal superhero.

"Hi, Nesrin. I'm Sander, as you've probably figured out."

I laugh, nodding. "Nice to meet you."

His brown eyes light up with mischief. "I've heard so much about you," he teases.

I arch an eyebrow at Lukas, asking Sander, "You have?"

Lukas smirks, giving me a shrug. '*Nothing bad, I promise.*'

Sander flashes him a grin. "Yes. And from what I've heard, you're proving to be a great luna."

"I'm glad you think so," I reply.

My smile falters for a second as I see a shadow move across his eyes. I narrow my eyes, searching for what I saw, then shake my head. I must be imagining things.

"I'm glad you're finally home." Kyra hugs him around the waist. I've never seen her smile so bright. I'm so happy for her and the boys.

"Longest assignment ever," he groans, rubbing his hand over his short hair, before wrapping his arm around her shoulders.

"What do you do?" I know he works for a security firm, but doing what exactly?

"I work for a security agency in Portland. I'm their hacker."

My eyes widen and I stare at him for a moment, unblinking. *A hacker?* "So cool!" I reply in awe. The room erupts in laughter in response to my statement.

"I'm glad you think so. I specialize in cyber security," Sander replies, his tone seeming to have changed suddenly. I can't put my finger on what exactly I'm sensing though. Something buzzes just out of grasp. I must just be on edge, wired from my two cups of coffee.

"Well, Nesrin and I will head off and leave you guys to it," Lukas says, stepping forward and shaking Sander's hand.

I glance around the room looking for Astraea and Malachite. There's movement under the kitchen table and I crouch down, my eyes locking with a pair of bright violet eyes, no blue in sight.

"What are you doing down here?" I ask, pushing down my unease. I watch as Astraea's gaze moves past me to Sander and she chews on her lip. It is such an odd thing for her to do that I'm left confused. Malachite, sensing her unease, has perched himself protectively in front of her.

"Astraea, you can come out. Everything's fine," I say, beckoning her.

She shakes her head and I'm even more befuddled. Suddenly, Nissa is there, her tiny body vibrating in outrage. Startled, I straighten up, even more confused than before. What's going on?

Turning to Lukas, I shrug. '*I don't know what's gotten into them.*'

Lukas takes a few steps toward the table and crouches down. "What's up, little star?"

Astraea shrinks further back, and Malachite lets out a huff of steam. I've never seen him do that before. I stare at Nissa. "Do you know what's going on?"

The sprite moves faster than I thought possible, straight for Sander. Kyra steps back in shock, dragging the boys with her. Sander doesn't flinch as the sprite stops an inch from his face. I watch in horrified realization as Sander's eyes shift, the warm brown fading into milky white, a sneer transforming his kind, handsome face into a nasty scowl. Slowly, ice lines my chest, making my breathing uneven.

"What are you going to do?" Sander mocks menacingly at Nissa. Lukas straightens to his full height, his fists clenched at his sides, and slowly steps forward, positioning himself between us and Sander.

"Sander?" Kyra chokes out. I can hear the uncertainty in her voice.

"That's not Sander," I answer.

Magic hums along my skin and through my veins begging to be released so it can take care of this threat, but Sander is pack. I won't do anything that would hurt him. This may not be Sander speaking, but it must still be his body, and he is still in there somewhere.

Nissa speaks next. "Why are you here?"

Whoever is controlling Sander laughs. The sound is so horrible it makes me want to cover my ears. It makes my skin crawl. It's a mixture of Sander's voice and that of whoever is controlling him. "Like I'd tell you anything. Traitor." He tried to hide it, but his eyes kept shifting to the table behind me, revealing his true intentions. If it's Astraea he's after, he can think again.

'Lukas, you're going to need to restrain him so I can find the object that is being used to control him.'

'Easier said than done.'

'Can you use your alpha command? Would that work?'

Lukas thinks about it for a moment. *'It's worth a try.'*

I stare at Kyra and concentrate on her until I find the thread that links her to me as pack, then follow it. *'Kyra?'* Her worried brown eyes snap to mine. This is the first time I've spoken to her telepathically. *'I need you to get the kids out.'*

She bites her lip, looking around. I can understand her hesitation. She's worried about her mate, but her children are more important right now. She meets my eyes and nods. I let out a small, relieved breath.

'Don't hurt him,' is her only request.

'I won't.'

Kyra motions for the children to follow her and they all edge their way to the door, Sander's eyes tracking their movements as they do.

Kyra tries to beckon Astraea, but she won't budge. She just shakes her head, blonde curls flying around her face.

'She's okay. Just get the boys out.'

Kyra disappears just as Gabe steps into the room nodding toward Lukas. Lukas must have sent for him. Who better to help Sander regain control than someone who can enter another's mind. My magic senses Gabe's as he draws it to the surface, making my skin tingle with awareness. I watch in amazement as the mist from outside starts creeping in through the crack under the door, swirling around our feet. It rises to my waist, and I panic when I lose sight of Astraea.

'Astraea?'

'I hide.' Her reply is barely a whisper in my mind.

Lukas's voice is hard and unyielding as he stares down at Sander. "You will stand there and not move a muscle while we do what needs to be done." His power is in full force, backing up his words. I cross my fingers, hoping it could actually be this easy.

Sweat beads at Sander's forehead and I can see the internal battle raging behind his eyes. Whoever is controlling him is trying to fight off the command. I hold my breath, my hope rising, but then I see a ripple of magic slide over Sander, and I know it didn't work.

Sander snickers. "Nice try, alpha."

Lukas growls and stalks forward, his hand extending to grab Sander, but Sander moves quickly, sliding back a step, making Lukas pause.

Lukas's head tilts and he lets out an inhuman growl. When he steps forward again, Sander raises his fist, lunging toward Lukas. A squeak falls from my lips and my hand shoots out, sending an invisible force pushing Sander across the floor and slamming him into the wall, pinning him there. Even though I know Lukas can take care of himself, I can't stop my primal need to protect. My eyes take on that white haze again as I try to control my building anger. Sander pins me with a lethal stare as he struggles against my magic.

"You cannot stop us," Sander says, his voice now so different from the one when he first walked in the door. The loving warmth is gone from his eyes as he stares at us with cold disdain.

Oh, goodie. The old bad guy speech.

Gabe's eyes cut to mine, obviously hearing my thoughts.

'Can you hold him there?' he inquires, and I nod, clenching my teeth. I can work some spells and perform various magic, but my strength lies in healing.

Gabe steps up to Sander until he is a foot away. Their eyes level. I know Gabe's eyes are glowing with his own magic now as he delves deep into Sander's mind to free him from the cage he has been confined to.

'Lukas, search him. He would have something on him that would give the person controlling him access to his mind. Ring, coin, pendant, anything.'

Lukas storms forward, fury rolling off his body in intense waves. He is furious someone has done this to his friend in an attempt to harm us. He crouches, starting at Sander's shoes and working his way up. When he gets to Sander's wrist, he spots a woven bracelet. Lukas frowns, untying it.

At the same time, Gabe whispers, "There you are."

Sander starts thrashing against my binds. "NO!" he bellows. Not a moment later, he sags forward. Twisting my hands, I use my magic to shake him a little. Gabe raises an eyebrow at me.

"What?" I shrug. "I was checking to make sure he actually passed out."

Gabe turns to Lukas, his expression turning grim. "That was mind control. I couldn't tell who, but someone was using him as a puppet. Sander couldn't stop him."

Lukas growls, slamming his fist into the wall. Plaster falls to the ground and Lukas storms across to the room, his fists clenching and unclenching at his sides. Just then, Astraea, Malachite, and Nissa emerge from under the table, all casting curious looks at Sander.

"Nissa, do you know who would do this?"

"Queen Anwyn."

I frown. "The Seelie Queen?"

She nods, settling on Astraea's shoulder and absently stroking her hair. "They're up to something, I'm sure of it."

"How did you know something was wrong?" I ask her.

Nissa looks to be weighing her words before she answers. "Astraea called for help."

I jolt at her words. *What?*

"How?" Lukas demands.

Nissa eyes me warily. "The mist was my first indication she was uneasy. Then she called to me. You know she's a telepath."

"Wait, *she* made the mist?" I blurt.

"Yes, it's part of her heritage."

"What?" I am so confused right now. What is Nissa on about?

The sprite flutters back a few feet and lands on the table. "This is not important right now. You need to destroy the talisman and ward everyone who comes and goes from pack land." With that, she takes off out the door as the mist disperses.

Lukas is outside comforting Kyra and the boys. Gabe's hand rests on my shoulder, squeezing. I sigh, considering Sander, who is still pinned to the wall, unconscious. "What should I do with him? He is no threat now. With the bracelet removed, they won't have a link to him."

I hold my hand out for the bracelet. Gabe raises an eyebrow and drops it in my palm. I mutter an incantation under my breath and blow on it. Blue flames erupt in my palm, engulfing the bracelet. Within seconds, it is gone.

Lukas walks back in, rubbing his face, and motions for Gabe to grab Sander. With little effort, Gabe does as he asks, allowing me to release my hold, then carries Sander into the next room and places him on the sofa. I'm going to have to step up my wards and get to work on some safeguards for everyone, just as some added protection. They have targeted one of ours, and I don't like that. I think Lukas is taking it especially hard. I can feel his anger and frustration as if it was my own. Astraea moves over to my side, and I lift her into my arms.

"You knew, didn't you?" I ask her.

She nods her little head and lays it down on my shoulder. I rub her back and my eyes connect with Lukas's. *What do the high fae want with us? What does it have to do with Astraea?*

I sift through my cardboard boxes in Lukas's garage, feeling for the supplies I need. It's been a long day, but I still need to make some more protection charms. My jeans are caked in dust from all the kneeling and crawling I've had to do while sorting through my boxes.

"This isn't going to be enough." I sigh to myself as I stare at my meager supplies.

Running my hand through my long, thick hair, my fingers tangle in some knots. My mind drifts to Sander, and the look on his face when he finally regained consciousness after being freed from the mind control. He felt a deep sense of shame at what happened. I'm so grateful that the kids didn't get hurt in any way. Initially, the boys were hesitant, but with some gentle encouragement, they were soon laughing and playing with their father again.

Still, there's the big question about who exactly did this. And are they under orders from the queen?

"Everything going okay in here?" Asena's voice asks from the doorway.

I twist at the waist and see her walk in with Kate on her heels. Asena's pale blue eyes regard me with worry. I give them a weak smile as I stand, brush the dust from my jeans, and grimace.

"Yeah. I'm just low on supplies. I was hoping to make up some charms to protect everyone."

Kate frowns slightly. "You think they will try again?"

I shrug, my fingers weaving my hair into a messy ponytail as I pull it up. "I'm not sure, but I'd rather be safe than sorry."

Sander hasn't been able to recall who gave him the bracelet, which means he was likely glamored into forgetting. That is dangerous, and I am not taking chances.

I bend down and pick up the old leather-bound grimoire. It practically sings in my hands, magic tingling my skin and pulsing through me as I hold it.

"I understand," Kate says, peeking into one of my boxes.

"I've still managed to charm some crystals with protection spells. I will definitely need to head into the city to get more supplies if I'm going to have enough for everyone."

Asena crosses her arms over her chest. "Ugh. It was already bad enough worrying about the coven and the Order. And now the high fae are sniffing around."

Guilt slithers through me, and I bite down on my lip. Kate looks at me with a sympathetic smile.

"I think we should go after them," Asena continues.

I shake my head. "We can't. Not yet, we need more facts. Plus, Marcus and Claudia are working on the coven. Leila remains a part of the Council. We cannot give her away. Her place there will be vital once this is over. If they are planning anything, one of them will let us know."

"Will they?" Asena's response is tinged with doubt, her uncertainty evident in her tone.

My head snaps in her direction. "Of course. I trust each of them."

Kate comes over and puts an arm over my shoulders. "How about a break? Coffee?"

I melt into her. "Coffee sounds amazing."

Asena shifts on her feet. "We can compile a list of supplies you need, and Lukas and Zee can grab them when they go into town."

"Not fair," I say, looking over at her.

"What?" she asks, her pale blue eyes widening.

"I was getting angry with you, and you go and butter me up with lists."

Asena shakes her head, her laughter filling the air as her thick, wavy black hair frames her face.

We turn and walk toward the door that leads into the kitchen to get started on making coffees. Asena starts with the list as I rattle off what I will need.

Lukas strolls into the room, freshly showered, his dark hair still dripping with water. "I'm heading into town with Zee to see if we can find where these fae are hiding. Or at least how they're coming through the barriers."

I watch, transfixed, as he comes to a stop next to me. He grabs the barstool I'm seated on and turns it to face him, stepping between my legs.

I hear the girls' soft chuckles, but I am captivated by Lukas. The air is filled with his distinct, woodsy scent of sandalwood and cedar, and his full, inviting lips are almost too tempting. I reach up, cupping his face, feeling his stubble against my palm.

His stormy green eyes flicker with a hint of yellow, and he brings his face closer to mine, his nose trailing along the length of mine until our eyes close.

"Lukas," I breathe against his mouth.

Suddenly his palm cups the back of my neck, and his lips are on mine. I felt my stomach tighten as a mass of butterflies flutter in my stomach. Lukas's lips are hot against mine and I am consumed by the fire of his kiss.

Pulling away, Lukas smirks down at me. "Your eyes are glowing freckles."

Blinking, I pull back. "Well, I blame you."

"You two are perfect together." Kate sighs, holding her coffee cup with both hands, a dreamy look on her face.

My cheeks heat and I reach for the list Asena's making. "Here. This is what I'll need from town to make the rest of the charms."

Lukas plucks the paper from my hands and his eyes flicker over it. "Okay."

"Be safe," I whisper, grabbing his hand and squeezing it.

His hand comes up and grazes my cheek, the warmth of his palm radiating against my skin. "I will, freckles."

Zee storms in the back door with a look of thunder on his face. "We going?"

Lukas gives him a nod and steps away, but I thread my fingers through his and lift one of his hands to my mouth, kissing his knuckles. His hand slides around my neck and he pulls me close, kissing me gently on the lips.

"Can you stop in and check on Joseph and Sophie? They said everything was fine when I called–"

He leans in, leaving a lingering kiss on my forehead. "I'll stop in and see them." His words ease the pressure in my chest. The young troll family has become like family to me, especially after I helped deliver baby Rose. Astraea is still so unsettled after what happened, so I'm planning a night in with her.

"We will head off. If you need anything, just call out." Kate says, giving me a small wave. Asena drains her coffee cup and sets it in the sink before turning back to us.

"Anything! Pumpkin spice, you call." With a wink, she follows Kate out the back door.

Lukas turns to leave, and we find Astraea blocking the doorway. Her tiny arms are crossed, a stern look set on her face. Malachite is standing next to her, trying to look equally fierce.

Lukas crouches in front of her. "I have to go, little star. I need to see what I can find out."

She shakes her little head and grabs his hand, trying to pull him back toward the living room. My heart cracks, a dull pain settling there. She really doesn't want him to leave. Lukas stops her and goes down on one knee. "I need to go. It's my job as an alpha. I need to take care of my pack, but most importantly, you and your mom. You are the most extraordinary star in the universe. I love you."

She stares at him for a full minute before wrapping her arms around his neck. Lukas hugs her back and stands, taking her with him. He hands her off to me, kissing each of us on the head before turning and walking out the door.

"Okay, sweet girl, what should we do first?"

She simply shrugs, looking so sad. I hate seeing her so down. So much for a fun evening with my girl. Malachite is quite excited about the idea, and has already found his spot on the sofa waiting for us to join him. His beautiful blue and green scales glow brightly in the warm firelight.

A soft knock on the door pulls my attention away, curiosity getting the better of me as I move to answer it.

"Nikolas! I wasn't expecting you. Astraea, look! Nikolas is here."

Nikolas looks unsure, almost shy, as he explains, "Lukas said you might want some company, ma reine."

My smile is instant. "Yes, of course! Come in."

Astraea's mood lifts a little, but as we settle in to try to watch a movie, her eyes constantly stray to the door, waiting for Lukas. Nikolas notices, and worry lines his face before he quickly types out a message on his phone and pockets it. Astraea's is at the window, looking out into the night, when her head spins our way, her curls flying, and she gives Nikolas a soft smile. She moves for the photo album Kate and I had made for her of her mom and dad. It's filled with photos Finan and Kate gave me of Hunter, and the few I found on the cloud of Niamh and me. She climbs onto the sofa between us and starts showing Nikolas the photos, glancing up at him every now and again, smiling or nodding. I know they must be communicating, and it makes my heart burst that she trusts him enough to do that. She may not want to speak out loud, but she is still communicating.

'What did you say to get her to come away from the window and relax?' I ask Nikolas through our bond.

Nikolas's eyes lift to mine, the blue and silver swirling with emotions, *'I told her I messaged Stephan to watch over Lukas and the others tonight.'*

Tears of gratitude line my eyes and I lean my head on his shoulder, then we all look through the photos in silence. Malachite finds us and jumps onto my lap, his head pushing Astraea's arm up so he can rest it on her leg. We stay like that for hours, Astraea refusing to sleep.

She whispers into my mind, *'Not till daddy's home.'*

When Lukas gets home just after two in the morning, he's surprised to find us all awake and waiting. Astraea runs into his arms the second she sees him, and he hugs her close, whispering into her hair. Nikolas stands and walks over, clasping Lukas's shoulder. They each give the other a silent nod, and Nikolas heads for the door.

'Goodnight, ma reine. It was a pleasure to spend the evening with you.'

'Thanks, Nikolas. For everything.'

Lukas strolls over and takes a seat with me on the sofa. Turning, he lays down against the arm, pulling me down beside him, his arm wrapping around me and Astraea on his chest. I feel his contentment and love through our bond and sigh deeply. His scent wraps around me, the stress of the day easing now that I'm in his warm embrace. I glance over and notice Astraea already asleep, a smile on her face.

'What did you find out?'

'Not much. The fae have been coming through a gateway in the forest. There have been plenty of sightings of them, but no one can say where they are holed up or what they are planning.'

'I don't like it. The fae showing up can only be bad news. With the coven already making our life difficult, and Hera out for blood, we don't need this.'

'We'll figure it out. I've got Gabe and Asena digging for more information. They will hopefully turn something over.'

'Did you manage to see Sophie, Joseph, and baby Rose?'

Lukas's arm pulls me in tighter. *'Yes, they're fine. The baby is healthy, and they are all keeping a low profile. Joseph offered to help us find out what the fae are up to, but I told him we have it handled.'*

'Thank you.'

The last thing I want is to get them involved. Lukas is well aware that I don't want them to be affected by the chaos I'm caught up in. Not again.

CHAPTER TWENTY FOUR

I strap my sheath around my waist and secure my dagger. Astraea walks over and hands me my other dagger that I fit around my thigh. I'm dressed in all black tonight, hoping to blend in with the night. I asked Lukas if I could come on patrol in the city tonight. We haven't seen many of whatever monsters escaped the underworld, and another set of eyes on patrol can't hurt.

"You're sure you're okay with me going?" I ask Astraea, who is climbing onto my bed where Malachite is already sleeping.

She turns toward me, her bright violet eyes sparkling with joy. *'Yes.'*

"You'll be okay with Aunt Kate?"

Astraea nods her head, blonde locks falling over her shoulders.

I shove my hands in the pocket of my jacket, feeling unsure. I really don't want to let her out of my sight. The bedroom door creaks open and Lukas walks in, already dressed for a night on patrol.

"You ready?"

I nervously bite my lip, my gaze shifting back to Astraea.

'I can feel your unease, sweetheart. What's wrong?' Lukas asks, one of his hands sliding around my waist.

I lift my gaze to meet his, and the warmth of his eyes envelops me. *'I just hate leaving her.'*

199

When he looks over to Astraea, his eyes hold a warmth that shows his understanding. I feel his love and reassurance flow down our bond, and it soothes my frayed nerves. I follow his gaze to see Astraea's radiant smile, and I'm confused.

'What's going on? What am I missing?'

"Nothing, sweetheart, but we better go. The others are waiting." Letting go of me, he walks over to Astraea and kisses her on the head, his lips moving to her ear as he whispers something that makes her giggle.

Even more confused than before, I walk over. "Okay. I'll see you in the morning." I lean down and kiss her cheek. Her tiny hands stretch up, her fingertips barely brushing my ponytail as she tugs gently.

'Loves you.'

'Love you, too, sweet girl.'

I turn to follow Lukas down the stairs, my eyes lingering on his jean-clad butt. A throat clears and I raise my gaze to find Lukas looking over his shoulder at me, amusement lighting his eyes.

"Eyes up here, freckles."

I shrug. "It's a great butt."

Lukas chuckles, and the warm feeling of happiness spreads through my chest as he opens the front door. We step out into the cool evening breeze where Zee and Sander are already waiting. It's been a week since Sander returned home, and in that time he's helped secure the packlands with surveillance cameras.

"Hey," I greet them as I approach the car.

Zee gives me a nudge in the shoulder. "Hey, honey. Come to see where all the action is, eh?"

"Sure, why not? I can't sit at home all the time. I gotta put the training you guys are putting me through to the test some time, right?"

Sander chuckles, opening the door for me, and I climb in the front next to Lukas, who already has the car started. I just close my door when I see Jameson come jogging up to us.

"Lukas winds down his window and leans out. "What's wrong?"

Jameson stops at the window. "Alpha, I was just hoping I could join you tonight."

Lukas shakes his head. "No patrol off packlands until you've completed training."

"But I think I can–"

Lukas holds up his hand. "No."

I watch as Jameson's head drops and a lump forms in my throat. He longs for the opportunity to demonstrate his strength.

"Jameson!" I call out before Lukas can roll up the window.

He turns and looks at me as I lean forward past Lukas's large form. "Can you watch over the house? I hate leaving Astraea here without me, and it would go a long way to making me feel better."

Jameson's eyes light up and the dimples on his cheek pop. "Sure thing, luna."

Jameson takes off toward the house, the men in the car snickering as the car accelerates down the driveway. When I look at Lukas, I see his head shaking ever so slightly, with a smirk playing across his lips.

"What?" I ask, feeling better that I could have an extra set of eyes on Astraea and give Jameson a task.

"Nothing, freckles. You just made the kid's night. Thank you."

My heart swells, and I grin back. "He just wants a chance to prove himself."

"I know."

"Did Finan call today?" Zee asks.

"Yes," Lukas and I reply in unison.

Finan has called every day as promised. He's been kept pretty busy sorting out the issues that arose while he was here. Kate groans about his overbearing ways, but I find it sweet. My vision still remains in the back of my mind. I have no clue if it will come to pass or not, and it has me on edge. We pull up on the outskirts of Portland city near the cemetery and pile out. Together we walk into the busier part of the city. Zee and Sander going one way, Lukas and I the other.

As we walk past the city library, I think back to my little shop, a sadness sweeping through me. I brush off the memory as I feel Lukas's warm palm slide into mine, leading me up the wide steps of the building, away from the others on patrol. A thrill goes through me at the promise of being alone with him. Sander and Zee are patrolling the next block over. Sander was understandably furious after what happened, and has spent the last week trying to prove himself even though he doesn't have to. We all understand it wasn't him. But the fact that the Seelie Queen was behind it certainly doesn't fill me with warm fuzzy feelings.

Turning abruptly, Lukas spins, bringing me from my wandering thoughts. His palm rests on my abdomen, almost covering it entirely with warmth, as he pushes me backward. The heat from his body is contrasted by the coolness of the stone pillar I'm pressed up against. A cloak of darkness envelops us as we gaze at one another. My heart races as I feel the intensity of his gaze burning into me. Our desires intertwine like a single thread through the bond.

"Nesrin."

My heart skips a beat at the rumble in his voice. His hand reaches up, tugging on some of my hair. "I'm not good at this stuff. The words. I show you my love with actions." He emphasizes this with a thrust of his hips and I stifle my moan, keeping my eyes locked on his. His hands move and take hold of my hips, squeezing lightly.

"I told you I wanted it all with you," he says. "It's only ever been you. It will only ever be you." Those emerald eyes blaze with affection. I open my mouth and shut it again, deciding to just nod, not trusting my words to come out coherent.

"You two are my first priority. My pack knows you're mine, that we are mates. I want to make you my wife so the world will know," he finishes. His intense gaze makes my heart thump wildly in my chest, so much so that I almost think it might burst free. I can do nothing but nod, unable to focus with his words plummeting my heart and his hands burning into my skin through my jeans. Lukas shuffles even closer until there is barely any space between us, blocking out the whole world.

"You are the light of my life, Nesrin Carson. I don't deserve you, but I will try every day to be the man you need, the kind of man who deserves you. You walk headfirst into danger to protect the ones you love. It is infuriatingly painful, and probably bad for my health, but it's you, and I would never change that. You shine your light on the world, Nesrin. You are beautiful, sweet and kind. You never turn anyone away who needs help, your compassion shows no bounds. You made friends with Cerberus of all creatures, a beast that usually would tear anyone but Hades and his kin apart. I want you to be mine in every way. You are my mate, but will you be my wife?"

Tears sting my eyes and blur my vision. I wasn't expecting this. I can't quite catch my breath. A smile moves over his handsome face as I nod my head dumbly.

"I'm going to need the words, sweetheart," he coaxes, his eyes filled with so much warmth, hope, love.

Passion heats the bond as we stare at each other, the charge so electric my skin seems to hum in response. He adjusts his position as a soft light highlights his features, and I have a feeling my eyes have started to glow with my overflowing emotions.

"Of course, yes. I'll be your wife," I choke out.

Lukas makes a sound deep in his chest that vibrates through my body, making it throb with need and fill with love. The mate bond is overflowing with our emotions, mixing together, overwhelming my senses.

I smile up at him. "I'm yours in every way," I whisper.

The smile he gives me is downright sinful. "I have a ring," he says.

I jerk back, surprise and excitement bubbling up inside of me. I can't keep it from my voice. "You do?"

Lukas laughs, reaching into his back pocket. "Yes."

Hands clasped in front of me, I bounce on my toes as he reveals a small black box. An indecipherable noise escapes my mouth as he opens the box, turning it toward me. My eyes widen as I stare at the ring, speechless. It is beautiful and unique, very antique looking. The stone is an emerald cut moss agate. The wisps of green running through the gem are no less than breathtaking. The gold band is adorned with three sparkling teardrop cut diamonds on either side of the gem.

"It's beautiful," I whisper in awe.

"Astraea approves."

My eyes fly up to his from the ring. "What?"

"Astraea approved the ring, and me asking you to marry me."

Tears fill my eyes, making my nose sting. "You asked her?" the words are choked.

"Of course." Lukas lifts the ring out of the box and takes my hand, sliding it onto my left ring finger, then brings my hand to meet his mouth where he places a kiss on the ring. Lukas's eyes burn as he brings his hands up and slides them into my hair. I tip my head back further, resting it on the pillar behind me so I can keep eye contact as he leans in slowly. Unable to wait a moment longer to feel his lips on mine, I move up on my toes, my arms going around his neck as our lips meet in a desperate kiss. His hands drop to my ass, and he lifts me up, my legs wrapping around his waist as he pushes me harder into the pillar. His erection presses against me, and I wish more than anything we were naked right now.

'I wish you were naked, too.'

Lukas's tongue slips into my mouth and I groan, my stomach fluttering wildly as he explores my mouth. We break apart, panting, Lukas's eyes blazing like jewels as we look into each other's eyes. I can feel his need and love as if they were my own. He closes his eyes and sighs, his lips moving to kiss my forehead, then he slowly slides me back to my feet, his chin resting atop my head.

"I will not fuck you out here, but as soon as we are home . . . " He lets his words linger in the space between us and I grin, a giddy feeling sweeping over me.

Wrapping my arms tighter around him, I whisper into his chest, "I love you." My chest fills with warmth as I stare at his green eyes. "I . . . want you to adopt Astraea. You are her father now. She loves you so much, and I know she thinks of you as her dad. I want to know that, if anything happens to me, you won't have to fight to keep her." My throat grows tight at the thought.

Lukas's hands move to my shoulders and he moves me away from his body to cup my face, my hands landing on his chest. His emerald eyes glow with a fierce intensity, and I can feel the steady beat of his heart beneath my hand.

"You know I will, sweetheart. You are both my girls. And just so you know, I would win whatever fight there was to keep her. But nothing is going to happen to you. I will protect you with my life, so will our pack."

'Hey guys, I hate to break this up, but I need you back here now,' Zee's voice comes through the pack link. His voice is edged with concern.

'Everything okay, Zee?' Lukas demands, switching into alpha mode.

'No. Sander's down.'

My heart thumps hard in my chest at the thought of the others in danger. Lukas and I turn, sprinting to where we left Zee and Sander. A coldness trickles down my spine as my pulse skyrockets. As we draw closer to where the others are, ice begins forming in my chest. This is bad, very bad. Fear fills me with nervous energy, and I push it down as we reach the entrance of the alley and turn the corner. Both of us skid to a stop, Lukas's arm shooting out to stop me from advancing. Zee and Sander are cornered at the end of the alley, a large shape looming over them. Zee is in his wolf form, snarling and snapping at the creature in front of them, shielding Sander who is lying in a heap behind him. I think he's unconscious, but it's hard to tell from here. As I step further into the dark alley, I squint my eyes in an attempt to adjust to the darkness. Slowly, Lukas and I inch forward, and I can feel his arm tense as he keeps it protectively in front of me, ready to push me behind him at any given moment. My body tenses up and a small squeak escapes from my mouth as I get close enough to see the creature. It looks exactly like a praying mantis, but its size is that of a small car, making it all the more intimidating. A shiver runs up my spine and the skin on my arms crawls. I really do not like bugs.

The creature's head spins in our direction, its gaze zeroing in on me. I stand on frozen legs, staring in captivated horror. Its beady black eyes blink once before it turns toward us on legs that are as sharp as blades, its body divided into three parts, the head, thorax, and abdomen. Its two larger forelegs are shaped like hooks, and its mouth is open in what looks like an expression of glee, showing rows of sharp teeth.

That's not normal.

I fight off tremors as I stare back, searching its rigid exoskeleton for any weak points.

"What is . . . " The words die in my mouth as the creature starts advancing on us, Zee and Sander forgotten.

Lukas steps in front of me, shifting in the blink of an eye. I barely have time to register the shift, my own body wanting to follow suit and shift with him, but I am still too scared. I watch in horror as Lukas advances on the creature, his black fur glinting in the moonlight, a growl tearing from his mouth. I dart to the left, hoping to sneak past and get to Sander while Lukas distracts it. But it locks those creepy black eyes on me, Lukas and Zee barely registering to the creature. It's me. It wants me. My fight-or-flight response kicks into high gear as my mind races to find a solution. Bloody hell, why did it have to be a giant bug? Swallowing over my fear, I straighten my shoulders and flex my fingers. Bring it on. I take a step to the side and it follows my movements, taking a step in my direction, my body locking up in fear. Lukas and Zee leap into its path, and the creature draws up short.

'Nesrin, leave!' Lukas demands.

Even down the bond, the words carry the authority of the alpha. I feel the magic push in the words, commanding me to listen. It cuts through my moment of panic, and I shake off my fear. I will not leave them. These monsters were released because of me. I will not allow everyone else to clean up my mess. Determination fills me as I straighten my shoulders and face the creature.

"No. If I run, it will only follow."

'Nesrin!' Lukas growls, ducking under a swinging arm.

"I'm not leaving," I refuse again.

The creature scurries forward, swiping out at Zee who somehow manages to leap back in time. Lukas leaps for the mantis, but is knocked to the side by its large body. Lukas lands on all paws, skidding across the wet road. His head is lowered and he snarls as the creature turns to rush at him. I scream his name as Zee barrels into the creature from the side, knocking it over. Lukas flings his body to the side to avoid the collision.

Think, Nesrin. Think . . .

The best way to kill a bug is to squish it, right?

Heart pounding wildly, I glance around the alley and set my eyes on the dumpster. I whisper an incantation, my hands stretched out toward it, and the dumpster lifts off the ground. Perspiration dots my forehead with the exertion of lifting something so heavy with my magic. I turn with my hands out in front, sending the dumpster flying toward the creature. It sees the massive projectile coming, and moves only enough to grab it and swing it instead toward Lukas and Zee. The dumpster hits them both and comes to a stop against the wall, the two of them trapped behind it. A cry falls from my lips as I stare in horror, a wave of icy dread rushing through me.

'We're okay,' Zee grunts.

Lukas's howl rings through the alley, the sound filled with rage and vengeance. *'Give it hell, sweetheart. We will be there soon.'*

My heart swells with hope and fear. They'll be okay. While the creature is distracted, I try to move around behind it. But it's no use, even with its attention on the others. It still seems to be following me with its eyes, eyes that are full of unnerving intelligence. Maybe I can tase this thing with my magic. It could work. I hope. I gather magic, a sparkling white ball of light forming between my hands. But the bastard seems to read my intentions and moves out of the way before I can stun him, its creepy legs scurrying to the side and up the wall of the building before dropping back down in behind me.

It turns those sharp teeth my way, its mouth stretching into a smile that will haunt my nightmares for a very long time. Moving quicker than I would have expected, it strikes out with its foreleg, the barbs cutting through my jeans at my thigh. Excruciating pain tears through my leg, stealing my breath as it slices through my skin.

"Nesrin!!" Lukas shouts through the link.

My vision blurs around the edges as I fight to stay upright. A savage howl that trips my heart rips through the air as Lukas and Zee free themselves. The dumpster tipping over, they charge for the mantis-like creature. Lukas leaps onto its back as Zee goes for its neck. Still, neither is able to sink their claws or teeth in. Its razor sharp legs and impenetrable armor make it impossible to land a single blow, making it too dangerous to approach. Lukas's fangs close over one of its antennae, ripping it from its head. The creature throws them both off, letting out an inhuman scream. My hands snap up to cover my ears, as it withdraws further down the alley, Lukas and Zee pushing it back.

Sander tries to stand, and I notice the blood soaking his jeans. Shit. His eyes, full of pain, meet mine. He stumbles and collapses again. Looking back at the others, I see Lukas is studying Sander as well. Taking advantage of his distraction, the mantis lurches forward, slashing out with one of its bladed legs. A warning scream tears from my throat, but Lukas is quicker. He swiftly moves out the way just in time, the razor sharp leg missing him and embedding instead in the dumpster behind him. Lukas slides on all fours and spins, jumping onto the mantis's back once more, this time going for its throat. I hold my breath, waiting in terror. My stomach cramps at seeing my mate so close to danger. The mantis easily rips its leg free from the dumpster, swiping at Zee and flinging Lukas from its back, sending him rolling across the alley.

The beady eyes of the mantis look up and meet mine. An involuntary shiver runs through me as I read the intent there and I sense my magic taking over, my vision clouding white. Since I began wearing the necklace Althaea gave me, I've been able to channel my magic more easily and I'm able to control the flow, but I am exhausted, barely running on fumes at this point.

The mantis charges, leaping over Lukas and Zee straight for me, a hair-raising screech coming from it. Raging fire courses through my body as I screech my frustration. Pushing past the pain burning its way through my leg, I straighten. The world tilts and white coats my vision entirely as words tumble from my lips. I run at the creature, my magic forging a blade of light in my hand. That's new. At the last second, I drop to my knees, sliding over the wet pavement. I barely register the pain as fabric and flesh are shredded. Without thought, I throw up a shield around myself and lift the blade with both hands above my head, as I slide under the mantis. It overshoots me and the blade slices like butter through its underbelly. Black blood, guts, and gore hit my shield, sliding off. Thank the goddess.

I can faintly hear Lukas yelling my name, but my attention is on the body of the mantis falling into a heap behind me, twitching and spasming on the ground, its blood seeming to eat away at the pavement around it like acid.

"Nesrin!" Strong hands are hauling me up and patting me down, looking for injuries. I can't take my eyes off the remains of the creature. It is barely recognizable anymore, its own blood bubbling away at its remains.

A gentle hand grips my chin, turning my head away from the gory sight to meet the stormy green eyes of my mate.

His voice is rough when his words come out. "Are you okay?"

I take a few long blinks, the world blurring in and out of focus. When I don't answer, Lukas shakes me a little.

"Nesrin, look at me. Open your eyes."

I didn't even realize I had them closed. I obey, and my eyes connect with his again. His face is only inches from mine with eyes that hold a concern so intense and wild it verges on feral.

"Yes," I croak, my voice coming out tight and scratchy. Lukas's shoulders seem to drop in relief as he pulls me against him. I hear him groan and feel through the bond what he has been covering up. He is hurt. I gasp, pulling back, my eyes searching over his body.

"Where?" I demand as panic rises, making my voice sound desperate.

"Nesrin," Lukas says, trying to still my movements with his hands.

"Where? God damn it!!!" I screech, the fear and dread choking me. My mate is hurt, and I can feel the pain through the bond. Lukas always tries to shield me from his pain, so I know it must be bad for him to let it slip.

Lukas tries grabbing me, but I step out of his range. I am trembling, so many emotions riding me right now.

Lukas's eyes soften, "Sweetheart," he says in a calming, reassuring voice, which does absolutely nothing whatsoever to calm or reassure me.

"No, Lukas!" I snap, then growl, "Tell me where you're hurt."

The pressure building inside of me at the thought of him being hurt is too much. I need to see it with my own eyes. Now I understand why he hates seeing me hurt, how easy it is to lose control in moments like this.

Lukas sighs in resignation and slowly lifts his t-shirt, the black material slick with blood. There is a long, deep gash running the length of his abdomen. I step forward, drawing in a pained breath, "Why isn't it healing on its own?" I ask as I examine the wound, my fingertips brushing his skin.

Lukas sucks in a sharp breath and pulls his shirt back down stiffly. "I would say its barbs were poisonous. It's preventing my self-healing. I need to wash the poison out, and then I should be able to heal on my own. It'll just take longer. I'm okay."

"No. I will do it." I begin summoning my magic, but before I can make contact with Lukas's stomach, his hands grab mine, holding them away from him.

"Nesrin, stop."

Tears fall down my face. I hate seeing him hurt, and thanks to the bond I now know the pain he is hiding. Pinning my hands with one of his, he reaches up with the other to wipe away my tears.

"Sander needs it more," he whispers, his eyes searching mine. "You don't have enough for both of us. You need to recharge, sweetheart."

I blink, startled, and glance around. Sander?

I spot Zee crouched over him further down the alley and run over on shaky legs. Before I can get down on my knees beside him, Lukas grabs my arm, stopping me. He slowly, and judging by the expression on his face, painfully takes his jacket off and folds it, placing it on the ground.

"You hurt your knees," he notes, running a hand down my arm. I glance down, and sure enough, my knees are scraped up, but somehow I don't feel any pain. They are healing just fine. Since unlocking my magic and having shifted into my wolf, my body heals pretty quickly on its own. My thigh though—that stings like a bitch. Lukas is right, the barbs were poisonous.

"Yeah, that was badass, Nesrin. Where'd that wicked sword come from?" Zee asks, doing a long whistle. His blonde hair has been ripped from its bun and hangs disheveled around his face. But his blue eyes still sparkle.

"I don't know. The words just came to me like muscle memory and the sword appeared. It was weird. Once the creature was disposed of, it vanished." I shrug. I wasn't actually aware of what my magic would do when the words came to me.

I kneel on Lukas's jacket and run my hands over Sander. He looks pale and pasty. Sweat beads his forehead, his body racked with tremors. My healing magic warms my hands with little effort. This is the magic I am meant to do. Healing comes so naturally to me that I barely have to try anymore. I gently place my hands over the gash on his leg. Once that is healed, I move up to his chest and shoulder. As I work, the color returns to his face and the shivers subside. He slowly opens his eyes, the warm brown connecting with mine.

"What did she say?" Sander groans, moving into a seated position. His clothes have seen better days, but then again, looking around at all of us, we are all in pretty rough shape.

Lukas just smirks down at me. "She said yes."

"Of course she did," Zee laughs.

I roll my eyes and stand on stiff legs. My jeans are ripped at the knees and the huge gash on my thigh is still oozing blood. We need to get back home and wash these cuts. A raindrop hits my face and I smile, tilting my face upward and closing my eyes. The sky opens up and I soak in the feeling of the water washing away the blood and gore. The sound of several cars pulling up to the entrance of the alley has me opening my eyes. I watch Kyra run for Sander, her brown corkscrew curls flying wildly around her face. Her usually warm brown skin is sickly pale with worry.

"Sander!" she cries, jumping into his arms.

Sander barely stumbles as his arms circle around his wife. I smile, feeling happiness surge through me. We got lucky tonight. I'm sure Kyra would have known something was wrong through the mate bond and was able to alert the others.

A hand lands on my shoulder, and I turn to face Zee. "How are you doing, honey?" he asks, wrapping an arm around my shoulder and pulling me into his side. I rest my head against his chest.

"I'm okay. Tired," I mumble.

He places a soft kiss on the top of my head. "Then let's get you home."

"What about the others?" I ask, feeling my eyes grow heavy. I really need some sleep, and soon. The excitement from Lukas's proposal still lingers in the back of my mind, but we have other things to worry about right now.

"They will stay and do clean-up."

I lift my head and search the small crowd for Lukas. *"Lukas?"*

"I'm here, sweetheart. Go wait in the car. I'll be there soon."

"Lukas wants me to wait in the car. I'm not sure how long I can stand, anyway."

Zee nods, leading me to the car and shutting me inside before walking back over to the group. I rest my head back against the seat and close my eyes, my breathing evening out and my shoulders relaxing. That's the last thing I remember as sleep takes hold of me.

CHAPTER TWENTY FIVE

I wake to the sound of raised voices coming from downstairs. I groan as I try sitting up in bed. Shit, my head hurts. And there's a dull ache in my thigh. I lift the sheet to see that someone—probably Lukas—has cleaned and wrapped my leg. He must also be the one who put me in one of his shirts. I lift the collar up and take a whiff of rain and sandalwood.

"You could have been seriously hurt! Can't Hades tell us how many of these things escaped?" I've never heard Kyra so mad before. Guilt slithers through me. This is all my fault.

'It is not. Don't you dare feel guilty.'

I jump at the sound of Lukas's firm words resounding in my head.

'How can I not? If I would have just, I don't know . . . left? Never come here? Everyone would be safe.'

Lukas's anger comes rolling through the bond. I can almost taste the bitterness those thoughts bring him. *'Don't talk like that. I would do anything for you. But letting you leave would never have been one of them.'*

A deep sigh leaves my lips and I push up from the bed. I walk over and grab a pair of loose track pants and drag them on. Looking around the floor for the fluffy bed socks I know are here somewhere. Finding them,

I pull them on before padding down the stairs. It's still dark outside, so it must be early morning.

Everyone is gathered in the lounge room, a fire lit to ward off the chill. Sander, Kyra, and the boys are here along with Zee. A moment later, Suzy walks through the door from the kitchen with two mugs in her hands.

"Suzy?"

Her smile doesn't quite reach her eyes. "You're going to turn me gray before I'm even legally allowed to drink. You know that?"

I can't help the snort that slips free. "Sorry?"

Suzy rolls her eyes, still smiling, and hands me a mug.

Zee walks over, ruffling my hair, "Good to see you up and about. We were worried the toxins might prevent your healing."

I'm about to answer when I remember Lukas's injury. My heart thumps painfully in my chest as I swing my eyes to his.

Lukas's face softens. "I'm fine."

I place the mug down on the coffee table and approach him. My eyes dart to his shirt, looking for blood. "Show me."

"Sweetheart, I don't think–"

"Now, Lukas," I say, uncompromising, and trying my best to keep my tone even. I won't panic. Who am I kidding? I'm already panicking!

Lukas sighs, and I hear everyone behind me snicker—Zee being the loudest—but I ignore them. Crossing my arms, I wait. Lukas lifts the bottom of his shirt and the gash revealed there is barely healed. The angry red mark has stopped bleeding, but has turned blackish around the edges, the wound festering. I whip my gaze up to his, a snarl on my lips.

"WHAT THE ACTUAL FUCK, LUKAS!" I bellow.

"It will heal. There's nothing to be done."

Suzy steps closer, and I hear her intake of breath. "Shit. You should get that looked at," she says, pointing out the obvious.

Zee mumbles something to Sander and Kyra before wandering over. "Holy shit, Lukas! Why didn't you say anything?" The bewilderment in

Zee's voice has me turning to him. "Well . . . fix him!" Zee says, pushing me at Lukas.

Suzy's arm whips out, backhanding Zee across the stomach. His soft oomph is satisfying.

"Don't tell her what to do, you big oaf!" she snaps angrily.

"No one asked you, Hufflepuff."

Suzy gasps and my lips twitch as they throw insults back and forth. I rest my hands on Lukas's side, tendrils of magic already seeking out the injury.

I look up into his stormy green eyes. *'You should have woken me.'*

'No, you need rest. Need time to heal.'

'You should have woken me,' I repeat.

'I should have shifted. I would heal faster in my wolf form.'

"Oh my god. You're healing him?" Suzy's voice cuts through the room.

My head drops, and I watch Lukas's skin smooth over as if nothing ever happened.

" . . . Yes?"

"You never told me you could heal people!" she shrieks, inspecting Lukas's stomach closely.

We haven't really discussed what my magic is, what powers I possess. I've only told her I'm a legacy. Alex is the one who outed the whole shifter thing to her, after losing her temper and shifting during a dinner Suzy was at. It was hilarious. Emotional control is one of the first things witches learn about when using magic. Because shifters can be unpredictable at the best of times, they train hard to be able to control their wilder side, so it surprises me that she doesn't have better control. Before I can answer her, the howl of a wolf sounds in the night. We all exchange looks. Lukas straightens up, his arms uncrossing as he cocks his head, listening. Another howl sounds, this one deep and guttural. *Wounded.*

"That's not one of ours," Lukas mutters, pulling his shirt down.

Zee walks over to him, and they both look out the window.

"What do you want to do?" Zee asks.

Lukas turns around, his eyes finding mine. "Ward the house. No one is to enter. Zee, Gabe, and I are going to check it out."

I step forward, ready to argue, but he holds his hand up, stopping me. "Please, sweetheart."

I falter and glance over at the others, seeing that Astraea has come downstairs. Kyra gives me a pleading look, and I relent. I can't leave them, even if I ward the house. I look back to Lukas and nod, "Okay."

His shoulders fall with relief and the door bangs open as Gabe storms in. The wolf's cry sounds again, this time further away, more subdued. They need to leave now if they are going to catch whoever is out there.

Lukas takes three large steps to me and pulls me to his chest, giving me a kiss. "Ward. Now." He turns and storms from the house, Zee and Gabe following close behind.

The silence in the room is deafening. Tense, we all sit listening out into the night. I close my eyes, muttering an incantation under my breath. In my mind's eye, I watch magic drift from me, covering everything: walls, doors, and windows. Slowly, the spell grows to cover the entire house, sealing the world off.

We sit in silence for a while, the kids drifting off to sleep by the fire. Their soft snores ease my frayed nerves. I wish I could sleep but I'm too wired to relax, my knee bouncing nonstop. The sudden sound of paws clicking on the porch alerts me to something outside. I brace myself, climbing to my feet and crossing the room. The moon is still high in the sky as storm clouds come closing in, ready to swallow the moon. In the dim light, I can see down to the river and the outline of the distant forest. But I can't see anything on the porch. Did I imagine it?

I sigh and stare out over the valley. *Where are they?*

"They'll be back," Suzy says, coming up behind me.

"I know," I whisper.

She rests her head on my shoulder and I grip her hand, leaning my head on top of hers as we keep our attention out the window.

Bang!

We all startle as a loud bang comes from the door in the kitchen, the one that leads to the backyard. The sound of scratching follows.

Liam's wide, brown eyes swing to me. "Well, that scared the swear word out of me!" he says in an alarmed voice.

I bite my lip to keep from smiling. Kyra pulls him to her chest, her worried eyes meeting mine. Astraea and Noah still sleep soundly by the fire. But Malachite is now on alert, pacing in front of them protectively.

Another bang rings through the house and sounds of scratching follow, like claws being dragged across the wood. Whatever is out there wants in, but my wards will hold. The door rattles and Sander pushes to his feet. Suzy and I follow him into the kitchen, while Kyra stays with the children.

I grip Suzy's hand in mine firmly, both of us refusing to let go. I can hear the first drops of rain hit the ground, the wind picking up. Looks like the storm is here. The door stands still, as if whatever was out there has left.

"Is it gone?" Suzy whispers.

Sander holds his hand up to us as he cautiously approaches the door. Slowly, he pulls the curtain aside and looks out the window at the top. I move next to him, peering out. I can see the rain falling in heavy sheets, and the sway of the trees in the distance as lightning lights up the night. A figure stands not forty yards away, glowing red eyes looking directly at us. I draw in a quick breath and Sander curses, dropping the curtain.

"What? What is it?" Suzy whispers frantically.

Sanders's eyes glaze over, and I grip his arm, realizing he is trying to contact the others. Another flash of lightning has the lights in the house flickering. Suzy squeaks.

I squeeze her hand. "Go back and wait with Kyra and the kids."

Suzy's wide blue eyes swing to mine, and she nods. When she's gone, I step forward to pull back the curtain again. I don't see a thing.

I anxiously bite my thumbnail. "Sander, what do you think it is?"

The doorknob rattles, and I drop my hand from the curtain, taking a huge step back, magic flickering to life inside me as I watch the door shake. The wards will hold. There is no way that thing is getting in here.

'Lukas?'

He must be too far away to communicate. I hate that he, Zee, and Gabe are out in this weather . . . with that creature.

"Nesrin, come away from the door." Sander says, gripping my arm and pulling me further away.

"You didn't answer me. What is it?"

"A feral wolf. He has lost all sense of who he is. The animal has taken over, but not in a good way. I think it had help to draw the others away so it could get in here."

From the other side of the door comes a deafening bang. It rattles the hinges and Sander leaps forward to brace it.

"It can't get through," I say to reassure him.

Sanders's soft brown eyes lock on mine. Another bang shakes the door, this one just as loud. I wish it would just go away.

"It's weird, though," Sander muses.

"What is?"

"Feral shifters rarely pair up or work with others. They have usually lost all sense."

A snarl sounds from the other side of the door. Then a yell followed by a hard thump. Silence reigns as Sander and I wait, our eyes glued to each other.

After a minute, there is a knock on the door. Startled, we move to the window and slowly pull the curtain back to reveal Nikolas. His eyes are completely silver now, and his hair is soaked from the rain. I grip the knob and rip the door open. "Nikolas, what are you doing here?"

Nikolas motions to the dark lump behind him. "I felt your emotions, and I came to see what was going on."

"Oh . . . " I reply dumbly.

A howl sounds not far away, and I relax. Lukas is back. I wave Nikolas inside, but he shakes his head. "I'll wait out here with him." He motions to the lump on the ground.

"He's alive?" I ask, raising an eyebrow.

Nikolas shrugs, explaining, "I thought you might need answers."

Lukas and the others come into view as thunder rumbles overhead, a flash of lightning quickly following. Lukas's black wolf stalks around the wolf on the ground. From here I can't make out the coloring, but I can see that it's about half the size of Lukas.

Lukas barks out at Zee, and both he and Gabe shift and move to pick up the wolf. Lukas trots over to us, shifting. His clothes soak through instantly.

"Nikolas."

"Lukas."

Sander moves aside, pulling me with him so the two can enter.

"I'm going down to the lockup to see what's going on with that wolf," Lukas says, not stepping inside.

"Should I come?" I ask.

Lukas just shakes his head. "We can handle it."

"Okay."

We stare at each other for a moment. Then he turns, disappearing into the rain.

Nikolas rests a hand on my shoulder, squeezing. "I will leave now that everything is okay."

I nod, realizing that it will be dawn soon.

"Yes, of course, go. Thank you, Nikolas." I draw him into a hug. The vampire's arms wrap around me, holding tightly for a few moments.

"I'm happy to help, ma reine."

The bed dips as Lukas slides in behind me. He pulls the cover up and over us, tucking it around us, then moves right in behind me, his body curling around mine perfectly. His hand reaches out, stroking Astraea's head of curls next to me.

'*What did you find out?*'

'*Not much. We know he was being controlled, but not by whom.*' He sighs. '*He killed himself before we could question him.*'

My eyes fly open, and I try turning, but Lukas holds me firmly against him. '*What do you mean??*'

He takes a deep, comforting breath. '*As soon as he woke, he started thrashing about. He was holding his head. Clawing at it. When we tried to stop him . . . He turned and ran so fast into the wall he broke his own neck.*'

My stomach rolls at the imagery. We are silent for a moment.

'*But that shouldn't have killed him.*'

'*No, it shouldn't, but whatever happened to him made him too weak to heal.*'

'*What happened out in the woods?*'

'*Nothing. Dead end tracks. It was a lure.*'

We lie silent for a while, but on the inside my mind is whirling. What happened to him? What could have sent him crazy?

"Get some rest, sweetheart. It's almost morning," Lukas whispers out loud, kissing the top of my head. I groan. There's no need to remind me. I snuggle deeper into the blankets, but sleep doesn't come. The sun slowly rises as I listen to the sounds of Lukas breathing.

CHAPTER TWENTY SIX

Today has been a good day. I stand, brushing the dirt from my jeans, and turn to help the others set up for our bonfire by the river. Zee and Asena are making their way down the hill with some chairs. Lukas has taken the birthday girl, along with Noah and Liam, looking for firewood. I can't believe Astraea is two years old. Time has flown by, especially in the last five months. She is absolutely thriving here.

The tension between Zee and Asena has been easing over the last month, both settling into friendship. I never knew what exactly their relationship was, but it has to have been more than friends. I smile as I approach them. "I'm going to help Kyra and Sander bring the food down."

I freeze at the sound of Asena's gasp and glance up at her. Her wide-eyed stare is focused on something behind me.

What now? I groan internally.

I don't sense any danger at present. And yet a look of pure thunder comes over Zee's face as he vaults over the chairs, storming past me at an impressive speed. I spin on the spot and stumble, my eyes finding someone in the river.

My brain short circuits for a moment. *Wow!*

Emerging from the water is a very large, very handsome man. His dark skin ripples over muscles as he moves through the water, making his way to the shore. The light seems to glisten on his skin as the water drips down his naked torso. Golden eyes hold laughter. The dimple on his cheek says he is amused by our reactions. With one hand, he reaches up, running it through his midnight black hair, the water dripping from the ends. His hair is so long. Like, really really long.

Tattoos cover most of his body from his temple on one side of his face, down his neck, across his shoulders, arms, chest, and down his impressive six pack and further still. I quickly avert my gaze, my eyes clashing with a stunned Asena. I widen my eyes and mouth.

"What the fuck?"

Asena is shocked mute. She looks back at the man in the river and continues staring, her mouth agape. I snicker at her reaction. It's like she's never seen a half-naked man before.

"Who the fuck are you?" Zee growls, and I turn back to the river quickly as the stranger emerges from the water.

I realize too late that he's not half naked at all. He is, in fact, *fully* naked. Completely naked. There is a whole lot of skin on display. I immediately avert my eyes again and spot a blanket on the ground. Snatching it up, I throw it at the stranger as he approaches. He catches it with a smirk, wrapping it around his waist. I can't help but watch his muscles flex as he does.

"Nesrin, is this one of your friends you haven't told us about?" Zee accuses, a bite to his voice.

I glare over at him. "No."

The stranger doesn't say a word, his curious golden eyes taking in our exchange. I squirm under his intense stare, clearing my throat, and use my best luna voice.

"Who are you?" I ask, hoping he'll answer before Zee loses his shit.

My pendant hasn't flared yet and there is no ice present in my chest, so I figure he must be safe. I take in the swirling tattoos across the left side of his face and over his entire chest. They seem to move on his skin as if they were alive. My eyes follow the flow of the patterns, finding that they look like magic threads or spells inked onto his skin.

"She asked you a question," Zee snaps.

The man looks over at Zee appreciatively and gives him a wink, riling Zee up even more. I choke on my laughter as Zee sends a glare my way. Before things get out of hand, I take a step between them and put my hands on my hips.

I raise an eyebrow at the stranger. The stranger lets out an exaggerated huff and looks away. I squint my eyes, cocking my head. That huff is familiar. Where have I– Oh. *Oh*. Oh my god. No way . . .

"N–Nero?" I stammer, completely dumbfounded.

I realize that Pucas are magical shapeshifters like the wolves or any other shifters. But I guess I just thought Nero was either stuck in his horse form or that the shifting was a myth. I didn't think he could actually change forms. A blush works its way across my skin. I've been brushing him and feeding him for weeks. I've taken rides on him, built a bond with the horse. Now I feel stupid.

He turns back to me, his smile on full force. And wow, that is one killer smile. He is gorgeous. I hear Asena sigh behind me and smother my laugh. Yes, he is gorgeous, but he is nowhere near Lukas level, I remind myself. Zee growls in response to the man's behavior.

The stranger inclines his head. "Yes."

"Fuck, no," Zee snaps, his hands cutting through the air aggressively.

I spin on him. "Zee!!" I admonish.

"What? There is no way that is Nero," he says, gesturing at the stranger.

The stranger chuckles softly. "I am Nero."

I turn back to Nero. "I believe you."

Zee huffs. "Of course you do."

I frown, but ignore Zee. "Have you always been able to shift into a human?"

"Of course he has. He's playing you, Nesrin," Zee snaps.

"Zee!" I bark.

Closing my eyes, I take a deep breath, counting to ten.

"What?"

"Stop. Just stop." I rub at my temples.

'*What's wrong?*' comes Lukas's voice through our bond. Crap on a cracker. Lukas is going to blow a gasket when he sees Nero. I try my best to calm my nerves so Lukas won't come barging down the hill.

Opening my eyes, I meet Nero's gaze. "What's your name?"

"Nero."

"No. That's the name I gave you. What was your name before that?"

"A fae's name is sacred, the name Nero is fine," he says, bowing his head to me.

Confusion sweeps through me as I absorb his words. Not a second later, Malachite comes bounding down the hill towards us. The sound of the children returning follows him. He darts up the back of my legs and winds around my stomach and chest, his head peering at Nero from over my shoulder. My long hair hides him from sight. The only parts showing are his tail, which is wrapped around my middle, and the tip of his nose over my shoulder. Malachite lets out a small huff, a small amount of mist pouring out of his mouth. He must sense the tension in the air and is reacting instinctively to it.

Nero bows his head at the dragon, a slight gesture of respect. "Your fae heritage allows you to bond with these creatures. It is why they all come to you. They gather with the daughter of light, ready for the change to come."

"What are you talking about?"

"Mythical and supernatural creatures are drawn to you because of your fae heritage. They can sense you. Sense what is to come. You are a beacon of light and hope. The star of light."

"I don't understand," I reply.

Aren't I just like the others, only with goddess blood? The shifters are part fae. That's where they get the magic that allows them to change at will, and as I've finally learned, keep their clothing intact.

A crease appears between Nero's brows as he stares at me. "You really are clueless."

I exchange a glance with Zee, and he shrugs, seeming suddenly less annoyed than a few minutes ago. Because, of course.

"Then clue me in, Nero," I reply, trying not to sound offended.

When Nero's eyes meet mine again, they begin glowing with magic. A bright flash surrounds me, and I bring my arm up to cover my face. When the light fades, I drop my arm, looking around.

Uhh, where am I?

The world around me looks faded, washed out. My gaze swings around, stopping on two figures standing next to the shore of a lake, their backs turned to me. The water gently laps the edge near their feet, the sound relaxing me slightly. I start forward, my eyes jumping from one to the other as I approach, then it occurs to me that I'm having another vision, and by the clothing the couple wears, it's one from the past. As I get closer, they turn to face me, and my heart stutters in my chest. My eyes take in the male first. He has closely cropped dark hair and a clean shaven square jaw. A scar runs from his temple across his cheek to the corner of his mouth, but it doesn't detract from his appearance. If anything, it makes him look more handsome, almost dangerous. Two piercing blue eyes watch me coldly. They flash violet, reminding me for a moment of Niamh and Astraea. The part that draws my attention are his pointed ears; high fae. My mouth drops open, and I swing my gaze to the female wearing the red hooded cloak. She pushes the hood from her head, her long auburn hair flowing around her shoulders as she smiles softly at me. *Blanchette.*

Then, turning, she looks at the male, nodding once. I watch in awe as magic swirls around him and a large gray wolf bursts to life beside her. They stand side by side, a red-hooded woman and an extremely large gray wolf. *Shit, we really are descendants of Little Red Riding Hood.*

Our surroundings change again, and we are all standing in a large circular room with a glass dome ceiling showing a beautiful sunset. Vines creep along the walls from floor to ceiling, and from what I can see, there are no doors or windows. Fireflies hum around the room, casting a soft glow that makes it seem so magical. One firefly breaks away from the wall of vines and floats closer to me. I lift my hand up, and the firefly lands in my open palm.

"Wow," I whisper in awe, leaning in.

Looking closer, I realize it isn't a firefly at all. It's a fairy, but it is absolutely tiny, no bigger than a grape. Its delicate face, adorned with two little antennae, tilts up to mine as it regards me carefully with large blue eyes.

"They are devas, small fairies that look like fireflies," Blanchette explains, drawing my attention to her.

Blanchette and Leopold, now back in his human form, stand watching me curiously, which is odd because usually I have been an invisible bystander in these visions.

"It's good to see you, Nesrin. I've been waiting a long time to meet you." Blanchette's voice is soft, sweet, with an air of authority. She seems to glow ethereally as she stands in front of me.

I look around, perplexed. "I don't understand. How can you see me? Where are we?"

Her laughter rings out around us, airy and light, as Leopold grins, the scar on his face stretching with the motion. Moving forward, she places her small, slender hand on mine.

"We have been waiting for a moment like this to bring you to us and tell you what should have been passed on to you long ago. Seems information was lost in all the fleeing and hiding."

"Okay? What am I missing? Because I'll admit I feel like a freak already."

Leopold steps forward, putting a hand on his wife's shoulder. She steps back from me to stand at his side. There is kindness in his harsh blue eyes as he looks down at me. "Nesrin, you are a legacy, but it's not that simple."

"Never is," I laugh dryly.

Blanchette chuckles, the sound wrapping around me, calming my nerves. Energy buzzes in me, making my body hum with anticipation.

"Very true," Leopold says, his face growing serious. He gestures to a small table and chairs I didn't notice before. There are glasses of water on the table, and I quickly glance around, not seeing anyone else. We make our way over to the wood carved furniture and take a seat. I lift the glass to my mouth and sniff. It doesn't smell like it's been tampered with. I tip the glass up and flavors burst across my tongue. It is the most refreshing water I have ever tasted, with hints of fruits I can't possibly name. I drain the glass and glance back to Blanchette and Leopold, who are smiling at me.

"Sorry," I say, my cheeks heating as I place the glass back on the table.

"It's fine," Blanchette says softly.

Leopold leans forward, his elbows resting on his knees. "My mother was a Selkie."

I clear my throat. "Right, straight to then."

Ignoring me, he continues, "She was young when she met my father and fell in love. She thought he was mortal and decided to give up her life of the water, for one with him. It wasn't until he had her seal skin, that he showed his true colors. My father was a cruel man, not at all who he pretended to be." Blanchette tenderly lays her hand on top of his, giving it a gentle, reassuring squeeze. "My father, as it turned out, wasn't a mortal man but a member of the Unseelie Court, a high fae. I have both unseelie and seelie blood running through me. Mix it with the blood of a goddess. And our bloodline would no doubt be powerful. No one knew of my mixed blood. My father had kept my mother locked away. Only those who were living on our estate knew."

My mouth opens several times with so many questions on the tip of my tongue. I'm not sure I am totally understanding what's happening here. I know nothing of Fae politics.

"So, I'm a legacy, but also have fae blood from both courts as well? But wouldn't it have been watered down through the generations?"

"You would think, but because shifters are also fae, it stayed heavily present throughout the generations. After your display of power last week summoning the sword of Nuada, and then your niece conjuring the féth fíada, we thought it was time to meet. Your father sadly wasn't aware of his lost heritage."

My heart thrums wildly in my chest as I speak. "My Dad?"

Leopold leans closer, his eyes fully focused on me, it was unnerving. "Yes, he was a direct descendant of a race we thought was lost forever."

I let out a humorless laugh, rubbing my hands over my face. "I didn't even know he was a shifter until this year, and now you're telling me he was . . . what, exactly?"

"A descendant of King Nuada," Blanchette answers, her eyes taking me in carefully, probably to check for any signs of a mental breakdown or see if I might run. Both are highly plausible.

I clear my throat, searching for the words I need. "So, let me get this straight. You"—I point to Blanchette—"are a deity turned witch. And you"—my finger shifts toward Leopold—"are full blooded Fae from both courts. You had a child together who also mated with a shifter. This went on for generations, the women in the family mating with wolf shifters, making a long line of legacies. Then my mother found her mate, who was a descendant of King Nuada of the Tuatha Dé Danann. Is that about right?"

"Yes," they say in unison.

"Okay." I nod, my finger curving around my mouth as my hand cradles my chin. "And that makes us what, exactly?"

"You, Astraea, and Leila are legacies, but with the added power from your father's bloodline. Nesrin, *you* can finally put a stop to the council's laws and injustices. It is why creatures are gathering around you, you are a beacon of light to the creatures of the magical world. You have also been chosen to inherit Althaea's powers by the Moirae. To stop Hera once and for all," Blanchette says.

"You are all extremely strong. You are the first legacy in centuries who has been able to shift into her wolf. I think it's possible because of your higher fae blood," Leopold adds.

I rub my temples. This is way too much information. Why can't things ever just be easy?

"That's all you want from me? To overthrow the magical council and get rid of Hera? Sure, sounds like a piece of cake."

"It won't be easy. And we know it will take time. But Nesrin, if anyone can do this, it's you," Blanchette says reassuringly. At least one of us thinks I can pull it off.

"And what of the fae?"

"You need to remember when it comes to the fae and the courts that neither side is good or evil. They are merely happy to go whichever way benefits them personally."

"It's the same with you and your sister. You are neither good nor bad. Yes, one of you is light and the other dark, but either can be good or bad, depending on the situation," Leopold adds.

Blanchette stands and walks over to take a seat at my side, picking my hands up to hold in hers. "We all assume light is good, and we want to have light and happiness in our lives at all times, but we wouldn't exist without darkness, either. Darkness is our reprieve from the brightness. To balance us out. This is how you healed Nikolas's soul. You balanced the darkness with light."

"They bonded you and your sister from conception. You cannot defeat Hera on your own. It needs to be together. Darkness and light together," Leopold urges, and I laugh, the sound rough and scratchy. I feel my emotions getting the better of me.

"What about Niamh? We were triplets."

Blanchette and Leopold share a look. Blanchette sighs before looking back to me, her face grim. "Your sister's death was a tragedy. One that wasn't expected. Niamh had one purpose, and that was to bring Astraea into the world. She did that, and by releasing her magic when she died, she was able to fulfill her duty, allowing both you and Astraea to escape the magic that was trapping you in the house."

Tears clog my throat. It seems so pointless. Why give me a sister and take her away like that? Why are the fates so cruel? Why Astraea? I have so many questions. Questions I know I'll never get answers for.

"We can't even begin to guess at the intentions of the fates. Just know that Astraea is important," Leopold says gently. The tenderness in his voice almost has me breaking down right here. "As Blanchette said, your sister's death was a tragedy. It seems fate's paths came to a crossroads where Niamh was concerned. Her purpose was to ensure Astraea's survival, the path chosen was one that ensured that outcome. The Moirae weave the threads of fate in a way that no matter what choices you make, the end result will be where you are meant to be."

"Meaning the only way for Astraea to live was for Niamh to die?" I draw in a deep breath, trying to center myself once more.

Darkness tempers the light, for light is all-consuming. As will light balance the dark, for one can get lost in the dark without the light.

Grace's words ring in my head. I can't recall what we were discussing when she told me that, but I do remember that she was serious. The thought of Grace sends a pang through my chest. I miss her so much.

"What will it mean to have such strong ties to our fae heritage?" I croak.

Leopold's voice is soft, as if he can read my emotions. He probably can.

"However you choose to see the fae is the way you will see them. It's because of fairy tales people believe they are kind and good. In reality, they are not that. They are instead both *good* and *bad*. You need to be on guard, because they will deceive you if given the chance. Duality is at the core of our nature. Fae are highly unpredictable, changing from one side to the next instantly and rather often. You see the best in everyone, and therefore, many have shown themselves to you. But only a few can be fully trusted."

"This is crazy," I murmur. This cannot be real. I must've fallen over and hit my head on a rock. All this is . . . is my imagination. I put my head in my hands.

"This is a lot. I understand, but we want you to know you have allies. The fae that surround you are on your side, and you will need them. The courts will be looking for you. And not everyone can be trusted. They will use you to their advantage. The sprites will help to conceal you from the Seelie Court, and Nero has sworn to you his protection."

"You said before that I am their beacon of hope. What did you mean?"

"You will bring forth change. What that change will be is yet to be seen," Blanchette replies.

"I'm imagining this. I'm hallucinating," I say, trying to convince myself. I start braiding my hair to keep my hands busy.

Leopold's voice is serious when he replies, "I can assure you, you are not."

"I can never participate in my visions. This is all in my head. You're dead. Or am I dead?" Great, now I'm rambling.

"This isn't a vision. You're not dead. We are not dead," Blanchette's musical voice replies.

My head whips up and my eyes lock on hers. "Wait, what?"

"This is Faerie," she replies with a shrug.

The faerie world . . . The Unseelie Court . . .

"As cruel and heartless as my father was, he wouldn't see his only child murdered by witches, so he portaled us out of the cabin and brought us here. But we cannot leave Faerie. We are not quite prisoners, but neither are we free," Leopold says, leaning back in his chair.

Legend says that Faerie is rather close to our world and is where most of the fae folk live. It's almost as though we live side by side with the fae, but we're in a different dimension, close enough that we can still interact. There are those who have chosen to live in our realm, and those who have accidentally wandered through portals and become stuck on either side. The troll family I helped in Portland moved here seeking a new life in our world after having their home robbed and burned in the Faerie.

"Then how did you bring me here?"

"Nero."

"What?" I hate how my voice wobbles.

"Nero was able to portal you to us, and we took you from the lake to our home. Nero is a good friend," Blanchette says, waving her hand around us.

Just then the vines move, pulling aside like a curtain as a petite girl with bright blue hair and soft shimmering wings walks in holding a tray, her long white dress flowing around her with every step. She looks to be around fifteen years old, though I know she's likely much older. She bends over, setting the tray on the table before lifting her silver eyes to mine and smiling shyly. I feel like a deer caught in headlights as I take in her high cheekbones, sharp pointed teeth, and pointed ears.

I force myself to return the smile. I'm sure the resulting expression is awkward as I'm not sure how to manage it at all. But if the girl—or whatever she is—notices, she doesn't show it. Turning without a word, she leaves the room, and I let out a long breath, sagging in my chair.

"What was that? I mean, who was that?" I quickly amend, rubbing my hands over my legs in an attempt to ease my nerves. This place is making me uncomfortable, especially now that I know it's actually real. Everyone back home must be freaking out, wondering where I went. They probably have Nero locked up. I need to get back. I can feel my heart rate gaining speed as I begin to spiral. As if reading my thoughts, Blanchette leans forward and places her cool hand on my leg. "Nero has everything at home under control. Don't worry."

"And that was Silver. She is one of the pixies who stays here with us. My father has many servants, though none are loyal to him. The ones here are loyal to only us." Pride shines in Leopold's eyes.

"They are unseelie?" I ask.

Leopold nods. "Most of my loyal friends are. I can trust them."

My eyebrows inch up my forehead. This is just getting weirder. I need to get back on track. Returning my focus to Blanchette, I straighten out my thoughts. "Why did you leave Mount Olympus?"

Blanchette's smile slips and she casts a quick glance to her mate before swallowing and replying, "My mother informed me of Zeus's interest in me. He had been awfully friendly in the past, but I was too naïve to know what was happening." She takes a breath before continuing, "Everyone knew what Hera was like, how jealous she could get. Zeus never believed his wife could do the horrible things the rumors had said. But we all knew. She cursed many people. All mistresses and children of Zeus. That man had more illegitimate children than anyone I know." She laughs bitterly.

"One night, my mother and Hecate came to me and told me that Zeus was planning to seduce me. I freaked out. I told them I was leaving, that I couldn't stay there anymore, so they helped me. Together, they helped hide me from the gods. They made a pendant to protect me and keep my magic hidden." She glances to the pendant around my neck and smiles wistfully. "I ended up using that pendant to protect my daughter and store my magic and energy for other generations. I knew we would have a long and powerful bloodline to follow us. But things went bad. A mage showed up, claiming to be the love of my life. I had never met the man before, but he was so sure of his claims that I was convinced he'd been put under a spell. He was obsessed with getting to me. Once he found out about Leopold, he exposed us. As you know, relationships between magical creatures of different races are forbidden, punishable by death. He gained ground and a following, managed to convince them to form a secret order to hunt down all who had broken that rule and burn us to the fiery depths of Tartarus."

Without thinking, I move to sit on the edge of my seat, my leg jumping up and down at the words she speaks. "So, who was he? Do you think Hera was behind his crusade? Or is it still you they hunt? This Mage was under her spell? What–"

Blanchette holds up her hand, halting my tirade. "Hera had spelled the man, yes. For what reason, I haven't a clue even to this day. I had left. It had been months, and I had not slept with Zeus. She had no reason to follow me. This Order of Tartarus is hers. They do her bidding. She is the hand that wields the blade responsible for our suffering."

Leopold reaches out, wrapping an arm around her shoulders, and I'm reminded of their embrace in that fiery cabin. Their farewells, their looks of despair. Hera didn't succeed at killing them, but she still managed to take their lives. They lost their freedom and their daughter. They were forced to stand by while generations of their descendants were hunted and killed.

"I think I know why."

Both spin their gazes to me. "What do you mean?" Blanchette begs.

"I think your mother wanted you out of Olympus, but not for the reasons she gave you."

Blanchette frowns. I swallow under the weight of their stares.

"Did Althaea ever tell you who your father was?"

Blanchette straightens and pulls away from Leopold. "No."

"We think Zeus was, I mean, *is* your father. That Hera found out about your lineage and Althaea panicked. She tried to hide you, but it was too late. Hera had followed you."

There is a long silence as they both absorb this information. Blanchette gets up and starts pacing. She shakes her hands and mutters under her breath. I feel bad for dropping this on her, but I think she deserved to know.

"It makes so much sense. I never felt like Zeus was trying to seduce me. He was never anything but kind. Do you think he knew who I was?"

Hope is clear in her voice, but I have no answers for her, so I shake my head and shrug my shoulders. There is one more thing I need to know, and maybe they can help me.

"Can a god be killed?" I blurt.

Both of them startle at the abrupt question. Leopold appears contemplative while Blanchette's expression is more one of concern.

"I . . . believe there is a way," Blanchette replies slowly.

Leopold's head cocks to the side for a moment before he turns his gaze to mine. "You need to leave now. He knows, and he is coming," he tells me as he takes two quick strides to my side.

I stand, moving my attention to the doorway Silver used before. "Who's coming?" I ask.

"My father." Leopold squeezes my hands before dropping them.

Blanchette moves in front of me, her icy hands clasping my cheeks, a small sad smile on her face. "I am so sorry you have to deal with this." She reaches down and taps my heart, urging, "Trust your heart. It will guide you." She rests her forehead on mine and whispers softly, "You are stronger than you know."

The world around me swirls and my legs give out, but before my knees hit the ground, powerful arms wrap around me, and I peer up into a set of glowing golden eyes.

"Nero," I choke out.

Pulling me up, he holds onto me until he is sure my legs are steady under me. I shoot him a grateful smile and glance around.

"Um, what's going on?" I question.

Everyone is just standing there . . . smiling. It's exceedingly creepy. Malachite comes dashing forward and weaves his way back up my body, and I reach up, running my hand over his smooth scales. When he nuzzles into my neck, I tilt my head so my cheek rests on top of his head. Still waiting for Nero to answer me, I turn back to him. "Well?"

"I wasn't sure how long you would be, so I laid an illusion over them. They are all having a pleasant time, I promise."

My eyes widen as I swing my gaze over my friends again. "You can do that?"

"I can do many things."

"Obviously. Can you undo it, please?"

"Of course," Nero lifts his hand and clicks his fingers.

Zee spins, his desperate eyes looking for me. When they meet mine, he relaxes only slightly. Seems that, despite the illusion, he was aware something wasn't as it seemed.

Asena blinks several times, glancing around and frowning. "Well, that was weird," she mutters. She makes her way over to the chairs, her long black hair whipping around her as she walks.

Not a moment later, Lukas comes stalking over the hill and toward us, his lethal gaze locked on Nero. Oh man, I know that look. He is about to go alpha male on Nero. I step forward, placing myself between them.

Nero's massive hand lands on my shoulder. "It's okay, daughter of light."

Lukas's growl rumbles from his chest as his gaze zeroes in on the hand on my shoulder. His gorgeous green eyes flash yellow as the rumble from his chest continues like thunder. Inching forward another step so Nero's hand will fall, I move into Lukas's personal space and put a hand on his chest, letting my love flow through the bond, willing him to know that there is no threat here.

"Everything is fine, Lukas," I whisper.

He doesn't break his stare from Nero when he breathes, "Who is this? He smells familiar."

I place my hands on his neck, feeling the tension there but hoping the touch will calm him somewhat. "It's Nero."

Lukas is a statue. There is no outward reaction whatsoever to my words. "The Puca?" he asks, his voice a pitch lower.

"Yes," I reply, dropping my hands.

"You could change this whole time? Were you spying on us? On her?" Lukas demands, gesturing to me. His voice is edged with another growl, an alpha ready to shred his enemy.

Nero shakes his head. "I was drawn to her. After she healed me, I felt a pull toward her. A feeling that she needed my protection. She and Astraea will always be safe with me. I would give my life before anything happened to either of them."

I am taken aback by the conviction in his voice, and I think Lukas is as well, his anger slowly beginning to dissolve. Lukas's hands go to his hips as he warns, "If you do anything to harm anyone here, I will end you. If you do anything to harm my girls, I will make you suffer while I end you."

Nero bows his head again. "I know," is all he says.

Zee comes strolling over and throws some clothes at Nero, who catches them, dropping the towel. Quickly, I turn to face Lukas, wrapping my arms around his waist and lifting up onto my tiptoes to kiss the underside of his jaw.

"I love you," I whisper.

Lukas's arms wrap around me, pulling me flush against him, his face tightening. "I don't like that he deceived us."

I rest my cheek against his chest. "I know."

"But I believe him," he admits with a sigh.

"Me, too."

CHAPTER TWENTY SEVEN

I startle awake, my heart hammering in my chest. Swinging my legs off the bed, I drag in a ragged breath. The room is dark and quiet, almost too quiet. I peer over my shoulder at Lukas—still sound asleep, stretched out on his stomach with his arms under the pillow, the position putting his well-defined back on display. I sit, trying to place where the feeling of unease is coming from. If anything were amiss, Lukas would be the first to know.

Standing, I pad over to the window and peer out into the darkness. My nerves are on edge, my body tense. My eyes scan the area for the two shifters on watch tonight. Jameson, a mountain lion, and Trevor, a wolf. There's no sign of either of them though. Searching down the pack bond, all seems normal. But then what woke me up?

A noise comes from outside the room—the top step of the stairs, to be precise. The floor there always squeaks. My whole body tenses with the sound, but I force my breathing to slow so I can listen. Astraea's piercing scream echoes through the house and I snap into action, running for the door. Flinging it open, I slam into a hard body and sway backward.

"Shit!" I exclaim as I land painfully on my ass.

My heart pounds against my ribcage as I look up into a set of emotionless, icy blue eyes that make me shudder. The man's pale skin has a slight shimmer to it, and his pointed ears peek out through long snowy hair that falls past his shoulders. He cocks his head in a predatory manner, sending my already wild heartbeat skittering. This is no man. This is a high fae.

"You are not supposed to be awake," he says in a musical lilt, an air of arrogance surrounding him.

"Bit casual for a break and enter," I snap, gesturing to his attire. The jeans and white shirt nearly make him appear human, but the ears and skin are a dead giveaway. Well, for me they are. To someone without magic sight, he probably blends in fairly well. The cold, emotionless look in his eyes doesn't help either.

Where is everyone?

The fae smirks as if reading my thoughts and looks over my head into the room where Lukas lies sleeping. I quickly get to my feet, wishing I had my dagger, but I do at least have my magic. I reach for it, but nothing happens.

My eyes widen as I snarl, "What did you do?"

Suddenly very aware of the absence of the icy sense of danger I usually have, my panic rises quickly. Dammit, I do not want to be without my magic. Desperation twists my insides as a sense of urgency takes over. I need to get to Astra. I've never heard her scream before, the sound automatically sends fear racing through me. She must have seen the fae coming. My palms start sweating as I try drawing on my courage. Whatever this fae has done, it has taken out everyone in the vicinity and my magic.

A loud screech comes from Astraea's room down the hall just before Malachite charges out of the room, heading straight at the fae. I see Astraea poke her head out the door, her wolf hugged close to her chest. I hold my hand up, telling her to stay.

Malachite doesn't stand a chance against the fae, he's just a baby. Before he can get himself hurt, I use the distraction to my advantage, jumping on the fae's back and covering his eyes. My legs wrap around his middle, my feet hooking at the ankles so he won't be able to throw me off easily.

"Malachite, no!" I yell.

At the sound of my voice, the dragon stops in his tracks.

'Astraea, take Malachite and find somewhere safe to hide.'

The fae desperately tries to fling me off his back. But I dig my heels in, one arm around his neck, the other over his eyes. Goddess, I hope he's the only one in the house. I watch as Astraea runs past, Malachite wrapped around her body.

The fae reaches back, gripping the fabric of Lukas's old t-shirt that I wore to bed, and pulls. The sound of the shirt ripping mingles with our panting, but I manage to stay on his back. My arms are wrapped firmly around him like a monkey. Roaring in frustration, he rams backward into the wall, slamming me hard into the drywall, knocking the wind out of me. He does it three more times. Each time, a sharp pain explodes through my back and my grip slips a little more. The fourth time, I lose my grip and fall to the floor. The fae spins on me, his eyes wild and full of rage. He pulls his leg back to kick me, but I bring my arm up, preventing the blow.

"Kicking a girl when she's down? That's low even for a fae," I pant.

"We don't fight fair."

"Noticed," I snarl, jumping to my feet before he can land a hit.

We trade blows, moving closer to the stairs. His fist clips my jaw, knocking me off balance. I stumble into the wall. Bringing my arm up, I block his next blow and manage to grab his hair with the other hand, pulling hard. It distracts him from the perfectly placed knee to the groin. The fae doubles over and I take my chance to race down the stairs. I need a weapon. The kitchen is my best bet. I'm sure a kitchen knife would work just as well as my dagger.

My heart hammers away in my chest, adrenaline pushing me to move faster. I just reach the bottom of the stairs when the fae lands on my back, sending us both sprawling across the foyer floor, the wind knocked out of me. I roll onto my back, staring up at the ceiling. Shit, it feels like I've popped a rib out. I wheeze as I try to pull in a breath, but my chest feels too tight. My body both wants air but is rejecting it at the same time. The fae crawls over me, sitting on my stomach, his face sneering down at me.

"You should have stayed asleep," he hisses, wrapping his icy hands around my throat and squeezing.

Panic hits me square in the chest. I am already struggling for breath. If I pass out, he will get Astraea. My hand lifts, wrapping his long white hair in my fingers, and I pull. My strength is nothing compared to his, though. A palm strikes me across the face, dazing me. His hands go back to my throat, but before he can tighten his grip, we hear a pounding of hooves approaching from outside. Nero.

The fae looks up, startled, and jumps off me with a preternatural grace, landing a few feet away. I scramble to sit up, scooting backward until I reach the wall. Astraea's head peeks out from around the sofa and the fae spots her, his cool eyes narrowing as he stalks toward her.

There is a loud roar from upstairs, filled with enough power that it shakes the entire house. The fae halts, his head tipping to the ceiling. Astraea takes a chance and runs into my arms. Holding her, I slowly stand, my legs a little shaky. My t-shirt is torn up, and only scraps of cloth now cover me. I am so glad I decided to wear panties to bed.

Small miracles, right?

I tighten my grip on Astraea as Lukas thunders down the hallway to the staircase. The fae's face is frozen in shock, his eyes dilated with fear as he looks toward the door.

"How?" he murmurs, as if Lukas waking up is a mystery.

Lukas launches himself over the banister and lands in a perfect crouch. His muscles bulge and his fists clench as he straightens up. Lukas lifts his head, his body trembling in fury. The green of his eyes fully fades away to the luminous yellow. His eyes clash with mine, taking in my state. I'm sure I look to be in worse shape than I am.

A snarl works its way up his throat as he narrows his gaze on the fae. In one breath, he is across the room in nothing but his gray sleep pants, his muscled chest on full display. Lukas grabs the fae by the throat, lifting him off his feet and, unbelievably, the fae's pale skin goes even whiter. Lukas's fury bleeds through the bond. He is *pissed*. Pissed that the fae was able to get past our defenses. That we have become a target once again.

Lukas throws him across the room where he hits the wall above the fireplace, then falls to a heap on the floor, glass shattering around him from the objects on the mantle. With purposeful strides, Lukas moves forward, a snarl rising from his throat. He exudes power and danger, it clung to him, making him look every bit the fierce predator.

Without hesitating, he grabs the fae by the shirt and rips him back to his feet. "Who sent you!?" he roars.

The front door bangs open, and Nero prowls in, his unclothed human form coiled and ready to fight. I cover Astraea's eyes immediately.

"Nero. Clothes!" I snap.

His luminous golden eyes swing my way, and he pauses. I'm not sure if the accompanying growl is in response to my request or because of my appearance, but a moment later a pair of loose track pants form over his lower half. His shiny, long black hair hangs loosely around his shoulders. I release a breath and nod my thanks before I remove my hand from Astraea's eyes, noticing Malachite is still around her neck.

Lukas throws the fae again, this time at Nero's feet. Nero's sparkling golden eyes are focused on the fae with ruthless intent. Trying to back away, the fae looks around frantically, but Lukas moves in, preventing his escape.

Nero crouches down, tilting his head to the side as if he were studying an insect. The unfolding scene intimidates even me, apprehension twisting my stomach as I watch. This fae must be shitting himself.

I step forward, damning the fae with a whisper. "He was here for Astraea."

Lukas's head swings my way, only just now becoming aware of Astraea's presence. His eyes are wild as his chest heaves. The shift struggles to take over, but he manages to keep it reined in. I send tendrils of reassurance and affection down the bond, letting him know we are okay. His eyes close briefly as they reach him.

Nero clicks his tongue, addressing the fae, "Why were you after the child?"

When he doesn't answer, Nero's eyes flash in warning. "Surely, you know who her mother is? One cannot simply contain the daughter of light with a sleeping spell. She carries the *Claimh Solais* and *Sanans Sidus Lucis*, after all."

The fae's eyes whip to mine, genuine fear within them, and I frown. *Claimh solais?*

"The sword of Nuada has long been lost to time," the fae chokes. The name Nuada has me jerking forward a step.

Nero mirthlessly chuckles. "I ask again, why the child?"

The fae's cold blue eyes turn back to Nero, his face pained. "They paid me to bring the girl to the Tallulah Gate and portal her to the other realm."

Nero's face tightens along with my grip on Astraea. Lukas moves to guard us, creating a wall of muscle. If the fae wants Astraea, he'll have to get through Lukas, then me, but I doubt Nero will give him the chance.

"Who?"

"Who?" the stupid fae repeats. Nero clenches his fist, rising to his full height, his tattoos swirling over his body as his eyes glow in the dark room.

"Don't make me ask again," his voice rumbles through clenched teeth. I don't think I've ever seen Nero so angry.

The fae's voice wavers, "Anwyn. She seeks the hybrid-born legacy."

Nero's eyes meet mine across the room. I have no idea who Anwyn is, but judging by his expression, I'm sure Nero does. I place a hand on Lukas's back, needing to feel him. His muscles bunch under my hand.

"Tell your queen this is not something she can have. Find another toy."

Before Lukas or I can react, the fae vanishes from the room. I glance around. "Where did he go?"

Nero walks toward me, his expression softening as he focuses on Astraea. "I sent him back to the Seelie Queen."

"You did WHAT?!" Lukas roars, his eyes blazing.

I clench my jaw hard enough to hurt and glare at Nero. "Why? I needed to know what he did to make everyone stay asleep, to nullify my magic and–"

"Calm down, daughter of light," Nero says, laying a hand on my shoulder, squeezing gently.

I take a step back, letting his hand fall from my shoulder. "Nesrin. It's *Nesrin*, Nero. I've told you this!" I snap, raking a hand through my messy hair.

The front door bangs open again as Jameson and Trevor come bounding into the room, skidding to a stop in their animal forms. Zee and Leila materialize next, and the room suddenly feels crowded. I remember my state of undress and embarrassment floods me. Lukas, sensing my dilemma, steps in front of me, shielding me from view.

Zee's voice is loud, cutting above the rest. "What happened?"

"I'm so sorry, alpha. We didn't mean to go to sleep."

"What's he doing here?"

"Enough!!" Lukas's voice rings through the room, silencing everyone.

Leila suddenly disappears into a mass of shadows, startling me. I blink, looking around the room. Then, suddenly, she reappears a few moments later, causing me to squeak in a very childlike way. She holds out some clothes for me and I smile at her gratefully.

"Thanks," I whisper, trading Astraea for the clothes.

Malachite jumps to the floor running up Lukas's back. To Lukas's credit, he doesn't even flinch as the dragon scales his exposed torso, settling across his shoulders. I shake my head while I slip on the shirt and pants. The room stays quiet while I dress. When I glance up, I see Nero is now reclined in a chair, holding a drink. Where on earth did he get a scotch from that quickly?

Zee is pacing by the window, throwing dirty looks Nero's way. I really wish those two would get along. Stepping around Lukas, I move to take a seat, but Lukas's arm snakes out, wrapping around my waist, and I'm pulled into his warm body. His thumb and forefinger grip my chin, gently lifting my face to his. His eyes take me in, slowly cataloging every injury.

"I'm fine," I whisper.

A rumble works its way up his throat.

"I got way more hits in. He wasn't expecting me."

Lukas's lips twitch. "No one expects you, sweetheart."

'*Yeah, you may be small, but you're tough.*' Zee's voice says down our link.

My chest inflates at the praise, and I face Nero. "Why can't I feel my magic?"

Nero's golden gaze lifts to mine. "Your magic will return. It was a simple nullifying spell. It will run its course."

"How was someone able to get past us?" Jameson asks, stepping forward. The young shifter is only eighteen, but he has guts and heart. Kid is going to break some hearts.

Nero moves his focus to the young shifter, and to Jameson's credit, he doesn't falter or back down. A shot of pride washes through me when he lifts his chin a fraction. I must have sent that out down the bond, because Jameson's lips twitch.

Lukas bends to whisper in my ear. "That kid's life is made now. He knows his luna is proud of him." My chest warms, and I move closer to Lukas.

"The high fae have many tricks up their sleeves. I believe he would have needed the help of a powerful witch, though. To hold the entire pack under for even a small amount of time would require a great deal of power."

"Who would join with the high fae?"

Nero simply shrugs, taking a sip of his drink.

Lukas snarls, making Malachite nuzzle into his neck in an attempt to calm him. I reach up, stroking the dragon, his tail wrapping around my wrist.

Zee is staring out the window as if seeing the answers we all need. Through the link, he sighs, '*Incoming.*' I can almost feel his eyes roll.

Before I can respond, the front door bangs open for the third time tonight and Nikolas appears in the room. His eyes are fully silver and have a crazed edge to them.

"Ma reine. You're okay?" He rushes forward, ignoring everyone else in the room.

I smile, stepping out of Lukas's embrace toward the vampire. "Yes, Nikolas, I'm fine. We had a little trouble, but we handled it." He visibly relaxes and grins at me.

"I was worried."

"For me? Pff . . . " I laugh, bringing him in for a quick hug.

Nikolas turns to take in the room, his silver cerulean gaze halting on Nero. His eyes flash, surveying the half-dressed shifter. Nero is most definitely breathtaking. You just can't help but to stop and admire him. So I don't blame Nikolas one bit for his ogling. Nero doesn't mind either, by the looks of it. His golden gaze seems to sweep over the vampire and fill with heat.

I try but fail to mask my amusement at these two blatantly checking each other out. Lukas clears his throat and moves over to an armchair, pulling me along and then down onto his lap. Malachite moves from Lukas's shoulders to my lap, curling up in a ball. Leila and Astraea are curled up on the larger couch where Zee moves to sit beside them. That leaves Jameson, Trevor, and Nikolas standing. Jameson takes the wing-back armchair in the corner and sits down cross-legged, making himself at home. The kid wants to be brought in on the inner dealings, it seems. I bury my grin in Lukas's neck.

'*He is brave,*' Lukas remarks down the link.

'*Well, it's not like you've dismissed them.*'

'*Still . . .*'

'*Let them stay.*'

"Are you two done?"

I pull back, and Lukas's eyes flash with annoyance at Nero. Trevor moves to sit and Nikolas is now at the window, his back leaning against the frame.

"So, what happened tonight?" Nikolas begins. "All I knew was that Nesrin was in trouble."

"I woke up feeling that something wasn't right. Astraea screamed, and when I ran to see, I found that fae in the house. He was surprised to see me, though. I think he assumed I'd be asleep like everyone else. He was after Astraea. We fought, and when he heard Nero, he backed off. Then Lukas woke up."

My eyes stray to where Astraea is burrowed into Leila's arms, her eyes closed. She appears to be doing okay despite the tension in the room. I thought she would be on edge like everyone else.

'*I taught her to breathe through it, to push all thoughts from her mind and focus on one thing that makes her happy,*' Lukas answers my unspoken question.

"Where is he now?" Zee questions.

"Someone sent him home." Lukas glowers at Nero, who, of course, is completely unfazed. I admire his sense of calm.

"What?" Zee narrows his eyes.

"I won't apologize for it. It would have done us no good to keep him here."

"Why did you let him go?" Zee demands.

"He was Queen Anwyn's grandson. If you had hurt or detained him there would be a price to pay."

Leila shifts on the sofa. "What about our price for them coming here and trying to take my niece?" she inquires, her fingers gently stroking Astraea's head.

"And hurting my mate?" Lukas adds, his tone becoming deadly calm.

Nero shrugs. "Things work differently in the fae courts. We don't want a war. Trust me on that."

"This is the second time they have gotten past our defenses and onto my lands," Lukas growls.

No one has anything to say to that. The fact that the Seelie Queen is after Astraea doesn't sit well with me.

It's Zee's turn to speak, pinning Nero with a curious gaze. "How did you know Nesrin was in trouble?"

"The same way I suppose all of you did, I felt it," Nero shrugs.

Leila and Zee trade a glance, and Lukas's arms tighten around me.

"What?" I ask, looking at each of them.

"That's the thing. We didn't sense anything from Nesrin. It was Lukas's anger that called to me," Zee replies.

Lukas relaxes back in the chair, his hand stroking up and down my back idly. I lean into the touch. As I consider Zee's words, it occurs to me that Leila and Zee arrived together. They weren't on pack lands before they arrived. If they were, they would have been under the spell with everyone else. Lukas chuckles, likely picking up on where my thoughts have gone.

'*Not now, sweetheart.*'

'*But–*'

Jameson's voice interrupts me. "So, why couldn't the pack feel our luna when both a vampire and Puca did?"

"Yeah. Before we passed out, we didn't sense anything wrong," Trevor agrees, looking extremely uncomfortable with the realization. He's also one of the younger shifters—around eighteen, I think.

Nero leans forward in the chair, resting his elbows on his knees. The movement makes the muscles in his back flex, and I watch with amusement as Nikolas fixates on Nero's torso.

"My only guess is that our connection wasn't targeted. They don't know about the vampire or me. I think they thought the only ones to worry about were the other shifters living here."

Well, that would explain why the fae seemed so surprised to see Nero. But . . . "Why would they want Astraea? Why not me?" I ask.

Hearing her name, Astraea lifts her head and looks around the room. Leila strokes her hair back and smiles down at her sweetly. When Astraea spots Nero, she hides behind her wolf, bashful.

Nero chuckles. "Astraea is a legacy, same as you, born of a strong fae lineage. Being a descendent of the Tuatha Dé Danann makes her a prize. One that is easy to be molded into a weapon. You are too old to change. They can't mold you."

Too old, my ass, I think, and everyone chuckles. Ugh, why do I keep doing that? Heat fills my cheeks and I shrug.

Something the fae said has me curious. "He mentioned the sword of Nuada. What is that?"

A smile pulls at Nero's full lips and he stands to his full height, running his hand through his long black hair as he explains, "The sword of light is a powerful and mysterious weapon which belonged to King Nuada. We also knew it as *Claimh Solais.* The sword was one of four ancient treasures of the Tuatha Dé Danann. It is told that once the sword was summoned, no one could escape it. It could enforce the law and distinguish the truth from lies"—Nero takes a drink from his glass, lifting his eyes to mine—"in order to mete out justice."

Silence has descended on the room. I can sense Zee's eyes on me. That creature I killed in the alley. I used a sword made of light that night. Was that this *Claimh Solais* he's talking about?

"Like a lightsaber?" Nikolas asks innocently.

Laughter bubbles up and my eyes widen as a chuckle slips from my mouth. Lukas's mouth quirks, and Zee tries his best to hide a smile.

"No, bloodsucker. It isn't a lightsaber," Zee quips.

Annoyance flashes across Nikolas's face. "How would you know?"

"I've seen it."

"You have?" Nero says, looking up from his drink.

"It is pretty badass, and you look super-hot wielding a sword, by the way," Lukas murmurs, placing a soft kiss on my neck. I lean into him, wanting nothing more than to trace my finger over the tattoos on his chest, but instead I curl my fingers into my palm.

Now is not the time to feel up my fiancé.

"You can feel me up anytime, freckles," Lukas whispers, and the heat in his eyes has my stomach tightening.

Damn it! That was out loud again. I groan, letting my head fall to Lukas's chest.

Saving me from my embarrassment, Jameson pipes up, "Who are the Tuatha Dè Danann?"

"They were immortal beings acknowledged for their magical abilities. I thought them to be a supernatural race that evolved into faeries. It was said they ruled over Ireland four thousand years ago. They were envied for their power, charm, elegance, and cleverness," Leila answers.

Of course, typical traits of the fae. *Beautiful and dangerous.*

"Precisely," Nero agrees. "Well, since all is done and I'm no longer needed, I will take my leave."

Frowning, I stand up. "You're leaving?"

"Yes. There is nothing else to be done tonight. Now we wait."

"But–"

Nero shakes his head as he walks toward me and places his hands on my shoulders, squeezing gently. "Your wedding is in thirty-five hours. Get some rest. I will find out what is happening with the queen."

Lukas's body presses to my back as he nods his thanks to Nero. Nero turns and winks at Nikolas, whose brows rise in surprise.

"Maybe next time we meet, we can get to know one another better," Nero purrs before turning on his heels and strolling out the door.

Turning to Nikolas, I chuckle, teasing, "Someone has an admirer." I wiggle my eyebrows, and I swear the vampire blushes. *Is that even possible?*

Lukas sends Jameson and Trevor home but asks Zee and Leila to stay. I don't think I'll be able to go back to sleep, but Lukas leads me upstairs while holding a drowsy Astraea. Lukas places her in the middle of our bed and I climb in, snuggling under the blankets. I gaze at him over Astra's blonde curls.

"I love you."

"I love you, too."

Hugging Astraea between us, I fall asleep to Lukas's stunning green eyes blazing with love and affection.

CHAPTER TWENTY EIGHT

Lukas

Everything is set. The garden is beautiful. The girls really have outdone themselves. They set the barn up for the reception, the double doors held open with empty wine barrels wreathed in flowers. Two long tables running the length of the barn on either side are filled with food and drinks. A dance floor has been set up in the center of the barn, fairy lights and lanterns draped overhead in the rafters inside and branches outside. Tables are scattered inside and out, allowing everyone to mingle.

Grand bouquets of colorful wildflowers in mason jars line the main table and smaller bouquets are arranged in the centers of the other tables to add color. The same flowers line the makeshift aisle leading from the barn to the arch we set up down the hill closer to the river where I now stand waiting.

Considering I am already mated to Nesrin, the thought of making her my wife has me filled with a sort of excited anticipation. I have been waiting for this day since I first met her. I've found that she occupies all my thoughts every day. That first night I saw her, she was running like the wind through the forest, her long auburn hair in a tangled braid streaming behind her. I could sense her fear then, but also her exhilaration. She was soaking in the thrill of the chase. I gave orders to the pack to escort her out of our territory, but not to engage. My pack was confused at first, and so was I, but she intrigued me. Her presence tugged at something deep in my chest. I followed her that night, trying to understand why I felt that way. When those amber eyes met mine in the dark, they were haunted. There was no trace of the excitement from the chase anymore. I felt a strange pull in my chest, and it took everything in me not to go to her. I walked away, thinking it was for the best, only to have fate decide differently.

Movement from the barn at the other end of the aisle draws my attention. Astraea comes walking out first, petals flying from her tiny hand, a gigantic smile on her sweet face. I'm not sure how, but miraculously, her white dress has actually managed to stay clean. Spotting me, she grins, her crystal blue eyes lighting in excitement. I can't believe it has only been six months since I met her. I feel like she's always been in my life. Half a dozen forest sprites are dancing around her. Astraea's blonde curls bounce along with her steps as she makes her way to me. I pick her up when she reaches me and she nuzzles into my chest, melting my heart.

"*Besk days ever,*" echoes in my head as she looks up at me.

"I agree, my little star," I murmur, pressing a soft kiss to her head before placing her on her feet and fixing up her flower crown. I glance up and see Kyra appear. She is dressed in a light green flowy dress. Her eyes are on Sander, who winks at his wife, and I suddenly can't wait to see Nesrin. Leila rounds the corner next in an emerald green dress that sets her bright red hair alight. I glance over at Zee, and his eyes are fixed on her intently. Suzy comes afterward in an even darker dress, the color setting off her vibrant purple hair.

Nesrin asked Merve to walk her down the aisle today. She was nervous about asking him, especially with how closed off he's been since Grace's death. But I don't think she realizes just how loved she is by everyone. Merve thinks of her as family, so of course, he said yes.

The music changes and my heart speeds up. Butterflies fill my stomach, making me—the fucking alpha—shift on my feet with nerves. Merve appears first and then there she is, her bright warm smile hitting me square in the chest. I feel like I can't breathe with the full force of it.

I couldn't tear my eyes away from her even if I wanted to. The world could be ending, and I wouldn't be able to take my eyes off her. She grins, laughing a little, and the sight blinds me. She is so goddamn gorgeous, and for a moment I forget anyone else exists. Her face is absolutely glowing with happiness. It flows from her in waves, and I feel her love, stronger than ever, pouring down the bond. The sun shines off her auburn hair, the color standing out against the white halo of flowers set atop her head and the white of the dress. Her long hair is pinned back at the sides, and the rest is curled and flowing down her back and over her shoulders. My eyes trace down her face and skim along her body. She wears a long-sleeved white lace dress that hugs those soft curves I love so much. The v-neck front is cut low, her moon and star pendant on display between her breasts. The dress flares slightly at her knees and is edged with an intricate lace pattern. It suits her perfectly.

As she turns to give Merve a kiss on the cheek, I notice the low cut of the back of her dress. My fingers twitch with the need to run them along her spine, to touch the softness of her skin.

Kyra moves behind Nesrin to adjust her skirt, which trails behind her as she comes to stand next to me.

"You are absolutely stunning," I whisper. It is taking all my willpower not to throw her over my shoulder and make for the house.

As if reading my thoughts, Nesrin flushes. "Thank you. You don't look too bad yourself, handsome," she says, reaching up and brushing some hair from my forehead. I capture her hand as she pulls it away and place a soft kiss on the inside of her wrist.

Nesrin's intense amber eyes shine up at me. I notice the flecks of white in them that only show up when she is highly emotional, much like when mine turn yellow close to a shift.

Time seems to slow and speed up before I hear a throat clear behind me. Blinking, I turn to Blue, who is officiating the wedding. His bright blue eyes hold mirth as he waits for me.

"Sorry?" I ask sheepishly. I can feel Nesrin's amusement roll over me like a gentle wave. I shoot her a smirk and hear the soft laughs from the gathered crowd of pack and friends.

Blue looks at me knowingly. "I said, Lukas Black, do you take Nesrin Carson as your wife?"

Shit, how did I miss the whole beginning of the wedding? Clearly, I was just so mesmerized by this beautiful woman in front of me.

I clear my throat. "I do."

"Do you promise to love, honor, cherish, and protect her, forsaking all others, and holding only unto her forevermore?"

"I do."

Blue nods approvingly before turning to Nesrin, his eyes softening. "Nesrin Carson, do you take Lukas Black as your husband?"

"I do."

"Do you promise to love, honor, cherish, and protect him, forsaking all others, and holding only unto him forevermore?"

"I do."

Blue looks to Zee and Leila. "Now for the exchange of rings and vows."

Leila steps forward, handing Nesrin the ring, winking up at me before taking her place behind Nesrin again. Nesrin looks up at me, a timid smile on her lips, lips I want to kiss so badly.

She slides the ring on my finger, not taking her eyes from mine. Her voice is soft as she speaks.

"I never thought I'd be so lucky to find someone who would love me, even when I'd been shattered in a thousand pieces. You made me believe I could be whole again." She takes a shaky breath before going on. "You helped me glue those pieces back together, just like you promised. There are cracks in those pieces, some things that will never fully heal, but you made me whole again. You made it possible for me to heal. To know love can exist in the most imperfect, lost, and broken people. I love you with my whole being, Lukas Black."

My heart is hammering in my chest as I hold the hands of this beautiful and amazing woman in front of me. I reach up and wipe away a stray tear from her cheek. She is all mine. And I am hers, irrefutably hers.

Zee steps forward, placing the ring in my hand. I barely notice him moving until I feel the cold metal against my palm. I take the ring from him, and place the gold band on her finger, looking into her captivating eyes.

"Nesrin, you are the light of my life. I give you my heart, my promise, that I will love and protect you until the day that I die. I want to be there when it's messy, when it's hard, when it's fun, and when it's rewarding. We will walk hand in hand, together for the rest of our days. Whether or not you're in a thousand pieces, I'll always hold you together. I'll be your glue."

Tears line her eyes, and her smile is so bright I blink in surprise. I can't believe she is real. I reach up and cup her face. It is only the two of us in this moment. My lips touch hers as I softly explore her mouth for what seems like the first time. Her hands are gripping my wrists tightly, as if she is afraid I'll let go. She never has to worry about that. I'm never letting her go. I'd go to the ends of the earth for this woman.

I ease back, taking my time, the world slowly trickling back into focus. The sounds of cheering and clapping reach me. Nesrin's eyes shine with amusement and her cheeks flush with the cutest blush.

"Jumped the gun there, big boy," she grins.

"Not sorry, freckles," I tell her, leaning down for another kiss. Blue clears his throat and I remember my surprise. I give Nesrin a squeeze and wink before turning and kneeling in front of Astraea. Her wide violet blue eyes regard me with curiosity.

I pull a necklace from my pocket. It's a gold chain with a pendant of a wolf's head. The wolf is intricate, with an emerald for an eye. I had it specially made for the sweetest little girl, to prove to her that she is never alone.

"Astraea, I hope to show you every day what kind of person you deserve to have standing next to you one day. Until then, I will care for you every day and I will give you everything you could possibly want. You are safe and protected always. I promise that I'll always believe in you." Her face crumples up, her emotions getting the better of her as I continue. For such a young age, it still surprises me she knows exactly what is being said. I grip her hands in mine. "No matter what, I'll always hold your hand. I will be right beside you, encouraging you every step of the way. You're never alone, because you'll always have me. I will be by your side, even when you spread those wings and fly. Even when you find your own true love."

My heart swells as I watch a tear fall down her face. I let go of her hand and unclasp the chain, and fasten it around her neck. "And if you get lost, look at this pendant and know I will search to the end of the world for you. Don't ever forget, you are my daughter. You are the most special star in the universe."

I lift her curls from under the necklace a moment before she launches into my arms. '*I love you, daddy.*'

Fuck, that word rips into my chest in the best way.

Wrapping my arms around her, I stand and bring my other arm around my wife, the three of us now and forever a family. Nesrin has tears in her eyes and I lean down, kissing her softly on the lips before laying a kiss atop Astraea's head. I would die for these girls.

CHAPTER TWENTY NINE

Leila approaches us, a soft smile on her face. Placing her hands on my shoulders, she pulls me in for a hug. "I'm so incredibly happy for you." When she pulls back, she looks at Lukas, who hasn't left my side. "Both of you."

"Thank you," I say, drawing her back in for another hug. When I let her go, she is grinning from ear to ear.

"I don't know if I will ever get used to that," she whispers so softly.

"What?"

"Hugging you, being part of your life again," she replies.

My heart speeds up. "Me too," I whisper back.

"Now, show me this damn ring! These two wouldn't let me see it," she says, casting a stink eye at Lukas and Zee.

Laughing, I hold out my left hand, showing her the gold band that sits perfectly against the engagement ring. It is simple and has a pattern of vines around it, with a message etched along the inside.

Lukas's hand lands on my waist, and I tilt my head up to look at him. The emotions raging in his gaze steal my breath. He leans down to murmur into my ear the words he had engraved on my ring: *Light of my life.*

Goosebumps scatter over my body from his warm breath on my ear and hearing the words etched on my ring.

"My heart is yours," I whisper back my own message.

Leila lets go of my hand and steps back. "You two are so sweet. Your ring is gorgeous, Nesrin."

A squeal escapes my throat as Lukas wraps his hands around my waist and spins me away and into a dance. I laugh as he glides me across the floor with ease. I'm lifted in the air as he twirls us in a circle. My hands rest on his shoulders as I grin down at him. Goddess, I am so happy, this man, these people. It is a dream come true.

Lowering me to my feet, Lukas's mouth claims mine, his palms gently holding my face. Pulling back, he looks down at me, craning my neck as I stare into his intense green eyes. Our bond is overflowing with emotions; so much love and passion and wanting.

Lukas's hand slips around my waist, his warm palm soaking into the bare skin on my back as he tugs me closer. I snake my hand around his neck as our wedding song starts. Lukas pulls me closer, taking my other hand, and begins sweeping me around the dance floor. The crowd blurs and fades into the background. I see nothing but Lukas's bright green eyes, his scent of sandalwood and rain form a cocoon around me. We spin around the dance floor, and my feet barely touch the ground as he leads me in twirls and steps, keeping me close. His hand leaves my waist and trails up my back, lightly cupping the back of my head, his fingers threading into my auburn curls. Leaning his head down, he captures my lips with his. The kiss is tender and sweet. I feel dizzy, almost drunk off him. The song ends and so does the kiss. He rests his forehead on mine, our eyes closed as we bask in each other's presence. I feel my heart beating in tandem with his, his soul linked to mine. We are connected; body, mind, and soul. The first thing I notice is the dead silence. It doesn't sound like anyone else is here. Even the music has stopped. I pull back and look to the side and gasp. Lukas and I are several feet off the ground, floating in the air. I am glowing and the magic floating in the air around us is like ribbons changing colors. I know everyone can see because I can see the colors of magic reflecting off their faces as they all look on in awe.

My wide gaze swings back to Lukas, and his eyes are already locked on me, the green glowing with flecks of yellow as he regards me.

"How do we get down?" I ask.

"I believe magic is your domain, sweetheart."

"How did we even get up here?"

Suzy is pushing to the front of the dance floor. Nero takes lengthy strides as the crowd parts for him. Nikolas flashes to his side. "Nesrin, close your eyes and imagine your feet touching the ground," he says, stopping under us.

I do as he suggests, and not a moment later, I feel the ground beneath us. I open my eyes and count to three. Which is exactly how long it takes Suzy to be at my side.

"Uhh, so you can float now?"

I have a smile on my face as I answer, "First time for everything."

Suzy swipes at my arm, laughing. "If you start flying, I want a ride," she quips.

Lukas's arm wraps around my waist and he pulls me closer. Suzy's gaze is warm, and I swear I see little hearts in them. I smother my laugh and grab her hand. "I can do that."

"My best friend is magical," she squeals happily. I laugh and pull her in for a hug. My eyes meet Sophie and Joseph across the room where they are feeding Rose. They both give me a smile and wave, their glamor perfectly in place. I don't think Suzy is quite ready to see trolls walking about.

A throat clears next to us, and we all turn to see Zee standing there. He does some elaborate bow before speaking. "May I cut in?" he asks, a smirk tugging at his mouth.

"Yes," I say at the same time as Lukas says, "No."

I pat Lukas on the chest. "You'll be fine. Mingle," I suggest.

Lukas grumbles under his breath, making Zee chuckle as his hand takes mine. Zee pulls me into another dance. Shock must show on my face, because he chuckles, "You seem surprised."

"I am. I didn't know you could dance."

"Many things my mom made us learn."

I can just imagine Nadia making Lukas and Zee do all kinds of things. Lukas mentioned once that Nadia taught him how to cook. She really is like a den mother, making sure they all knew how to take care of themselves and their mates. She was a great help with setting up for today and making certain things ran smoothly.

"I'm so proud of you, honey."

I wrinkle my nose at him. "Why?"

Zee reaches up, tapping my nose. "You've grown. Learned to trust. Bonded with the pack. Fallen in love."

Looking over at my husband, emotions clog my throat. When I rounded the corner and saw him waiting for me at the end of the aisle, tears filled my eyes from the intensity of the emotions shining in the depths of those green eyes. I love this man with all my heart and soul.

I watch as he picks up Astraea and spins her around the dance floor. Her laughter floats toward me, and I feel Nissa land on my shoulder. The sprite is also watching Lukas and Astraea dance.

"You are exactly where you are meant to be, daughter of light."

"I hope so," I chuckle.

Nissa lifts from my shoulder, and Zee and I turn to face her.

"I pledge my allegiance to you and yours. You have my word as queen."

My mouth drops open, an unintelligible noise falling from my lips. Zee cracks up laughing, and I can't help but smack him in the stomach with the back of my hand.

"I'm sorry. It's just nothing is ever boring around you."

Finally getting my mouth to work, I blurt, "I'm sorry. What?"

"I'm Queen of the Woodland Sprites."

"But why would you be hanging around with us if you were queen? That makes no sense."

Nissa's eyes move to take in something behind me and I turn at the waist to see what she's looking at. Astraea is still dancing with Lukas. Her blue eyes have a slight violet glow to them, just like Niamh's used to. Turning back, unease blossoms in my stomach.

"Why?" I ask again.

"She is important."

I knew this already from Blanchette and Leopold. But as I stare at the sprite, I wonder if she could tell me why? I'm almost afraid to ask.

"How is she important?"

Nissa smiles softly, sensing my anxiety, and floats closer. "It's nothing like that, nothing bad. *I promise.*"

I draw in a sharp breath. Fae never make promises lightly. They also can't lie. Of course they can omit the truth and trick you, but somehow, I don't think that's Nissa. I relax, if only slightly, and realize I've been gripping Zee's arm fairly tightly. I look up at him in apology.

"Didn't feel a thing," he winks.

Suddenly the air ripples, and the barn grows darker. Zee grips my arm, pulling me closer to him. "You feel that, right?" he asks.

"Yes."

Nissa turns in a circle and points to the middle of the barn. Shadows are forming in thick masses there. Suddenly, Lukas and Astraea are next to me, Suzy with them. I see Sander, Kyra, Alex, and Roan on the other side of the barn, eyes wide, worry bleeding from every pore. I am much more in tune with my close friends than the rest of the pack.

"What's happening?" Suzy whispers.

Leila simply moves toward the shadowy mass and crosses her arms, a look of annoyance on her face. Cerberus is the first to appear, causing everyone to gasp and stumble back a step. Not everyone saw him the last time he showed up here. Astraea's joy is easy to read, but Lukas keeps a tight grip on her. Suzy's nails bite into my arm as Hades appears, the tall imposing god dressed impeccably in a light bluish-gray suit. His golden eyes take in the room. Next second, Nikolas blocks my view of Hades as he flashes in front of me, a menacing growl rumbling from him. I reach forward and place a hand on his back as Nero strolls over, looking as if he were taking a walk on the beach.

"Nikolas, it's okay. He's not here to hurt us," I assure him, but Nikolas is like stone, unmoving.

"Who is that?" Suzy chokes out.

Before I can answer, Leila's voice rings out over the silence. "You promised."

Hades's golden eyes take in Leila, and he smiles. "You look beautiful, daughter."

Leila deflates a little. "Thanks."

Hades moves forward and places a soft kiss on her head before moving our way. Cerberus is still standing stock still where he stepped out of the portal. Astraea must say something to him, because all three heads lock on her across the room, and he moves forward a step. Nikolas crouches, ready to attack, but Nero is there, whispering in his ear. I don't take my eyes off Hades, but I can see Nikolas relax and move back a step to my side. I reach down and grip his hand, giving it a squeeze.

Lukas's palm lands on my waist as he stands beside me with Astra. Zee on my other side, with Nissa on his shoulder.

Hades stops a few feet away, taking in the group, his eyes stopping on me. "Hades," I speak.

Hades's golden eyes flare for a moment. "Nesrin. Lukas. I wanted to stop by and say congratulations."

"And you couldn't send a card?" Nero quips from the side. I glance over at him and arch an eyebrow.

Hades chuckles. "Been a while, old friend."

Nero steps forward to shake Hade's hand, and I think we are all in shock.

"You know each other?"

"Yes," they both reply.

Hades comes closer, Lukas's hands spasm on my waist and Zee and Nikolas stiffen at my sides.

'*It's alright,*' I send to all of them.

Nikolas trembles with restraint. We can all feel the power rolling off Hades, but I need him to remain in control. Lukas must read me, because he moves forward, pushing Nikolas back behind me with Suzy. A silent command.

"I didn't mean to cause a scene."

"Sure, you didn't," I reply, rolling my eyes. "But thank you. And for bringing Cerberus."

Having heard his name, Cerberus whines. I glance over at the hellhound and smile. Turning, I motion for Astraea. Without hesitation, she leaps into my arms, and we walk over to him. A murmur starts as the guest watch us approach the hellhound. Cerberus's tail whips back and forth wildly in excitement.

Leila chuckles, "He has missed her."

"I can tell."

I reach my hand out for him, and all three heads shove to get the first pat. Astraea launches out of my arms, and I hear Nadia squeal in shock as Astraea grabs a hold of the hellhound's neck, another of its heads using its nose to push her up and on their back. My heart melts at the sight of such a terrifying beast adoring my little star. Leila stepped over to me and intertwined her fingers with mine. I rest my head on her shoulder as we watch Astraea and Cerberus, her warmth radiating into my body.

'*Hades says Hera's not at Olympus. She hasn't been seen in a week,*' Lukas's voice sounds in my head.

I don't show any outward reaction to this. '*Does Hades know where she is?*'

'*No.*'

'*What else did he say?*'

'*He said Eris is also missing.*'

Anger floods my veins. Of course, it would be Hera and Eris, the goddess of discord.

I can sense when Hades approaches, and Cerberus whines, obviously realizing playtime is over. I pull away from Leila and we turn as one to the god of the underworld. Leila gives him a hug, and he murmurs into her hair. She nods and steps back. Hades's golden gaze locks on mine and I smile softly. Hades bows his head. "Take care, Nesrin. And congratulations."

"Thank you."

Lukas leads me up the stairs and pulls me to the end of the hallway, past our bedroom. I frown. Where is he taking me? Stopping in front of a wooden door, he draws a key out of his pocket and unlocks it. He pulls me up another flight of stairs and we step into a large room, painted in a shimmering black and emerald. The ceiling has massive skylights, and the smell of paint clings to the air.

Cupboards line one wall, a long work table set beneath, but what draws my attention is a beautifully carved stand near the window that holds my family's grimoire. My throat tightens as I realize what I'm seeing.

"You still need to add your own personal touches, but this is yours."

I step further into the room in complete awe. My eyes take in every detail. I must have been quietly standing here for longer than I thought, because Lukas's voice is hesitant when he asks me if I like it.

Turning, I fling myself at him. "It's perfect."

His arms come around me, holding me tight against him. "So happy you like it, freckles."

"Like it? I love it!" There are no words to describe how I'm feeling. Today has been wonderful, and now this? This is more than I could ever ask for.

Stepping back, Lukas cups my face, his eyes searching mine. The intensity of his gaze steals my breath. Leaning down, he crushes his lips to mine. I kiss him deeply, his hunger matching my own. His hand roams over my body, his fingers moving to the zipper of my dress. So slowly, he pulls it down, his finger tracing my bare skin as he does. My lips skim over his neck as I try my best to suppress my shiver at his touch. My hands trail down and under his shirt, my fingers tracing the hard muscles of his abdomen, making him suck in a sharp breath. I smile against the underside of his jaw, nipping the skin there. A rumble sounds from his throat and his hands move up to my shoulders, pushing my dress down my arms. When they are free of the dress, I lift his shirt, but I'm not tall enough to push it all the way, and the buttons will take far too long, so I grip it with both hands and tear it open. Buttons fly everywhere and Lukas eyes light up with lust and amusement. My body turns to liquid fire as I shimmy out of my dress, letting it pool around my feet.

Lukas steps back, surveying me. "So beautiful," he murmurs.

Slowly, he toes off his shoes and undoes his belt. I watch as the muscles in his arms and chest flex with each movement. Undoing his pants, he kicks them off, while I stand there trying not to squirm under his intense gaze. He steps forward, scooping me up, and carries me over to the bed in the corner. How did I not notice this before?

Laying me down gently, his lips graze mine before trailing down my throat to my chest. My pulse kicks up as his green eyes burn into mine as he gazes up at me.

"I've been dying to get you out of that dress all night."

Before I can reply, his mouth covers my breast, licking and nipping before moving to the other.

I gasp, my heart racing as his fingers brush against my skin. The sensations unleash a flood between my legs. Releasing my breast, he inhales sharply. "You smell amazing when you're turned on, freckles."

His words send a rush of warmth through me, making me squirm beneath him. Warm hands float over my body, a hot tongue following their path as Lukas moves over me, and I sink my hands into his already ruffled hair, reveling in the sensations he brings. Making his way back to my mouth, he presses a scorching kiss against my lips, causing my toes to curl with pleasure.

Pulling back, our eyes lock. *'What are you waiting for, husband?'* I smirk.

Lukas's gaze darkens. "Just making sure you were ready, wife."

His eyes burn into mine as he pushes in, stretching me slowly. Too slowly to relieve the ache of my arousal. I lock my legs around him, needing him closer. When his lips touch mine again, I am lost. Completely and utterly lost to this man. I open my mouth to him, and our tongues collide. A guttural growl rumbles from his throat, sending a flutter of wings free in my stomach, as we devour one another. Our bond is filled with so much love and passion, the feeling so satisfying, so fulfilling, that I don't think we'd even need air to survive.

It doesn't take me long to fall apart, my moans floating on the air. Lukas keeps a steady pace, drawing my pleasure out as long as he can. Suddenly, his hands grip my hips, and he pulls back enough to flip me over, pushing back in. I inhale sharply as he presses firmly into me, grinding against my backside. I push up on my hands, arching my back as his palms glide up my spine and thread through my hair. His pace is relentless, our sounds echoing through the room. Lukas's other hand grips my hip, firmly directing my movements as he draws me over his length, each thrust sending waves of pleasure coursing through me.

Letting go of my hair, his arm bands around my chest pulling me against him, so that I'm kneeling in front of him, his cock still buried deep inside of me as his hips pump. He bites down on my shoulder, a feral growl rumbling in his chest as he comes, his body going momentarily rigid and breathless as he fills me, his grip tightens on me, keeping me on his cock as I buck from the explosion of my own orgasm.

CHAPTER THIRTY

Lukas

"Y ou sleepy?" Nesrin whispers.

I pull her closer to me on the bed, my hand slipping down her back, and trace the outline of her spine. "No. You?"

Sliding her leg between mine, her amber eyes ignite. "No."

Today has been absolutely perfect. I married my soulmate, and now she is mine in every conceivable way, as I am hers. I can sense her happiness and contentment as her heart beats in tandem with mine. Flattening my palm, I glide it lower, smoothing it over her ass. Her own palm trails down my chest, her fingertips tracing my tattoos along my side.

We continue slowly, caressing each other's bodies, exploring every line, swell, and dip as if we were rediscovering each other after a long time apart. It is an exploration full of curiosity, worship, and intimacy, and neither of us wants to rush it.

"I love you," she whispers.

My smile is instant, and I reach up, threading my fingers through her hair. "I'm so glad you went running in the forest that night."

The brightest smile crosses her face, making me blink. "I'm sure you would have found me, even if I hadn't," she replies. She's right, the fates couldn't keep us apart. I love this woman more than anything else in this world.

"Kiss me?" she murmurs softly.

She doesn't have to ask twice. I roll her onto her back and slide on top of her, caging her with my arms. I trail my teeth along her jaw and take a deep breath to steady my racing heart. God, she smells so good. She tastes of sugar and strawberries and wine, and I want nothing more than to devour her. I take her bottom lip between mine, sucking on it, savoring the sweetness. She presses her tongue into my mouth, and I groan, deepening the kiss. The taste of her mouth drives me wild.

As much as I want to sink into her again, there is something else I want to try. I pull back and stare down at her, her lips swollen from our kisses. My dick throbs between us with a need so intense, I want to claim her again. The way her amber eyes fill with unveiled lust doesn't help matters. I drop a quick kiss to her lips and stand from the bed. She frowns at me, confused, and then I watch as her eyes roam over my body like a warm caress. I tip my head back and bite back my groan as she licks her lips unconsciously.

"Sweetheart, stop looking at me like that. I wanted to try something."

When I look back at her, she has moved to sit on the end of the bed. Nesrin arches an eyebrow. "You want to tie me up?" she asks.

My eyes widen and a shot of lust zaps through my veins. I'm not sure if it's hers, mine, or both.

"No, but if that's something you wanted . . . " I trail off.

Nesrin smiles coyly but doesn't answer.

I shake my head to clear it of the dirty thoughts she's sent running amuck. "I want to go on a run with you."

"Now?" her voice is incredulous as she gapes back at me in horror.

I manage to contain my smile, but only barely. "Yes."

"No. It's our wedding night. I'm not getting dressed to go running at two am."

"I meant to shift into your wolf and go on your first run with me."

Nesrin's mouth opens and closes several times. "I don't know, Lukas. What if I can't change back?"

"Not going to happen. You have me here."

She stares at me, considering. I can sense her fear and worry, and I understand it. Slowly, she stands, running a shaky hand through her hair. "Okay."

My heart leaps. "I'll be here the whole time."

Nesrin

Lukas sends me a wink before shifting, his body seamlessly changing form. He stands in front of me in the form of his gorgeous black wolf; the coat shining in the low light.

I can do this.

Taking a deep fortifying breath, I close my eyes and will the shift to happen. I feel the soft push of Lukas's wolf pressed up against me and I gasp as the change begins, as my fangs elongate, and I feel every tiny thing with my eyes closed. Lukas's love and comfort flows down our bond, drowning out the panic that is battling me. I inhale sharply at the feel of my skin tightening and pulling, changing form. It takes a few moments before the pain subsides and I open my eyes, blinking against the brightness surrounding me. I marvel at the sharpness of my vision, the smells that overwhelm me. And the crispness of my hearing.

Lukas's head nuzzles against my side and continues up to my head. He presses us tightly against each other, and I turn my head, nuzzling under his chin. I catch our reflections in the tall window across the room and stare in amazement at the contrast. Midnight black and pure white wolf standing side by side. Lukas is much larger than me, but we are perfect. Lukas's eyes are glowing yellow, but mine . . . mine are still amber.

'Why aren't my eyes like yours?'

'I don't know.'

'Were they like this last time?'

'Yes.'

Lukas pads over to the window and nudges it open.

'*Come on,*' he beckons and moves to the small balcony before jumping from the roof. I dart forward in shock, my paws skidding on the wooden floors. I glance over the railing to see Lukas staring up at me.

'*You want me to jump?!*' *I exclaim.* Last time I jumped from a window it went badly.

Lukas chuckles. '*Yes. Come on. You'll be fine, I promise.*'

I take a deep breath and launch myself over the railing. My stomach flips with the rush and the feeling of falling. My paws hit the ground lighter than I would expect, and a rush of excitement hits me. I bound away, spinning and letting out a playful yip. Darting forward, I nip at Lukas's leg. His nose lowers, and he nudges me back, sending me stumbling sideways. I laugh playfully. But the noise coming from my mouth is odd. Is this what wolves sound like when they laugh?

Lukas turns and trots toward the woods. I follow right on his tail. When we reach the tree line, we break into a run. The excitement and adrenaline coursing through me feels amazing. I have never before felt so alive. A feeling builds in my chest, and without thought, I lift my head and howl. Lukas lifts his head and lets out a howl of his own. I grin, my tongue lolling out, when I hear several answering howls rise from the forest.

'*This is amazing.*'

CHAPTER THIRTY ONE

The drive takes over ninety minutes to get to Cascade Rocks on the other side of Portland. It is where Lukas's other compound is, the one Alex was sent to when I first arrived at Lukas's. Today I'm heading out there for a change in scenery. I let out a breath as we pull off the main road onto a small dirt road. After another ten minutes, we come to a large gate. Alex jumps from the car and runs over to a keypad next to it, entering a code, and the gates slide open a second later.

"Fancy," I murmur as we drive through the enormous gates.

Alex shrugs. "They don't have the protection of living with the alpha on the same land as we do."

"I suppose it does come in handy living close to the alpha."

"If an attack were to happen, they would probably hit here first, being the easier target," Asena agrees, and my stomach sours at the thought.

"How many people know of this place?" I ask.

"Well, only the pack, really. It's not widely known. Lukas likes it that way, as most of the shifters who live here are families."

"Good."

"So what's it like being Mrs. Black?" Alex says smiling over at me from the driver's seat.

"Good. Really good." I grin. And it has been, Lukas has spent every spare moment with me. He has even gotten me to shift a couple more times, each time the process getting easier.

Asena laughed from the backseat. "I better it has. I can't believe it's been a week already."

"I know."

The girls must pick up on my edgy tone because I feel their eyes on me.

"What's wrong?" Alex asks, looking back at the road.

I let out a sigh, picking at my nails. "We have no clue where Hera is. The coven has been laying low. The fae sightings have stopped, and I'm just waiting for the other shoe to drop."

We wind around trees and long grass until we reach a clearing with a dozen small cabins, similar to those around Lukas's land at home, each nestled into a group of trees. A larger common building sits further up the hill where the trees are thicker. This compound feels open and relaxed. The long grass sways in the wind. Everything is quiet, natural, beautiful.

"This place is beautiful," I breathe.

Alex smirks over at me, putting the car in park and pulling her short, colorful hair back into a ponytail. "Wait till you see the waterfall."

My eyes widen, and excitement fills me. "There's a waterfall?!" I squeak, bouncing in my seat.

Laughing, the three of us pile out of the car, and I take a big breath of fresh air.

"Come on, the others want to meet you. Most couldn't attend the wedding," Alex says.

"I wish Kyra and Kate could have come with us," I murmur. The girls nod in agreement.

Alex's phone dings with a message. "Roan is so worried," she replies. Shaking her head at her phone, she sends off a quick text before pocketing it.

"He's newly mated. Give him a break," I tease, bumping my shoulder into hers.

A pink blush spreads across her face, and I turn, linking arms with Asena. "Okay, my fire agate friend, lead on," I joke. Fire agate is one of my favorite gems, with its brown iridescent layers. It offers a sense of calm and stability during times of chaos and emotional upheaval, and I've decide that is Asena.

"Oh, is that how it is?" she laughs. "Well, pumpkin spice, I shall take you on an adventure," she says, tugging on the end of my ponytail before linking her other arm with Alex. Together we make our way over to the common building. I have a feeling today is going to be a great day. Just what I need to get my mind off the witches and the gods trying their damnedest to ruin my life.

We round the main building and I take in the sight of thirty or so shifters gathered. A mixture of women, children and men. The group shifts as a burly figure with a powerful stride comes forward. His face is lit with a huge smile that radiates such warmth I feel it down to my toes. He halts in front of me, his hand extended.

"Luna, I'm Kian. I run things here. I'd like to welcome you to our home. We are honored to have you here today."

I reach forward and shake his hand, his completely engulfing mine. "Kian. Thank you for having us," I reply, blushing slightly, nerves getting the better of me, as all eyes point our way.

'*She is so pretty,*' one unknown voice filters through the pack link and I suppress my smile.

"Alex says she's planning to show you around. Maybe take you to the waterfall today?"

"Yes."

Kian nods and gives Alex a grin. "Hear you went and found yourself a mate?"

"Yep," she replies proudly.

"Good. You deserve it." Then, looking back to me, Kian says, "Please tell me you plan on staying for dinner?"

"Uhh . . . " I look at Asena and Alex, who just smile and wait for me. "I would love that," I finally reply.

"Good, we won't let ya go until that belly of yours is full." Kian laughs.

Alex clasps my arm and yanks me toward the throng of people. "I will introduce you to everyone, then we can go hiking."

I stop along the path and take a moment to breathe in the fresh air, the sound of the waterfall fading behind us. The fresh breeze brushes along my skin, calming my nerves and mind. About an hour ago, a sense of dread filtered in over me. Though, I didn't tell the others at the time, not wanting to ruin our time away. I glance toward the compound about eighty or so yards away from where we're standing now, and my stomach rumbles. The sun is setting and I am more than ready to head back and get some food. The others promised us full bellies before we left. Alex comes to stand beside me, taking my hand in hers. I look over, noticing that the scars on her face are now no more than silver lines across her skin. The serious expression on her face gives me pause. *What's wrong?* Does she feel what I do?

"Thank you for forgiving me," she whispers, tears gathered in her eyes.

I don't hesitate to step forward, wrapping my arms around her.

"Alex, this is all in the past."

"I feel so guilty all the time about how terribly I treated you in the beginning." She sounds so torn up, and I hate that. She shouldn't be carrying this guilt around anymore.

I squeeze her tightly. "You made it up to me by saving my life. And really, you weren't *that* bad," I reply. We stand in the embrace for a long moment, both absorbing the comfort we each offer the other. Alex and I may have started out as enemies, but we have become great friends, and I won't let her beat herself up about the past. I glance up, seeing Asena making her way over, her gaze darting between us. Giving her a wink, I pull away from Alex, and we all make our way back through the field of long grass. About halfway to the compound, I abruptly stop.

Ice hits my chest like a stab wound. I actually look down to see if I'm bleeding. My gaze swings out over the field. My eyes scan the area, trying to find anything that might explain my growing anxiety.

Asena grabs my arm, her face grim. "What is it?"

"I– I don't know. Something's wrong," I stammer.

My focus is drawn inward, on the feeling in my chest, hoping to pinpoint the danger. Taking a deep breath, I close my eyes and follow the feeling. Snapping my eyes open, they connect with a pair of yellow eyes, crouched in the grass. *It's a shifter.*

"Alex. Asena."

They follow my gaze and curse. Without taking my eyes from the leopard shifter in front of me, I step in front of my friends. My mind is buzzing as fear beats steadily in my chest.

Grabbing my arm, Asena pulls me back. "Oh, no, you don't, pumpkin spice. We are in this together."

Trying for reassurance, I smile. Despite the fear clenching my insides, I am worried for my friends. Suddenly, the world bursts into movement at the same time as screams and yelling rise up from the compound. The leopard is charging us at full speed, launching itself in the air, claws extended. Alex shifts instantly, leaping in front of me, taking the force of the impact. Using my magic, I hurl the shifter off Alex and turn to Asena.

"Run!" I tell her, my eyes whirling to the compound.

She hesitates and I shout, "That is an *order!* We have this. Go help the others." Asena's eyes widen. It's the first time I have issued an order as her luna. She takes off down the hill, shifting into her lynx, as she runs. My gaze goes back to the leopard shifter as it prowls in a circle around Alex and me.

My magic is swift as it rises and pulses through me, humming along my skin like a live wire. The leopard pounces again. I react without thinking, throwing up a shield with an electrical current. The shifter bounces off it, spasming and rolling in the grass. Alex is on it a moment later, her mouth going for the neck.

"No!" I yell, moving her away with my magic.

Quickly, I cage it in a magic bubble. I require answers, which means I need it alive. Yelling reaches my ears and I turn, running for the compound, the unmistakable sounds of fighting rising over my panting. I make it to the clearing and pull up short, seeing a mass of violence, shifter against shifter. I close my eyes and will myself to calm enough to focus on identifying friend and foe. When my eyes open, the ice in my chest pinpoints each of the threats. I run forward, throwing my hand up to send another feline shifter soaring back through the air. My shift calls to me, my body begging to change. A blow to the side takes me off my feet and I skid in the gravel, pushing up as I come face to face with a leopard, its yellow eyes gleaming. I suppress a shiver and slowly stand. My magic hums along my skin, my hands glowing with a brilliant white light that forms into my sword of light. The leopard attacks without hesitation, and I lift my arms in an arch, the sword slicing across its chest. I step aside as it lands in a heap next to me. I can't bring myself to give the killing blow, so I mutter a few words before laying a magical net over it's body, yellow eyes stare up at me in panic and pain.

The ground seems to shake beneath my feet. I bring the sword up as Alex's wolf comes to a stop at my side. I do a double take as a big brown bear comes lumbering toward us. Alex's voice sounds in my head. *'It's okay. He's one of us.'*

This is the first bear shifter I've ever seen, and he is absolutely enormous. He lets out a roar that stops my heart as the ground shakes beneath his paws. Massive claws swipe out, knocking a shifter away from a group of children. The other shifter slams into a tree, lying unconscious in a heap. The bear lets out another roar and charges another. One of the feline shifters tries to launch onto its back only to be swiped away, the bear's claws dragging across its face, leaving bloody gashes in their wake. The remaining two feline shifters look my way and hiss before running away. Well, then.

Surveying the damage, we have six feline shifters captured, including the one out in the field. Asena's Lynx comes padding up to me, winding her way around my body.

'*Are you okay, luna?*' she asks mind to mind.

"I'm fine," I say, looking around at all the scared and angry faces. This is all my fault. They are being attacked because I came here.

I peer over my shoulder at the massive grizzly bear. '*Are you okay?*'

'*Yes, Luna,*' he replies gruffly.

I watch as my pack begins to shift back and huddle around the children. My anger rises swiftly, and I spin to the closest feline shifter. I grit my teeth against the magic struggling within me to heal the injured snow leopard.

"Shift!" I command.

The snow leopard hisses at me, backing up a step only to realize another gigantic brown bear is blocking its only exit. A frantic, almost wild look enters the shifter's eyes as they dart back to me. I let my magic brush against my skin, causing a faint glow to appear.

"Shift," I growl, this time borrowing some of Lukas's alpha magic and infusing it into my words.

The leopard tries to fight the command, twitching before she shifts. I take a menacing step forward, my magic flaring across my skin, making my fingertips tingle. A white haze moves over my vision and a faint glow lights up my arms and hands. In front of me is the woman from the mall. Her short brown bob is a mess, and she has blood running a path down her chest from the gash there. Annoyance blazes in her eyes as she stares at me, her chin lifted defiantly.

"You," I snarl, the sound vibrating up my throat, sounding more animal than human.

Surprise flashes across her face, and she lowers her head.

Asena steps forward, back in her human form. "You know her?"

"She stopped and had the weirdest conversation with me that day we were shopping in the city."

Alex prowls closer to the girl, a low growl coming from her. I step closer, running my hand over Alex's back, smoothing down the hackles. My anger directed at the girl,

"What's your name?" I demand, then amend, "Your real name?"

"Why does it matter? You're only going to kill me, anyway," she snaps back.

"What makes you think I'm going to kill you? I have killed no one here, only trapped them. I don't kill."

Shock flashes in her gaze, followed by stubbornness. "Your mate will."

I forcibly keep my body relaxed, though my knee jerk reaction is to zap her ass. As I step forward again, her eyes dart around nervously. Good. She should be worried. "My mate wouldn't harm anyone without cause, and yes, attacking innocent people is a cause for his wrath. He wouldn't outright kill you unless it was self-defense. That's not who he is."

"But–"

"But what?" I growl clenching my hands into fists.

The young woman shifts on her feet. "S– she told us you had to be stopped."

My eyes narrow. "Who?"

Another feline shifter stands up, her words near-frantic as she answers, "She is in our heads. She won't stop whispering to us."

"She told us your pack was evil. That you're an abomination. She wouldn't stop until we agreed to kill you," another whispers hoarsely, tears streaming down her face as she sits in the dirt.

Asena steps forward, her long dark hair a mess, her light blue eyes as hard as ice chips. "She is a fierce warrior and fights for those who need her protection. We would die for her, just as she would for us. Nesrin is *no* abomination," she snarls.

"We tried to ignore it, but the voice wouldn't stop. I purposely ran into you that day to get a sense of you. There was nothing evil about you, but you . . . smelled different. A scent of something sweet—different, but not evil. We tried leaving the city, but she wouldn't let us. We are trapped here," the girl from the mall says, trying to push down her fear, but I can smell it, we all can.

I run a hand through my hair. I can sense that they're telling the truth, but if this voice has been driving them to do things they didn't want to do, I have to detain them. They'll be dangerous until we can figure out how to release them. Like the wolf who went mad on our lands about a month ago, clawing at his head before running into the wall.

Could this be the same thing?

I turn to Asena. She's covered in blood, but all her wounds have healed. My healing magic doesn't detect any serious injuries, so at least that relaxes me somewhat.

"Is there somewhere we can put them that's secure until we know they no longer pose a threat?"

She nods, motioning for others to help escort the feline shifters to a building on the other side of the clearing. *We have a room that will hold one of us. It will do until Lukas arrives,* she replies in my head.

A bone-chilling howl rises from the woods behind the compound. We all turn in unison. That was not a howl from one of our pack. My chest grows cold again, and I close my eyes. Without warning, something inside of me snaps, like an elastic band breaking. My magic bursts from me, lighting up every life form in my vicinity. It's like staring into the galaxy, every life a flicker of light in the dark. I focus on that icy presence, on following it across the forest, and watch in horror as a creature born of nightmares comes crashing through the woods toward us.

Breaking me from my vision, the feline shifter speaks. "I can help."

Blinking my eyes, I try to formulate a plan. "No, you will go with the others."

"But–"

I don't have time to argue with her.

"No," I growl, infusing the luna power behind my words. My command hits its mark, making her head drop.

The howl sounds again. My body vibrates with the need to shift. To fight teeth with teeth. Closing my eyes tightly, I will the shift to happen. I inhale sharply as the first bones crack and reshape, my skin tugging and pulling.

When I open them, the world around me is sharper. My nose instantly picks up on the approaching creature. It cannot be allowed to make it to the compound. There are too many people here. Too many families. I lift my head to the sky and let out a long howl, a call to arms. Those who will fight to protect those here can follow me if they so choose.

Alex howls next to me, then nudges my side. Asena's smaller lynx rubs against my other side. I look behind me to see five other wolves and the brown bear joining me. I bow my head in thanks and howl again before sprinting toward the tree line. We need to intercept this creature.

Bounding into the woods, we make it about five minutes before we slow. I lift my head, sniffing the air. We are close. My gaze moves over the darkened forest, my eyes passing over a tall dark figure between the trees. I snap my gaze back to it and gasp. A set of red eyes blink back at me.

The creature is like nothing I've ever seen before—well, maybe in bad horror movies. It looks like a hideous, demented wolf standing on its back two legs. The front claws are long and sharp, its arms long and gangly. Saliva drips from its elongated muzzle. Is this a werewolf? If so, it isn't fully night yet, or a full moon. How was it able to change?

The shifters let out a chorus of growls, spreading out and around the creature. Alex and Asena stay beside me as we meet the creature head on. As the creature launches forward, one of the wolves moves in close, snapping at its legs, but the creature pays it no mind. Its eyes are solely focused on me. Wasting no time, I leap forward, going for the neck, but the creature swipes out with a clawed hand, sending me flying into the closest tree; the wind knocking out of me. I can't breathe, and I am pretty sure I've cracked at least one rib.

Another wolf runs to my aid, helping me to my feet, pushing their body against my side until I'm stable on my feet. I can already feel my ribs mending, the bones fusing back together. I crouch low, snarling at the werewolf whose attention has turned toward the bear, wanting to take him out first. I dash forward and jump, my teeth sinking into its arm before it can land its hit. As it tries to shake me free, I hold on to it with all my strength. Its other arm swings out, slashing at my belly. I unclasp my jaws, whimpering as I drop to my paws. Alex and Asena are there, one going for the front, the other from the back. Distracting the werewolf from me, Asena leaps forward, but it catches her by the neck mid-leap and throws her aside. I hear the sickening crunch of her body hitting a tree.

Anger burns deep in my belly as I dart under its swinging arm and bite into its thigh, my fangs tearing into its flesh. The werewolf falters as its claws sink deep into my shoulder, and I howl in agony as I stumble away. We need to take this creature down, but it just keeps batting us away like flies.

I hear a loud growl as the werewolf stumbles away and knocks me aside. I give my head a shake as I stand up again.

The sound of Asena's pained cry has my eyes snapping open. The werewolf looms over her. Blood drips from its teeth and claws. I can feel her pain as Asena shrinks back. She has multiple wounds, not to mention her leg is broken, her shoulder dislocated, and a lung is punctured. Suddenly, the bear comes barreling forward, knocking the werewolf aside. Two more wolves leap forward, going for its legs in an attempt to get it on the ground. The werewolf bellows, and the trees quake with its frenzy. On shaky paws, I run forward, sinking my teeth into its arm, and tugging it backward. It just flings us all away and we go skidding across the gravel road. I didn't even realize until now that we've moved so close to the road.

Jumping back up, I shake the gravel loose from my fur and turn, snarling at the werewolf as it stalks toward me. The first drops of rain hit my fur as the werewolf and I stare each other down. I spare the others a quick glance and see Asena lying now unconscious a few feet away. My vision narrows, a white haze taking over. I barely register Alex vaulting on the werewolf's back, its long claws reaching behind, sinking into her back and flinging her off. It turns on her, stalking toward her. One of the gray wolves steps in its path, but it's knocked aside. With a growl that starts from deep in my throat, I charge forward, a red-hot rage burning in my stomach. My wolf moving faster than I thought possible, I am on the werewolf within seconds.

I leap onto its back, my claws sinking into its shoulders as I latch onto its neck. The creature stumbles back away from Alex, its clawed hands trying to swipe at me. All I feel is a rage that consumes my mind. All the pent-up emotions from the endless attacks over the last six months have finally pushed me over the edge.

I sink my teeth deeper into the creature's throat, relishing in its pain as fury builds inside of me. The werewolf's legs give out, and we hit the ground, the werewolf landing on its knees. Warm liquid coats my mouth and muzzle as I press down hard on its neck. I almost gag at the taste of its foul blood filling my mouth.

Shaking my head, I feel the tearing of muscles and tendons as I rip at its throat, more blood spraying around me. I feel the life leave its body as it falls heavily to the ground with a sickening thud. I pry my jaws open and back up quickly. Even in this form, words float through my head, and I whisper them faintly but firmly, '*extermino adolebitque.*'

Smoke immediately rises from the body lying mere inches from my feet. Flames erupt a moment later. I raise my eyes up over the burning corpse to Alex's face. Her shocked, pain-filled gaze meets and holds mine.

My eyes water from the putrid scent of burning flesh as smoke billows from the werewolf's body. My panting slows as the rage retreats. I look down at myself and see blackish blood covering my white fur and shiver with revulsion. My stomach revolts and I have to fight back the vomit that rises in my throat.

I snap my head to the road, hearing the rumbling sound of an engine getting closer and see a motorcycle, Lukas on it, speeding down the road toward us. The rain is falling in torrents now. Skidding to a stop, Lukas jumps from the bike, letting it fall to the ground, and rushes over to me.

I close my eyes and attempt to shift back into my human form. Next thing I know, his hands are on either side of my face, his soft, warm lips claiming mine in a desperate kiss. Breaking the kiss, he pulls me into his arms. I wrap my arms around his neck and cling to him, my chest heaving with adrenaline and my body protesting from multiple wounds. As we kneel here in the wet dirt, my emotions at last begin to trickle in. I feel Lukas's worry, anger, and sorrow through the bond, and lower my brow to bury my head deeper in his neck as I feel out the pack. Alex is fine, a little banged up, but okay. Asena . . . Asena, her link—her connection—is in tatters, her golden thread dissolving. I jerk back, my eyes frantically searching the area. Lukas's warm hands cup my face, bringing my gaze back to him. "I'm so sorry, sweetheart."

Tears spring to my eyes instantly.

"No!" I cry hoarsely as fear and horror erupt inside of me.

The expression in Lukas's eyes says it all.

"NO!" I scream as I rip my head from his grasp. I am a healer, I can heal her. She *needs* to be healed. I stand on shaky legs and stumble toward where Alex is leaned over a body on the ground near the tree line. I trip, falling to my knees, and crawl the rest of the way to her. I pick up Asena's cold, limp hand, but I feel no life. She is gone. There is nothing remaining for me to heal. Tears streak down my face. Her absence is tangible, that spark of life gone. Her lifeless blue eyes stare unseeing up into the darkening sky, her beautiful brown skin pale and her body limp.

"No," I sob, resting my forehead on her chest.

Above, the storm rages, dark clouds growing to blanket the world with their dark, ominous presence. Lightning flashes overhead, followed by a loud rumble of thunder. I lift my face to the haunted sky, and scream.

I scream for those we have lost.

For what I am.

I scream so loud that I will never forget those who are gone.

Branding their memories into my soul forever.

The next crack of thunder drowns out my scream.

The sky opens up and rain comes pouring down, soaking me in a matter of seconds.

A ripple of energy strikes the air around me as white hot coils of agony tear through me. Wind rages, rolling over the ground, kicking up debris everywhere it goes. Trees sway and bend, giving in to the storm around us. Alex's hand lands on my shoulder and squeezes. My gaze snaps to her tear-stricken face and we wrap our arms around each other. My fingers dig into her shoulders, trying to find purchase to keep me grounded. It seems death follows me everywhere. Everyone I love seems to be taken from me. *Who will be next?*

This is why I stopped making friends and connections when I came to Portland. I was doing fine until I found Lukas and the pack. Now I have people I care about again. People to lose.

I'm not sure how long we cry over our lost friend, but nobody disturbs us. I can feel worry and affection from Lukas like a soft caress down our bond. The rain slows and the wind dies down, leaving behind a darkened sky.

My face is puffy, my eyes swollen by the time we pull apart. Lukas and the others are standing close by, guarding our backs. Lukas's eyes lock with mine and the emotion shining back at me almost makes me start crying all over again.

"I'm sorry, sweetheart."

"Me, too," I hiccup, wiping at my face.

Lukas helps me to my feet and walks me over to a truck waiting not far away. I climb into the back seat with Alex, gripping her hand in mine, and staring out the window as Lukas and Gabe get in the front and start the short journey back to the compound.

As I sit here, everything rages inside of me—anger, guilt, sorrow, loss, so many emotions. I won't hide, I will fight, I will do what I have to do to make sure this Order is a threat no more. Astraea *will not* grow up with this hanging over her head, she will not lose another person she loves to them. I will find Hera, and I will destroy her.

"She will pay," I promise through clenched teeth. Hera declared war in her attempts to kill me, in sending others to attack these innocent people. My people. I will not hide who I am anymore. I am going to fight.

Lukas turns toward me, a mask of fury taking over his expression, our emotions adding fuel to each other's rage. His gaze burns into mine and his body goes rigid, an alpha ready to take on the enemy. I push down the rising well of emotions and wrap my anger around me like armor. We have a goddess to find.

CHAPTER THIRTY TWO

The drive back to the compound was quick, the scenery blurring past the window. When the cars finally come to a stop, we all clamber out and the sound of car doors slamming echoes around us. Lukas's arms go around me, leading me into the warm barn. Gabe goes to Alex, guiding her inside towards a seat by the fire. The small community that lives here has gathered, waiting. Children are huddled among the adults, the fear in their little faces hard to miss. They've had their haven compromised. They look relieved at the sight of us returning. A few of them can't hide the shock on their faces as they look at me, and I realize I'm covered in a mixture of black and red blood.

Another car pulls to a stop outside, gravel flicking up, and the next second Roan is rushing through the doors, his eyes wildly scanning the area, until he finds Alex. She hasn't said a word on the drive back, but then again, neither have I. There's nothing to say. We lost Asena. She is gone. My eyes follow Roan as he storms over, scooping Alex into his arms, his head buried in her neck. The red haired shifter takes a seat, Alex bundled in his arms, her face hidden in his neck. My heart lurches at the tender moment causing tears to spring to my eyes.

Lukas turns me around, guiding me into a chair, and crouches in front of me. His hand reaches up, pushing my hair over my shoulder.

His gaze is so heavy with emotion that my tears spill over. I watch as his eyes follow their trail then travel to my blood-soaked shirt. A noise of distress escapes him, and he rips his shirt over his head. Then he reaches for mine, lifts it over my head, and I have no energy left to bother being embarrassed.

Next second, his warm shirt is pulled down over my head. I close my eyes, pressing the fabric to my nose, soaking in his comforting scent.

'*I'll be back,*' he whispers, as I felt a light brush of his lips on my forehead.

Lukas stands and looks over to Gabe, pointing to me before he turns and strides outside, shirtless. I assume he's going to get a spare shirt from the car. I glue my eyes to the door, waiting for him to return when Gabe takes a seat next to me, holding out a bottle of water. Blinking, I look up into his warm brown eyes.

'*Thank you.*'

I don't think I can formulate any words at the moment. The lump in my throat is the size of a boulder. Gabe nods and I can't seem to get a read on him. It's like he's shut himself off from me.

I sense Lukas entering the barn again and peer up, watching him approach us while tugging a shirt on.

"I need you to come with me to interrogate the Salem pack," Lukas says, stopping in front of us. I stand, my legs tremble at the movement, seeming weak. I am drained both physically and emotionally, but I refuse to sit this out.

Lukas shakes his head. "No, I meant Gabe."

Frowning, I glance to Gabe, then back to Lukas. "I'm coming."

"I want you to get some rest."

"No."

Lukas sighs. "Nesrin."

My heart clenches when he uses my name. I can't remember the last time he called me by my name. It's always *sweetheart* or *freckles*. The hurt must show on my face, or he senses it through the bond, because he steps forward, hands clasping my cheeks as he cups my face gently.

"You're exhausted. You need rest. Gabe and I can handle this."

"But I need to be there," I whisper.

He bends so we are at eye level, his face close to mine as he studies me. "Why?"

"So I can feel like I'm doing something." I hate the way my voice cracks. But I can't just sit here doing nothing.

"Gabe needs to get into their minds, sort through their memories and thoughts. See if he can sort the truth from lies. It's not something I want you to see."

I understand, but there is no way I am going to be sitting around, not when I can be helping. I owe as much to Asena to find those responsible for her death.

A loud commotion outside stops Lukas from replying. He drops his hands from my face, and I immediately miss the warmth of his touch. The three of us swiftly make our way outside to see a wall of shifters facing off against Nero and Nikolas. When my eyes lock with Nero, he visibly relaxes. His golden eyes take me in, and I know he senses something is wrong.

Nikolas is visibly trembling, sensing my distress because I've linked us, not only as pack, but as part of me. Nikolas takes a step toward us when a wolf snaps at him, making my heart lurch.

Lukas's voice is commanding when he speaks, "They are family. Let them through. I promise no harm will come from them."

The shifters all spin to gape at their alpha. I can sense their unease and concern, but I want them to know they are safe. I'm not sure how to get that point across, though, especially given the attack a few hours ago.

Lukas stands tall, letting his power roll over everyone, his dominance easing their fears. The shifters back away, parting so Nikolas and Nero can approach. They move slowly, not wanting to startle the shifters that are understandably already on edge. Nikolas's arms go around me, and I take comfort in his embrace.

"Ma reine, what happened?" he begs, his chin resting on top of my head.

His hand moves up and down my back as I simply shake my head, burying it deeper in the vampire's chest. I can't speak right now. If I did, the dam would break, and I'm not sure it would ever stop.

Lukas, reading me well, speaks for me. "The Salem pack attacked the compound. They are claiming they were forced. We are unsure by whom, but we will find out." He releases a long sigh before continuing, "Then a werewolf attacked. Nesrin and some others fought it and were able to kill it, but . . . Asena died." Lukas's voice catches on her name and I squeeze my eyes closed.

Nikolas's hand stalls on my back. "Oh, I'm so sorry, ma reine."

"Where are they?" Nero growls.

The wave of magic coming from him has me lifting my head. His eyes soften when he sees me looking at him, and I step away from Nikolas. A single tear slips down my cheek, and I quickly move to brush it away. But not quickly enough. Nero's eyes zero in on it before I can wipe it away and a rumbling noise comes from him.

Lukas's arm goes around my shoulder as he pulls me into his body. His grief from the loss of his friend and pack member is easy to feel. He is trying to shield me from his pain, but it's there as if it were my own. Sharp and deep. Being the alpha means he has to hide those feelings. Everyone's eyes are on us, on him. The alpha.

I reach down our bond and flood him with love and support, Lukas's arm spasms around me. Bending, he places the softest kiss on the top of my head. I may be heartbroken, but so is he. I can also feel his guilt. Guilt at his relief that it wasn't me lying motionless on the road.

"We have them locked up. I was on my way to interrogate them," Lukas replies.

"I'm joining you," Nero states. I watch as he clenches and unclenches his hands, a mask of authority rolling over him.

"This is Lukas's territory. He will decide, Nero," I reply. I don't need the other shifters thinking we have lost control of our lands.

Nero bows his head. "Of course. I apologize, daughter of light, alpha."

Lukas looks over to a building that stands alone off in the distance, away from the other houses and common areas. That must be where the Salem pack is being held.

"You can come," he tells Nero. "I think we will need your help. From what I was told, they are being particularly forthcoming."

"I can wait with Nesrin," Nikolas offers, and I shake my head, pulling away from Lukas.

I glance at each of them as I speak. "I'm coming."

"Sweetheart, I don't think–"

"I'm *coming!*" I snap before he can finish. Pulling my shoulders back, I ignore the crushing sadness currently seizing my chest. I notice pride shining in Nero's eyes as he observes me, but all I feel is a lead ball of guilt sitting in my stomach.

"Okay," Lukas relents with a sigh. He grabs my hand, threading our fingers together, and motions for the others to follow. The five of us make our way to the building where the Salem pack is being kept. We are silent as we walk, each of us absorbing the impact of the day. When we push through the doors, we're met with an open room. There are two doors on the far end, which I assume lead to the kitchen and toilets. This must be some sort of function center.

I draw my eyes to the girls seated along the back wall, their hands and feet bound in iron. I frown. "Who put the irons on?" I ask.

"We did," the leopard shifter I met at the mall tells me.

I frown, stepping closer. "What's your name? You never answered me before."

She tips her head back, resting it on the wall behind her. "Beth."

"Why did you chain yourselves up, Beth?" I ask, curious as to why they would put themselves through that sort of pain. Especially before they can fully heal from their wounds. I can feel the tremors working through their bodies, my healing magic aching to reach out to them. I push it down. Now is *not* the time for that.

"To show you we're not a threat," she replies.

Lukas growls from behind me and Beth lifts her head from the wall, taking in the four men surrounding me, her eyes widening in shock and fear. Some of the other shifters drop their shoulders, hunching in on themselves, intimidated by Lukas, I know from experience how formidable Lukas is.

"You said someone has been whispering in your heads that they made it so you can't leave the area until we are dealt with?" I question. My tongue is heavy in my mouth, my jaw tight. I release a deep breath, trying to calm myself. I can feel the beginning of a headache forming behind my eyes.

Beth's eyes dart back to me. "You. We only had to eliminate you."

Lukas snarls, and Beth drops her gaze. Nero steps forward and crouches down in front of her. Beth's eyes slowly track up his frame to his face. She swallows, fear shining in her eyes. Nero's hand reaches out, and she jerks back her head, hitting the wall behind her.

Nero stiffens. "If you bite me, it will be the last thing you do," he warns. "If you don't hold still, it will be painful," he adds as an afterthought.

Beth sits stock still, she doesn't blink or twitch. I don't even think she's breathing at this point. Nero's palm lands on her forehead, his eyes closed, and I watch in fascination as a golden light hovers around their connection. Nero's tattoos swirl over his skin like smoke. We all stand here holding our breath as Nero . . . does whatever it is that he's doing. After a long minute, he pulls back. His hand drops and he twists to stare at me, his eyes glowing with magic. He is most definitely a powerful fae, so why he's helping me is a complete mystery.

"She is telling the truth. There is a curse on this pack. Whoever placed it made sure they could enter the pack's minds and torment them with thoughts and images, driving them insane."

"How do we break it?" I ask, feelings of defeat rising in me, and I want to cry again, but it will do no good.

Lukas steps forward, his fists clenched tightly at his sides. "I want you to tell me everything you know. Everything she whispered to you. If you do this, we will free you of this curse and let you leave."

'Lukas, how are we meant to break the curse?'

'Sweetheart, I have faith you can do it. I've watched you make a vampire part of the pack, so this will be a piece of cake.'

My eyes bug, and my mouth drops open. Like, I love that he has so much faith in me, but . . .

"Me?" I say out loud, and several eyes glance my way. I blush, shooting Lukas a look.

"And if we don't?" Beth inquires, fire in her brown eyes.

The cut on her chest has barely healed, along with her other injuries. The chains aren't helping; they're slowing their healing. My hands itch to heal the wounds, but I curl them into fists.

Lukas's eyes gleam with promise and Gabe steps forward, shifting in a swirl of golden mist. Watching him shift is amazing. His is a different type of magic than what we have.

"If you don't, *he* will get in your heads. He will make you wish you'd never set foot on my land."

The Salem pack sits staring in horror at the kitsune standing before them. Everyone knows what kitsune are capable of, and as nice as Gabe is, not even I like to test how far he can go.

"I thought kitsunes were a myth, but he's real," one shifter whispers.

"I thought they had been hunted to extinction," another says in awe.

Beth sits forward, baring her teeth. I can see she's about to say something to make things worse. I step forward, crouching in front of her. A storm brews inside of me, a whorl of guilt, shame, anger. It's a maelstrom of emotions. I survived, but Asena didn't. I wasn't able to keep her safe.

Next thing I know, words burst out of me with so much force my chest aches. Magic pushes to the surface, and I know my eyes are glowing by the reflection in Beth's eyes. "Asena died today, she *just* died. And for what? I lost a friend, and I *won't* lose anymore!"

Beth's eyes widen, and guilt flashes across her face. She hangs her head, her brown bob forming a curtain over her face. "I'm sorry you lost your friend," she says, her voice softening.

"Thanks," I whisper back.

"I will tell you what I know," she says, looking me in the eye.

'Take the chains off them,' I say to Lukas.

'Sweetheart, maybe–'

'No. I can't have them in pain while I'm here. My magic is desperate to heal them.'

Lukas and Gabe move forward to start removing the chains. They don't seem to have much effect on the two of them. I regard the feline shifters carefully, sensing their relief at being freed of the chains.

The cut along Beth's chest, the one my light sword caused, starts to heal, the skin stitching back together. I can see that her body wants to sag against the wall, but she's holding back.

Lukas grabs the chains from Gabe, who moves over to a massive chest in the corner, opening it up. Lukas strolls over, biceps bulging as he lifts the chains to place them inside. Nero and Nikolas stand silently by the door, watching the scene.

When Beth finally notices Nikolas, she gestures to him, inquiring, "Why is there a vampire here?"

I shrug. "It's none of your concern."

"Shifters rarely associate with the bloodsuckers, and if they do, it's for business. Do you plan to wipe our memories?"

I jerk back in surprise. "Why would we do that?"

Beth shrugs, looking over at Nikolas. "It's what I would do."

"Well, that's *not* what we will be doing." I glance over to Lukas. "Right?"

Lukas's lips twitch, ever so slightly. "Right."

Relieved, I turn back to the Salem pack and take in the others. There are a dozen of them, all young—I'd place them in their twenties, but with shifters, age can be difficult to guess.

Lukas picks up a chair and places it in front of Beth, gesturing for me to take a seat. I smile gratefully. My legs wobble, and I'm sure they'll give out at any minute.

Lukas's worry trickles down the bond and I send my affection back. I'll be fine. I can rest later. This really can't wait, plus, I need them off pack lands as soon as possible. I won't have our pack feeling unsafe by making the shifters who just attacked them need to stay any longer than necessary.

"Where are you from?" Lukas asks, crossing his arms over his broad chest.

Beth's gaze falls upon him, her eyes brimming with reverence.

"My pack resides on the edge of Salem, in a large home with plenty of acreage. We are all outcasts and runaways, all thirteen of us."

"Are you the Leader?" he asks.

Beth inclines her head. "I am. It is my job to look after my pack, and I failed. We were taken advantage of by a crazy woman, since I didn't recognize the threat until it was too late."

"It's not your fault," one of the girls whispers.

I lean forward and rest my hand on Beth's arm. "What happened?"

"An old lady showed up at our doorstep one afternoon. I let her in, assuming she was merely lost. I had made plans to take her into town. The last thing any of us remember is her face before everything went black. We woke up much later on the floor."

Beth's gaze travels over her pack, and she sighs heavily. "It took us a while to get our bearings, but once the fog cleared, we knew something had happened that the old lady wasn't who she had seemed. We kept getting visions and flashes of you."

"Her voice whispering in the back of our minds, telling us about all the terrible things you've done."

"We tried ignoring it, but we were slowly going mad," one girl says, finally lifting her gaze. Geez, she couldn't be older than fifteen.

"The voice grew quiet for a while once we relented and got on the road heading for Portland. Once we got here though, we had orders to take you out. 'Destroy the witch responsible for casting the spell over the alpha and manipulating the Portland shifters. Ruthlessly slaughtering innocent magical creatures for her own gain,'" Beth says angrily. "She picked us because all we had was each other. No big pack, no family. We were loners."

"Hera's been tormenting you for a while, huh?" I ask.

"Hera?"

I give a slight dip of my chin in acknowledgement.

"Like, Hera the goddess?" Beth asks incredulously.

"One and only," Nero says sarcastically.

"I came to you that day on the streets to understand you better. From the time we'd spent watching you, we didn't see any of what this voice was saying. You were kind and loyal. You stood by your friends. We saw when you healed a few magical creatures and demanded no payment in return. Now, you have a vampire, a kitsune, an alpha, and whatever he is at your back," she says, gesturing to Nero. "All ready to kill any of us if we so much as breathe the wrong way in your direction."

A sense of pride washes over me that I recognize as Lukas's emotions. I glance over my shoulder at him, seeing admiration shining in his eyes.

Turning back to Beth, I can't suppress my next question out of plain curiosity. "Why were you acting so weird that day at the mall?"

Her cheeks seem to redden in embarrassment as she stares at me. "She wouldn't stop talking. She was insistent that I kill you then and there. I was struggling to block her out. I was just about ready to claw my ears apart," Beth confesses.

I've heard enough, and so has this pack. They have been victimized by the cruelty of Hera. I close my eyes, letting the magic rise to the surface. This is the goddess's magic. Opening my eyes, the world has taken on that different hue. I've been finding it easier to distinguish between the powers residing inside of me. Which is goddess, witch, and fae.

I blink at the feline shifters in front of me, each just sitting with their backs against the wall. Surprise and shock shows on each of their faces.

Beth tilts her head, regarding me. "What are you?" she whispers.

"A healer," I reply, fixating on that swirl of red and black magic surrounding her mind. I wasn't able to see it before, but now I can. The curse clings to each of them, and I frown, searching for the threads that make up the curse. I slowly begin picking at them one at a time, sweat beading my brow as I work tirelessly to free each shifter from Hera's snare. Lukas's hand lands on my shoulder at one point, and I realize I am sagging in the chair. He lets his magic flow freely into me, lending me his strength, and I am so grateful I could weep.

When the last thread falls away from the last shifter, I release a deep breath. My eyes falling shut, Lukas's arms wrap under my knees and behind my back as he lifts me from the chair. His voice is distant, as I hear him direct Nero and Nikolas to see the shifters home.

I think I hear Beth whisper her thanks, but I can't be sure as I drift off to sleep cradled in my mate's arms, hoping to wake up to find that all of this was just a really bad dream.

CHAPTER THIRTY THREE

I 'm still cradled in Lukas's lap when the car pulls to a stop at our house. Gabe opens the door for us, and Lukas steps out, keeping a firm grip on me, and carries me through the silence of late night into our home. I don't even bother arguing that I can walk. I know he won't release me.

"Roan took Alex home," Gabe says, closing the door after us. Lukas places me on my feet and I feel a strong urge to race over to Alex's home and make sure she's okay, but I know Roan will take care of her. I am probably the last person she would want to see, anyway. Suzy stands from the sofa where Astraea and Malachite are curled up asleep.

"Nesrin," she whispers hastily, moving around the sofa and wrapping me in her warm arms. I bury my head in her purple hair, breathing in the scent of strawberries.

"It's all my fault," I croak.

"No, it's not. You can't take that blame, Nesrin. This is the work of a crazy person."

"I couldn't save her."

"You can't be expected to save everyone, Nesrin," she says, pulling back and gripping my shoulders, giving them a little shake.

"What good is my magic if I can't save the people I love?" I hiccup.

"Oh, Nesrin." Suzy's eyes fill with her own tears.

There is a sudden change in the air, charges of electricity prickling my skin. Someone is portlling in, which means it's either Leila or another fucking god.

Suzy drops her arms and Lukas immediately steps forward, wrapping an arm around my middle and pulling me into him. Not a second later, Leila steps out from a mass of shadows.

Without looking up, she brushes dust from her arms. "Hades sent me a message to meet tomorrow night. He found Eris," Leila tells me, her eyes lifting to scan the room.

She hesitates before asking, "What happened?"

"Asena is dead," I whisper, raising my eyes to hers.

She is across the room in a moment, pulling me into her arms. "Oh my god, Nesrin. I'm so sorry," she coos in my ear.

Resting my head on her shoulder, I squeeze my eyes shut to hold the tears at bay. Leila pulls back and grabs hold of my hands. "We will get justice for everyone who has suffered Hera's wrath, I promise."

The front door flies open, and I pull back in time to see Kyra race into the room, her mass of curls in disarray around her head, as she skids to a stop. When she sees me, her hands move to her face, covering her mouth, as she shakes her head.

"I'm sorry," I choke out, my face crumpling.

Sander appears behind her, wrapping his arms around her as she falls to the floor, a horrible wail falling from her lips. Sander's warm eyes lock onto Lukas for confirmation, then his head sags, his arms wrapping tighter around his wife.

"Where's Zee?" I ask the room, wiping my eyes. Zee is going to take this hard. Even though he called things off with Asena, they were still good friends, and they still shared a bond.

'He needed space, time to grieve,' Lukas tells me down the bond.

I hate that he is hurting and there is nothing I can do to fix it. I can't help the way my bottom lip wobbles and I take two giant steps, leaping back into Lukas's arms. He wraps his arms around my middle, holding me off the ground, then he guides my legs around his hips.

'You need rest, freckles.'

'I know.'

"Suzy, could you stay and take Astraea to her room if she wakes?" Lukas murmurs over my head.

"Of course," Suzy nods, whispering back.

Turning, Lukas moves through the room, carrying me up the stairs to our room. He walks straight to the bathroom and turns on the shower, getting the temperature right, all while I hang on to him like my life depends on it.

Gently placing me on my feet, he cups my face, his soft lips dropping to mine in a tender caress. Slowly, he slips his shirt from my body, tossing it onto the floor. He undresses me with such care I want to cry again, but I don't think I have any more tears left in me. My hands land on his shoulders to steady myself as he slips off my jeans. Lukas's warm hands trail up my legs and pause at every bruise, letting out a low menacing growl before laying a soft kiss on each one. Lukas's massive hands encircle my waist as he stands and turns me toward the shower. I step in, hearing the rustling of his own clothes before he steps in behind me, his arm brushing past me to reach for the shampoo.

Slowly and gently, he lathers my hair. Tears track down my face, and I let my head fall back. Lukas turns me to face him and backs me into the water, rinsing the bubbles from my hair. My eyes fall closed as he works to clean the blood and dirt from my skin. With my eyes still closed, I feel the soft touch of his lips on mine, and my lips part in a sigh. He pulls me into him, our bodies pressed together, not an inch of space between us. I run my hands up his soapy chest and loop around his neck. Lukas's soft touches turn possessive, and electricity runs over my skin, making my nipples pebble.

My mind and body want nothing more than to get lost in his touch. To forget tonight ever happened, if only for a moment. I push the sob down in my throat, the feeling making pressure build in my chest, as if it would crack apart at any moment. I deepen the kiss, letting all my emotions go before they overwhelm me.

I moan into his mouth as his hands move to my ass, lifting me so that my legs can wrap around his waist. He spins, pressing me against the shower wall, and the contrast of his hot body and the cold tiles makes me gasp.

Breaking the kiss, Lukas peppers kisses down my neck and shoulder, grinding his erection against me. I dig my heels into his ass, lifting so I can have him inside of me. My nails claw at his shoulders in my desperation to get him closer. I need to feel him, all of him, to remember I'm alive, he is alive. I'm panting, my skin flushed with need and desire. Lukas nudges my entrance, staring into my eyes as he pushes inside of me, his eyes glowing with otherworldly power.

'I thought I was going to lose you,' he murmurs, resting his forehead on mine. He moves at a gentle pace, not taking his eyes from mine.

'Never.'

'When I felt your fear and pain, I–'

My fingertips graze his cheeks as I peer into his eyes. "I'm okay. I'm here," I reply out loud.

I need to forget. To escape the pain before I drown in it.

The thought must be conveyed to Lukas because his mouth drops to mine. Our lips meet again, this time more desperately, his thrusts increasing in strength. A tremble works its way through me, loving the wet slide of our bodies as we move together. I keep kissing him, not wanting to pull away for fear of the tears that will come. My sorrow and heartache seem to pour out of me with that kiss, my emotions like a whirlwind inside of me. Lukas's hands squeeze my ass, tilting my hips. The slight change in position has him hitting that spot deep inside of me. I break the kiss, dropping my head against the wall, my eyes rolling back as waves of pleasure surge through me. My inner walls grip Lukas as my climax rips through me. Lukas doesn't pick up the tempo, he keeps a steady pace as he pounds into me. The water beats down on us as I ride the intense waves of pleasure. Lukas drops his forehead to the wall next to mine, biting down on my shoulder. The suddenness of it tearing another orgasm from me. I gasp, my muscles clamping down hard on Lukas. He grunts against my skin, his movements becoming frantic and it brings a flood of emotions to the surface. Lukas's groan echoes around us as he floods me with his cum, his breathing ragged. Our arms wrap tightly around each other. The warmth of our embrace combined with our panting breaths feels comforting.

CHAPTER THIRTY FOUR

The following night, we meet Marcus at the entrance to Forest Park. It seems like forever since we last saw him. But he's been lying low, trying to locate his father and the rest of the coven to no avail. Claudia got out while she could and is staying with Marcus, along with some other witches and mages, who realize something isn't quite right with the coven.

Before getting out of the car, I shrug on my leather jacket, checking that all the potions and hidden dagger are sorted. Then I reach down, fastening the strap around my thigh to hold my favorite dagger. My gaze moves to Lukas, and I catch his deep green eyes observing me.

"Are you ready for this?" he asks softly.

I shrug, tightening the strap a bit more. "We'll find out," I reply honestly.

I sense Gabe and Jameson as they approach the car and twist reaching for the handle. Lukas's palm lands on my leg, stalling me. I turn to glance over my shoulder at him. His expression is full of worry. "Please don't put yourself in danger tonight. Let's just get the information we need."

I feel my throat constrict and offer a small nod of agreement.

Reaching over, Lukas grabs me around the middle and hoists me over the middle of the car so I can sit across his lap. Before I can speak, his hand slips into my hair and his mouth is on mine. The kiss is slow and sweet. The rigidity in my muscles melts away and I relax in his hold. There's a tap on the window and I glance up to meet Gabe's eyes. Okay, I guess it's time to go. I move to get off Lukas's lap, but his hands hold me still.

His voice is firm and full of resolve as he promises, "We will end this. I won't lose you."

I lean forward, brushing my lips over his. "I love you."

Lukas's desire flows down our bond, but it's still accompanied by worry. We get out of the car and make our way toward where Marcus is standing at the entrance to the park. His hands in the pockets of his pants, rocking back on his heels, he takes in the four of us.

"Should I have brought my own backup?" he says casually, though I can see the worry lines around his eyes. He doesn't like being outnumbered, which I can understand, because I wouldn't either, but he knows I won't let harm come to him unless it were warranted.

"We have been having a bad run, so we didn't want to be caught off guard," Lukas replies.

Before anyone can say more, Hades and Leila step out of a portal, the former taking in our small group and smirking as he adjusts his cufflinks.

Hades' intelligent golden eyes meet mine. "Ready to meet another god?"

"As ready as I'll ever be," I mutter dryly.

Hades cocks his head, raising an eyebrow in question. I flush and gesture for him to lead the way. There is something in his eyes, something I can't place, that makes me uneasy.

Lukas chuckles, '*So fearless.*'

We all follow Hades into Forest Park. The meeting place is in an area of the forest referred to as the witch's castle. It's a set of old ruins dating back to the 1950s. The area is thought to be haunted, but I know better. As we approach the ruins, I scan the area. It's so dark in the forest and, unlike the others, I don't have amazing night vision. I summon an orb of light and send it ahead. Hades looks over his shoulder at me, the light playing with the angles of his face. I can't quite make out the smirk on his face, but I know it's there.

Looking up ahead, I see a woman pacing in circles and muttering to herself. Her long brown hair cascades down her tall and slender frame. Her skin had an unearthly glow that seemed to mesmerize me. Brown eyes widen in surprise as she takes us all in. "Hades, you brought company?"

"Yes. I'd like you to meet my daughter, Leila, and her sister, Nesrin. They are unfortunately Hera's current conquest, the bloodline cursed to die."

There's a heavy thud in my chest at that little bit of information, and I watch as Eris's already pale face drains of color.

"Your daughter?" she stammers. She looks between the two, as if trying to piece it together.

Hades shrugs, unfazed at the fact that he just outed his secret. "Adopted daughter. I saved her from a fire that would have claimed her life when she was only a child."

Eris bites her thumbnail, which doesn't strike me as a very godlike thing to do. I arch an eyebrow, casting a look up at Lukas, his expression set in a frown directed at Hades and Eris.

Eris seems to be considering something, then her eyes cut to Hades. "You . . . " she says, trailing off.

I see Hades's eyes flare in warning at Eris. I glance to Leila to see if she notices it as well. She is frowning at the two.

What is that about?

"Eris thinks she knows something, but she doesn't," Hades says by way of warning, setting my nerves on edge. I've given up at this point trying to keep my inner thoughts to myself.

"What does she think she knows?" Leila asks. But Eris turns, pacing again, muttering under her breath.

"This is all my fault," Eris whispers.

"Oh, is it?" I snap, getting frustrated with her.

"I didn't realize it would get so out of hand," Eris says, her long brown hair seeming to almost float around her as she turns to look at me, shifting nervously in front of us. I'm not buying her innocent act.

"That's bullshit, Eris," Hades snaps. "Haven't you learned your lesson?"

"Hades," Eris pleads.

"No. You know what Hera is like. How jealous she gets, especially over Zeus and his lovers. She can't control herself," Hades growls, making Eris flinch. I have no sympathy for her.

"I know, I know. I'm sorry. I didn't think when I . . . I mean . . . " Eris stutters.

Rage clouding my judgment, I step forward.

"What did you *do?*" I grind out through clenched teeth. My hands ball into fists at my side, magic buzzing under my skin, rising with my temper. Everyone is tense, poised to strike. Both gods turn to me. Eris has a look of surprise on her face, but Hades just looks perplexed by my outburst.

"I . . . told Hera that Althaea's descendants were Zeus's. It is the truth, after all. Hera obviously can't touch Althaea without consequence, so she set her sight on the descendants. Especially after I told her Zeus would give her up to claim them. That Blanchette's descendants would cause her ruin."

"And she believed you?" I ask incredulously.

"Well, I think her actions over the last few centuries would say she did," Eris replies mockingly. Crossing her arms, her facade of innocence falls away as she attempts to stare me down.

I am not so easily intimidated.

My anger flares, burning a path over my body. Leila steps to my side, raising her chin. Eris looks us both over before continuing. "It helped that Zeus was smitten with Blanchette, and for once it was never in a sexual way. I think he knew on some level she was kin. Then Blanchette disappeared, and Zeus asked after her for a while, but he's fickle. It didn't take long for him to forget all about her." Her voice drips with disdain.

Indignation ignites in the pit of my stomach and my hands tremble as I unconsciously summon my magic, that white light, to the surface. "Why? Why do any of it?" I demand as my light sword forms in my hand, an extension of my magic, my soul.

Eris's eyes widen as she takes in the blade. Her gaze swings to Hades in question.

Hades shrugs. "Answer her question, Eris."

Eris looks back at me, fear in her eyes, and that makes me feel good. Damn good. Her voice is meek when she answers, much different from the confidence she spoke with moments ago. "I'm the goddess of chaos. I saw an opportunity and took it. Blanchette, she got what she deserved, she left me. She decided that a life in this world with these lowly mortals was better than me, than Olympus. And I would do it all over again," she replies, squaring her shoulders and raising her chin, looking down at me.

I see her hands moving, just slight movements, but I catch a glimpse of the sickle. I don't even realize I'm moving until I've buried my blade deep in Eris's chest, her eyes widening in shock, her mouth gaping open. As I stare into her eyes, my mind flitters back to the fire that killed Niamh and Hunter. To Asena's lifeless eyes staring up at the darkening sky. To Grace's funeral, and how losing her caused Astraea to have a magical meltdown.

"You'll get what you deserve as well." I push up to my toes and whisper in her ear, "I hope you burn in hell."

I push my magic into the blade, and it begins to vibrate with light. Fractures of light move outward from the blade, spreading like cracks splintering the ice. Eris's body seems to be covered in them before her whole body becomes only light. A pulse of energy shoots outward, knocking everyone off their feet. I am the only one left standing. Eris is gone, reduced to embers floating on the wind. My blade blinks out and silence reigns around me.

I just killed a god.

Hades stands fluidly and regards me carefully, his head cocked to the side, and his emotions, as always, locked down tight. "That was unexpected."

"She fucking *deserved* it," I snap, glaring at Hades and daring him to say differently.

"I didn't say she didn't. Merely stating that I'm shocked you killed her."

Lukas breaks our stare off. His features are cold and murderous, even in the dark. "What happens when a god dies or is killed?"

"A new one is born to take their place, though no gods have been killed in a very, very, long time." Hades eyes me suspiciously, "Gods are almost impossible to kill. Seems that fancy sword of yours is powerful enough to kill a god."

Crap on a cracker.

I keep my mouth shut. I don't think Hades knows about my family's ties to Tuatha Dé Danann. Unless Leila's said something, but I don't think she has. My mind drifts to the shock in Eris's eyes when she realized what I'd done. That image is going to be burned into my brain forever. I've never killed anyone before now, but my anger at all the pain she caused generations upon generations of my family and others overtook me. I swallow over the knot forming in my throat. Lukas reaches out and grips my hand in a subtle move to show he is with me.

Leila and Lukas move to my side. Leila's hand links with mine and squeezes. Lukas's arm brushes mine, and that small touch has me feeling so much.

It's Gabe who asks the question we all wanted to know the answer to. "How do we find Hera?"

Marcus coughs, drawing our attention. "My father is meeting with the head of the Order on Sunday night."

That's three days away.

"Then we will just have to be ready." My focus turns to Lukas. '*I need this to be over.*'

Leila and Hades shadow away, leaving the rest of us to walk back to the car, which is fine by me. It gives me a bit of time to process what just happened. I can sense Jameson's eyes on me, and do my best to ignore it. Gabe and Lukas lead the way, and Marcus walks by my side, his gaze every so often looking my way, but I pay them no mind. I am not in the mood to talk.

Lukas and Gabe stop abruptly, causing me to stumble. Marcus grabs my arm to steady me, making Jameson growl low behind us. I peer around them to figure out what made them stop.

"Well, well, well. What do we have here? Midnight stroll for the Scooby Gang?" Anna mocks, pushing off the side of Lukas's truck. My hands clench at my sides. She really picked the wrong night to torment me. Marcus takes up a position in front of me alongside Gabe and Lukas.

"What are you doing here, Anna?" Marcus growls.

As she steps forward, a coldness blossoms in my chest and a thread of light shoots from me toward her, much like it did with Nikolas in the club. No one else reacts to the trail of magic, so it must just be me who can see it. Although, Lukas likely does sense my nerves through the bond, because I watch as he stiffens and turns slightly toward me. I draw in a shaky breath and move around Lukas's bulky form, getting a good look at Anna under the streetlight. She seems about the same as last time I saw her, that smirk firmly in place. From one blink to the next, my vision shifts, and I can see the darkness invading her soul. The mass almost seems unnatural, like it's more than just the darkness that naturally resides within her. I gasp as I realize she's under a compulsion spell.

Marcus stops arguing with Anna and his attention moves to me, his brow furrowed. "What is it?"

I don't speak as I push past the men and take a few steps toward her. I see the moment she realizes I know something is off. Her smirk slowly melts away and fear overtakes her eyes.

'Gabe.'

Gabe seems to understand what I need, and he uses his magic to paralyze her. Through my mate bond, I sense Lukas's surprise then understanding.

Marcus, though, is still confused, and more than a little worried by how tensely he's standing. Marcus moves to intercept me as I make my way forward. I lift my hand, freezing him in place. "I won't hurt her. Trust me."

"What if she hurts you?" Jameson pipes up, unease clear in his voice.

I turn my eerie white eyes his way and he holds his hands up. "Point taken."

Marcus looks to his sister and then back to me. I see the worry there. He did just watch me kill Eris. The tug in my chest is becoming harder to ignore, but I need him to trust me before I proceed.

"Marcus?" I snap, beads of sweat forming on my brow.

His head dips and his eyes close, understanding what I need. "I trust you."

I drop my hand, my entire body warm as a sense of purpose hits me in the chest. I move forward, approaching Anna, coils of Gabe's magic holding her still. Anna's eyes dart around frantically then land on Marcus.

"You can't let her hurt me. Marcus!!" she shrieks.

I don't worry about anyone else; Lukas has my back. My focus is entirely on Anna as I take that last step. My hands raise to grip both sides of her head, and she screams, trying in vain to break my hold. Fear and frustration well in her eyes as I close the gap between us. My hands sink into her hair, my thumbs pressing into her temples. I close my eyes and release the hold on my magic. It flows freely into Anna, the brilliant bright light surrounding her mind, eating away at the compulsion spell. The spell fights back, but my power is stronger. I grit my teeth, pushing more of my light forward. I can hear her wailing as I continue, but it sounds so far away. Marcus yells from behind me, and I feel Lukas's guilt slithering down the bond, and I falter for a moment. That moment costs me, giving Anna the opening she needs to free herself from Gabe's grip on her and take me to the ground. My back hits the pavement hard, but I tighten my grip, willing myself not to break our connection again. I'm not sure what would happen if I did. I grunt, trying to keep her still. My eyes widen as Gabe suddenly materializes behind her.

Panic hits me square in the chest. "I can't break the connection."

He seems to understand and helps me to roll her under me, so I am straddling her, my hands fused to her head. My eyes burn into hers as I wrap the light around the spell, unraveling the last of the compulsion spell. I tilt my head, studying her as I work the spell, and then I see it tucked away in the back. It's like a cage. It isn't a compulsion spell at all, it's a *containment* spell. Frowning, I move through Anna's mind, slowly approaching the cage. I lift my hand, running it over the bars when I hear a noise inside, I step closer to peer inside, and gasp as I stare at Anna huddled in the corner.

"Anna?"

Anna's gaze snaps up to mine and she jolts forward, her eyes pleading, hands wrapping around the bars.

"Please, you have to kill it."

"Kill it? The spell?"

Anna shakes her head and points behind me, I frown and spin around just as a dark shape comes darting toward me and collides with my chest, the impact knocking me backward and I fall past the floor of her mind, landing back in my body. My eyes snap open and I growl, anger surging through me like hot lava.

Incantations fly from my mouth as I drive my magic deeper into what isn't even a containment spell holding Anna hostage. A fucking demon has been taking her body hostage, and I plan to expel it.

The demon is strong. It won't let go of Anna easily. My light seems to hurt it, so I wrap it around the demon, making it coil tighter and tighter while I simultaneously work on unraveling the spell keeping Anna prisoner in her own mind.

When the last of the containment spell falls away, Anna bursts forward, driving into the demon from behind. The combination of our magic and will is all it takes. The demon shrieks and thrashes violently as its form disappears bit by bit until nothing remains.

I come to, my body sagging on top of Anna, my lungs squeezing and heaving with air. Panic set in and I quickly set about checking to make sure I didn't make her pack the way I did with Nikolas. Lukas must have read my expression, because he lays his palm on my back.

"You didn't form a bond with her. Relax, freckles. You did good."

I want to weep as his reassurance sweeps over me. Anna's eyes blink up at me, and I gently let go of her head and slide off her. She sits up slowly, her eyes darting to Marcus, who lies unconscious a few yards away. I stare up at Lukas in question.

He shrugs. *'He was panicking.'*

'I bet you enjoyed that.'

'Not as much as I thought I would.'

I remember the guilt he felt while I was trying to break Anna's compulsion before I realized there was a demon in there keeping her locked away. It all makes sense now. I never understood before how she could be so damn cruel and vicious.

"Thank you." Anna's voice is meek, and cracks on the last word.

My gaze swings to her and I frown. "Are you okay? I didn't hurt you, did I?"

She shakes her head vehemently. "No. Well, my throat is sore from screaming, but that wasn't you," she says hoarsely, rubbing her neck.

"I can fix that," I say, moving toward her.

But she raises her hand, stopping me.

"No, it's okay. I'm fine. I'm happy to be free. That spell . . . it took over. I could still think, still feel, but I lost all control. I was like a passenger in my own body. The things it made me do . . . " Anna starts sobbing.

Gabe comes over, taking his jacket off and draping it over her shoulders. My heart aches for her. For what she had to endure. Trapped inside her mind while they forced her to do horrible things.

Marcus groans, and I hear him curse as he tries standing. He stumbles over, glaring at Lukas. "Was that really necessary?"

"You're a powerful mage. So . . . Yes."

Marcus grumbles under his breath and then kneels down by his sister. "Anna?" his voice softens when he speaks to his sister.

Anna launches herself into her brother's arms, burying her face in his neck as she cries. Marcus's surprised gaze meets mine.

"She was locked away in her mind, a spell keeping her contained while a demon controlled her," I explain.

"I'm so sorry, Marcus. I'm so sorry," she says between sobs.

"Shh. It's okay," he assures her, stroking his hand through her hair.

"I can't go back there. I won't. If they find out I'm free . . . " she fervently protests.

"You don't have to. You can stay with me."

Anna nods, and Gabe helps her stand, while Marcus swiftly climbs to his feet.

"We should probably head out before the cops come. All that screaming might have drawn unwanted attention," Jameson points out.

"He's right," Lukas says, helping me to my feet.

My head is spinning and my knees buckle. Next thing I see is the pavement rushing toward me. I would have hit the ground hard if it wasn't for Lukas sweeping me up into his arms. I try speaking, but my tongue feels swollen, my body begins tingling, almost like pins and needles all over. I moan, trying to flex my fingers, but everything feels heavy. Something is wrong. I can feel it deep down in my bones. A sharp stabbing pain pierces my skull and I cry out in pain.

"What's wrong with her?" Jameson asks anxiously.

Lukas frowns down at me, and it's Gabe who comes over, pressing a cool hand to my forehead. "She's burned out," he explains softly.

"Burned out?" Lukas questions.

"Magically. She used too much," Marcus clarifies. "She'll be okay with some rest."

I notice very little after that, as darkness sweeps me away in its cool embrace.

CHAPTER THIRTY FIVE

Leila

D arkness. That's all I can make out at first. The only sound I can hear is that of my steady heartbeat. My brows pull down in confusion, and I slowly turn in a circle. Nothing.

Where the hell am I now?

Unfortunately, this isn't the first time I've woken up somewhere I shouldn't be. Damn, I must have shadow portalled in my sleep again. Melinoe warned me this could happen in times of stress. Hades's daughter is my best friend, and although at times I question her sanity, she knows a lot about the shadows.

My eyes close as I take a deep breath through my nose, letting it fill my lungs, and release it slowly. I do this several more times. Concentrating on that spark of magic in my chest.

Nothing.

I huff in annoyance, opening my eyes.

"Hello?" I call out into the darkness. My voice echoes through the empty space and I wrap my arms tightly around myself. I listen and hear a faint shuffling noise behind me. Spinning, I call out again, "Who's there?"

My heart rate picks up, beating painfully inside my chest. Shuffling comes from the left now, and I turn with it. Whatever's there is circling me. Observing.

I sensed a tug on my night shirt, and my heart quickened as I spun around in alarm. Claws drag across my calves, and I dart to the side. My other senses are sharpening with my lack of sight. Movement to my right has me sidestepping. I hear the soft 'whoosh' of air behind me. Then the hair around my face moves and I freeze. I hold my breath, listening, but the only sound I can hear is my heartbeat.

Suddenly I'm shoved hard in the chest, and I tip backward, my arms pinwheeling as I go down. I wait for the force of the ground to hit me, but it doesn't come. I let out a gasp and tense as I fall past where the floor should be and keep falling. A scream lodges in my throat as I continue to fall. My long red hair streams around my face. There's a loud rushing noise in my ears, as I slow a second before landing with a thud on the ground.

Sitting up, I blink my eyes, trying to adjust to the light. I glance around, confusion twisting my stomach. The deafening sound of waves crashing is all around me as I sit in the middle of a grassy plain. I push to my feet, spinning in a slow circle. Deep green grass surrounds me, swaying in the crisp, salty breeze.

There is something so relaxing and mesmerizing about it. I take several steps forward, the ground soft beneath my feet. The smell of the ocean air hits me in the face as the wind turns sharp and cold, whipping around me. I stop at the edge of a steep cliff and look down at the ocean furiously crashing against the rock face below. I walk along the cliff, and when I turn around, the meadow is gone, replaced instead by a small pillar in the middle of the raging sea.

I am trapped, alone, and feeling a little desperate. The feeling of being isolated, cut-off from the world causing my panic to build.

I look out at the horizon, turning in a full circle as the wind picks up, howling in my ears.

The softest whisper floats in the breeze. "You were meant to be used as a pawn."

I spin around. "Hello?"

"Weak but strong. You were formed as a weapon."

The voice seems to come from all around me. Everywhere but nowhere.

"One that could kill a god."

Closing my eyes, a tear slips free, tracking a path down my cheek.

"It was all lies," the voice hisses in my ear.

Suddenly, I jolt awake, my heart thumping wildly in my chest. Zee stirs next to me, but doesn't wake. Relieved, I take a few calming breaths. It was just a dream. I stare down at Zee, his blond hair ruffled from a roll in the sheets. I slowly reach out and let my fingers glide over his forehead, brushing away the strands there. He sighs in his sleep, his arm wrapping around me and pulling me down to him. I don't fight it, content to snuggle into his warm, comforting chest and hold on tightly to my mate.

I asked him to wait to complete the bond until Hera has been defeated. I have a feeling I might not make it out alive, and I will not have him lose me like that. To lose a mate is said to be an unbearable loss. It would send him crazy. I should have done what I was supposed to and stayed hidden. But when I saw those wraiths stalking the children, I just couldn't any longer.

Zee is my mate. The word *mine* is burned into my mind and carved in my heart. We may have had a rough start, but I realize now soulmates aren't the ones who make you happiest. No, they are the ones who make you feel the most, who inspire you to get up and fight every day. Even with all their jagged edges and scars they are worth it all. Zee has never been afraid of my darkness, my shadows. It was hard not to fall in love with him when he saw the deepest, darkest parts of my soul and didn't run away. I love him, and now we need to end this so I can finally start living the life I want for us.

CHAPTER THIRTY SIX

Nesrin

I slide out of bed only to be growled at by Malachite, who is curled up by my feet at the end of the giant bed. One of his golden eyes opens in protest at having been disturbed. I roll my eyes at him and head into the bathroom. I barely slept, so of course I woke with a pounding headache and dark circles under my eyes. Man, I look like absolute shit. I thought being a legacy would grant me supernatural powers of flawless skin and beauty; *I guess I was wrong.*

My mind keeps playing over the events of the previous night. The shock on Eris's face when the blade sliced through her chest. I shake off the thoughts. What's done is done. She deserved no less. The knowledge doesn't stop the guilt from gnawing at my stomach and the pounding behind my eyes from growing more intense.

The last few days have been hard to say the least. Between losing Asena, the attack, and Eris, my mind is a mess. Marcus has sent me at least a dozen messages thanking me for what I did, and asking how I knew.

I haven't responded yet.

I also haven't answered Stephan and Nikolas's calls.

319

I can't muster the energy. I feel like I'm drowning, literally. My lungs burn, my body is heavy, my mind foggy, and I can barely break the surface. I have been trying so hard to push these feelings down so as not to burden Astraea with them.

I grip the bathroom sink until my knuckles hurt, the burning in my eyes too much to take. A stuttering gasp falls from my lips, and I turn for the shower. Stepping in, I turn the water on. I don't bother undressing as I slide to the floor. Tilting my head back, I let the water cascade over my face and mingle with my tears.

'*Sweetheart?*' Lukas's worry floats down our bond, causing more tears to flow. I don't answer, I can't. Anything I said would be a lie.

Not five minutes go by before I hear the bedroom door bang open followed by the bathroom door. I blink through the water as I watch Lukas's form stalk toward the glass shower doors. Swinging them open, he reveals a look of pure thunder on his face, his eyes a swirling storm of emotions as he takes me in.

He steps into the shower fully clothed and sits next to me, pulling me onto his lap. We don't speak as we sit together, the water soaking both of us.

Finally, I pull back, breaking the silence. "Sorry."

Lukas's hand grips my chin, lifting my face. He stares into my surely bloodshot eyes and makes a noise of distress in the back of his throat. His lips descend on mine. The kiss is sweet and gentle, but it stokes a fire deep inside me, turning my core to liquid fire. I move to straddle him, my hands sinking into his hair as I rock my hips. Lukas groans, his fingers digging into my hips, pulling me down hard against him. The kiss turns wicked as I try to forget the pain in my chest. Tongue and teeth clash as we desperately rip the clothes off each other. I end up on my back, Lukas hovering over me as he sinks inside of me. I arch my back, a loud moan falling from my lips as the water cascades over us. My legs wrap around his waist, and he scoops me up, lifting me in his arms and sitting up. I ride him as he thrusts upward, our bodies rocking and grinding together. We stare into each other's eyes the whole time, our bodies, minds, and souls connecting.

Asena's body is released to us the following day. Lukas has planned and organized the funeral. Asena left behind a detailed will regarding her burial. She wanted to be cremated on a pyre. Of course, we had to get special permission for this. And then the shifters spent all day collecting wood for the pyre, which we've set up down by the river.

Lukas and I head downstairs, hand in hand. I sense Suzy sitting out on the porch swing with Astraea and Malachite. I watch as cars pull in and park down by the common buildings.

I take a deep breath, and squeeze Lukas's hand tightly. Lukas has his own emotions firmly locked down. And I don't want to go down there and face everyone any more than he does. Before we leave, Lukas turns me to him, his warm palms cupping my face, tilting it up to him. He doesn't say a word, just takes my mouth in the sweetest kiss.

He pulls back, kissing my forehead gently. "You ready?"

"Never," I whisper in return. The lapels of his jacket gripped tightly in my fists, I rest my forehead on his chest.

His hand cups the back of my head. "I know, sweetheart."

A shriek from Suzy has us breaking apart and racing out the front door. Joseph and Sophie stand on the step with baby Rose. Their black void eyes are wide in fear. I rush forward. "Suzy, it's okay. They're friends."

Her shocked blue eyes whip to me. "What?!"

"This is Sophie, Joseph, and baby Rose. They are trolls," I explain, giving the troll family a small smile and mouthing *sorry*.

Sophie steps onto the porch, Joseph one step behind her, eyeing Suzy warily.

Shit, I really should have warned Suzy.

321

"You think!" Suzy quips, and I realize, as usual, I said that for everyone to hear.

"Hi, Suzy," Sophie says softly, and I can see she's trying not to show the rows of sharp teeth in her mouth.

I step forward to take a peek at the baby. "Gosh, she's grown," I breathe in wonder at the cute bundle in her arms. Black eyes blink, taking me in, one little hand reaching for me. I hold out my hand and Rose wraps her fingers around my finger. My heart swells. "And so strong," I laugh as she pulls me closer.

Sophie and Joseph both beam, their sharp teeth on full display.

"If it weren't for you, she wouldn't even be here," Joseph says.

"Want a hold?" Sophie asks me.

I nod eagerly and reach for the baby, taking her in my arms and smiling at her. "You are going to grow up beautiful and strong," I whisper to her.

Rose has grown, her grayish skin is tinged blue like all trolls until they reach adolescence. She has the cutest dusting of black hair on her head and no teeth that I can see. She gives me a grin and reaches for my face.

Lukas has been silently watching the exchange from the door. I turn to him, and give him a soft smile. "Isn't she cute?"

Lukas's smile reaches his eyes as he watches me. "Yes."

I look to Suzy, who still has a firm grip on Astraea, her eyes screaming, *Are you fucking crazy?*

I crouch down so Astraea can see, and Suzy lets go of her. Slowly, Astraea approaches and peeks at the bundle in my arms. Surprise shines in her eyes as she peers up at me in wonder.

"Astraea, I want you to meet Rose."

Astraea reaches up and gently strokes Rose's head. Rose reaches for her hand, a small babbling sound coming from her. Astraea lets Rose hold her finger and smiles softly at the baby. My heart might actually burst from this interaction. It's exactly what I need to get myself through today. Standing, I turn and hand the baby back to Sophie. Lukas's arm wraps around my middle. "It's time."

Our somber expressions wipe away the happy ones from moments ago. We all head down the hill toward the river to the pyre. Alex and Roan meet us on the way down the hill. Alex's eyes are puffy and red, and Roan's arm is firmly around her, keeping her tucked into his massive body. Alex has barely spoken to anyone in the days since Asena's death. I see Kyra and Sander down the hill, the boys standing next to their parents quietly, heads down. I've never seen them so still. My heart picks up as we near the gathering, everyone turning their gazes on us.

We stop at the front of the pyre. It's bigger than I expected. Asena had no family, only her pack. So Lukas, Zee, Sander, and Gabe carry her to the pyre. I watch as they gently lay her on top. A line of people make their way past, laying flowers, gifts, and other offerings on her. When Lukas, Astraea, and I get there, I can only stare at my friend.

She looks so beautiful, so peaceful laying there. Her long dark brown hair is laid out around her head like a halo, and she's been dressed in a white robe. A bouquet of lilies has been placed in her hands on her chest. My hand drifts forward and I gently touch one of the lilies as my gaze slowly lifts to her face, where her once rich brown skin is now pale and dull. Void of life.

How could I let this happen? Asena shouldn't be dead.

"I'm sorry." My voice cracks but I go on, "Thank you for being such a good friend. For accepting me, letting me be my unapologetic self. You're going to be missed," I whisper.

Moving back, we take our place. I spot Merve toward the back, his expression subdued. He meets my gaze and nods his head in sympathy. I close my eyes and stare back at the pyre as Gabe walks forward with a torch, his body moving stiffly. He is in pain. We all are. I move closer into Lukas's side, Astraea in his other arm. I reach up, holding her hand.

'You okay, sweet girl?'

'I okays. I's block out feelings,' she replies softly, her voice like butterfly wings along my mind.

We all stand there silently, watching the flames engulf the pyre. Movement from the forest has my eyes darting in that direction as several animals and fae creatures make themselves known, Nissa and her sprites front and center. They all bow in respect and watch on silently, some from the forest's edge, others gathered on the other side of the river. My eyes find Merve's and he smiles sadly, before he looks pointedly to Astraea.

What was that about? Did she call them here?

Tears burn my eyes and trace down my face as the pyre blazes. My gaze lifts to the forest when a sweet melody drifts from the trees. The sprites are singing. I don't recognize the song, but the haunting melody makes a sob break free. Lukas pulls me into his chest, his arms wrapping tightly around me. Astraea and Malachite huddle in as well, and together we watch the fire burn for hours. Slowly, the pack drifts back to their homes. The only ones left standing are Lukas, Kyra, Sander, Zee, Leila, Gabe, Alex, Roan and me. Suzy took Astraea home to bed. Joseph and Sophie left a couple of hours ago. Merve came and hugged me before he disappeared into the forest with the other creatures.

"I can't believe she's gone," Zee murmurs into the silent night, the only sound the crackling of the dying fire.

"Me either," Kyra replies, wrapping her arms around herself. Sander looks down at his wife before pulling her closer.

Alex and Roan murmur their goodbyes as the last of the fire dies out, the others turning and following them back up the hill. Lukas and I remain, his arms around me. I rest my head on his chest.

"I don't want to do this again," I croak, my throat raw.

"I know, sweetheart. I can't promise you that we won't, but I can promise I'll be right beside you."

CHAPTER THIRTY SEVEN

Lukas said he wouldn't be long, but it has been over an hour since he left. I nervously pace the length of the closed shop of Blue's café, biting my fingernails.

Where is he?

A flash of movement across the street catches my attention. The lights are off in the café, so nobody can see me. But still I duck down, creeping toward the window and pulling the sheer curtain back slightly. I hold my breath as I watch three mages I recognize hurrying down the street. *I wonder what they're doing?*

Shit. I know what I'm going to do before I open the door and close it behind me, magically engaging the locks. I quickly make my way down the street, hoping to catch which way the mages went. I just make it to the corner in time to watch them turn down the small side street. Looking around, I hastily make the decision to follow. My feet are silent as I move down the street toward the small side street known for their more eccentric shops.

I stop at the entrance to the small cobblestone street and gather myself. My fingers hover over the dagger strapped to my thigh, even though I have magic and a sword at my fingertips, I can't help going back to old comforts. I do miss my trusty taser, though, what I wouldn't do to be able to tase one of these buffoons.

Peering around the corner, I see the mages standing at the entrance to a store known to deal with black magic. I frown, my fingers sliding over the hilt of my dagger out of habit. *Why would they be there?*

I draw in a breath as I watch the high priest stroll out of the shop with another man on his heels, carrying a bag. They all turn, making their way further down the street, before turning into an alley. I quickly dart forward, making my way to the mouth of the alley and sneaking around the corner, keeping to the shadows as much as possible.

I'm about twenty yards away when my phone rings. The volume's turned down, but in the quiet night it's like a car horn blaring. I fumble for it in my pocket, switching it off. Cursing myself, I watch in horror as the high priest and his entourage stop abruptly. They all turn as one in my direction. Everything in me freezes at the sight. *Fuck.* I am so screwed. My entire being screams to run like my ass is on fire. I am definitely the prey in this scenario.

"You got this, Nesrin, just blend in with the shadows, just like Leila taught you," I mumble to myself. If I can somehow manage to make it the twenty yards down the alley to the busy street, I'll probably be fine. Safer in public, right? The *Sanans Sidus Lucis* pulses in warning and my chest grows cold as I edge my way along the wall toward the end of the alley. The high priest's men fan out, all moving swiftly toward me. My hands shake with adrenaline, the need to run so strong. I just have to avoid them. They can't see me, but that doesn't mean they won't feel me or hear me if they get close enough.

I slow my breathing, not taking my eyes off the men as I slowly edge my way down the alley. In my concentration, I don't see the empty bottle on the ground. My foot knocks it, and it's like a gunshot in the middle of the night as it rolls across the road. I jerk in place, the pounding in my chest almost painful.

"There you are, my little mouse," the high priest drawls, waving his hand.

The shadows I wrapped around myself disappear and I'm left standing here, exposed. The priest's eyes fall on me, and I narrow mine in return. The high priest is an older version of Marcus, his dark hair turning silver on the sides. Smug superiority oozes from his pores, which has my teeth grinding. I am trapped now. At the back of my mind, I scream my frustration. Why did I have to follow those damn mages? Lukas told me to stay at Blue's shop until he got there.

"What? Nothing to say?" the high priest taunts.

"Look, let's just keep the bullshit to a minimum, okay?" I say, keeping my tone bored. He doesn't scare me anymore. I am itching for a fight. Maybe that's why I chose to follow them. The high priest's eyes flash, and I see it again. This time I *know* I saw it. His eyes shifted. The other mages sneer and I let anger take hold.

The world around me blurs as I charge toward the closest mage. I shift my weight, putting one foot forward and adding magic to my punch. I aim for his chest, sending a current of electricity into him. He drops to the ground unconscious, as I spin to the next target. All eyes assess me a little more carefully this time, their smirks and sneers gone.

One mage steps forward, our eyes locking. He is so much larger than me, so, it's a good thing I've spent so much time training with Lukas. I wait for him to make the first move, ducking under his arm as he swings at me. I sidestep his next punch, and grabbing his arm, I pull him forward and off balance. Growling, he spins on me, I dance backward out of reach, but he moves quickly. I block several hits, one landing on my ribs, I grunt and duck under his next punch. Popping back up, I land a punch at his stomach, he grunts, faltering a second. Not wanting to waste the opportunity, I reach up and put both my hands behind his neck, kneeing him in the ribs twice before he grabs my thigh, lifting me off the ground with a yell, and throwing me off him. I land hard on my back, sliding across the rough pavement.

Crap, that hurt.

"It's going to hurt a lot more," the mage taunts.

Grumbling, I push to my feet as he approaches. His face is a mask of fury, his brown eyes have a crazed twinkle in them. I quickly look to see the others spread out around me while the high priest stands out of harm's way. Hate blazes in his dark eyes as he stares at me. If he could burn me alive with just that look, he would. I have no doubt.

Snapping back to my surroundings, I dodge another blow aimed at my face. Baring my teeth, I take a step back, lifting my boot to land a well aimed kick to the mage's chest. Stumbling back a step, he regains his balance, snarling. All four mages advance on me this time, all coming at me at once. I see a spell forming around us. But a faint fluttering sensation in my chest makes me pause. Lukas and Nikolas are close. Magic hums along my skin, pulsing outward, pushing the mages back a step.

A blur of movement has one mage flying across the alley. The sound of his body hitting the opposite wall makes me cringe. The mage in front of me doesn't hold back this time, not that I think he ever was. His fists are throwing punch after punch. I raise my arms to block each blow one by one. He is driving me backward across the alley, and I try to not stumble on my feet. Slightly lowering my arms, I go for a strike and his fist connects with the side of my head, sending me sprawling to the ground.

Groaning, I roll onto my back, blinking up at the dark night sky. *Crap on a cracker, that hurts!*

A sneering face blocks my vision of the sky, and magic warms my palms and along my skin in response. It flares to life, lashing out at the mage, who is leaning over me. His brown eyes flare wide, and I send him flying through the air. Jumping to my feet, I see Lukas bound forward in his wolf form. He brushes up against my body, his bond reaching out to make sure I'm okay.

'I'm fine, Lukas.'

'Ma reine, you should leave.'

'I'm not leaving.'

I can basically hear both men roll their eyes at me. Well, they really should know me better by now. I've never run from a fight. I lift my hands and watch them glow with a brilliant white light. I turn my palm skyward and watch as tendrils of light waft upward like embers from a fire. The two remaining mages and high priest form a wall in front of us.

"What are you going to do?" I growl. "You don't stand a chance against the alpha, a vampire, and me." I let my magic flare in my palms in response.

The high priest chuckles, "Oh, child. You have no idea how much I'm going to enjoy watching you burn."

Lukas snarls, snapping out at the three men blocking our way out. The two remaining mages step forward, wielding their magic. One of them has swirls of orange magic streaming from their fingertips, while the other has vibrant green sparks.

'Nesrin?'

I'm startled by the sound of Lukas's voice echoing in my head, *'Yes?'*

'I think you're lending me your gift. I can see their magic. It's like the spell you did over the river.'

My thoughts are running at a thousand miles an hour, and my mind is buzzing. Could I be transferring my magic to him? It's possible. My thoughts are racing as I try to figure out how I am doing it. I'm snapped from my thoughts as the mages move forward.

Lukas and Nikolas don't waste any time. Both men leap forward together. Lukas going for one, Nikolas the other.

I send my magic across the ground toward the high priest, making it curl around his ankles like a snake wrapping around its prey. I smile to myself when I see his startled expression.

With the mages dispatched, Lukas and Nikolas circle the high priest, but he doesn't seem as concerned as he should be. Which strikes me as odd. Something isn't right.

Suddenly someone lands on my back, taking me to the ground. I land hard, not at all like Gabe taught me. The air leaves my lungs at once and

I wheeze, struggling to draw in a breath as pain spreads through my chest. A hard blow lands on my ribs before I can recover. Instinctively, I curl up into a ball, my hands going over my head to protect it, but a kick to my back has me crying out. I scramble to bring up a shield. Anything. But the next blow is to my head, and it has me seeing stars. The onslaught of kicks stops, and a sharp pinch of a needle hits my neck. *What was that?*

I lay there, assessing the damage as I wait for my breathing to go back to normal. I'm pretty sure I have a few broken ribs, as each breath is excruciating. A numbness starts to take over, causing my fingers and toes to tingle. The warmth of my magic dulls in my chest, almost to a non-existent hum. The world buzzes in my ears, my vision blacking out. Slowly, sounds filter back in around me. I hear Lukas make an animalistic sound that cuts right through me, sending my heart into overdrive. Lifting my head from the ground, our eyes connect across the alley.

Oh my goddess.

My heart drops and panic claws at my insides.

Two mages are on either side of him, chains coiled tightly in their hands as they wrap them around him. He's back in his human form, his shirt gone. They've pulled his arms behind his back, his muscles bulging as he fights to free himself. The man I love more than anything is on his knees, surrounded by a dozen mages. *Where did they all come from?* I frantically search around for Nikolas, but I can't see him. He isn't there when I search the bond. I hold back a sob. Surely he isn't dead, right?

I watch as the chains are wrapped around Lukas's neck. His jaw clenches as he strains against the chains. Blood tracks down his torso and the muscles in his arms and neck flex as he pushes against his restraints. The chains must be made of a mixture of iron and silver. Only iron could weaken him this much that he can't fight back. I see a mage walk up to him, a dagger in hand. I watch in horror as it flashes in the moonlight before sinking into Lukas's stomach.

NO!!!!!

My arms try pushing up, but they only tremble before collapsing under me. Frustration and despair well up inside of me. My mate needs me. Now is not the time to be weak. Black wisps lick at the edge of my awareness, threatening to carry me off into oblivion.

No.

I shake my head, desperately trying to dispel it.

'Run, sweetheart.' Lukas's sweet damn voice floats to me through the bond, accompanied by a wave of warmth.

Lukas is not sacrificing himself for me. I know he will die for me, and that I will have to carry that for the rest of my life. I can't let that happen. The world slows down as Lukas watches me, silver chains coiling around him. His face twists in pain and his body shudders.

'Lukas, I'm here. Fight.' Through the bond I feel some of the pain, but I know he is shielding me from the worst of it.

'I love you, Nesrin, and I will always fight for you. But I need you to run. No matter what happens, we will always find our way back to each other.'

A wave of calming and loving energy floods the bond. I can almost feel his warm protective arms wrapping around me. It gives me strength to push up and stand on shaky legs.

"You will pay for this," I seethe through gritted teeth. The mages lift their faces to me as if surprised to see me standing.

"You gave her the nightshade, right?" one of them asks the other.

The assholes injected me with nightshade?!

I take an unsteady step forward. I fucked up. I should not have followed the high priest. I knew better. Now Lukas is paying the price for my stupidity. A twinge of warmth hits my chest at the same time as a dash of ice hits it. My magic is replenishing. The nightshade they injected me with is fading fast, my magic burning it out of my system.

'Lukas, my magic is returning. You need to fight!'

'I will, sweetheart, but I need you to use your magic and get away, please.'

'No! I won't leave you. They will kill you.' I sob. I am so focused on Lukas, I don't see one mage pull out a gun. The sound of the gun going off makes me jolt. I watch in horror as blood spreads across Lukas's bare chest.

They shot him.

They shot him.

They fucking shot him.

He's been shot in the shoulder, no doubt by a poisoned bullet. *What bloody magic-wielding dickwad uses a gun?*

"These dickwads," the mage answers with a predatory smirk on his ugly face.

Even Lukas's inner voice is raw with pain as he gives a final, *'Be strong,'* before he collapses, his body going slack, his eyes closing.

A feral scream tears from my throat. "NO!!!"

A contemptuous laughter fills the air. I jerk my eyes up as the mages part and Hera steps through. She wears a slinky red dress, the slit indecently high. Her smirk makes me want to go ape shit, to claw her to pieces with my bare hands. The high priest stands by her side, his eyes black voids, a cunning smile on his face.

Hera casually strolls right up to Lukas and motions to the mages. Two of them run forward and pull Lukas up so he is kneeling again. Hera leans over, one hand sinking into his hair, ripping his head back. A snarl rips from my throat as I watch, unable to do anything until my magic has fully returned.

Smirking, she doesn't take her eyes from mine as she digs her fingers into the wound in his shoulder. Lukas eyes fly open, his face twisting in agony as a muted roar leaves him. I jerk forward a step, but Hera shoots me a warning look.

"You care about him?" she sneers.

"You know I do," I snarl.

Fire fills my veins, demanding retribution. My eyes briefly flit over to Lukas. His eyes are barely open as he wavers in and out of consciousness. I test my magic and my heart leaps when a little more seeps through. It's still not enough to use as a weapon, but I know I won't have to wait much longer.

'Lukas, please hold on a little longer. I can get us out of here. My magic is almost back. I can feel it.'

'You can't fight them and save me. You need to run.' His lids flutter open, his storm green eyes pleading with me.

I am so sick of people telling me to run. I am not running. I will never leave him.

Hera's eyes glint as she leans closer to Lukas, her tongue darting out to lick the side of his bloodied face before she stands tall. A satisfied smile on her face, she lets go of Lukas, his body crumpling to the ground.

"Hmm, that's too bad."

My stomach plummets at the sight of the sardonic smile that stretches across her evil face.

There's a sudden shift in the air and Leila is behind me, her fingers digging into my arm, pulling me back. The world swirls violently around me.

"No!" I scream in fury, realizing why she's here. I won't leave Lukas. I struggle in her grasp, but it's too late. We land in the kitchen at home. Several sets of eyes turn our way as I whirl on Leila, rage burning in my gut like molten lava.

"*Take. Me. Back!*" The words come out feral, barely human.

Leila shakes her head, standing her ground. I lunge forward, my hand wrapping around her throat and I push her hard against the wall. Magic swells in my chest as I squeeze her throat in warning.

"TAKE ME BACK TO MY MATE!!" I scream, my pain intensifying until I feel nothing else but the loss of my mate. I can't feel him. The mate bond has gone excruciatingly silent.

Leila doesn't break eye contact. "No."

A raw, animalistic scream rips from deep within my chest. I feel movement at my back and throw up a wall of magic.

"Nesrin?" I can feel Zee's eyes boring into my back. I don't answer, my breath sawing in and out roughly.

"Nesrin, it's okay," he says, coming closer.

"It's *not* okay!" I snarl, not taking my eyes from Leila's. My fingers spasm around her throat as emotions choke mine.

"No, it's not. But Lukas wouldn't want you to go back for him."

He's right. Some part of me knows that, but I don't care. I need to go back. I need Lukas.

My eyes fill with hot, angry tears. "She has him."

"I know, honey. We will get him back. I promise," Zee says. I glance over my shoulder at him and snarl. I feel a ripple go through my body, the urge to shift taking over.

My eyes frost over as I stare back at my sister. I *hate* that she took me and left Lukas. The image of his stormy green eyes pleading with me to run flashes in my mind and I drop my hand. Bending at the waist, I brace my hands on my knees, taking deep, sobbing breaths. Zee moves past me, grabbing for Leila, but she pushes him aside, moving closer. Brave.

I look up into her eyes before straightening.

"I'm sorry," she whispers, before she disappears in a swirl of shadows.

A wave of desperation hits me square in the chest, and my head begins to swim. My hands spear into my hair, grabbing each side of my head, and a guttural scream claws out of my throat as I pour out all my anguish.

My mate. My husband.

She has him.

Zee's muscular arms wrap around me, pulling me into his chest, but I don't want to be comforted. I pull away, swiping at my face as I look round the room.

Zee, Gabe, Kyra, and Sander all stare at me with varying expressions. Their emotions combined with my own are too much to handle. I spin on my heels and run like the devil himself was chasing me. I make it outside and change form mid leap. My heart throbs savagely in my chest as I let out a mournful cry. I run for the woods and keep running, having no idea where I am headed. I just need to run. To clear my mind so I can find the right path forward. Movement catches my attention, and I lift my head, sniffing the air as I run. *Nero.* The black horse breaks from the trees, running at my side. Nero keeps a steady pace with me. My shadow. My companion.

'Are you okay, daughter of light? I can feel your heartache as if it were my own. What has happened?'

I slow my pace and then stop, turning toward him, changing back into my human form. He trots over, nudging me with his nose. And, even though I know he can shift into human form, this form brings me comfort. I lay my forehead against his and breathe him in. The scent of cedarwood and evergreen oils, such as cypress or fir needle, fills my lungs. I can never put my finger on which, but it's so calming.

"She took him," I answer on a shaky breath.

'Hera?'

Her name sends fire burning through my body. I hate her. I hate her with the fire of a thousand stars. My chest warms as my mind fills with thoughts of the goddess who has destroyed so many lives, murdered generations of my own family, along with countless others, all of them damned by her jealousy alone. I feel my magic building and my breathing coming in rough pants as my heart races. My every muscle trembles as I feel adrenaline pumping through my veins. A sudden awareness sweeps over me, and with it a sense of impending doom. Is this an anxiety attack? A pulse of light bursts from my chest as I stumble against Nero. I turn, staggering over to the closest tree as the vision hits me with the force of a tidal wave crashing on the shore. It comes from out of nowhere, and I falter, knees buckling. When I look up, I am somewhere else. Somewhere beneath an endless red and orange sky. The barren landscape before me is filled with an army of monsters and soldiers in black. My heart thumps hard at the sight.

I turn around and see myself standing opposite the army. Behind me stand the shifters, Nero, Nissa and her sprites, trolls, kelpies, vampires—all awaiting my command. I feel the anticipation of the order thrumming in the air.

Turning back to the dark army, I study them, the claws, fangs, and wings amongst the soldiers. That's when I see her at the back, standing behind them. Hera.

A horn blares and the army begins moving forward, an inhuman battle cry rippling through the ranks, sending tremors running through my body. The ground shakes beneath my feet. The shifters and magical creatures behind me shout their own battle cries, and I watch on as the other me raises her light sword into the air and charges forward.

A pulse of pure white light erupts around me, and everything fades away. I faintly feel my body fall and land on the hard ground. Then nothing.

CHAPTER THIRTY EIGHT

I slowly open my eyes and blink several times. My head is pounding and nausea swirls in my stomach. Muffled voices come into focus, and I frown. I'm lying on my stomach, and I feel warm. Overly warm. I lie still, waiting for my head to stop spinning and the nausea to disappear.

"What should we do?" a familiar female voice asks.

"How the fuck should I know?" an angry male voice barks.

Zee, definitely Zee.

"We can't leave her there." I recognize Gabe's voice. He sounds worried. I hear shuffling and growls erupt around me.

"Back up, Zee," Alex snaps.

Kyra's voice comes out unsure. "Would they really attack us?"

"Want to take that risk?" Zee snaps. I can just imagine him running a hand through his blonde hair in agitation.

What on earth are they all talking about? What's going on?

I try rolling over, but that's when I realize I'm wedged between two large bodies.

"Nero, I know you understand me. Let us near her, man," Zee demands.

"I think they are protecting her," Kyra says in a softer tone.

I roll my head to the side and see Nero's shiny black coat. I move my hands under my chest and push up onto my hands and knees. My stomach lurches violently and I pant through it, waiting for it to pass. When I'm certain I won't lose the contents of my stomach, I raise my head up slowly and gasp in astonishment. I'm surrounded by a barrier of creatures including: Nero; Malachite; a kelpie; some sprites, though I can't see Nissa; a few smaller forest creatures; and . . . holy shit, is that a griffin?

I sit back on my knees, my legs folded under me, and look around at the creatures that seem to be guarding me. I reach up to stroke Nero as I look beyond the creatures to where a small group of people have gathered. Zee looks pissed, Gabe looks on in wonder, Kyra seems nervous, and Alex is gaping at the griffin.

Looking down at my wall of creatures, I feel extremely grateful for them. I would have frozen to death out here on the forest floor without them. Still, I wonder why they've come? What brought them here?

Zee takes a step closer, drawing my attention and the attention of the creatures around me. He pauses, his eyes assessing the situation and how best to get to me.

"It's okay, I'm okay."

I'm not sure if I'm talking to Zee or the creatures guarding me, but everyone seems to relax. The creatures move aside as I stand up, letting Zee step closer to help me. Nero shifts into his human form, standing for all to see as naked as a newborn baby. I faintly hear the shocked inhales from Kyra and Alex and stifle my laugh.

Zee rolls his eyes. "Dude, can't you, like, magic up some clothes or something?"

"No," Nero replies, entirely unfazed, his tattooed body on full display.

The creatures all move to leave, each one nudging my hand before turning to walk away. The griffin, to my surprise, rubs against my legs, almost knocking me over. I watch on in amazement as the creature only moves a few feet away and sits, regarding us. Griffins are beautiful, amazing creatures. They have incredible strength and unshakable protective instincts. Best of all, they have zero-tolerance for evil. It's like my superhero of mythological creatures. And there is one standing a few feet away from me right now.

"You called them all to you. They were protecting you," Nero says, breaking me from my internal wonderings.

Frowning, I swing my head his way, doing my best to keep my eyes focused only on his face. "Huh?"

"When you had your vision. You sent out a distress call."

"The pulse?" I question as the vision rises to the surface of my mind again. I can't let it come to that. Too many people will die.

Nero nods. Zee grabs my shoulders, his gaze roaming my body. "Are you hurt?"

"Physically, no," I reply hoarsely.

I still have a gaping hole in my chest where Lukas should be. Zee's hands pat my head and move down my body like he's searching for injuries. Brushing his hands away, I step back.

"I said I'm okay."

Zee grunts. "I wanted to make sure."

Kyra and Alex make their way over, linking their arms through mine. "She said she's fine, Zee. Drop it," Kyra says.

Gabe approaches the griffin and crouches before it, examining it closely.

"I will leave you with your pack now, but if you need me, just call," Nero tells me with a bow, his long black hair falling over either shoulder. Standing, he gives me a small smile and turns.

"Wait! Nikolas. He was with me last night. I don't know what happened to him," I choke out.

Nero's steps falter, and his dark eyes grow stormy. "I will find him." He turns, shifting fluidly into his magnificent black horse and trotting off into the woods.

"Really wish he'd wear some clothes," Zee grumbles.

"Don't be a hater, Zee," Alex quips.

Kyra's cheeks turned a rosy hue as she laughed.

Ignoring them, Zee refocuses on me. "Let's get you home."

My heart sinks. *Home.* Home is Lukas. He has become my home. I need to see Astraea.

CHAPTER THIRTY NINE

"Are you sure that's what you saw?" Marcus asks for the hundredth time tonight. His pacing is doing my head in. I put my elbows on the table, resting my head in my hands. It's taking all my willpower to keep my anger at bay. It's always the same with Marcus. He just doesn't seem to get it the first hundred times.

"Yes, Marcus. Why do you always ask me that?" I retort, pushing my auburn hair behind my ears. I feel a gentle nudge against my leg under the table and reach down, running my hand over the griffin's head. When I realized he has no intention of leaving anytime soon, I named him Talon. Since then, he has refused to let me out of his sight, which makes sense, as, judging by his size, he's still quite young.

Sinking into the chair across from me, Marcus sighs, running a hand through his pitch-black hair. He looks wired. Something else is bothering him, I'm sure of it.

"If you have a vision of this, we have to assume it will come to pass."

I shake my head, shuddering at the thought of the vision of the barn and all those dead bodies. It hasn't happened yet. My visions don't have a timeline, and I hope that if we are able to stop Hera, the horrors that vision showed me will be prevented.

"Not necessarily," I mutter.

Marcus heaves a deep breath, his dark eyes intent on mine. "Well, I sure hope not. But if it does, you know we're on your side, right?"

"Yeah," I whisper.

Kyra squeezes my shoulder as she walks past, taking a seat to my left. Alex has already gone home, and Gabe is out getting pizzas from town for dinner.

'Ma reine?'

I jolt in my seat, the shock of Nikolas's voice sending a flurry of emotions barrelling through me. I close my eyes, focusing on our link.

'Where are you?'

'At Stephan's'

'Oh, thank the goddess. I was so worried. Has Nero found you?'

'Yes.'

'Are you okay?'

'I will be. I'm almost at full health. They hit me with the nightshade as well.' There is a slight pause before he speaks again, *'I'm sorry about Lukas.'*

I can feel his sorrow down the bond, and for the millionth time I wonder why I can feel him more strongly than anyone else in the pack. Why can we communicate over long distances when I can't with the others? Lukas is the only one who has a stronger tie to me.

'I will get him back,' I vow.

'There is no doubt in my mind, ma reine.'

I feel someone grab my hands and my eyes snap open to meet the stare of a set of onyx eyes. Marcus looks tired. We all do.

"I'm sorry about Lukas. We will get him back," Marcus says softly.

Pain claws at my throat, and I struggle to push down my tears. I can't shake the fear of what they're doing to him.

Zee slams a cup down on the bench behind me, making all three of us jump. "Damn straight, we will. Your fucking high priest is dead when I get hold of him."

My mind filters back through my vision. I don't recall seeing Lukas there. What does that mean? Dread fills my chest, and I block out those thoughts. I can't feel him through our bond, but I know he's still alive.

The connection is still there. I think about the shift in the priest's eyes, the way his eyes blinked, the blackness bleeding through the white until they were completely void.

"Uhh, Nesrin, you're glowing," Marcus's deep voice seeps through my haze.

I look down to my hands and realize I am, in fact, lit up like a light bulb. Shit. Taking slow, deep breaths, I close my eyes. Marcus's hands are still gripping mine, which really isn't helping. I want it to be Lukas's hands. Before I snap, I pull my hands from his, and stand to pace the room.

"I don't think it's your father. Well, not anymore, anyway," I assure Marcus, turning to face him.

His brow slams down, clearly confused as to what I'm saying. He peers at Kyra, who simply shrugs. I continue, obviously needing to elaborate.

"When I was first captured, I didn't remember, but I later had a dream about my time at the coven. In particular about your father's eyes. An eyelid slid from the outer corner to the inner corner. I thought I was going crazy. That I was seeing things, or my imagination just conjured it up. But the other night in that alley, it happened again. His eyes shifted. They turned fully black. I knew then I hadn't imagined it at all. I think a demon possesses your father, or it's not him at all."

Marcus is staring at me dumbfounded, and I look to Zee, who seems to be just as speechless.

"Didn't you wonder why he hated you so much?" a voice asks from the doorway.

I go still. I know that voice. A small sigh leaves me as I look over to find Hermes leaning against the door frame, his arms crossed over his chest, and those boyish features set in a serious expression. How long has he been standing there?

"Hera planted her minions everywhere. Though, you can usually tell them apart by the pure unadulterated hatred seeping from their pores."

"Hermes, what are you doing here?" I ask.

Pushing off the door, he walks into the room. Marcus and Kyra sit stiff in their chairs as the god moves closer.

Not Zee, though. Never Zee.

"She asked you a question, god," Zee snaps, stalking toward Hermes.

Zee is looking for a fight, and I won't let him pick one with a god. I step between them, Zee's chest pressing against my back. Hermes's eyes flash, and my body vibrates in warning at the energy filling the room.

"Popsicles!! Would you two knock it off before you set the house on fire!" I snap.

Hermes tilts his gaze down to mine, his blue eyes kind. "I thought I'd bring you some help, cousin. Someone who has their own vendetta against Hera."

My eyes widen at the word cousin, and I'm struck speechless. This man has a disturbing way of surprising me. In my kitchen, no less. Hermes raises an eyebrow at my silence.

"Could you repeat that?" I ask, wondering if I heard him right. He has someone who can help me. And, cousin. Does that mean he knows about us being from Zeus's bloodline?

Tilting his head, his lips twitch slightly at one corner. "Which part?"

"All."

"Explain yourself."

Zee and I both growl at the same time.

I am getting tired, and I just want to find Astraea and curl up in bed, holding her as close as I can. Sensing my annoyance, Talon moves out from under the table and nudges my legs. I automatically reach down, running my hand over his head.

"Do you have bad hearing?" Hermes asks.

I've known he's stubborn from my last encounter with him. He also enjoys playing with his food before he eats it, and I am done getting messed around with. I narrow my eyes at him, and he lets a small smile show.

"Very well. I brought Athena with me. I assume that's the part that had you confused, right?"

"Athena. Like *the* Athena?" I keep my voice even. Those blue eyes settling back on me.

"Yes, I'm that Athena. Sorry I kept you waiting."

A tall blonde woman breezes into the kitchen, her sky-blue robes trailing behind her adorned with golden armor over her shoulders and upper body. Her face is a mixture of delicate and fierce. I stare at her in disbelief and awe.

Her blue eyes twinkle the same as Hermes and she pulls her full lips into a wide smile. "You're smaller than Hades mentioned."

I shift uncomfortably under her probing gaze.

Marcus shoots to his feet, his chair scraping across the floor. "What is happening right now?" I can sense his magic rising in defense.

I soften my gaze and lower my voice when I turn to him, "Marcus, it's okay. You can calm down."

His incredulous gaze swings to mine. I can see he wants to argue, but he manages to hold back. He remains standing though, ready to fight should the need arise. I'm still shocked sometimes by how he has stuck by me this whole time. His friendship has been unwavering. His goals align with mine, he wants change as much as I do.

Jameson chooses this moment to walk in through the back door, Astraea on his shoulders and Malachite bounding behind him. He draws to a stop when he sees the kitchen full.

"Oh, um . . . What's– what's happening guys?" he stammers, his hazel eyes growing large at the sight of two gods standing in our kitchen.

Astraea's eyes take in the group, then settle on me, and she reaches out. Jameson walks over, and as I'm annoyingly the shortest person around besides Astra, he bends so I can grab her.

'Daddy?'

My heart clenches. *'We're working on it, sweet girl.'*

Nissa flies through the open door, stopping short in the crowded room. Athena claps her hands, and we all turn to her.

"You have a problem, and we are here to aid you in the only way we can. Obviously, we cannot actually intervene. This would cause a civil war between gods, and that is not something we can allow. We have let Hera run free for long enough. We think you can stop her."

Athena's eyes scan the room, stopping on Kyra briefly before landing on Astraea. My eye twitches, and I want to turn, to hide Astraea from her view.

Zee clears his throat, and Athena blinks. "I will mark you. This will mean you are under my protection. Should you require aid, you can call upon me."

"What do you mean, mark me?"

Athena steps toward me, reaching for my hand. Zee, Marcus, and Jameson all move at once, prepared to defend me, but Athena holds up her other hand, seemingly freezing them in place.

"I'm not going to hurt her," she clarifies, glaring at the men.

I hand Astraea to Zee. "It's fine."

As soon as I have released Astraea, Athena grabs my hand. I suck in a sharp breath as a fiery pain works its way over my arm, an olive branch appearing in gold over the inside of my forearm.

Athena speaks softly as she watches the mark form completely. "It is a sign of peace and the symbol of light. My symbol. It will help guide you in battle. It will give you added strength." She runs her fingers over the mark. "If you need to summon me, just push your magic into the mark and I'll come."

Athena steps back to stand next to Hermes. My throat is tight with gratitude. "Thank you."

Hermes steps forward next, his hand taking mine. "I mark you with my Caduceus. It signifies the life force and power within you. It will help channel your magic through your body and mind. It will also alert me if your soul is in danger."

As he speaks the words, a searing pain shoots up the inside of my other forearm, and there appear two snakes winding around a winged staff. Both marks seem to glow a golden color, but are otherwise mostly translucent. Hermes releases my hand, taking a step back.

I feel the blood drain from my face, remembering Hermes is also the conductor of souls. He can move freely between the worlds of the gods and the mortals. His ability to access the underworld without consequence is unique among gods.

Hermes sees my reaction and smiles reassuringly. "One more thing. Hades asked that you consider forgiving your sister."

His words pierce my heart, and I look up at him, glaring. "I don't take orders from gods."

Athena's laughter is light and airy. "You shouldn't."

"I'm only the messenger," he says, hand over heart. "But Leila loves you, she spent most of her life in hiding, pretending she was someone she wasn't, and now she has a chance to be with her family and be herself, she wasn't willing to lose you."

I cross my arms in defense and glance over at Astraea. Her blue eyes are sad. She knows I'm in pain, and I'm struggling. There is no way I can hide it from her. I hate that she has to go through my heartache and anger. Without Lukas here, she hasn't been able to decompress as easily.

"I'll think about it," I whisper, returning my focus to the gods.

"That's all I ask." Hermes says, bowing. Athena rolls her eyes, then takes on a more serious tone.

"Hera is cruel and has no qualms about killing whoever she needs to in order to get what she wants. Be careful."

Athena goes to step forward again, but her eyes dart to Astraea and she changes her mind.

Hermes links his arm with Athena's and bows. "Till next time, daughter of light." With that, they begin to fade.

Jameson whistles low, and I glance over at him, arching my eyebrow in question. He shifts on his feet, ducking his head. "Sorry. But that was crazy."

Zee walks over and slaps him on the back. "Yep, it's never boring with Nesrin as our luna."

"Hey!" I exclaim.

I don't intentionally make everything dramatic. Trouble seems to always find me, it's not like I go around looking for it!

"It's true," Kyra laughs lightly. "That was intense."

Malachite and Talon come over and run their bodies around mine. "I wish this had never been an issue. I wish Blanchette could fight this battle, but she is trapped, safe and sound in Faerie. Why is it up to me and Leila?"

Kyra stands and pulls me into a hug. "You can't undo the past. We can only face the future."

"I feel so lost," I whisper.

"Through our struggles, we find who we truly are. I know you will get Lukas back. I know we will win this battle. You won't allow any other outcome."

I sniff, trying not to let my emotions overwhelm me. I miss Lukas. Asena is gone. Grace is gone. I feel like everyone is slowly being ripped away from me.

A tug on my shirt has me looking down at a blinking Astraea. Her wide blue eyes are glowing violet, her magic close to the surface. Emotions overwhelm me and I scoop her up in my arms, nuzzling her. She wraps her tiny arms around me. '*Tis kay, mommy. I'm here.*'

Goddess, bless my bleeding heart, this girl gets me. She is my angel, my shining star on a dark night. I have to end this for her. Even if I die in the process, she will not carry this burden.

CHAPTER FORTY

Leila

I storm through the castle halls toward my father's study. My boots echo off the stone floor. The castle is empty, but I know he'll be there, hiding from Milinoe. His daughter is in a mood, and usually she takes it out on Hades. It's funny that Hades, god of the underworld, fears his daughter. I used to feel bad for him, but not today.

Today, he will face my wrath.

Two guards step into my path as I approach the doors. I don't slow. Instead, I lash out with my shadows, wrapping them around the guards and throwing them further down the hall. Surprise flitters across their faces. I am usually the well-behaved puppet. It's Milinoe who causes trouble.

I reach up with both hands and shove the double doors open. I don't flinch as they bang loudly against the stone walls. Hades's head snaps up, a snarl forming on his mouth until he sees it's me. His brows slam down as he takes me in.

"Sunflower?"

The pet name does nothing to soften my mood.

"Father," I spit, my whole body vibrating in anger.

I overheard the kitchen staff talking eagerly between themselves about how Hades's plans are finally coming together. Usually, I wouldn't listen to the gossip of the staff, but when I heard my name, a pit formed in my stomach. I just hid there in the shadows, listening, unable to move.

Hades used me, trained me as a pawn in his battle of sibling rivalry with Zeus. He knew about Hera's plans all along, that Zeus had no idea, but he always pushed that it was Zeus behind everything. I believed he cared for me. I was wrong. He only cares about what I can help him accomplish.

Hades stands up, rounding his desk, his golden eyes never leaving mine. I swallow over the lump forming in my throat. "Is it true?" I bite out.

Hades stops short. "Is what true?"

I growl, taking a step closer. "Is it true what they are saying? Was I just a pawn in your stupid game with Zeus? That you only took me in so you would have leverage." Hades opens his mouth, but I steam on before he can speak. "That you only trained me so I could kill him. That if you got me to hate him as much as you do, that I'd kill him for you!" I'm yelling now. Tears burn my eyes as I watch Hades's face fill with regret. It's true. He used me. I turn to leave, but the door slams closed. I spin back on Hades.

"Let me out," I snarl, emotions twisting my insides. I can't believe I've been used like this.

Hades's golden eyes flash in anger. "No."

I growl, shadows forming around me. They slither over me, ready to attack at my command. I can't portal from within the castle, so I am effectively stuck until Hades lets me out.

"You will sit so I can explain," he clarifies, motioning for the chair across from his desk.

"So you can spin more lies."

It's Hades's turn to growl. His eyes grow brighter and the castle rumbles under our feet. In the back of my mind, I know I should be scared. This is Hades, after all. But I know he'll never hurt me.

"I will tell you everything. Now sit."

Reluctantly, I walk forward and sit stiffly in the chair as he moves to take his seat behind the desk again.

I stare into his familiar golden eyes and see the god I have grown to love as a father. My chest restricts painfully at the betrayal I feel.

Hades sighs, dropping his head a fraction. "I learned of Hera's plans when Hecate let it slip one night that Althaea had borne Zeus's child. I followed Hera for some time as she took this crazy curse of hers above and beyond. One night as I was watching, something pulled me to a house. It was like a sharp tug in my chest. I had never intervened before, and yet I found myself portaling into the house before I knew it. There you were, huddled in your grandparents' arms. Your wide amber eyes staring up at me, pleading with me to save you. I knew I couldn't leave you. I justified taking you as leverage with Zeus, but I never could make that offer." He leans back in his chair. "When I found out about your abilities and the magic you held. I thought if I trained you, made you think it was Zeus who had done this to your family, that you would kill him. Us gods are forbidden to kill each other."

Hades stands and moves to the chair next to mine, shifting my chair to face his. "Leila, I could never go through with it. I ended up loving you as if you were my own. I decided I would help you stop Hera and stop this damn Order of Tartarus. I love you like a daughter, and I am truly sorry I never told you the truth."

I feel my tears well up, and duck my head in an attempt to them. I am not some little girl who needs caring for anymore. I need time to gather myself. "Can I go now?" I'm proud that my voice doesn't waver.

I don't look up, instead waiting silently. Hades sighs, standing as I hear the doors swing open. Without hesitation, I leap out of my chair and walk out through the door. As soon as I'm far enough away, I break into a sprint.

CHAPTER FORTY ONE

Nesrin

Turning the handle, I pull the door open and glance inside to find a dark staircase leading down into the basement. A quick look over my shoulder reveals no one else nearby, so I slip in and shut the door behind me. I summon an orb of light as I make my way down the stairs. The last thing I need is to miss a step. When I reach the bottom, I spot the light and turn it on. My eyes widen at the large gym sprawling out in front of me. Lukas told me about the gym, but he never mentioned just how large it was.

This is exactly what I need to get my mind off everything. I reach into my jacket to pull out my phone and sync it with the sound system. Hitting play on my playlist, I shrug off my jacket, already in my black gym pants, sports bra, and crop top. My boots aren't workout worthy, so I slip them off. Barefoot it is.

I make my way over to the rower, and get my feet strapped in. I keep up a steady pace on the rower, my breathing at an even pace. I can feel my body warming up, my muscles burning in a good way. I relish in the burning of my muscles. I haven't worked out properly in a long time, and I know I'm going to be stiff and sore tomorrow. But, honestly, I couldn't care less.

The screen on the machine shows I've already rowed ten miles. Huh. I must have zoned out. My eyes wander over to the boxing bag in the corner. I loved the kick boxing classes I attended in Pittsburgh; I miss them.

I stop rowing and pull off my top, wiping my face. I unstrap my feet and stand on shaky legs to walk over to the boxing bag. Dropping my shirt on the ground, I search around for gloves, but I don't find any. Maybe shifters don't see that point in gloves, which makes sense. My eyes catch the mirror behind the bag. I've been avoiding looking at myself, but as I stare at my reflection, I'm not surprised to see that I don't recognize the girl in front of me. I look like hell. Dark circles cast shadows under my eyes. My skin is dull and pale, almost gaunt looking. No wonder everyone seems worried. My eyes don't seem to have any spark, they seem lifeless. It's been five days since Lukas was taken, and I have barely slept. Nightmares plague my sleep, and Astraea has spent every night by my side, soothing me when I wake. I'm so thankful, but still feel tremendous guilt for putting that on her. Zee and Gabe have spent every day organizing groups and patrols to go out searching both Portland and the magical community. They question everyone, but no one knows a damn thing, and if they do, they aren't saying a word.

I back away from the mirror and move over to the bag. A deep breath falls from my lips as I take my stance. I put my left leg forward, making sure my knees are slightly bent and my shoulder slightly forward. I bring my hands up to protect my chin, my left hand slightly out farther from the face.

Tuck chin and keep the mouth closed. My instructor's words float through me.

The music is throbbing through my body, making my soul sing. I start slow, jab, cross, jab, hook, jab, repeat. I match my pace with the music, letting it keep me in a rhythm.

I feel like I am drowning. Like without Lukas, I can't find the surface to catch my breath.

Jab, cross, jab, hook. I maintain my rhythm, following the flow of the music blaring in my ears. My breathing grows sharper as the smell of leather and sweat mixes in the air. My knuckles burn with each hit, and I soak in the pain.

I add my legs now. Jab, hook, knee, jab, cross, kick. My movements become faster, my combos are spinning out of control, no rhyme or rhythm. Just my body moving with the music.

A fire is burning deep in my chest. With every hit of the bag, the heat intensifies, becoming more desperate. My magic flares and I speed up my movements, my breath heaving, making my lungs burn. Sweat drips into my eyes, running down my back and chest.

I can't believe he's gone. I will get him back, though. Until he's with me again, I won't stop.

Green eyes full of love and mischief are front and center in my mind. I let out a growl, urging myself on.

Kick. Knee. Punch. Cross. Strike. Duck. Jab.

With the words of the song fueling the fire inside of me, I step forward and prepare a roundhouse kick, my body rotating. I raise the knee of the kicking leg up, my thigh parallel to the floor as I kick out, hitting the bag hard.

The song finishes and I send another kick at the bag. A satisfied breath leaves me at the force of the bag swaying. Panting hard, I watch as the bag swings back and forth, my eyes swaying with it, only to catch my reflection in the mirror again. My eyes are pure white glowing orbs, and without thought I step up to the mirror and pull my arm back.

A guttural scream rips from my throat. All the pain and anguish that have been building escapes me. I bring my arm forward to connect with the mirror over and over, shattering into a million pieces, just like my soul.

I expel all my rage, despair, and heartache on an endless loop. I double over, my hands sinking into my hair. A mixture of sweat mixed with blood drips down my arms as I grip my head. Squatting down, I let all the pain out, my screams becoming hoarse. A ringing fills my ears, and

I squeeze my eyes shut. My chest is being torn apart in the most violent of ways. A throb of magic leaves me, and I fall the rest of the way to the floor.

Suddenly, I am lifted into the air and cradled against a warm body, a familiar scent wrapping around me. Soft words are whispered into my hair, but my mind is beyond comprehending the words being spoken. Zee sits on the floor with me in his lap. Tilting my head back, my eyes find his bright blue stare.

Worry reflects back at me, "Are you okay, honey?"

I make a horrible moaning sound and drop my forehead to his chest, his hand coming up to stroke my damp hair. I am grateful he found me because I am utterly exhausted. It's as if my body is weighed down and I'm trying to walk uphill in quicksand.

"Stupid question," he murmurs.

We stay like that for a while, me leaning on him, and him stroking my hair. As my body cools and the air caresses my sweat-coated skin, I become vaguely aware I am sitting on Zee's lap in only my pants and bra, but I can't seem to summon the energy to care. Movement next to me catches my attention, and someone tenderly grabs one of my hands. I lift my head and stare into Gabe's warm brown eyes as he takes my hand and turns it gently over in his. His expression is filled with such concern my heart gives a hard thump. He's sitting cross legged in front of us with a bowl of water beside him.

"Does it hurt?" he asks, reaching for the bowl.

I shake my head because no, it doesn't hurt as badly as the pain I'm feeling inside. I am a crazy mess. I need Lukas back. I glance over to the broken mirror, the pieces lying shattered on the floor. Jagged, sharp, and bloody; exactly how I feel on the inside.

"You know, you might be a legacy, but you're not unbreakable," Gabe murmurs, pulling the bowl of water closer. I swallow around the lump in my throat at the kindness he's showing me.

"You're our luna, our goddess." Gabe chuckles at the look I shoot at him. I wrinkle my nose, frowning at him. I don't feel like much of a luna, and I am definitely no goddess.

Gabe points off to the side before going back to washing my hands in the bowl of warm water, inspecting them for shards of glass. I turn my head to the side and my body locks up at the meadowfoam flowers blooming where I was standing only a few moments ago, my tears and blood now nowhere to be seen.

"The compound at Cascade is filled with them now."

I glance away, biting my lip. I don't have the headspace to think about that right now.

Zee's hand is idly stroking my back. I can sense his concern through the link, and I hate how much worry I'm causing them. I am their luna. It's my job to be worrying about them.

"I'm a failure," I whisper my thoughts. Zee's body stiffens, his hand frozen. Leaning back, Zee's hands gently grab hold of my chin and tips it up to him. His luminous blue eyes are equal parts angry and troubled.

"You are not a failure, Nesrin. Never. We will get him back."

He brings his face so close, our noses almost touch. I was vaguely aware of Gabe still cleaning the glass from my hand.

"Lukas is strong, one of the strongest. He will be fine. We will get him back. There's no way he would leave you," Zee promises , his words searing my heart.

I'm terrified of what might be happening to him. The last I saw before I disappeared was Lukas being shot with a silver bullet, and wrapped in iron chains. The pain alone would turn him feral if not kill him. I'm not sure I'll survive either.

Lukas's green gaze flashes in my mind again. "No more. Time to make use of these powers. It's time to show them who they are fucking with," I growl.

"Atta girl." Gabe nods, lifting his fist and gently tapping my chin playfully. My heart fills with warmth. I may not have Lukas here, but my pack is here with me. I can lean on them.

CHAPTER FORTY TWO

I shower and change before heading down to the main barn for the meeting Zee has organized. When Kate told Finan what had happened, he got on the first flight out of Pittsburgh, so he should be set to arrive sometime later tonight.

Nikolas checked in earlier. He and Nero are still in Portland, seeing what they can find out. Someone had to know where Lukas was taken.

Considering my body is physically fatigued from my workout, I have copious amounts of nervous energy buzzing through me, making me jittery. I flex my hands at the reminder, the skin still feeling tight, the wounds not completely healed yet. I wonder if I'm somehow blocking myself from healing, as if I want to suffer, to cause myself pain because I know Lukas is going through so much.

I see they have propped the barn doors open, and the place is full. My heart hammers in my chest and tears spring to my eyes again. I haven't seen anyone since that night. Zee addressed everyone for me, giving me time. But I have really let everyone down. I sense a presence behind me, and Malachite dashes past me into the barn, darting between people before disappearing. A small smile pulls at my lips. He is really fitting in here. As I approach, there is a sudden change in the air. Conversation drops to an indistinct murmur. My anxiety flares, making my hands tremble. I'm terrified, but I keep putting one foot in front of the other. The crowd parts for me and I give a weak smile to those who make eye contact. Up ahead I see Zee, and make a beeline straight for him. A large form moves into my path, and I'm pulled into a massive chest. Powerful arms wrap around me as Finan embraces me. I don't know when he arrived, but goddess, I'm glad he is here.

"God, I'm so sorry, Nesrin. We will fix this," he whispers gently to me, and I swallow around the large lump in my throat. He places me back on my feet and pulls back enough to peer down at me.

"We got this. More importantly, you got this," he says.

"Thanks, Viking," I say.

A smile moves across his face, and he turns, placing a hand on my back to guide me to the front where Zee is waiting. Zee reaches out and squeezes my hand. I turn to face the pack, flanked by Zee on one side and Finan on the other. Everyone is watching me, waiting.

The silence is deafening. Standing tall, I do my best to suppress the urge to fidget. Before I can speak, Malachite and Astraea make their way to me. Astraea looks sad, her violet blue eyes duller than usual. She misses Lukas and has asked me constantly where he is, and why he isn't taking her for their runs through the forest with Astraea clinging to his back while he makes his way through the forest, his wolf form bounding through the trees with a toddler on his back. Her tiny hand reaches for mine, and I grip it tightly.

'We'll get him back, Star.'

'I know.'

I see Nissa perched atop Talon's head off to the side. The griffin had settled in comfortably, making himself right at home. I bring my attention back to the room, looking for a familiar face.

"As you all know, we have been through a lot lately." I clear my throat. "We have lost people who meant a lot to us. I want you all to know, I will do everything in my power to protect the pack and get Lukas back. Failure isn't an option; I *will* find him."

As I look down to Astraea and then around the room, I feel a surge of courage coursing through me and I stand up straighter, my voice stronger than before. "I'm not afraid of Hera, and I'm determined to do whatever it takes to win this war. Because we will win. We will not bow or break. Our strength will never be broken." My gaze slowly moves over everyone and I continue. "I will fight for our lives—every single life. My people inside the coven are trying to locate where they are keeping Lukas. I must ask that you don't approach the coven on your own. The high priest is not to be confronted. I can sense something off about him, and I don't believe he is who he claims to be. I believe a demon has possessed him." Pausing, I allow the information to sink in.

"I'm sorry I brought this to your home. This fight was mine to carry."

Zee's hand lands on my shoulder squeezing. "You're our luna, Nesrin. It was always meant to be this way. We couldn't ask for a better luna—more strong, brave, and caring. This is *our* fight."

I look around the room to see the family I have made, the friends I never thought I'd have, and I'm grateful and terrified at the same time.

I glance to Gabe, Jameson, Kate, Finan, Kyra, Sander, Alex, and Roan.

"Hera has finally made her move. It's time I made mine. I'm done waiting for the next shoe to drop. I'm taking this fight to her."

Kyra and Sander step forward from the crowd. "We are here for whatever you need," Sander pledges, bowing his head. I attempt a half smile, but don't remotely manage to pull it off. I feel like a fraud.

'These people trust you,' Gabe gently assures me.

As I look out at the mingling crowd, a sense of loneliness hits me in the chest. These are Lukas's people, his pack. I try rubbing away the feeling, but it doesn't work. A sense of calm washes over me, love and affection pulsing in my chest. I close my eyes and follow the feeling as my mind connects with Astraea's. I startle, my eyes flashing open and peer down at her. Her bright blue eyes have hints of violet flashing in the depths as she smiles up at me. I crouch down and pull her into a hug.

'I don't know how you're doing it, but thank you, sweet girl.'
'I loves you, mommy.'
'I love you, too.'

"Why are you lurking over in the corner?" I chide, coming to a stop next to Gabe, who is leaned against the barn wall, arms crossed over his chest.

His head swivels my way, his warm brown eyes appearing thoughtful, a small grin tugging at his lips.

"I'm not lurking. I'm standing in the shadows. There's a difference."

I lean my shoulder on the wall next to him. "Alone?"

He tilts his head down at me, as if considering my words.

"Mmmhmm."

I arch my eyebrow at his response, and our silent warrior chuckles, turning back to the room. "Okay, I might be lurking," he admits.

I grin. "Why?"

A shrug. "Just observing."

I've noticed this about Gabe. He is watchful, always a step away from everyone, taking everything in. He is always the first to pick up on things because he is removed enough, for the most part, to see the whole picture.

"How are your hands?" he asks without taking his eyes off the crowd.

I stare down at my hands and flex my fingers. The tightness of the skin is still there, but the pain has gone, and the cuts have healed. My emotions are wreaking havoc on my magic.

"Good. Thank you for cleaning them for me."

"That's okay. Try not to break anymore mirrors though. Okay?"

"I'll try. No promises."

I stare out at the room, at everyone gathered. Everyone is ready to fight to get their alpha back. Leila still hasn't shown up since she portaled me here. I want to apologize to her. I don't want there to be anything hanging between us. My heart can't handle the loss of my sister, I want a relationship with her more than anything. I know there will be losses in the upcoming battle, but I will do everything I can to prevent that. I sense Gabe go alert, and he straightens from the wall, stepping in front of me.

I open my mouth, but before I can ask him what it is, there is a loud scraping noise. One that reverberates through the large space. Everyone goes quiet, each sharing looks of confusion. The noise sounds again, and I cringe, goosebumps scattering across my body. Gabe has gone deathly still next to me, and I glance up. His eyes are glowing like suns.

An ominous feeling slithers through me, like a snake. Something bad is about to happen. I survey the room, the families gathered. My eyes frantically search for Astraea, I spot her with Noah and Liam by the fire, Malachite and Talon with her. The double doors slowly swing open, and the smell of rot hits me. It instantly transports me back to my vision months ago. I didn't notice it at the time, all I remembered before was the sight of blood, and the feeling of despair. The creepy feeling of eyes on me makes the hairs on my arms stand on end. But as I watch the double doors slowly move in the breeze and the darkness beyond, everything falls into place. This is my vision. *It's happening . . .*

A bloodcurdling scream rips through the night and cuts off abruptly, followed by a cackling sound. My pulse goes into overdrive as I share a look with Zee, Gabe, and Finan. That wasn't a scream from a pack member. Laughter echoes from outside the barn doors, followed by more scraping. It sounds like whatever's out there is running long, sharp claws along the wall. The sound makes goosebumps spread over my entire body, and I shiver involuntarily.

I swallow the fear building in my throat and try my best to push the images from my vision away. I won't let it happen. This is my call. I am in charge, and I need to step up. I take a few steps forward, raising my voice.

"Everyone grab the children!"

Then down the pack bond, I send everyone the rest of the message.
'Get into the back of the room! I'm going to put you inside a protective shield and cloak it.'

Everyone stands frozen for a few seconds before moving. That horrible icy grip seizes my chest with its sharp claws, and I gasp.

"HURRY!" I shriek.

An image flashes behind my eyes. One of scattered limbs and blood.

I watch in horror as two long gray arms grip each side of the doorframe. Three long-fingered claws scrape the wood on either side, leaving gouges in the wood. A head appears through the door next. The gaunt creature has a stag's skull for a head, sunken eyes, and skin that stretches impossibly tight over its bones. It's all gray and gangly. Its mouth gapes open in a silent scream, revealing long, sharp, serrated teeth. I stand frozen to the spot, everything in me trembling at the sight of this nightmare. The creature moves into the barn, its mouth opening.

"Look what a feast I have," it says in my voice.

"Nesrin!" Finan snaps.

Oh, right. Shield. They have gathered everyone where I ordered them. I start moving my hands, before remembering I no longer need to draw upon the elements. I just have to will the magic to come forth. Pulling magic threads from my core, I weave a tightly constructed shield around the pack. I watch the magic thread together and then I reinforce it, adding a failsafe just in case.

From the corner of my eye, I see Gabe swirl into golden dust and disappear before reappearing in front of me. My mouth drops open in shock, and I reach forward, poking him in the chest to make sure it's really him.

"Did you just turn into magic dust?" I ask incredulously.

Gabe's burning golden eyes swing my way, and he gives me a sharp nod.

What the actual fuck?

"I can teleport short distances," he explains.

Since when? I shake my head. Okay, I have a lot of questions, but that can wait. I glance back at the creature stepping into the barn.

"What is that?" I hiss, my heart skittering.

"A wendigo," Gabe replies, his gaze firmly fixed on the creature as it stands in the doorway.

Zee, Kate, and Finan race up next to me.

"What's the best way to kill this thing?" Zee's focus is locked on Gabe, waiting.

"Although it appears gaunt, it is extraordinarily speedy and strong, with sharpened senses and stamina. The four of us should be able to take it down, but we have to be careful not to let it slip away, or it'll come back with a vengeance."

"I asked how to kill it, not what its strengths were, Gabe. Fuck, man. Come on," Zee growls.

I have my eyes on the horrifying creature making its way inside, but I can see Zee's body vibrating from the corner of my eye.

The wendigo creeps closer, its eerie-as-fuck eyes never leaving mine. I wrinkle my nose at the smell drifting from its body. It's the putrid stench of a rotting corpse.

"We need to destroy its heart. Cut it out and put it in a fire hot enough to melt it. Well, so I'm told," Gabe replies, stepping slightly in front of me.

"Okay, sounds easy enough," I mutter.

Gabe's body glows golden as he calls on his unique magic. I do the same. I think my sword will be able to destroy its heart if I can just get close enough. Then I remember Athena's mark, she promises protection. I pull up the sleeve of my black shirt and draw my magic into the tattoo, watching as it starts to glow.

"Sammy! Sammy!" a woman screams from behind us.

Alarmed, I turn back to the group. Letting my magic go. I have made the pack invisible to the wendigo, but we can still see them. I feel calmer knowing I can see they're okay.

I watch as the mother pushes through the group, her eyes frantically searching the children. "He was right here. Where's my boy?" she screams.

My heart drops, and I feel the blood drain from my face. Is a child outside the barrier? I whirl, looking wildly around the room. Zee moves, his head tilted as he listens.

I look back at the creature. It has stopped moving, sensing something is amiss. I chance a quick glance back at the group and I can't see Astraea anymore. Panic hits me hard and fast.

'Astraea?'

'I gots Sammy. We near fire. Creature doesn't like fire.'

'Zee!!'

At the panic slamming through our link, Zee looks at me, his yellow eyes glowing bright with fury.

'Near the fire, Astraea is with him.'

Zee's face hardens even more, his fist clenching at his sides. *'I got them, Nesrin. I promise.'*

Zee shifts in an instant, his large gray wolf slinking into the shadows.

'Gabe, we need to draw the wendigo away from the fire now!' I order down our link.

'We should draw it close to the fire, not away,' he argues.

'Astra and Sammy are near the fire.'

'That's the best place to be, the wendigo won't get closer to the fire. It's a creature of winter."

'Gabe, just get its attention!' I command.

Gabe doesn't hesitate. His magic whips out like a lasso, the golden coil wrapping around the wendigo's leg. The wendigo lets out an inhuman wail, slicing its claws through the magic before stalking toward us, its claws scraping along the floor. *'Happy?'*

In a blink of an eye, Finan shifts, his white and gray wolf pacing in front of us. A shiver ripples down my spine as the wendigo's full attention lands on me again. Its eyes are voids, having lost whatever humanity it once had, the black depths sinking into an abyss of malice and ice.

Finan stops in front of me, his hackles raised, lips peeled back, snarling. From the corner of my eye, I watch as Zee's wolf creeps around the outer edge of the large barn. If the situation wasn't so dire, I'd think it funny that a wolf that size is trying to sneak around. All the while, I do my best not to look toward the fire, not wanting the creature to pick up on anything.

Zee reaches the fire and shifts again, his hands reaching for Sammy and Astraea. I hold my breath as I watch him lift them both into his arms. Zee turns, motioning to someone else. I'm about to growl at him to hurry when Malachite darts up his body and wraps around his neck. Moving fast, Zee runs for the shield. My heart rate rises as the wendigo spins, zeroing in on him. Ignoring us, it starts for Zee. Gabe swirls into dust again and appears in front of the wendigo, throwing up a shield. I watch in horror as it moves faster than possible and dodges around the shield to make it across the room. Its long claws swipe out toward Zee, and I let out a shriek. Suddenly, Talon screeches dropping from the ceiling and flying at the Wendigos face, the griffin wraps his talons around the wendigo's horns, yanking it backward. I hold my breath as the wendigo swipes out at Talon but misses.

I turn my frantic gaze to see Zee has made it to the barrier. I let out a breath of relief that they are safe. There's another screech, this one of pain, and I swing my gaze back to Talon just as the wendigo slams into the shield, the thunderous sound causing everyone to shriek in panic.

'*It can't get through,*' I assure the pack.

I search for Talon, but he's gone. Kate, Finan, and Gabe are still standing on the other side of the room with me. I hear gasps and snarls from the pack and turn to see shadows forming inside the barrier. Then Leila is suddenly there, scooping Astraea up in her arms, Cerberus stepping from the shadows behind her, his massive paws landing with a thud. A deep, menacing growl rips from the throats of all three heads as they sweep their crimson eyes around the space. They lock on the wendigo and six glowing red eyes ignite with fury, and my heart gives a little leap. The wendigo may not be able to see in here, but he can hear. It slowly inches away from the shield, its movements stiff, and I am filled with a steely determination that I can feel in my bones.

'Gabe, can you trap him?'

Without a word, Gabe lifts a hand, and a wall of magic goes up around the wendigo, trapping it where it stands. I watch as the wendigo realizes we trapped it and starts smashing against its confines. Gabe's eyes grow brighter as he struggles to keep the barrier up.

I grab Astraea's face and place a quick kiss on her head, *'Go with Leila.'*

I look up at my sister, her eyes shining with worry. "Take the children, get them out of here." I don't want them to see this.

Leila's amber eyes widen as she scans the room. Looking back at me, her apology is clear in her eyes. I shake my head at her, trying to convey my love and understanding. We will discuss everything later. Leila nods before making her way over to the children and opens up a shadow portal. A wave of relief hits me, as I watch the portal close behind them.

A loud roar shakes the barn, reminding me our troubles aren't over yet. I turn back to the wendigo and see the barrier flickering. I draw on my inner strength, that magic I keep hidden deep inside my chest, and run out of the shield, my sword forming in my hands, as I rush the creature. At the same time as the barrier falls, I lift my arms. The wendigo's long-clawed hand swipes at me, the claws dragging painfully across my arm. I scream in pain as it easily slices through my skin. Pivoting on my feet I bring the sword down, slicing straight through the wendigo's hand, severing it from its body. It rears back, stumbling a few steps and roaring in pain.

I breathe through gritted teeth and lock eyes with Gabe. My glowing white orbs meet his golden ones. Zee and Finan circle the creature in their wolf forms, giving me time to recoup. Suddenly, the wendigo bursts forward. It swipes viciously at Finan, sending him flying through the air. Kate launches forward, but the creature is fast, evading her as it collides with Zee.

Zee grunts as he pushes his paws against the wendigo's chest, desperately trying to hold it at bay.

Sword in one hand, I reach my other hand up and try to throw the wendigo off Zee with my magic. To my disappointment, I barely get it to budge. My frustration builds as I search around frantically. Suddenly, Cerberus snarls, the sound bouncing off the walls, making the ground quake. He stalks forward, all three of his heads low, saliva dripping from his maws. A wave of relief washes through me knowing Leila left him here to assist.

The wendigo's attention breaks from Zee to take in the new threat. Zee takes the opportunity and snaps his massive jaws at the wendigo. The creature stumbles off him.

The wendigo lets out a horrible screech, and I can't help but cover my ears, the sound deafening. Icy cold horror makes my whole body freeze as an answering call sounds from outside. There are two of them?

I look to the hellhound. "CERBERUS!" I scream.

All three heads whip in my direction, and I nod outside. He nods back before turning and bolting out the doors. A snarl and a crash sound from outside, but I know the hellhound will be fine.

I turn back to Zee, seeing him back in his human form. I open my mouth to shout, but nothing comes out. I watch in terror as the wendigo hurtles forward, sinking its claws deep into Zee's shoulder, then rips them out, sending blood spraying across the floor.

Lightning erupts in my veins, and someone screams in rage. It takes only a moment to realize it's me. I don't even know how I make it across the space, but I raise my sword, catching it off guard. Moving without thought, I swing my sword, spearing for its heart. There is no resistance as the blade slices through the body. The light pulsing from the sword never wavers as the wendigo opens its mouth in a petrified scream. The noise is so loud I swear my ears are bleeding. I send a pulse of magic through the sword, the light streaming from the wendigo's mouth. Gritting my teeth, I rip the sword from its body and swing again, the blade slicing through its neck. I watch in a haze of relief as it falls to the ground, lifeless.

The sword disappears, and I spin, running the few feet over to where Zee is sitting on the ground. "Are you okay?" I blurt out, my hands shaking as I reach for his shoulder. The trembling wracks my body with such intensity I can barely get a grip on his shirt.

Zee's hands cover mine and squeeze. "Honey, I'm fine. Relax."

I sit back a little, my eyes taking him in. I calm at his words, but he looks pale, tired. Blood still gushes from the wound. Without thought, my hands cover his damaged shoulder and warmth flows from me to him. Magic pulls and stitches muscles and skin together. I rest my head on his chest as I work, his palm on the back of my head holding me close. When I'm done, Zee wraps me up in his arms, setting his chin atop head.

Gabe comes over, clapping both of us on the back. "Well, I hope we never see another one of those again."

Kate visibly shivers as she approaches with Finan. I reach for him, already knowing he has several cracked ribs, a massive gash across his midsection, and internal bleeding. I wrap my arms around him and give him a hug while healing him, his body gradually relaxing as I heal his wounds.

"Thanks, Nesrin," Finan says, cupping my face and placing a kiss on my forehead.

"It's nothing."

A moment later, Cerberus comes bounding in through the doors, his three heads surveying the area for any threat.

"You did good, boy," I tell him as I walk over to scratch each of the heads. "Who's a beautiful boy? Yes, you are. Oh, I love you," I murmur to the hellhound.

The pack spends the next hour burning the carcasses and cleaning, while I tend to the injured, healing everyone. Luckily, Zee's injuries are the worst of it. Most have only small wounds which are already well on their way to healing before I reach them.

Gabe surveys the room carefully before turning his attention to me. "You knew what was going to happen."

Though there's no question in his tone, I answer anyway. "It was my vision, the one where Grace died. I thought– I mean, I was hoping it wouldn't come to pass with Grace being gone, but I was wrong."

"What tipped you off?"

"The smell."

CHAPTER FORTY THREE

The following night, I sit at the window downstairs, my hands gliding through Astraea's curls. Malachite and Talon are curled up at my side, and Kate is snoozing on the sofa. Finan is out on a run with Zee and the others. Jameson insisted on guard duty, so I watch as he moves around the yard, his mountain lion alert as ever.

After last night, everyone's on edge. Several patrols are running, and lookouts are posted around the homes. We aren't taking any chances.

It's oddly absurd that we have been so taken aback by the monsters that have surfaced. When you're a child, you don't question the existence of monsters. On some primal level, you know that they are real, that there are things lurking in the dark, just beyond your sight, waiting for the chance to grab you. We might not know what they're called, but we know they are there all the same. Our parents will comfort us with reassuring words that monsters aren't real and we are safe. The reassurance will work for a while, but we will still harbor doubts in the back of our mind. It's with those doubts, those thoughts, that the monsters will appear, as if we have somehow given them permission. Like the very thought of them has conjured them into existence.

I jerk out of my musing as my phone vibrates in my hand. Kate jolts awake, her wide eyes snapping to me. *Sorry,* I mouth to her before answering the call.

"Nesrin?" Suzy's voice comes through the phone, full of fear. I'm instantly on alert.

"Suzy, what's wrong?"

"I think I'm being followed."

I straighten up and slide Astraea off my lap. Kate is looking at me, worry in her eyes. I point to Astraea, and she nods.

I race toward the front door. "I'm on my way. Where are you?"

"I'm at home," she whispers.

"I'll be there in half an hour. I have warded your apartment, so nothing should be able to get in. Stay put, okay?"

"Okay," she whispers, fear coating her words. "Nesrin?"

"Yes."

"Hurry," she pleads.

"I will." I hang up and send Zee a message to get home and stay with Astraea. He will know I've left the pack lands, and I want him and Gabe here to protect the others.

'Nesrin, I don't like this. Take Gabe.'

'No. I want you both here. I will call for Nero and Nikolas if I run into trouble. They are both in the city anyway.'

'Fine. Be safe.'

'Of course.'

I jump in my car and get to the city in record time, though I don't recall the drive at all. I do my best to keep my nerves at bay. I can't let anything happen to Suzy. She's only in danger because of me. I pull my car to a stop in front of Suzy's apartment and jump out. Stopping, I glance around, casting my magic out around me. I don't sense anything. Quickly, I send Suzy a message that I'm here before racing up the stairs. Suzy opens the door as I approach, relief clear on her face. She throws her arms around me, and I hug her back.

"I was so scared. I don't even know why. I didn't see anything, but the feeling was . . . my blood froze, and my brain was just *screaming* I was in danger," she swiftly explains.

"It's okay. Let's get you packed. You're staying with us for a while."

Suzy nods, and we rush to her room, throwing stuff into a large suitcase. We climb into the car, and I turn the heater up before pulling out onto the street.

"You will be safer at our place. One of the guys can take you to your classes."

Before she can respond, a sense of dread washes over me, those icy fingers digging into my chest. Movement outside Suzy's window draws my attention.

"Something's wrong," I whisper.

Suzy looks up at me, frowning.

I put more pressure on the gas pedal and take the corner, skidding to the side in a move that frightens even me. I straighten out at the last second to avoid smashing against the curb. My poor little VW shudders. I should have taken Lukas's Escalade. Performance vehicle this is not!

Suzy's right arm is up, hand pressed firmly into the roof of the car while her left has a death grip on the old fabric seat, keeping her locked in place. She shows absolutely zero signs that she might let up, but on the plus side, she isn't screaming at me.

"You know if we get in a wreck, we won't get there at all, right?" she breathes, anxiety clinging to her words.

"Sorry."

I slow down a bit, keeping my eyes peeled. Suzy relaxes her grip, dropping her arm down from the roof. My breath seems to puff out in front of me and a cold sensation spreads from my chest outward. Whatever is following us is right on us now. I open my mouth to tell Suzy to hold on when something heavy lands on the roof of the car. The impact sends me swerving across the lanes. I straighten the car as something bangs against the roof.

'Nikolas! Nero! I need you.'

'Where?' is Nikolas's prompt reply.

'Heading down Monument Avenue toward home.'

My connection breaks as three enormous claws stab through the roof of my car, tearing through the metal as if it were cheap, flimsy fabric. Suzy and I both scream, ducking our heads on instinct.

"Suzy, keep your head down," I yell as I twist the wheel sharply, hoping to dislodge the creature from the car. Another clawed hand punctures the metal, and the creature peels the roof back bit by bit. Suzy and I are sitting ducks here, and I can't drive and use my magic to defend us at the same time. I slam on the brakes, pulling to the side, the creature's momentum sending it flying over the car to land heavily onto the roof of another car.

Alarms start blaring, and I push on Suzy's shoulder. "Out! Now!"

We both scramble from the car. I race around to her side and grab her hand. "RUN!!!"

We take off down the closest alley. I chance a glance behind, seeing the creature hit the wall of the alley as it turns to chase us. I fling my arm out, throwing up an invisible wall in front of it.

I watch in horror as the daemon hits the wall and bounces off. It gets up quickly, its long limbs coiling as it pushes off the ground, jumping over the wall. *Well, fuck.*

"Suzy, go!" I yell, letting go of her hand and pushing her forward.

She spins, her purple hair whipping across her face. "What?"

"Run!"

Alarm crosses her face, and she starts back for me, shaking her head. "Not without you."

"Suzy, please. I can't lose you, too." Her eyes fill with understanding, and she hesitates a second before she nods and turns to run.

Terror seizes me as the daemon drops to the ground in front of her. *How did it move so quickly?*

Suzy skids to a stop and backs up slowly.

A screech sounds from behind me, and I spin to see the first advancing.

There are two of them.

We are so screwed.

"Nesrin. What do we do?" Suzy's panicked voice makes my adrenaline surge, and I will my magic to the surface. I reach out toward the daemon approaching Suzy, sending out a pulse of magic.

"Suzy, drop!" I shout.

Suzy doesn't hesitate. She drops to her stomach fast, covering her head. The blast of magic hit its mark, sending the daemon flying through the air. It hits the building, and I pin it there, hoping my net will hold.

A cold, bony hand clamps down on my arm, and panic curls in my stomach. I cringe as its sharp claws cut into my skin. I twist, its claws tearing through flesh with the movement, and lift my leg, landing a kick to its chest. Surprised, it releases my arm, stumbling backward. Letting out a roar of outrage, it moves forward again. This time, I grab my dagger, pulling it free from its sheath. As the daemon approaches, I spin, bringing my dagger up. A contorted, clawed hand grasps mine, twisting the dagger away savagely. I hear more than I feel the bones in my wrist break for the second time this year. I grit my teeth against the strangled cry that is desperate to force its way from my mouth.

The daemon snarls, flinging my dagger away before swiping a clawed hand at my face. I feel the skin tear on my cheek and the sting of blood as it streams down my face. Hissing through my teeth, I raise my forearm, summoning my shield. A blue wave of magic bursts to life in front of me, knocking the daemon back. I have to hold it off until help arrives. Nero and Nikolas shouldn't be far away. I'm not so sure I can dispatch the daemon with a broken wrist. Healing takes too long when I'm using my magic.

Suzy moans in pain behind me, and I turn to look at her. It's a mistake. I let my guard down. The daemon flings its arm out, catching me across the chest. I sail through the air, landing in a heap twenty feet away. I roll over, pushing up on my good arm. Anger radiates through me. I spit a mouthful of blood onto concrete, making my stomach churn. *Fucking daemons.*

I manage to get my feet under me, swaying slightly as I turn. The blood drains from my face at what I see. Suzy is dangling a few feet from the ground, her small hands gripping the massive, clawed hand holding her by the throat. Her wide blue eyes are frozen in terror as she stares at the creature. Something in my chest explodes outward, and I call on my fae abilities, willing the sword of light to me. In the next second, my vision shifts and I'm moving more swiftly than I ever have before. I bring my sword up over my head as I leap forward and plunge the sword through the daemon's chest. Surprise flashes across its hideous face and it drops Suzy. She lands at its feet and crawls away. I step forward again, slicing upward in an arc, taking off one arm. It stumbles forward, its other arm weakly reaching for me. I scream in anger, spinning and slicing through the other arm. Falling to its knees, it lets out a horrifying shriek which cuts off with my blade slicing through its neck, the severed head rolling one way as its body collapses the other.

Heaving, I remember the other daemon. I turn swiftly and race down the alley, but it's gone. *Damn it!!*

A soft groan reaches my ears and my vision clears. Suzy! I race over to her and fall to my knees at her side. My hands run over her body, frantically looking for injuries. Carefully, I lift her blouse, finding a gaping hole in her stomach. The daemon must have pierced her with its claws before I could get to her. This is all my fault. Anguish rises as I frantically try to think.

Shit. Shit. Shit.

My hands tremble and shake as I apply pressure to the wound. I already have my magic brimming along the surface, and I push it into her.

She will be okay. I can heal her, she will be okay.

I repeat this over and over, but all my magic is doing is moving in waves over her body.

Come on, heal her. I let out a hoarse scream of frustration.

There is a shift in the air, and I feel the hair around my face move. I open my eyes to a set of liquid silver eyes.

'*Ma reine, she is gone.*'

'*No! No, damn it! She can't be. Why can't I heal her?*'

'*I'm sorry.*'

No. I shake my head. *No.*

I stare at the wet blood coating my palms. So much of it that no mortal would survive this much blood loss. I can't breathe; can't think.

'*There is another way, ma reine. She can be turned.*'

I jerk my head up and gape at Nikolas. I can't focus on anything at this moment. It's like I have overloaded my system and it's frozen.

'*Ma reine?*'

"Do it," my voice cracks and I shut my eyes.

'*Are you sure?*' Nikolas's voice is soft in my head, hesitant.

'*Yes,*' I reply just as softly.

I'm not sure if this is something she would want, but I can't just do *nothing.*

'*Okay.*' Nikolas nods his head and picks Suzy up in his arms, her tiny body cradled against his chest. Her purple hair, dripping blood, hangs over his arm. I hear hooves pounding on the road. Not a second later, Nero rounds the building into the alley. I turn back to Nikolas, but he is gone, Suzy with him.

My hands fall uselessly in my lap. What have I done?

Nero nudges me with his head. '*Climb on, daughter of light.*'

I can't move. If I do, I'm afraid I will fall into a thousand pieces, and Lukas isn't here to put me back together. There is a shift in the air, and Nero's massive arm slides under my knees, the other behind my back, lifting me off the ground, cradling me against his chest. He carries me as he walks for what seems like an eternity before I hear a truck approach. It slams on its brakes to come to a stop in front of us, headlights blinding us.

"What the fuck happened?" Zee's voice bellows, and I hear several car doors open and close. Pounding feet reach our side and I feel Zee's hand pushing the hair from my face. "Honey? Nesrin, talk to me. Where are you hurt?"

His warm hands tip my face up to his, his blue eyes searching mine.

"It's not mine," I whisper, even as my wrist throbs at his question. I'll heal soon enough, but what of Suzy?

"What's not yours?"

My heart races, and I feel the bile threatening to rise. "The blood."

His questioning gaze shifts to Nero, who answers for me, "It was Suzy's."

"Was?" Zee croaks.

Nero replies in a gentle tone, but I zone out. I can't hear or see anything. I'm in a void. Nothing but pain and loss surrounds me. I'm cursed. Everyone I love is taken from me.

"Nesrin, calm down." The voice is distant. It seems to fade away as I pull further into myself. I am slipping, falling, losing myself to grief all over again. It's too much.

"Nesrin!!"

Hmm, what a nice name. I'm pretty sure I've heard it somewhere before. It means *wild rose.*

I close my eyes and let myself float on a wave of light. My body warms and I smile softly. This is nice. The light fills me, and I become uncomfortable. It's too bright, too warm. I squirm as my skin tightens and pulls, prickling with magic. It's too much. Suddenly, a cool hand moves over my face, two hands cupping my cheeks. I sigh at the touch, at the tenderness behind it. The coolness seeps into me, pushing down the heat, dulling the light. I take a breath of relief.

"Nesrin, can you hear me?"

"Hmm . . . " I answer.

"Nesrin, open your eyes."

Aren't they already open?

"No, they aren't, honey. Open your eyes."

Zee's voice sounds worried. I should probably see why. I concentrate on my eyelids. They feel heavy; as heavy as the rest of me. My eyes flutter open to see Leila and Zee huddled over me. I'm no longer cradled in Nero's arms, instead lying on the side of the road, on a patch of grass. Leila's shadows are swirling around us, so thick I can't see anything beyond them. They seem to reach for me, stroking my body, and that's when I realize I'm lit up like a glow worm. The shadows are interlacing with my light, balancing the overflow of magic before it consumes me.

"What happened?"

"Your emotions took over and you shut down. It allowed your magic to take over your body completely."

For light is all-consuming. Dark will temper the light, as will light balance the dark.

Frowning, I try to sit up. Zee's arm goes behind my back, helping me. I shoot him a grateful look before looking down. As I take stock of my body, my hands tremble at the sight of blood. My breathing picks up and I feel lightheaded.

"Suzy?" I croak.

"Shh. It's okay. Nero has gone to see Nikolas."

"I . . . told him to turn her."

"I know, honey."

I tip my head back to peer at them. "What if I made the wrong decision?" my voice cracks on the words.

Zee and Leila both share a look. They both seem lost for words. Because if Suzy's transition works, she will be a vampire. And new vampires stay in a bloodlust for the first few months of their change. Suzy won't be able to leave the house, she won't be able to be around others until it all settles. No more sun, food, or coffee. My goddess, she is going to kill me.

"Nesrin, you're hyperventilating. Just breathe," Leila coos, trying to soothe me.

"She won't be able to drink coffee," I moan, going to cover my face, but the sight of all the blood covering my hands stops me. My vision blurs with tears, and Leila grabs both my hands in hers.

"Nesrin, look at me."

I stare up into her whisky honey-colored eyes just like mine and see warmth and sadness there. "Suzy will forgive you."

I let out a sob, my hands grasping her shoulders tightly, as I pull her to me. We take a few moments to appreciate each other's embrace, feeling the closeness of our bond. Then Zee guides me over to the car and Leila hops in with me, the warmth of her arms embracing me as she softly runs her fingers through my hair. I am so thankful she's here. With a heavy sigh, I close my eyes, feeling the weariness of exhaustion.

All I want is my mate.

CHAPTER FORTY FOUR

Leila

Darkness closes in from all sides. Though, it has never been something to fear. Even as a child, I always took comfort in the dark. But as I look around now, I feel cold and vulnerable. The shadows move, follow, and reach out to me. They are part of me, part of my soul, and I would be lost without them. They encircle me, wrapping me in darkness, cloaking me from the world as if protecting me. I once felt safe, secure, and hidden amongst them. Nothing could touch me; not even the ghosts who seem always to linger. But now the darkness seems suffocating, everything seems too much. What if Nesrin and I can't stop Hera? What if we fail?

How can I protect myself from the possibility of countless losses? I can't. In a world filled with an unending supply of threats, it just isn't feasible. As for protecting Astraea, how can I when the risks are endless? Everything seems impossible.

Growing up in Hades had its challenges, but it was also where I needed to be. It took me a long time to overcome the grief and anger of losing my family, but Hades was there for me every step of the way. He was surprisingly patient and kind, considering he's the god of the underworld. Hades trained me as a warrior, focusing on my abilities, since he himself can't stop Zeus or Hera. If he tried, he would start a war. A war that would tear the realms apart. So, he gave me the necessary tools to do it myself. When he figured out I am a phantom caster and have shadow magic, he taught me everything I needed to know in order to hone those abilities.

Whenever I would doubt myself or feel myself getting lost, he would tell me, *Darkness will balance the light. For light is all-consuming. As will light balance the dark, for one can get lost in the dark without light.*

I always took comfort in those words. I looked up to Hades and trusted him completely. That was how I felt . . . until I discovered his reasons for training me were selfish. I could feel the cracks forming, threatening to crumble the foundation I built so carefully when I was a child. It will take time for me to forgive him. I know I will, but just not yet.

CHAPTER FORTY FIVE

Nesrin

I spend the next day on my bed, the comforting weight of Astraea, Malachite, and Leila beside me. All content to remain in our cocoon, the four walls of the room providing safety and comfort. I miss the sound of Lukas's voice. I want to storm Olympus, tear the heavens apart and demand Zeus find his wife. With every beat of my heart, my magic pulses in my chest, demanding payback and retribution for the millennia of pain and suffering she has caused. I feel an overwhelming urge to scream until the heavens echo back my grief, the void in my chest growing ever larger without my mate. I want them all to suffer along with me. The mating bond lies dormant in my chest, the connection still there, but quiet. So damn quiet. I hate the quiet.

Tap, Tap, Tap, sounds from the window, breaking me from my thoughts. I lock gazes with Leila to see if she heard it, too. We get up slowly and make our way to the window, where we find Talon perched outside, his feathers rustling in the light breeze. The baby griffin has been gone for a few days, his absence leaving a noticeable silence. Fear had made knots of my stomach as I contemplate the possibility that he may have been taken. I struggle to swallow the lump in my throat, raw as it is from crying.

A sharp pain rages through my back, and I jolt forward, swinging open the window. "Quickly," I call to him, realizing it's his pain I am feeling.

With a piercing screech, he flies into the room, crashing to the floor, an arrow sticking out of his back. I can't move. Can't speak. I can barely breathe as panic rises swiftly, bringing nausea with it. Leila races over to him and crouches down, assessing the wound.

Standing, she turns to me. "I'll get some towels. That arrow needs to come out before you can heal him!"

The door banging against the wall as she runs from the room snaps me from the paralyzing fear. I dart over to Talon, dropping to the ground beside him, and run a trembling hand over his head, trying to soothe him. Warmth spreads through the both of us, following the path of the magic. Astraea has a hold of Malachite on the bed, her curious eyes tracking the griffin's every movement.

The door swings open as Leila returns, Zee close on her heels. "Geez, Nesrin. What the hell?!" he shouts, taking in the bloodied griffin.

"Shut it, Zee!" I snap.

"Yes, be useful and get over here and hold him so we can remove the arrow," Leila directs, her face etched with worry.

Talon's head swings toward Zee. *'Eeeekkkk,'* he squawks softly, desperately, his beautiful golden body now soaked in blood from the wound. We need to hurry.

Zee huffs and walks over, looking down at Talon. The griffin's big golden eyes blink up at him, and I see the moment Zee's eyes soften. Zee places his hands on either side of the griffin, and I keep a hold of his head. My hands run over him in soothing motions, tempering the pain as much as possible. Those big eyes blink up at me before Talon buries his head under my arm. Leila and I nod. Leila grips the arrow, and carefully—as gently as possible—pulls the arrow out. I'm so focused on the arrow I don't notice Astraea wandering closer. My magic is instant as it finds the injury, stitching Talon back together and repairing the damage. It isn't something I even need to guide or think about anymore, the magic just knows what it needs to do. I notice Astraea on her knees next to me, her tiny hands running through the feathers on Talon's head. The griffin stares intently at her, as if the two are communicating.

I make my way down to the kitchen, spotting Zee and Gabe sitting at the table, an apple pie in front of them, and my stomach rumbles on cue. Both heads turn to me as they stand abruptly.

"How is Talon?" Zee demands.

I smile. He's smitten with the griffin, though I know he won't admit it. "Resting, but healed. I would like to know who shot him, though."

"Me, too. I was planning on heading out soon to see if I could pick up any scents," Gabe replies.

"That would be great. Thanks."

"Mom dropped by while you were sleeping. She left the pie," Zee tells me, moving to the fridge and pulling out a large container of ice cream.

"Thank the goddess. I love her pie."

After grabbing a bowl from the cupboard, I head back to the table and help myself to a generous serving. I plonk down hard on the chair, putting the biggest spoonful in my mouth. I can sense both Gabe and Zee's eyes on me, but I refuse to look at them. If I did, I might cry again, and I am sick of crying.

The air in the room cracks, and I feel a wave of electricity floating through the air. Zee and Gabe stiffen before their massive forms close rank in front of me.

"Who are you?" Zee's voice demands.

Wait, who's here? I slowly stand, wanting to be on my feet if we're about to be attacked.

"I am Silver."

Silver? I push past my friends and come face to face with the fae I met briefly in Faerie.

"I am here to help Nesrin," she explains.

Her blue hair is longer now, though her sharp teeth are just as scary as the last time I saw her. The fae cocks her head to the side as she regards me. Some sort of black substance is painted around her eyes like a mask, and she stands in a warrior's stance, a sword slung across her back. How she manages that with those wings, I have no idea. She looks nothing like the timid woman I saw before. Now she looks every part the warrior.

Tilting her head, she regards me with open curiosity. "You've changed," she says.

"So have you," I reply.

The guys stand, wedging me between them. I can sense their agitation, ready to protect me should she step out of line.

"Why are you here?" I ask.

"To help you find your mate." The room goes silent, no one so much as breathes as she takes a calculated step forward. Zee's body is trembling with unease. After everything that has happened over the last two weeks, I can't blame him. I softly place my hand on his arm, feeling his muscles tense. Down the bond, I send a wave of comfort and security.

"Can you help us locate Lukas?" I ask.

"I can. I know where he is being held, and how to get there. But there are other things you need to know."

She can take us to Lukas? My mind whirls, hope filling my chest. "How do we get to him?"

"In due time," she answers coolly.

I try my best not to growl and make demands. Zee, though, has no qualms doing just that.

"Tell us how to find him," he snarls. "We don't have time to play your games."

Her chin raises a fraction in warning. "I'm only visible to you, shifter, because I allow it. Don't push me. I *will* bite." She grins then, baring her sharp-pointed teeth, and I shiver. I do *not* want to be on her bad side.

The guys, however, both growl their displeasure, pressing in closer to my sides.

I calmly regard her. I don't know her, but Blanchette and Leopold said she is loyal to them. And at this point, we don't have any clue how to get Lukas back if not this. If she can help us, I'd be stupid to say no. I am going to get him back, even if it takes making a deal with the devil.

Before I can speak, Finan and Kate walk through the back door, freezing on the spot at the sight of us standing in the kitchen. Finan's eyes lock on Silver and his gaze turns cold, making those blue eyes seem frosted over.

"Who are you?" he growls, taking a menacing step forward. My Viking brother-in-law seems to grow in size as he stares down at Silver.

Ugh, these men are not helping.

"None of your business," Silver answers, crossing her arms.

Zee's flat stare turns incredulous, "Are you fucking kidding me?"

"Finan, back down," I bark, taking a step between the two.

"She is fae. She cannot be trusted. You need to leave, now!" he growls, fists clenching at his sides, as he directs the last part at Silver.

"So, this is the hill you're choosing to die on?" Silver croons, a dagger appearing in her hand out of thin air. She touches the tip to her pointer finger, twisting the dagger around. "You know you're no match for me, wolf boy. I'll have you gutted in a second."

Finan's snarl filled the air as he shifted in an instant. Silver's teeth gleamed dangerously as she bared them in challenge.

"Stop!!" I shout, my luna magic whipping through the room.

Everyone goes still at my command.

I glare at them, daring anyone to speak. "That. Is. *Enough*. All of you. Goddess help me, Finan, we *need* her. She can help us get Lukas back. And I will not let you jeopardize that. And you"—I point my finger at Silver as our gazes lock—"are not gutting anyone, so put that away."

Finan paces behind me, his paws clicking on the wooden floors.

I peer over at Kate. "Can you get him out of here?"

She eyes Silver nervously. "Sure. Are you okay here?"

My gaze is unwavering as I nod. I have Gabe and Zee at my back. I look Finan in the eye.

"I will be fine. Go with Kate and do a run of the perimeter."

Finan huffs out a hot breath, casting one last look at Silver before trotting out the door, Kate following on his heels.

"Where do we start?" I ask.

Zee opens his mouth to argue, but I grip his hand in mine. *'Don't. Please.'*

Silver winks at Zee and approaches us, moving for the chair. Spinning it around, she takes a seat, straddling the chair. The position, I'm assuming, is meant to accommodate her sword and wings. Her arms cross over the back of the chair as she waits for us. I take my seat again, Zee and Gabe pulling their chairs next to mine like overprotective brothers, and I can't help but roll my eyes. They are treating me like I am defenseless instead of the powerful luna I am. Silver sees, and she smirks. Gabe huffs out a breath, running a hand through his hair and tugging on the ends. He looks exhausted. We all do. Lukas being gone has, understandably, had us all on edge.

"Well?" I ask, growing impatient.

Silver's eyes flash and she turns to the door just as Leila walks through. She halts midstep, her wide amber eyes taking in Silver. "Who's this?"

Zee answers before I can, a bite to his words. "This is Silver. She's here to help get Lukas back."

"Can we trust her?" Leila asks me.

"Yes."

Silver moves then, faster than any of us are expecting, and grips my chin with her thumb and forefinger. She lifts my face to hers, her eyes glazing over as she stares at me. A vision appears in my mind, a courtyard with a beautiful garden and a balcony overlooking it. Then fire, blood, screams, and the world cracking around us as the sky turns the deep red of fresh blood. A scream is trapped in my throat as blood flows through the cracks on the stone floor.

Silver blinks, breaking the connection. Her fingers let go of my chin, and I fall back in my chair, panting. Zee and Gabe seem frozen in their chairs, and I realize Silver has contained them. Knowing them, it was likely the right call, even if it irritates me. She regards me a moment before releasing them. Zee moves to stand, but I place a warning hand on his arm.

"Don't. It was fine. I'm fine."

I can only assume that was another vision.

Silver's voice is curious when she breathes, "You're bonded to a vampire." It isn't so much a question, more of a statement, and how she knows, I have no idea.

"Yes."

"Call him here."

"Now?" I ask, looking at the setting sun. It will still be light out for at least another hour.

"Yes."

"But–"

"He will come," she cuts in.

I frown at her, but do as she says nonetheless.

'Nikolas?'

'Ma reine?'

'I need you.'

Silver chooses that moment to pull her sword, aiming it at my throat, fear punching through my stomach. And it must have been carried down the bond, because Nikolas's response is immediate and rushed.

"He's coming," I inform her, swallowing roughly. Silver smiles, flashing her sharp teeth. Sheathing her sword, she takes a seat again. Zee and Gabe are frowning at her, and Leila is sitting there, eyes wide in shock. Or maybe it's confusion. I'm really not sure at this point. Probably both.

"Good. Just wanted to make sure the message was taken seriously."

I gape at her. Is she for real? Fae can be ruthless creatures, sure. Even I know that. But my dealings with them have barely begun to scratch the surface. I clearly have a lot to learn. I wish Nissa were here.

"Your bond with him is different from that of the rest of the pack."

"How'd you know?"

"He imprinted on you, as his new master. It is different than the pack accepting you as their luna."

"Why don't we move to the living room? We can sit and talk more comfortably," Leila suggests.

I look around the kitchen, and all the throwable objects. Probably a better idea. The living room is more open and spread out, preventing anyone from getting too close to each other. I nod and stand, making my way into the other room without waiting to see who follows.

Before I can ask more questions, Nikolas barrels through my front door. I stare at him, dumbfounded.

"You came? How?" I look to the window where the sun is still visible.

"What is wrong?" he demands, ignoring my question. His steps stop abruptly when Silver steps around the corner, a smirk on her face.

"Nesrin is in need of your family's heirloom." Then she turns to Gabe in the corner. "As well as your special ability," she adds sweetly.

My eyes widen and I glance around the room, thankful to see everyone else just as confused as I am about this. What does Silver know that we don't?

The sound of hooves approaching means Nero will crash through the door at any moment. Nikolas is on Silver in the time it takes me to blink, gripping her around the throat and lifting her off her feet. I jerk forward a step, ready to intervene when a flash of silver catches my eye. *Fuck.* Silver has a dagger positioned over Nikolas's heart. My mind empties and I lash out with my magic, sending both of them flying. They each slam against opposite walls where I hold them a foot from the ground.

'Mommy, your eyes are pretty.' Astraea's voice startles me, and I look over at the door to see her standing there with Malachite in her arms and Talon next to her, his head tilted curiously as he regarded me.

The front door indeed crashes open right on cue as Nero strolls in, ruffling Astraea's hair as he passes. Zee, Gabe, and Leila have stood silently behind me this whole time, letting me handle this situation, and I'm extremely grateful because I really don't need Zee and his smartass mouth making things worse.

'Thanks, sweet girl. Why don't you take Malachite and Talon with you to the kitchen and get a snack?'

Astraea smiles and nods before turning down the hall, making her way to the kitchen. I release Nikolas and Silver and both land on their feet, glaring at each other.

Nero walks over to Nikolas and blocks his view of Silver. I don't hear what is said between them, but I feel Nikolas's hurt and shock through our link. He takes a step back as if Nero has slapped him. I walk over and grip Nero's arm, pulling him away.

"Leave him alone," I scold.

Nero looks down at me, his eyes flashing a bright gold, his displeasure clear. The dark tattoos seem to move across his bare skin as he regards me. I don't care if he thinks I'm overstepping. Nikolas is mine to protect. I step between the two, putting my back to Nero. I stare up at Nikolas and smile. "Hey, I'm sorry. I didn't know it was going to be an ambush."

Nikolas's blue eyes fall to mine and soften. "I know, ma reine. This isn't your fault, it's his." He glares back up at Nero.

I turn, still wedged between the two, and glare up at Nero. "What did you do?"

"I merely passed on information that could be useful in helping you retrieve your mate." He states it with no emotion whatsoever. Then it clicks. He betrayed Nikolas's confidence to help me. Guilt and frustration whip through me.

"I won't force him to help. It will be Nikolas's choice if he tells me his secrets, not yours." My anger at the situation gets the better of me. As much as I want Lukas back, I won't ruin my friendships to do it. Trust is far too important.

Nikolas's voice is tired and withdrawn. "I'm a dhampir. Born from a vampire and mortal. That's why I can walk in the sunlight. I kept it a secret, as my kind are rare; usually hunted or forced to become hunters themselves." I turn to peer at him, and he offers me a small smile. "I don't have the same weaknesses as full-blood vampires, but I still can possess their abilities, depending on how strong my father is."

"Who is your father?" I whisper. I grab his hands in mine. Then, "You don't have to tell me."

Nikolas pulls me over to the sofa and takes a seat, pulling me down next to him. All but Silver and Nero take their seats around the room.

"I have lived hundreds of years. I was born in the year 1547."

I balk. I mean, of course I knew he was old. But . . . I quickly do the calculations. "You're four hundred seventy-four years old!" I blurt.

Nikolas chuckles and Zee whistles. "Dude, you're old."

"I may be more mortal than a vampire, but I can still live for hundreds, if not thousands of years. But, back to your question. Stephan is my father."

My mouth drops open, and I gawk. "Wow. Okay. Now his reaction to me bringing you into the pack makes substantially more sense."

Nikolas dips his head. "Stephan fell in love with my mortal mother and they married, but war broke out, and she was killed when I was five. After that, Stephan took my safety very seriously." He pulls a chain out from under his shirt. "He had this made for me by a witch. I have never taken it off. The protection has never worn off, the spell using my life force to replenish."

My brain is still in shock, because I can't quite seem to move on from the whole *Stephan is my father* thing. "Stephan's, like, your actual father?"

Amusement fills Nikolas's gaze. "Yes."

What the fuck?

"You say that a lot, you know," Leila teases, making a feeble attempt to hide her smile.

"Hence the mug," Gabe quips with a wink.

I lean forward and poke Nikolas in the chest. "I can't believe it. You're like a unicorn!"

Nikolas's eyes turn incredulous. "You did *not* just call me a unicorn."

"I did. I totally did," I admit, still gaping at him.

Nikolas shakes his head, a small smile tugging at his lips. Pulling the chain over his head, he holds the pendant out to me.

"I won't take that from you," I refuse, holding up my hands.

"I want you to use it. If it will help you get Lukas back, take it." He grabs my hand, turning it over and placing the amulet in my palm, the metal surprisingly warm. My pendant pulses in response.

"Who made this?" I whisper. It's a mirror image of my own pendant, but hanging from Nikolas's moon is a red star, whereas mine is blue.

Nikolas gives me a lopsided smile. '*Ma reine.*'

I lift my pendant from where it hangs beneath my shirt and hold them next to each other. They contain the same essence. My eyes dart back up to his. "Was it Althaea?"

"Hecate," he answers.

My pendant has held my magic in it for a long time. It has helped me hone my abilities and seek out those at risk of darkness consuming them. Althaea said it also offers protection. I just assumed she meant warning of impending danger. Apprehension twists my stomach as the pendants seem to hum in my palms, lifting from my hands. I watch in fascination as the two essences light up and begin to merge like threads of magic reaching for each other. The pendant reforms into an intricate full moon with a single purple star gem in the middle. It drops into my palm and dims, resting normally in my hand. The room is so silent you would hear a pin drop.

A crash from the kitchen startles us, but the giggle that follows has me sagging in my seat. My worried eyes meet Nikolas's. "I didn't know that was going to happen. Nikolas, I'm so sorry."

Nikolas's hand reaches out, cupping mine, and gently closes my fingers over the pendant. "Nothing to apologize for. It's yours. I gave it to you."

"But–" I start, but he simply shakes his head.

"No, buts,"

"Wait. If you're dhampir, how did you change Suzy?" Zee pipes up, breaking our moment.

Nikolas drops my hands and rubs the back of his neck. "Stephan carried out the change. It is not something I can do."

"Wait! Is she okay?" I ask.

Smiling softly, Nikolas's eyes swirl with silver, the change in color mesmerizing. "She is actually adapting very well for a newbie."

The relief that sweeps through me is swift. I let out a long breath.

"Now it's your turn, foxy." Silver holds out an arm to Gabe, clicking her fingers.

Stunned by her abruptness, I glance over at her and growl, "Stop ordering my friends around."

Silver shrugs nonchalantly and looks at Gabe. "You need to help fortify her mind. She cannot be near Hera without first building up her defenses. Hera will slice through her mind like a sword slicing through flesh."

"Nice analogy." Gabe smirks.

Silver shoots him a grin. "Once you're done," she then sets her eyes on Leila. "You will test her."

Leila stands abruptly. "But–"

Silver holds her hand up. "But nothing. She *cannot* do this if her mind becomes compromised. You are the only one who can test those barriers properly, and you know it."

Leila worries her bottom lip, her eyes catching mine. "I don't want to hurt you again," she whispers.

An image flashes in my mind, a memory of the first time she broke through my mental shields. The pain then was so excruciating I passed out.

Faking bravado, I assure her, "I'll be fine. If it helps me get Lukas back, I'll do it." Zee squeezes her shoulder, and to my surprise, she leans into him, accepting his offer of comfort. Lifting my gaze to Zee, I see he is just as surprised by her actions.

"Good, it's settled," Silver chirps, clapping her hands together. "Now, I'll leave you with Gabe to work on fortifying those shields. I'll be checking the perimeter."

Before I can protest, Silver is gone, the front door closing behind her.

Nero steps forward, his eyes on Nikolas. "Can we talk?"

"No. We have nothing to talk about. You could have spoken to me about this, but instead you chose to go behind my back," Nikolas answers. The raw pain in his voice is unmistakable. Nero's golden eyes flicker, and I wish I knew what he was thinking.

"I'm sorry," Nero says, walking toward where we're seated, "but I need to talk to you." With no warning, Nero reaches out and grabs Nikolas's hand, pulling him into his chest. Before anyone can react, they both disappear. *What the absolute fuck?*

We all stare at the spot where Nero and Nikolas disappeared for a moment until Zee mutters under his breath, "Fucking fae," and turns, leaving the room. "I'll take care of Astraea and the strays!" he calls back to me over my shoulder.

Leila takes the seat next to me on the sofa. "Nesrin, are you sure you're okay with this?"

Grabbing her hands, I give her a small smile. "Of course, I know what needs to be done, and if I stand any chance of rescuing Lukas, we need to do this. I need to be strong. Hera will take control the minute she can. I can't give that chance."

Leila nods. "I'm worried."

I open my mouth to reply when I'm suddenly sucked into a vision. My eyes are slow to adjust as I take in my surroundings. Immediately, I recognize where I am. I have been to this field of meadowfoam flowers before. I turn in a circle, my steps faltering at what I see. Leila and I are lying side by side amongst the flowers. A flash of light blinds me, but before I can move closer, Hermes appears. He turns, looking directly at me, and I'm suddenly ripped away.

Slowly, the world comes back into focus, and I see Leila's glazed-over eyes. She blinks and stares at me a moment. "You saw that?" I question.

"Yes," she croaks, letting go of my hands to twist her red hair over her shoulder. Her fingers idly move through the strands. Gabe's voice startles both of us. "What did you see?"

Gabe and I spend the next three hours working to strengthen the walls around my mind. There is no way I am letting anyone get through these walls. We've been training for weeks, Gabe talking me through the process, building it brick by brick. But this time he tells me to reinforce each brick with steel. I thought my barriers were good before, but they were nothing compared to this. No wonder Leila was able to get into my mind so easily back when the coven captured me. I've added my own special touch around the wall as well. An electric current now runs over every inch of that barrier. Anyone who tries to use compulsion or manipulate my mind will be in for a shock. Literally.

"That's a nice little extra touch you have there, Nesrin," Gabe quips warily, having just tested my walls and gotten a small zap for his efforts. If he were digging deeper, the shock would have been even worse.

"I thought so," I chuckle.

Gabe runs his hands over his face. It's late, and we need to get some rest, or we will all be walking zombies tomorrow. I can feel fatigue dragging me down. And not just from the dinner Zee and Leila made for us earlier. I still can't help but chuckle at the memory of poor Zee trying to bathe the little ones earlier. Unfortunately for Zee, Malachite is a water dragon, so he can make bathtime seem like an underwater adventure for the whole family. The laughter causes the sleeping Talon to stir, his head pressing against my side and his feet digging into Gabe's side. The little griffin has been wedged between us on the sofa since after bath time. I lazily stroke my hand over his wings, my fingers tracing the soft feathers in hopes to lull him back to sleep.

"Are you still okay with Leila testing this out?"

Shit, I have been so focused on making my mind impenetrable, I forgot who was testing it. I stop mid stroke over Talon's wings, and his head pops up to nudge my hand in protest.

"I forgot. Do you think we need to test it? You said it was good, right?"

"Well, yeah . . . but we still need Leila. She is a phantom caster, after all. If anyone might have a chance to get through those barriers, it's her."

I stand and start pacing. Rubbing my hands on my jeans, I shake my head. "No, it'll be fine. I don't need the testing."

"Yes, you do."

I spin toward the door as Leila walks in, Zee right behind her.

"But–"

"But nothing. I said I'd do it. I will be fine."

I bite my thumbnail. This will most likely hurt both of us. I cringe, thinking about the last time, but know she's right.

"Tomorrow," I counter. I need a good sleep if we're going to do this.

"Now." Silver appears out of thin air, ready to shut down negotiations. Growls erupt from Zee and Gabe, while Leila and I both let out embarrassing squeals.

"Can't this wait till morning?" I try again, crossing my arms.

"No."

"Look, I think . . . "

"I don't care, and neither does Hera. You need to do this now. Do you think Hera will wait for you to be well rested before attacking you? This is the best time to test your defenses."

She's not wrong, and I have the sense to feel ashamed for my reluctance. I need to get this over with. I need to focus on rescuing Lukas. I have tried so hard not to think about what he must be going through. The times I've allowed myself to think about it too much, I've felt my sanity slipping. And so, I nod and seal the room. I won't have everyone running in here wondering what's happening.

I turn my focus to Leila, but she is watching Silver carefully. So I walk over to grab her hand, then pull her over to one sofa before moving to sit on the sofa opposite her.

"Ready?" I ask.

"Ready," she sighs.

I stare into her eyes, the mirror of my own, as I feel the sharp nails testing the edge of the barrier. It feels like the spine-tingling sensation of scratching your nails across a chalkboard.

Tap, Tap, Tap.

We don't break eye contact as Leila pushes against my mental shields, testing, pushing, and scraping along each wall, looking for weakness of any sort. I have a trap set, a softer part of the barrier, and I pray she won't find it. If she pushes into it, she'll get a shock. Like, a real shock. I bite down on my lip, my fingers digging into my pants.

Leila edges closer to my trap and my eyes widen as she feels around it, testing. I shake my head at her, the movement barely visible, but she understands. But instead of backing away like I'd hoped, she pushes through the weak spot into my trap, my magic wrapping around her mind and sending jolt after jolt down the tether. Leila jerks in her seat, and I cry out, cutting off the magic before she gets hurt. I slide to the floor and crawl over to where Leila is doubled over on the sofa, Zee's hand rubbing circles on her back.

"Are you okay?" I whisper, stopping in front of her. She holds up a single finger, not lifting her head. I wait, casting Zee a nervous expression.

"Her mental shields are strong, stronger than any I've come across," Leila breathes.

"Perfect." Silver is clearly pleased, her sharp teeth on display. Her silver eyes stand out even more against the black paint on her face as they brighten with anticipation.

Gabe helps me to my feet and Leila stands with Zee's help, a weak smile on her face. She has a trail of blood coming from her nose. My hand reaches up and I swipe under my own nose, realizing I do as well.

"You did good, Nesrin," Leila croaks. I can see her muscles quivering and guilt slithers through me. Before I can formulate a reply, Silver steps between us.

"It's time to go."

Her hand grips my arm, and the world disappears.

CHAPTER FORTY SIX

My head is spinning when we reappear in a small, round room with stone walls. It only has one window, a bed, and a large hand-crafted wardrobe. Silver drops my arms, stalking over to the wardrobe, and flinging the door open. She reaches in, rummaging through it while I take slow steps toward the window. I feel like I have sea legs, the room swaying slightly as I walk.

"Where are we?" I ask, gripping the ledge of the window and peering out.

Great mountains rise off in the distance, snow coating their peaks. The sound of swords clashing below draws my attention, and I realize how high up we are. The room overlooks a massive courtyard and gardens, currently occupied by around thirty soldiers doing drills below. A massive humanoid creature with horns and leathery wings is pacing the lines of soldiers, bellowing orders.

"We are in Faerie. Here, put these on."

I turn just in time to catch the clothes she's thrown at me. I hold up the leather ensemble and raise an eyebrow.

Silver rolls her eyes and huffs. "It will offer you protection."

"I can't believe you took me without letting me say goodbye. You know they're going to worry."

Silver simply shrugs and moves over to a large chest in the corner I've yet to notice. I strip off my clothes and quickly change, surprised to find the clothes fit perfectly. I lift my arms, admiring how the suit looks and feels against my skin. It kind of reminds me of Catwoman. The sleeves go down to my wrist, and it zips up at the front. I bend to pull my boots back on, and stand. Silver tosses a sheath and two long daggers and I catch them with ease.

"Just in case." She slams the lid of the wooden box. "You know how to use them, right?"

I scoff and roll my eyes. "Of course."

"Good."

"So, where is Hera keeping Lukas?" I ask, getting to work at strapping the sheath around my waist.

"Argos."

I fumble with my strap and glance over at her. She's standing at the window, peering down at the soldiers.

"In Greece?" I clarify, confused at why Hera would take him so far.

Silver looks over, her silver eyes glittering in the sunlight streaming in from the window. Tucking her blue hair behind her pointed ear, she nods.

I swallow roughly as my heart picks up its pace. I finish strapping the daggers to me and run shaky hands over my waist. "Okay. Let's go. Oh, wait. One more thing." Walking over to my discarded clothes, I reach into my pocket and pull out the newly formed pendant and slip it over my head. I notice as a tingle of magic washes over me, and sigh.

Turning to Silver, I see her biting her lip. "What?" I question.

"One more thing." She disappears and I'm left standing on my own in the room. "What the fuck?" I growl. This damn fae is driving me crazy. I storm to the door and swing it open. I hesitate briefly before stepping out into the hall. I look left and see this is the last room in the hall. And when I look right, there is only a set of stairs leading down. Slowly, I make my way down the stairs. Silver technically hasn't told me to stay put, and I have a sudden burst of energy since arriving here. At the bottom of the stairs, there is a single door, which must lead outside, as I can see the sunlight outlining the door. I quietly open it. A gentle breeze lifts my hair, sending it across my face. Pushing it away, I move into the courtyard, keeping to the shadows and outer edges.

I move behind a tree just as the fae with the horns and wings turns my way, his head raising like he's sniffing the air. The breeze ruffles my hair again, and I curse silently, wishing I would've thought to braid it before I came down here.

Growling under my breath, I reach up and twist it over my shoulder. When I look back to where the soldiers are, a small yelp escapes me. The massive fae is standing directly in front of me. When did he move?

Crossing his massive arms over his chest, he leans causally against the tree. "What do we have here? Are you lost, little bird?" he asks in a rough, deep voice. His gaze holds mine. I freeze, unable to form any coherent thoughts. When his eyes flicker down, taking in my outfit, I take a step back, my hands slowly drifting to my daggers. His eyes watch the movement, a smirk tilting his lips.

"And what exactly do you think you will do with those?" he inquires mockingly.

I raise my eyebrow in challenge. "I'm sure I could get some hits in if I were given a reason to defend myself."

The fae straightens from the tree. "What are you?" he leans in closer, sniffing me.

"Rude," I chide, nerves jittering around in my stomach. His enormous wings flare wide, blocking out everything behind him.

His intense silver eyes harden. "You're the one walking around–"

The sudden appearance of Silver cuts his words off. Her hand grips mine, and she smirks at the fae.

"Sorry, Raiden. Gotta go!"

Raiden moves to grab us, but the world is sucked away, and we land back in her room. Nikolas's eyes widen as he stands there. Silver doesn't speak, just grabs his hand and winks us all out of the room again.

Oh, goddess, I feel sick. I breathe heavily through my nose. The moment my feet hit the ground, I fall to my knees, my head spinning wildly. I grip the long grass in my fist and hang my head. I feel Nikolas approaching me, crouching down with a palm on my back. He rubs slow, soothing circles, pulling my hair back.

'*Are you okay, ma reine?*'

'*Hnnh,*' I groan, pushing back to kneel, then speechless as I take in the surroundings. We are atop a hill overlooking the City of Argos and the mountains in the distance. Curiosity fills my mind as I contemplate what the mountains are called. My knowledge of this area is limited, but each and every part of it holds stories and history.

I admire the citrus groves covering the fields on one side of the city, and my mouth drops open in wonder at the sight.

It is beautiful. Nikolas helps me to my feet, and I relish the feeling of the breeze on my flushed face. The black leather suit does not suit this weather at all. I wish I were in a flowy dress with Lukas's hands in mine as we took in the scenery together. A sharp pang hits me in the chest, and I turn to Silver.

"Right. Where are we going?"

Silver smirks. "I will take you there."

"Where is there?" Nikolas questions. I can feel his distrust for the fae clearly.

"Heraion of Argos, also known as the Sanctuary of Hera."

I reach up to run my fingers through my tangled hair, wishing again for something to tie it back. "Why is Nikolas here?" I ask, dropping my arms and frowning.

Silver's eyes dart to the dhampir, and Nikolas folds his arms, waiting.

"He is the only one of your friends that Hera won't be able to control. Plus, I figured a little backup wouldn't hurt. The temple is in ruins, but that is just an illusion for the mortals. You will see what lies beneath the spell. Hera will have her followers there and her guards, so you need to be alert."

Sounds easy enough.

"It won't be. This is Hera," Silver admonishes, her wings fluttering in agitation. "Even if she isn't expecting you, she will be ready."

I lean into Nikolas, grateful for his presence. Silver's right, I need the backup. Silver reaches for us and smirks. "Hold on."

Before I can protest, we are disappearing again.

CHAPTER FORTY SEVEN

S ilver drops us in front of a set of large metal gates. I will never get used to transporting. I hold a hand over my stomach as it wrenches uncomfortably.

"I'll find you once you secure Lukas."

Before I can ask questions, she pops back out of existence.

I take a deep breath, my anticipation growing by the second. Lukas is in there somewhere. I am so close to getting him back. Nikolas grabs my arm as I take a step forward. I look up into his blue eyes, watching as specks of silver dance in their depths. He drops my arm, running his hand through his hair, making the blonde strands fall messily.

"Are you sure about this? We haven't even made a proper plan. We are just supposed to walk in and find Lukas, then by some miracle, trust Silver will pop up and get us out?"

"Yes. I don't have a choice. I'm going to get Lukas." The longer we are apart, the harder it becomes to breathe.

"I don't understand why the fae doesn't stick around. Are you sure we can trust her that she didn't just deliver us to a crazed goddess?"

Before we can say more, the gates swing open and a dozen guards run out, surrounding us. My hands linger over the hilts of my daggers, but Nikolas stills my hand.

'*Conserve your energy.*'

I nod and raise my hands, Nikolas doing the same. Two guards walk forward and push us toward the gates. I peer over my shoulder and growl, "Hands off!"

Surprise flashes in the guard's eyes before he regains his composure. "Move."

As they march us through the impressive gardens into the temple, I look around, noting all possible escape paths and the locations of every guard post.

'*I don't like how they are looking at you, ma reine.*' Nikolas's voice is filled with concern.

'*I haven't noticed.*'

Nikolas hums down the link. His hands clench and unclench at his sides. I look up at him, finding his face a firm mask of displeasure as we continue down a wide corridor.

Up ahead, I see a set of giant wooden doors, propped open to reveal another room beyond. The closer we get to the doors, the steadier my heart becomes. My body relaxes. As we approach those doors, I feel strangely at ease. No fear, or anxiety pounds in my veins. Nothing but a calm sort of rage burning in the very core of my being.

As we walk into the open chamber, we find her sprawled across a white velvet vintage sofa with carved gold legs. Hera turns her head toward me as I enter, her stare immediately connecting with mine. Her bright red lips curl into a sardonic smile, making me want to launch myself at her. She takes a sip from her wine glass, her unbreaking gaze trained on me.

Making me wait is a power play; one I will play. I cross my arms over my chest and cock my hip, not taking my attention off her for a moment. Hera raises one perfectly manicured eyebrow, letting out a small chuckle.

"Full of fire, I see."

I don't answer. I just continue to glare. Hera's eyes move to Nikolas, her gaze slithering over him. "I don't know you."

"You wouldn't." Nikolas shrugs, placing his hands in the pockets of his tailored pants in a casual move. But I can tell he is primed, ready for a fight.

Amusement lights her cold eyes as she makes an obvious attempt to pry into Nikolas's mind. Her eyes flare the second she realizes what he is. I see Nikolas flinch, and my protective instincts flare. Before I can think better of it, I have one of my daggers in my hand and send it flying through the air, end over end, toward Hera. She catches the blade with ease and simply pauses to examine it, testing the sharpness.

"Brave, but foolish," she remarks, smirking at me. She drops the dagger next to her on the sofa and flicks her wrist. I watch as a wave of magic rolls toward me. I brace myself instinctively, a shield of blue flashing into existence before me. The spell hits the shield and bounces back toward Hera. Her eyes widen and she deflects the spell. It hits the nearest guard full in the chest. His eyes widen as he staggers backward with a grunt, touching his chest. I stare at Hera, and I'm not sure who's more surprised by the turn of events. Where did that blue shield come from? I didn't will it into existence. Did I?

'Was Hecate, ma reine. The pendant works.'

'Huh.'

I lift the necklace up and admire the soft silver glow surrounding it. A noise from the guard has me dropping it back to rest on my chest. His expression is enraged. He clearly didn't enjoy whatever Hera concocted for me.

I feel a flutter along my mental shields and slowly turn my gaze back to Hera. It's my turn to raise an eyebrow.

Anger transforms her face as she stands. "Well, well. You've come prepared, I see."

"Where's Lukas?" I demand.

"Where's Eris?" she counters.

Alarm bells go off in my head at her words. "Not a clue," I reply casually.

Hera sighs, taking slow, deliberate steps toward us. Anger seeps into her features as she approaches us. I am done fearing this woman, done being a victim. I cross my arms over my chest, lifting my chin.

"Why did you kill my family? Surely you knew Eris was just feeding you lies." Resentment burns through me, but I have to keep myself under control, Lukas's life is at stake.

"I killed them because of the threat the child had on me."

"What?"

"You will pay for her death. Eris, I mean. She was a dear friend of mine," Hera threatens, circling me, her hand reaching up to twirl a piece of my hair around her finger. I hold still, frozen. Deep inside, I feel my power growing, thrumming through my body, ready to be unleashed, but I need to see Lukas first.

"As for the why. I was told by a powerful oracle that a child from Blanchette's bloodline would be the one to put an end to my reign. That they would release all those I had cursed by destroying me. Now, obviously, I couldn't let that happen. The fact that my husband was Blanchette's father made it even easier for me to hunt you all down."

I step forward, feeling a type of wrath stirring inside of me. My skin hums with magic, making my hands and eyes glow. Wisps and tendrils of light float around my palms as I stand facing Hera.

A chill snakes down my spine. "You gods are all the same. Spend your days cheating on each other, then seek revenge for the betrayal. It's pathetic," I spit at her.

Hera's eyes flare with anger. "You have no idea–"

"No. *You* have no idea. The amount of pain and suffering you have caused," I cut her off. Nikolas moves closer to me, his body tense. Hera's eyes move to him and something cruel and twisted blazes in them. Her lips curl into something wicked, and flicking her fingers, she sends a spell toward Nikolas. Without thought, I step in front of him, and once again, my pendant flares to life, magic pulsing outward in a shield, the spell bouncing off its surface. Only this time, everyone takes cover.

Hera's growl echoes through the chamber, but I keep speaking. "What about the pack of felines in Salem? Was that you? Just another group of innocence for you to torment?"

With a sly smirk, Hera lets her amusement be known. "Oh, yes. They were fun to taunt. It was so easy to dive right into their minds and play with them. Never could quite bend them to my will, though."

"They are not your playthings." Overwhelming rage floods me at the callousness of the remarks.

"Why are you so huffy about it? I didn't mess with your pack, now, did I? Plus, you broke my control over them," Hera replies, her face calm as she waves off my anger with a flick of her wrist, as if all she did was take my favorite sweater. I am so ready to teach her a lesson.

"I want to see Lukas. I won't be leaving without him." My voice has dropped an octave, my magic bursting at the seams to wipe them all out.

Hera gestures to the room. "Who said you'd be leaving at all?"

"I will be leaving here."

"Love is a weakness, you know," Hera tells me.

"No. Love gives you something to fight for," I correct her.

"Being loved by someone gives you strength, while loving someone gives you courage to face danger and persevere against impossible odds," Nikolas adds, voice rich with conviction.

Hera huffs in annoyance. "Oh, fine. You want your precious mate back? You will need to fight my champion. Win and you can have your mate. Lose and he is mine."

"What are the rules?" Nikolas inquires.

"Simple. No magic. Only combat."

Nikolas and I stare at each other. *'I can be your champion,'* he offers.

I jerk back, my eyes widening. *'No.'*

I will not allow him to fight on my behalf. Never. I look back to Hera, her smirk firmly in place, and anger burns in the pit of my stomach. She knows it, too. I will never allow someone to get hurt in defense of me.

And every time she looks at me, I can't help but want to wipe that look off her face so damn bad.

All that matters is Lukas's release.

I must have been glaring at her for longer than I thought, because she bristles, her pitch rising with each word. "Do we have a deal?"

I nod my head. "Deal."

Hera throws her head back and laughs before turning away. Waving her hand in the air, she exits the room and the guards move forward, motioning back the way we had come.

I look to Nikolas. *'I hope this works.'*

'You won't be able to use your magic in there. Nor will you be able to shift.'

I sigh, *'I know. I will figure something out. I can't lose.'*

'I know, ma reine.'

'I'm glad to see the pendant is working though.' I smile up at him.

Nikolas grins down at me. *'That was pretty epic.'*

"Enough, you two," one of the guard's growls, shoving us in the back.

Nikolas turns, snarling at the man. "Do. Not. Touch. Her."

CHAPTER FORTY EIGHT

I'm pushing through the gate into a small amphitheater, the stands mostly full, and when people see me, a deafening cheer erupts.

What in the actual fuck is going on here? Where did all these people come from? Where am I? This doesn't look like any place I've ever seen. It's like a smaller version of the Colosseum.

Hera made sure I would be without my magic in the arena, but thanks to Gabe, Zee, and Lukas, I have learned a great deal these last few months. I am more than my magic. I am a fighter. I am strong, and I will save my mate.

Though whatever she did may have hindered my magic, I can still feel it. Deep down, it lies waiting for the moment I need it.

The gate opposite me opens and Lukas strolls out, his face a mask of fury, his green eyes blazing with wrath. And it's aimed at me. My joy at seeing him melts away instantly when I realize *this* is her champion.

Primal fear twists my insides at the thought of fighting Lukas. I sweep my eyes over his naked torso, my breathing growing more ragged with every inch I survey. The wound from the gunshot still hasn't healed. They haven't so much as removed the bullet yet, and black veins of poison are visible across his shoulder and chest. His tattoo is crusted with dried blood, and he has several cuts that aren't healing on his abdomen.

My heart clenches and my first instinct is to run for him, but I hold myself in check. This isn't the Lukas I know; Hera has control over him at this moment, which ignites a hatred like never felt before burning in my chest. I send my senses forth through our bond, reaching out for him, but hit a wall.

'If you get him to shift, the fae magic will burn away her spell. He will be free. It's the only way.' Silver's words ring in my head and I glance around quickly.

Okay, so I need to get him to shift. That's the only way to break the compulsion spell and free him. But, of course, that's easier said than done.

I stare intently at Lukas, my emotions a jumble as I try to sort through my thoughts. My mind is racing as I try to recall the contents of my grimoire. I mentally shake my head. No matter how hard I attempt to come up with an idea, it's like my thoughts are just beyond my grasp. My pulse races as the cheering continues around us. Lukas's face twists into something dark and wicked.

A harsh, blaring horn echoes through the arena, the sound reverberating in my chest, and I falter, scanning the arena. My heart pounds in my chest, as I refocus on Lukas.

On instinct, I reach for my magic and I'm met with an empty void. This is what Lukas, Gabe, and Zee have been training me for all these months. Preparing me for when I couldn't rely on my magic to get me out of a situation. The crowd begins pounding their feet on the ground, the shock of it making my stomach sink.

My focus flies to Nikolas standing on the other side of the gate where I came through, his face set in a grim expression. He doesn't have the answer, either. Dread and anxiety claw at my chest. They do their best to overtake my ability to solve this puzzle, and I struggle for several seconds to take in a deep breath. With a loud clank, a rack of weapons slowly rises from the ground, the sound echoing around Lukas as a part of the ground opens up beside him.

Shit.

Lukas doesn't even spare them a glance as he charges forward, an animalistic roar ripping through the air. I ready my stance, waiting until the last second, then lunge to the side. Lukas misses his mark but pivots, his wild eyes tracking my movements with precision. We circle each other slowly, and I take the chance to attempt reasoning with him.

"Lukas, it's me." My breaths are coming out in pants, my gestures pleading with him as we continue with this terrible dance. "You have to know who I am. It's Nesrin. *Please.*"

Lukas sneers, "I know who you are. You're an abomination."

Pain lances my heart at his words, his unfettered disdain making it difficult to keep my composure. I do my best to ignore it. "You are the love of my life," I try to keep my voice strong, but it cracks on the words.

He swings out a jab aimed at my face and I duck under his fist, shifting my weight and kicking out at his legs, but it's like kicking a stone wall. Lukas doesn't so much as stumble. His hand shoots out, this time gripping my throat and lifting uncomfortably. My nails dig into his arms as I try to pry his hand from my throat. I gasp, trying to suck in any air I can. I stare into his beautiful storm green eyes, the tears from my own blurring my vision.

"Lukas . . . " I rasp out, my nails drawing blood.

He brings me closer, dragging my feet across the dirt toward him, his face now barely an inch from mine. There is absolutely no recognition in those beautiful eyes I love so much. I feel the heartbreak and rage bubbling up inside me, and my entire being begs to shriek out.

Lukas throws me backward without warning. I land hard on my back, and slide several yards through dirt and gravel. My chest heaves in the precious air, the muscles in my neck tender. I groan as I roll over and push up to my feet, rising slowly. Fuck. This.

I paint a smirk on my face, taunting, "That the best you got?" I may be exhausted to my core, but I will not give in. I refuse to let Hera win. To let her go on without suffering the consequences for her immortal lifetime of heinous actions. I will fight tooth and nail for Lukas. She can't have him. He is *mine.*

Bellowing, Lukas whirls to grab a spear from the rack then spins back, launching it at me. I force my breathing to slow, focusing all of my concentration on the spear. Time seems to slow down, drawing out the moment. I side step, and reach out, plucking the spear from mid-air. I follow through with its momentum, spinning on the ball of my foot, releasing it at just the right moment. It flies through the air, aimed perfectly for Hera's hideously beautiful head. If not for that *fucking* shield, it would have been her demise. I growl, baring my teeth at her, as loud gasps fill the air around me. Hera easily recovers from her shock, plastering a sardonic smile on her face.

Lukas snarls in response, the hairs on my arms raising at the promise of pain in the sound. He is not happy that I used his weapon against his master. He charges me again, and I allow my training to move through me as I block blow after blow, my eyes pleading with his.

"Lukas, stop!" I beg.

"Fight back!" he grinds out, enraged.

I grit my teeth, blocking another blow. "No."

I have trained with Lukas plenty of times, but I still can't compete with his size and strength. His next hit sends me sprawling across the ground. I push to my feet, swaying slightly. I feel the urge to shift rippling through me, and mercifully, an idea pops into my head. Thanks to Hera's spells, this will be hard, but if I can manage, it just might save us both.

Lukas stands across from me now, fists up and ready to strike as he tracks my movements. He must have been ordered to draw this out. To make a show of killing me.

Hera has somehow concealed her spell so that I can't see the threads, but that doesn't mean I can't still find a way to break it. Drawing every ember of my magic to the surface, I pour every ounce of my will and intentions into the shift. Black spots form in front of my eyes as I strain against the spell. A wave of dizziness hits me harder than I could have expected and I stagger forward a step. Gritting my teeth, I feel sweat bead across my forehead with the effort to remain focused on shifting. I can feel my skin as it begins to stretch, and my bones reform.

I close my eyes, focusing my breath to aid in the shift. The change is agonizingly slow this time, Hera's magic hindering my own. When I open my eyes, everything is clearer and my injuries feel a tad more bearable. I refocus on Lukas, who has stopped dead in his tracks, arms falling slack to his sides as he tilts his head, regarding me curiously, cautiously. I watch his fists clench and unclench with the war raging on in his head.

I bark out at him down our bond, *'Lukas, shift with me!'*

I try to get through to him, but a wall still blocks the pathway between our minds, our souls. I drop to my belly and crawl closer to him.

I can hear Hera shouting out orders, but I block out the sound, concentrating only on Lukas. I need him to shift. That's when I feel it; the pack. They are sending their strength to me through our link. Their unity, energy, friendship. I am not alone. I push their energy toward Lukas. His eyes flicker, and for a moment, hope fills my chest.

'Lukas, it's me, Nesrin.'

I watch as his body trembles, and I notice then as guards begin filtering into the arena.

'Lukas, you are stronger *than her. Block her out. Please come back to me.'*

I see it then. The moment Hera's compulsion breaks, Lukas's head tips back, a violent roar rumbling from deep inside his chest as he shifts, snarling and snapping at the swords pointed our way. I vaguely hear Hera's scream of outrage as she shouts orders to her guards.

Nikolas flashes to my side, the three of us turning our backs to each other so we can face off against this new threat.

'Sweetheart.' Lukas's voice floats down the bond, and I want to weep with joy and hold on to him, never letting go. But we have to get out of here first.

Instead, I settle on, *'It's so good to hear your voice.'*

The guards move as one, converging on us. With a sudden burst of energy, I pounce on the closest guard, tackling him to the ground. My anger overrides all else as I sink my teeth into his neck, just above his armor, shaking my head violently until I hear his spine snap. A wave of surprise ripples through the bond I share both with Lukas and Nikolas as I simply open my jaws and let the guard's limp body fall to the ground. Without hesitation, I spin on the next, the instinct to protect my mate sending possessive fury running hot through my veins.

I shift back, wanting to use my magic now that the containment spell has been broken. My magic crackles and ripples outward over my skin as a guard runs forward. I duck under the outstretched sword and spring up, kicking the guard in the back, sending him sprawling in the dirt.

Nikolas is a blur as he fights several guards at once. Lukas pounces on one, biting down on his neck. I hear the snap before he turns for the next. He is out for blood. I can feel his fury through the bond, and it only adds fuel to my own.

I spot a dagger on the ground and run to pick it up. I whirl back around and grunt with the effort to push away the next guard, my magic sending him tumbling. My other hand shoots out, dragging one guard from Nikolas to me. As I close my fist, the man falls to his knees in front of me and I drag the blade across his throat. Fresh blood sprays the air at the same time Nikolas snaps another's neck.

I throw my forearm up and a barrier forms between us and the remaining guards. Hera's face is a mask of fury staring down at us. In a blink, she is gone, only to reappear at the gate to the arena. Her stride is purposeful as she approaches. Lukas's rage bleeds down the bond and he lunges for her, moving beyond the boundary of my shield, his massive jaws snapping savagely. My heart leaps in my throat as Hera's hand flicks up and he goes flying backward. Lukas lands on his paws, sliding in the gravel until he comes to a stop next to me.

A flash of magic hits mine and I stumble, the shield blinking out for a second. I recover in time to re-erect another shield, and as I do, I feel a sharp pain steal my breath. I peer down, expecting to see something protruding from my chest, but there is nothing there. I glance at Lukas and see him crumpled on the ground, his agony causing me to falter.

'*Focus, ma reine.*'

He's right. His injury can't be the first priority. If I don't find a way to get us out of here, I won't be able to heal him anyway. I picture the large gates behind me and send my magic spiraling toward them. A blast booms through the arena as the gates are destroyed.

Through the dust and debris, Silver strolls in, lazily spinning her sword.

"Ready to go?" she asks as if this is an everyday occurrence, and smirks at me before surveying the massacre.

Nikolas picks Lukas up carefully, cradling him in his arms.

"Silver, can you transport all of us?" I ask.

"I'm offended!" she retorts, flicking her blue hair over her shoulder. She sheaths her sword and grabs hold of Nikolas and me. Hera's eyes promise retribution as I stare at her. I blow her a kiss as the world fades around us. I hear Hera's scream of frustration, and though I know we're not out yet, I allow myself to smirk, relishing in her anger. That smirk falters when I sense Lukas's pain fading from our bond. I try not to panic, telling myself over and over that it's just because we're between spaces, and nothing more.

We land with a thud outside our house. I double over, catching my breath. I watch as Nikolas gently sets Lukas down on the grass. My feet stumble as I race forward, falling to my knees.

I can't feel anything. No pain. No bond. Nothing.

Hysteria sets in, making it hard to breathe. I lift his head onto my legs, stroking his black fur. A sob catches in my throat.

"Lukas?" I croak, tears burning my eyes.

I hear commotion behind me as Zee and the others come crashing out of the house. But I ignore them as I hug Lukas to me, grief crashing down on me like a tidal wave. I shove my face into his black fur, letting the sobs come, letting my tears fall. Nikolas kneels beside me and rests his hand on my shoulder.

"Ma reine–"

"NO!" I shout, shaking his hand off me.

I bury myself deeper into Lukas's fur, hugging him even tighter to me. Until, suddenly, I feel that tug in my chest. That pull that lets me know my healing magic is preparing itself. I pull back, blinking down at Lukas. Shakily, I reach out and put my hand in front of his snout. I jerk back, looking at Nikolas in disbelief as white light erupts from me, surrounding Lukas and me unbidden.

I watch in awe as wave after wave of magic pours from me into Lukas, seeking out all his injuries. He may be injured and in pain, but that is *good*. Far better than the alternative. If he's in pain, it means he is *alive*. I can feel my tears tracking a hot path down my cold face. But I don't care. He is home, and he is alive.

His fur gradually changes to skin, and his chest begins moving rapidly with his ragged breaths. Strong arms reach up, wrapping around me as I watch the bullet slide free from his shoulder. The skin stitches back together behind it, the inky blackness vanishing from his veins. I pinch my eyes closed from the onslaught of tears. When I open them, Lukas and I are still surrounded by light. It slowly fades, and he sits up, pulling me into his lap. I grab his face and search his bright emerald eyes.

"Lukas?" My voice cracks on that one word.

"Freckles."

His hands sink into my hair and his mouth drops to mine, stealing my breath. Our heartbeats sync, and I can sense his beating right beside mine. He's okay. *We* are okay. We will win this fight. There is no other option. I won't give this up. His lips move over mine intently. I hear shuffling around us as a door bangs open.

'*Mommy! Daddy!*' Astraea's sweet voice shouts in my head.

We pull back to see her running down the steps straight for us. Both of us are covered in blood and dirt, but Astraea doesn't spare it any thought as she slams into us. Lukas's powerful arms wrap us both up in a warm embrace, his head dipping as he breathes in the sweet smell of

Astraea's hair, and we are content to sit here like this for a long time, none of us moving other than to whisper affection and lay kisses.

"Thank you for bringing me home," he whispers after a time, brushing his lips over mine.

"Always."

A sense of peace washes over me.

CHAPTER FORTY NINE

Zee and Sander help us inside and I want nothing more than to drag Lukas away. To go off somewhere, just our little family. But he is the alpha, and he has been missing for almost ten days. The pack—his friends and family—need to see him too.

"Nadia, stop fussing over him already." Blue's lips twitch slightly in amusement as he speaks.

"He was taken prisoner, Blue. I need to make sure he is okay," Nadia scolds, her blue eyes deepening with anger.

Blue's expression is apologetic. "I think it's time I take you home. Lukas is in excellent hands." Blue gives me a wink and mouths *'sorry,'* but I just smile and shake my head.

Lukas simply watches the older woman fondly as she busies herself, amused by her behavior.

"Fine," Nadia huffs, before turning to me and wrapping me in a warm embrace. "Thank you for bringing our boy back," she whispers.

Emotions clog my throat, and I simply nod, squeezing her back. Blue takes Nadia's hand and leads her out the door, but I'm pushed further away from Lukas as a few more people come in.

Astraea is still in his arms, refusing to so much as unwrap her little arms from around his neck. I can't say I blame her one bit for clinging to him, though. If it were socially acceptable, I'd be in his arms as well. But, as it is not, I stand off to the side as the others crowd their alpha.

I am still dressed in my leather outfit, earning a few curious looks. I stand at the back of the room, my eyes tracing Lukas's every move. Lukas's gaze flickers to mine. My breath catches the second our gazes connect, making my heart skip a beat. Lukas's gaze shifts away from me when another person steps up to him, breaking our connection.

I'm so immersed in watching Lukas, I don't notice Jameson as he comes to stand by my side. "Are you okay?"

I startle, surprised at being addressed, and my eyes dart to meet his. "What?"

Giving me a small smile he says, "I asked if you were okay."

My heart swells, and I have to look away. "You're the first person to ask me that," I whisper.

"Well, that's shit," he blurts, and I can't hide the slight pull on my lips, as I look back at him.

I sigh softly and shrug. "It's okay. Everyone's just so overwhelmed at having Lukas back."

We survey the room and Jameson bumps my shoulder with his. "Thanks to our kickass luna."

I feel my cheeks flush and I can't help but break into a gentle smile. "It was nothing."

"Bullshit. It was everything, and you know it."

I chuckle and rest my head on his shoulder. "Okay I was pretty kickass."

"That's better."

Gabe strolls over and pulls me into a hug. "You scared us when Silver whisked you away."

"She scared me as well," I murmur into his shoulder. Speaking of Silver . . . *where has she gone?*

Gabe steps back and grins, "Silver said she needed to get back to Faerie. Something about her commander being pissed."

My eyes widen as I recall the giant man with wings, what was his name? Raider . . . No, Raiden.

'*Ma reine . . .* ' Nikolas's voice floats through my mind.

'*Nikolas . . . where did you go?*'

'*I went with Nero.*'

'*Everything okay?*' I ask carefully.

'*It will be.*'

'*Thank you, Nikolas.*'

'*What for?*'

'*For everything.*'

There is a long silence before Nikolas responds.

'*You're welcome, ma reine.*'

A commotion outside draws my attention before Leila bursts into the room, her wide amber eyes locking on mine as she pushes through the crowd. She actually growls when Trevor doesn't move out of her way fast enough.

She reaches me and pulls me firmly against her, clinging onto me. "Zee called me. He said you were back! You need to stop, okay? Please, just stop."

Confused, I mumble into her hair. "What?"

"Disappearing. I can't take it! Next time, I will go with you. Promise?"

My heart thumps hard in my chest and my throat clenches with emotion.

"Promise," I whisper, gripping her.

Zee casually strolls over, stopping next to Leila and giving her a kiss on the head before sweeping me up into a bear hug. "Honey, she is right. I'm going to have to put a tracker on you."

"I second that," Sander says from behind him. My smile is instant as I pull away from Zee. I step forward, giving Sander a quick squeeze before going into Kyra's arms.

"You scared us all when you disappeared. Sander couldn't find any trace of you. I was so worried!" Kyra complains.

"I was in Greece. And Faerie, for a bit."

Kyra pulls back, her warm brown eyes widening.

"Well, slap my ass and call me George," Zee says, wrapping his arm around Leila's shoulders. I quirk an eyebrow at my sister, and she ducks her head, blushing. I smirk, lifting my eyes to Zee, and he winks back at me.

Shaking my head, I peer over at Lukas. A sense of longing hits me hard in the chest, causing an ache to start. I want to go to him, hold him.

Gabe senses my internal struggle and squeezes my shoulder. "Let's clear this place out. Our luna needs her mate."

"Gabe!!" I snap, my face heating.

Sander and Kyra chuckle. "No shame in needing your mate, luna," Sander says with a wink.

Kyra leans forward, giving me one last hug. "Please don't disappear on us again," she whispers in my ear.

"I'll try not to."

Kyra pulls back and keeps a hold of my shoulders. "I suppose the key word was *try*."

I chuckle and see that Zee, Gabe, and Jameson are rounding up the pack. Leila leans in, giving me another hug.

"We need to end this," she whispers.

"I know."

Pulling back, she smiles before turning and finding Zee. I wave to Finan and Kate, who are huddled in the corner with Roan and Alex. They have been sitting back like me, letting the pack reunite with Lukas.

My attention is drawn away when Gabe leans in, whispering in Lukas's ear, and for some crazy reason my stomach fills with nerves. Lukas's gaze lifts to mine. Those piercing green eyes hold me to the spot.

He adjusts a sleeping Astraea in his arms and addresses the room. "Thank you all for coming, but I need some time with my girls."

Protests rise all around, but Zee is quick to shut them down. "Let him rest!" Zee growls, ushering everyone out of the house.

'Jameson and I are patrolling tonight,' Gabe's voice says in my mind, easing my anxiety.

'Thank you.'

Lukas's eyes meet mine across the room and his ignite with desire that sends my pulse skittering. The leather suit begins to feel restricting as we stare at each other. Lukas turns abruptly, moving toward the stairs to carry Astraea up to her room. I follow behind, watching as he tucks her in, and swipes her curls from her face before softly placing a kiss atop her head. Malachite darts through the door, making me giggle as he bounds onto the bed, nudging Lukas's hand and face before curling up beside Astra.

Lukas straightens and backs out of the room, and I turn, walking down the hall into our room. I hear the door click shut behind me and then Lukas's hand grasps my wrist, my heart leaping at the contact. He spins me around before backing me against the closed door.

We're so close I can feel his breath brush over my face as he speaks. "Fuck, you're so beautiful. So perfect, so mine."

Before I can take my next breath, his lips are on mine. My legs nearly collapse with the sheer power of the kiss. And he tastes so good. My hands dig into his hair, pressing his lips deeper into mine. Goddess, I've missed him. Missed his touch.

'I missed you too, sweetheart.'

I didn't realize I spoke it into his head.

Lukas's hands trail down the length of my body. I can barely feel his touch through the leather, but the promise of it has me trembling. His hands squeeze my ass hard before pushing his rigid cock against my abdomen. His growls of desire make me even weaker in the knees. Lukas sucks on my bottom lip hard, nipping at it before pulling away. We are both panting wildly, the desire pulsing between us electric.

His hands raise to grab the zipper between my breasts, and he slowly drags it down, revealing my breasts and upper stomach, stopping at my waist. His fingers lightly drag back up, tingles spreading across my skin. He pushes the fabric off my shoulders sensually, tugging it down my arms.

"This is fucking hot. You are so sexy," he growls, gently nipping at my shoulder. My heart takes off in a gallop at his words.

Lukas drops to his knees and I draw in a quick breath as he kisses my stomach, tugging the suit down my body. He lays a kiss on each of my thighs as he removes my boots. I tip my head back, the sound of it hitting the door behind me echo's through the room. His nose runs along the seam of my underwear, and I pant. I hear the tear of fabric and I cry out his name as his mouth covers me, his tongue swirling over and over. Lukas grips the back of my leg, lifting it onto his shoulder, making me go up on my toes. I push my shoulders and head against the door as I rock my hips into his mouth. Sensations flood me, making my body heat. I don't know how much of this I can take. The need to feel him inside of me is overpowering. As if he's heard my thoughts, he growls against my flesh, his tongue slipping inside of me. Goddess, he is good at this. He seems to know my body better than I do. I twist my hands in his hair as he slides two fingers inside of me.

"Fuck," we both moan as one.

Lukas doesn't slow. No, he is driving me higher and higher. Licking, nipping, and sucking me to bliss as his fingers move inside of me. I'm trembling with the effort to stay upright. I moan as my orgasm rips through me, magic bursting outward, lighting up the room as my legs buckle. Lukas's free hand reaches around to grip my ass, holding me steady as he continues his onslaught. He slowly peppers kisses up my body, then devours my mouth.

Stepping back, Lukas shreds the rest of his clothes. "Fuck, sweetheart. I've missed you."

A spark of desire lights his eyes as he grabs my hips, guiding me to the bed. I lie down as he settles over me. Our eyes don't break contact as he rubs his cock between my legs. The friction builds there, and I think it might make me come again before he's even inside of me. Lukas's lips drop to mine in a long, deep kiss that sends my heart racing, my hands clawing at him, wanting him now. Lukas pushes up onto his hands, our gaze staying locked as he pushes inside of me. Our bodies move together, rocking into each other. I gasp as he picks up the pace.

Lukas's eyes flare, locking on my lips. Bending, he takes my mouth in the most beautiful kiss as he slides in and out, his thrusts becoming more and more. Everything in the world ceases to exist except us. Heart, body, and soul merge as one. Magic pours from us, light flickering about the room, hues of color dancing around our bodies.

Lukas's jaw clenches. "I want this every day. I want to be inside of you, claiming you, every damn day," his deep voice growls. His words push me over the edge. Wave after wave floats through me.

Lukas reaches down, lifting my thigh and hooking it on his arm, driving even deeper. He fucks me harder, my orgasm squeezing him tighter.

"*Fuuuuucccckkkk!*" he roars as he tenses, planting himself as deep as he can go before stilling.

Letting go of my leg, he collapses on top of me. Breathing heavily, I close my eyes, wrapping my arms tightly around him. I hold on as tightly as I can, refusing to let go. I won't ever let go again.

CHAPTER FIFTY

The following night, Lukas and I are standing outside Nikolas's mansion. I flex my hands nervously at my side before ringing the doorbell. Nikolas opens the door after a beat and I launch myself into his arms. He leans down, tucking me in his chest, returning my hug. I can feel Lukas's irritation through our bond, but ignore him. He has been extra possessive of me since his return.

"How is she?" I ask, pulling back and staring up at the handsome blonde vampire that I've come to love like a brother.

"Better. Her cravings have calmed down, and bloodlust seems to have passed. Which is highly unusual, given it's only been a few weeks. She has been asking for you."

I let out the breath I've been holding. I've been anxious to see Suzy ever since Nikolas took her bloody, torn body from my arms three weeks ago. Usually, it takes a new vampire months to get over their bloodlust, but Suzy has been different.

Lukas slips past me into the house, and Nikolas shuts the door. The three of us make our way through his large foyer into a sitting room.

A flash of movement catches my eyes as a blur moves down the stairs. Suzy draws to a stop at the bottom of the stairs. Her usually vibrant blue eyes are now glowing bright red.

Nikolas and Lukas both move to come between us, but I throw my magic out, freezing them in place.

Lukas's temper is hot and swift as it races down our bond. "Nesrin." He bares his teeth and growls, his arms trembling with restraint as he attempts to break my spell. But it won't work. He knows my spells are unbreakable, especially since he can now see magic like I can. Some quirky bonded mates thing we have.

"She isn't in control. I thought she could handle visitors," Nikolas explains desperately.

Ignoring them, I step forward and Suzy's eyes flash, the red gleaming in the low lights.

Lukas growls long and low. "Freckles, step back."

"Suzy?" I whisper hoarsely, taking another small step forward.

Suzy moves before I can take my next breath, surprise making me slow to react. Her body collides with mine and we both hit the floor, sliding into the sitting room. Suzy is on me the next second, her powerful grip pulling me up to my feet and her arms wrapping around my neck in a death grip. Her sobs reach my ears first, and I relax, bringing my arms up and holding her just as tightly.

I try to swallow my emotions before I release my spell on Lukas and Nikolas. I sense them moving closer, then further into the sitting room to give us privacy. We stay like this for a while before Lukas approaches us, causing Suzy to stiffen in my arms. Her head pulls back slowly and turns, snarling at the two men, her fangs glinting in the light. Nikolas's eyes widen and then flash silver, his answering growl one I've never heard him make.

Suzy's eyes drop immediately, and she rolls her shoulders inward. I don't like that. Not at all. I grab her hand in mine and pull her over to the luxury sofa. Nikolas really has nice furniture. All French provincial. It suits him.

"I'm so sorry," I say when we are seated next to each other.

Her head snaps in my direction, her eyes returning to their natural blue.

"No." She shakes her head, her purple hair flying everywhere.

"I stole your decision from you."

"Don't be sorry. It wasn't your fault, and you made the decision that would allow me more time. I could have chosen not to be turned. Nikolas gave me the options during the process and when I woke. I am grateful that you helped me."

I didn't know he had done that. I glance over to Nikolas, and he shrugs. It's a slight movement, but I catch it. Lukas is glaring daggers at Suzy, regarding her as if she were a threat.

'Knock it off,' I scold.

Lukas slowly turns his head my way. The smirk on his lips makes my belly flip.

'Or what?' he counters, silently waiting for my answer.

I have nothing, my brain momentarily frozen. *'Just stop looking at her like that.'*

Suzy breaks our silent exchange, taking my hand in her cold ones. "I will need your help."

"Anything."

"My brother." Suzy's voice drops and I can see she is trying to hold her emotions at bay. "He won't stop calling. I don't think I can see him yet, not by myself. I need you there to stop me if something happens."

I freeze and stare at Nikolas, but his face is unreadable. "Do you think it's wise to see him?" I ask.

"He said if I don't meet him this Friday, he's going to call the police. We meet every other week for dinner, and I've missed the last two. He's worried. There are only the two of us now, and he is protective."

"Okay, okay. We can sort something out. I'm sure it will be okay," I reply, rubbing her arm.

The front door opens, and Lukas raises his eyes to mine. The yellow flashing there tells me he isn't thrilled by the newcomers. Stephan strolls into the room, dressed impeccably as usual.

"Rose sauvage, so glad you returned from your travels safe and sound. And with your mate in one piece, I see." He flashes me a smirk. "That's too bad." He chuckles. I watch as Lukas's eyes flash in warning, his muscles flexing.

'Babe, you're the only one for me,' I sing sweetly through our bond.

He falters and his amused eyes flicker to mine. *'Babe?'*

'Yeah, it's finally decided.'

Suzy gently shoves my arm. "Stop flirting," she chuckles, and my face heats.

Goddess, I missed her.

"I missed you, too."

I tilt my head back to the ceiling on a sigh. The front door opens again, and I straighten as Nero appears in the doorway, a smirk on his face. He walks straight up to me, ignoring everyone else in the room, and lifts me off the sofa, squeezing me against his massive chest. Lukas's growl echoes through the space, making me chuckle. I pat Nero's shoulder, surprised he's actually fully clothed in jeans and a loose shirt. The only clothing he usually wears willingly is track pants.

He pulls back, and I watch the tattoos on his face move across his skin. It always fascinates me that they actually move. His hands land on my cheeks, drawing my attention to his eyes. "I'm so proud of you, daughter of light. You went in there and held your own."

"Yes, Hera is quite pissed. She's currently throwing a tantrum."

We all startle at the sound of Hades's voice coming from the bar in the corner. When did he get here?

"Now that I'd like to see," Nero chuckles, crossing his arms.

"It is very amusing. Especially because Zeus has no clue what it's all about. There is no way Hera will tell him she has spent centuries destroying one of his bloodlines."

"Why didn't Althaea tell him?" I ask.

I am curious about the politics of the gods. They don't seem inclined to go up against each other. The way they see it, they have pawns for that. I feel my anger rise at the idea of being used as a pawn to fight their wars.

Hades eyes flash bright gold as he pauses, considering me. "Althaea was in hiding herself. After getting Blanchette free of Olympus, she asked Hecate to hide her. Think she hoped for the out of sight out of mind approach. But Hera never forgets. After we took over from the Titans, a pact was made. We could not outright challenge each other or kill each other. All matters were to be discussed. As you can imagine, those discussions never went well."

"If someone"—I give a pointed look to Hades—"told Zeus, he could have stopped Hera."

Hades's rich, deep laugh is the only sound in the room. "Are you serious? Zeus is terrified of his wife. Plus, I assumed it was him doing it until recent events."

I glare at the god of the underworld. How can the king of the gods fear his own wife? Hades's face grows serious, looking down at the golden tattoos on my arms. "I see Hermes came through and got Athena to join your cause."

I glance down to my arm and rub over the marks there, "Yes. Athena said I'd have her backing me. That when the time came to fight Hera, she would help prepare me for the battle ahead. As the goddess of war, I can only hope she has an excellent strategy for me."

"For us, you mean," Leila amends, appearing behind me from her shadows.

Nikolas sighs and rubs his forehead. "Seriously, this is supposed to be Suzy's first small gathering, and now it's a meeting."

Suzy shifts uncomfortably on the sofa, her head cast downward. "I'm okay," she replies softly. I take my seat again and grab her hand in mine. Magic wafts from me to her, calming her nerves. Blue eyes shoot to mine in gratitude. I give a small wink and face the others.

"So, what's the plan? How do we stop her?"

Hades smirks. "Si vis pacem, para bellum,"

"You want peace, prepare for war." I frown, recalling my vision of the battlefield, all those magical creatures willing to die for my fight. That would not happen. I have to find a way to take Hera out without involving those I care about. I look to Lukas, then to the others around me that I love.

As I catch Leila's gaze, I feel a deep connection of understanding pass between us. We are determined to fight against Hera to the death, no matter what the cost. Together, we will merge dark and light to defeat Hera, a feat that would have been impossible to achieve alone.

CHAPTER FIFTY ONE

Leila and I meet down by the river, later that night when everyone was sound asleep, the sound of the rushing water providing a gentle backdrop. She has her back turned to me, watching the water. Her long red hair is intricately woven into a braid, contrasting my own, which I have hastily tied back in a ponytail. As she hears me approach, she spins round, her amber eyes taking in my all-black attire. I secure my dagger to my thigh and allow my pendant to glimmer between my breasts. Leila wears a similar leather suit, except it has no sleeves.

"How on earth are they so comfortable?" I ask.

My hands run over my waist and hips in amazement.

"Fae-made leather is actually quite comfortable," she chuckles lightly.

"Agreed."

I kept the suit Silver gave me to wear last time I faced Hera. She disappeared back to Faerie as soon as we were back home to help smooth over the bit of a stir I caused with Raiden, her commander.

She grins, but then we fall silent. "Are you ready for this?" I ask.

"As ready as I'll ever be."

Holding out her hand, I reach and grasp it. "Let's end this," I say, determination filling my soul. We will end this tonight. I close my eyes and summon my magic, infusing the golden symbols on my arms with it. Within seconds, they pulse with a response.

Opening my eyes, I watch as Hermes and Athena materialize in front of us. Athena is dressed in white robes, this time her long hair twisted into a soft braid. Hermes is in . . . I blink, thinking I must be seeing things, but nope, he's standing there dressed in a bright Hawaiian shirt and white shorts.

I shake my head and address them, "We're going to Hera. I want Hermes to take us to her private residence. He is the only one who can get us past her barriers, and Hades said you'd know the location."

Hermes and Athena glimpse at each other. It's Hermes who speaks first.

"Are you sure it's smart to go alone?"

"She won't be alone," Leila answers for me as she steps forward.

Hermes considers her, then me. He shakes his head in exasperation, his blonde hair falling over his face before he releases a deep sigh. "Okay. I will take you. But just so you know, I don't like this plan."

I feel his blue eyes pierce me, as if they are looking into my soul. "You need to be sure you're willing to do what it takes to win, because Hera will *not* let you leave again."

My heart races in my chest as I lift my chin and square my shoulders. It's time to end this. It is my responsibility to free all those cursed by Hera.

I see a glimmer of approval in Hermes's eyes as he nods.

Athena shifts forward. "This is wise. Take her by surprise. She won't be expecting you to show up at her villa . . . or alone."

Hermes genuinely looks worried, and Athena lays a hand on his shoulder. "It's a good plan."

Athena's eyes meet mine. "I will guard your pack lands. Nothing will harm those here. You both have shown true bravery. You, Nesrin, have lived up to everything the Moirae said you would be. A goddess of love, compassion, prophecy and protection." Turning her gaze on Leila, she continues softly, "And you, daughter of Hades, are a goddess of witchcraft and shadows, all things hidden and illusions. Both of you are strong and fierce, yet soft and kind."

"Thank you," we both say together.

"Just remember, even though this is a surprise attack, Hera is smart. She will be ready for anything. I suggest you combine your powers and use it to defeat her. She will not be defeated easily."

Hermes turns and links his arms with each of ours. "Shall we?" he asks.

"Let's do this," I reply.

Athena's voice floats over me, "Bono malum superate." *Overcome evil with good.*

"Hold on," Hermes warns as the world swirls violently around me. I try bringing my hand to my head, hoping to stop the spinning, but my limbs are heavy. When the world appears around me, I step away from Hermes and double over. Goddess, I really, really hate transporting. Portals are so much better.

When I recover, I see that we're standing in a large stone courtyard with a large fountain surrounded by a lush garden.

"This is where Hera's been hiding?" I whisper.

Hermes nods. "I know where the gods are at all times."

I turn to him. "Thank you."

His worried eyes study the both of us. "Are you sure about this?"

"We need this to be over," I reply.

With a long-suffering sigh, Hermes winks out of the courtyard.

All at once, guards burst in, surrounding us. I unsheath my daggers, sending my magic coursing into the blades. I don't take my eyes off the guards as they light up. Leila conjures her shadows, a dark whip forming in her hands. The first guard runs forward, but we're ready. I dive under the blade swiping at me, and engage the next man, leaving Leila with the first. I hear her whip crack and turn to see her shadows engulf the guard. Together we spin around the courtyard, keeping our backs to each other, covering each other. I fling three guards into a nearby wall and watch them attempt to stand.

Cold blossoms slowly in my chest, stealing my breath. I struggle to maintain composure as the feeling increases. Hera is coming.

The guard I'm fighting dodges my dagger, and I miss hitting his chest. But I manage an upward strike with my other dagger. Dragging the blade across his face, a thin red line follows. The guard pauses, bringing his hand up to swipe at his face. His eyes fill with rage at the blood. He bellows, charging me again.

His hand reaches for my arm, but I strike out with my light, sending him flying through the air. An electric current sparks across his limp form as he lands on the other side of the courtyard. I turn, looking for Leila, but find Hera instead. I growl and start toward her. Light ripples down my arms. She smirks, her arm shooting out to lift me from my feet and sending me flying backward. I slam hard into the stone wall. I hear more than I feel the stones cracking around me. Slumping to the ground, I struggle to catch my breath. My necklace seemed to have protected me from the hit. I have to thank Silver for this later. Hera sneers at me and I just bring my hand up and wipe at the blood dripping from my mouth.

"That's all you got?" I rasp, standing straight and squaring my shoulders. I want her anger. People make mistakes when they allow their emotions to take over. And I am counting on her to make one.

"Two against one is hardly fair," Hera clucks, flicking her fingers toward me. The air shifts, and Leila appears at my side.

"What? You scared?" I taunt. "Zeus and Althaea's bloodline too intimidating for you?"

At that, Hera's face transforms into something truly ugly. "You do not know how many of Zeus's lovers and children I have cursed or killed. *You* do not intimidate *me*."

For a moment, I think I might feel sorry for this woman. It must show on my face, because she laughs bitterly. "Don't feel pity for me, girl."

"We don't have to do this. We can just walk away. Make a vow and end this now."

I can sense Leila's hard stare on me, yet I can't tear my gaze away from Hera. Even though this isn't part of the plan, it also isn't in my nature to fight. Not like this. I desperately hope for a peaceful resolution. And I will take one if there is even a tiny chance we could end it without bloodshed.

Hera's wretched laughter echoes through the air as she tips back her head. The sound is like nails on a chalkboard, making my skin crawl. I can feel Leila's hand as it reaches for mine, and I clasp it firmly. The magic runs across our skin, binding together with an invisible thread. When Hera's eyes meet mine again, her disdainful sneer is unmistakable. There will be no truce. Not so long as she remains alive.

"Fine. We end this today," I growl.

Hera still doesn't know about Astraea, and I absolutely will not permit that to occur. Hera will not be leaving here. I would die to protect that little angel. As the feeling of acceptance fills my heart, the pendant around my neck begins to shine brighter. A tingling sensation spreads across my chest as our magic lifts and swirls around us. Our hands are clasped tightly. The pendant glows a brilliant blue and purple as the magic slowly moves over Leila and me, creating a sort of barrier.

One guard breaks rank and lunges for us, letting his dagger fly. Before either of us has a chance to react, the dagger hits my chest, falling uselessly to the ground. A ripple of magic moves over my body, as if it has only been slightly disturbed. I stare down at the dagger, its sharp edges gleaming in the light, before looking up at the man who threw it. I tilt my head, a smirk tugging at my lips, as I raise my free hand and send him flying backward into the fountain.

"Attack them," Hera orders.

I watch as several guards run toward us. Hera stands at the top of the stairs, smirking. My blood boils and I drop Leila's hand, reaching for my daggers. I whisper an incantation, feeling the power of the words on my tongue as my blades begin to glow purple. I duck under the swinging sword and swivel, slashing the guard's back. He hisses in pain, spinning on me. I hold the daggers in front of me, ready to strike. He charges, obviously thinking my tiny stature is easy to overpower, but I spin at the last second, coming around behind him again and stabbing him in both thighs. As he drops, I yank them free, stabbing one into his neck. Panting, I don't watch as he falls to the ground. I charm my blades to kill, so even a non-fatal wound will kill them. I turn and see Leila's shadows shoot out of her hand, wrapping around another guard, lifting him high into the air and letting him fall, taking out two others.

My body throbs with magic that saturates the air around us. I let it fill every cell in me until I can't even begin to tell where I end and it begins. It's an intoxicating feeling, a high I've never experienced before.

A growl rumbles in my chest and echoes through the courtyard as my vision turns white and my body hums, as if an electric current is running over my skin. Magic floats from me like wisps of light and embers. My gaze locks on Leila as tendrils of shadows and ash float from her. We are yin and yang; opposing forces that are interconnected. We balance each other perfectly, light and dark working together to create something truly wonderful.

Shouts reverberate in my ears as I feel a surge of magical energy coursing through my body. Glancing up, I am met with the sight of a monstrous creature, its wings spread wide and claws glinting sinisterly in the light of the full moon. I don't even need to think about it. My magic whips around me, writhing and striking out at the beast. It hits the creature head on, sending it careening into a group of oncoming guards; the impact sending them tumbling to the ground.

Leila and I stand side by side, our backs to each other, as the guards advance. Our magical defense is impenetrable, a barrier that nothing can break. We send guard after guard soaring through the air, before they get close enough to reach us. I pin the gigantic creature under a containment spell, its shrill cries echoing through the courtyard.

Hera's eyes widen in fear, all the usual confidence and cunning gone in an instant. Leila's shadows stretch and snake across the courtyard for Hera. Guards raise swords to attack them, but slice through nothing.

The shadows move more swiftly than before as Leila's magic coils around Hera like bands of steel.

I release the magical energy I've been holding. It bursts forth with a crackle, winding around Leila's shadows. Hera trembles in her restraints. All my emotions disappear as I stare at Hera. The world around me is smothered in white like a void; no color, no features at all. My pulse slows as I direct more magic into Hera.

Closing my eyes, I feel the warmth of magic radiating around me. Leila's voice echoes through the void, a gentle yet firm warning that it's too much. But the feeling of the magic and power coursing through her veins feels so exhilarating. I sense my magic extending, forming. When I open my eyes, I feel the familiar heat of the sword of light in my hand.

Slowly, I look up and tilt my head to the side, taking in the fear in Hera's wide, darting eyes. Leila lifts her hand, making Hera's feet rise from the ground, drawing her close to where we stand.

From the corner of my eye, I watch a guard shoot from the shadows toward us. Without thought, I plant my back foot and swing with both hands on the hilt of my sword. It easily slices through the guard, blood and gore splattering across Hera's dress and face. She flinches, but manages to keep her mouth shut.

Time feels as if it has stopped, and the air is infused with a magical, electric charge. The shadows bring Hera to a halt three feet away. Hera's eyes widen and her breath catches as she reads the intention in my gaze. Without wasting another second, I press the tip of my blade against her chest, drawing my arms back. I put all my weight on my back leg before transferring my weight to my front leg, thrusting the sword into her chest.

"You pursued me relentlessly. You targeted my family, and murdered those dear to me. You have done *everything* in your power to destroy my bloodline. Despite twice holding me captive and taking my power, you failed to achieve your goal. But you won't succeed in any further attempts. We're here to ensure that. I hereby liberate all those who have been afflicted by your jealousy and vendettas."

More of Hera's guards swarm into the courtyard. Some are not guards at all. Some are daemons. But Hera doesn't take her eyes from mine. Hera drags in a rugged breath, a small amount of blood trickling from her mouth as she speaks.

"I guess the oracle spoke the truth, after all. But if I go down, you'll come with me." Her eyes scan over her guards, sending them a silent order.

Growling, I push the sword deeper, feeling pressure building in my chest. Hera winces, pain lining her face as she glares back at me. Leila links her magic with mine, balancing the light inside of me. The sword pulses in my hands, wielding both light and dark magic. Blood roars in my ears and I tremble uncontrollably. Leila moves to press her back against mine, and I relax slightly.

We are immersed in a magical maelstrom of shadows and light.

Hera is fighting our magic with her own. She won't be as easy to kill as Eris was. I struggle against her power. Every part of me hums with magic, my hands tingling with a strange warmth.

Through all of that, I feel a brush against my mind, a gentle tug on the bond that resides deep in my chest.

Lukas is here.

How is he here?

Lukas and Zee burst into the courtyard, a snow leopard with them.

Beth?

My thoughts race as I attempt to understand what's happening.

How did they know where we were? How did they get here?

I catch a glimpse of white robes, but when I look, there is no one there. I growl. Athena must have brought them here. I watch as Nissa flies forward with at least two dozen sprites. Vines and tree roots rip free of the ground, spearing for the guards surrounding us.

I focus my attention back on Hera as battle rages around us.

I can sense Lukas and Nikolas trying to get through the bond to me. I haven't blocked it completely. But I have to finish this. Leila steps up to my side, and I look over at her. She can feel it, too. Our magic is draining us, taking everything we have to give it. Dark wisps lick at the edge of my awareness. *No.* I shake my head, trying desperately to dispel it.

If we want to end this, it has to be now. I let my power build as sweat drips down my face and my hands shake with the effort to contain the flow of magic. With my sword still piercing Hera's chest, I reach one hand out for Leila and pull, bringing her closer to me, resting my forehead against hers. "Whatever happens next, know that I love you," I whisper.

She pulls back, startled. "I love you, too."

I draw the last of my magic, infusing it into the sword, Leila doing the same. I battle against the combined flow.

We watch as Hera's eyes widen with shock, cracks and fractures appearing across her form still pinned in place by the shadows. Hera fights on, pushing back against our onslaught. Her mouth opens in a silent scream, light pouring from it. Dark shadows pour from her eyes and ears until we can no longer see her in a swirl of light and dark.

A throb of magic bursts outward, almost knocking me from my feet. Pain lances my chest, and I can't breathe. I close my eyes, my arms feeling heavy, then my arm drops. When I open my eyes, Hera is gone, nothing but a fading cloud of specks floating in the air.

Every part of me aches. The adrenaline burns through my body, energy giving way to fatigue as an exhaustion I have never felt settles over me. My world tilts sideways as we both collapse to the ground, hands still clasped together. Light fades around me, and in a swirl of shadows, Leila's red hair appears. It's come loose from her braid and is now scattered around her face. I try tugging on her hand, but mine won't budge. Nothing happens when I open my mouth. I try moving, but nothing. Panic doesn't set in. Only calm. Peace.

The last thing I see as my vision fades is the frantic expressions on Lukas and Zee.

Then my world fades to nothing.

CHAPTER FIFTY TWO

I blink my eyes open. I am lying on something soft and dewy. With my vision still blurred, I can't make out where exactly I am. My fingers curl, recognizing the feel of dirt and grass beneath my palm. The distinct scent of earth and salt from the ocean wafts over me. It's an odd combination, which only seems to confuse me more. I try shifting my position, but my body won't obey. My cheek is pressed to the damp grass, and I tilt my head back in effort to get a better look at my surroundings.

Where am I?

What happened?

I draw in a gasp at Leila lying next to me, our hands only inches apart. I grunt, struggling to close the gap between us. My fingers clench around hers and I squeeze.

"Leila." My voice is hoarse and rough.

There is no movement, no response. Her hand is cold under my touch.

Panic rises in me, my breathing becoming ragged. Everything feels cold, and painfully numb at the same time.

A slight breeze drifts over me, and I shiver as a chill moves up my spine. Suddenly, a pair of bare feet are in front of me. I try looking up, but once again, I can't. The person crouches down, face coming into view. Hermes.

He looks so sad, his eyes moving over me then over to Leila.

"What's happening?" I croak.

His eyes swing to mine, slightly flaring with emotion, "You're dying."

What? No.

I recall my vision and realize this is what I saw. The moment of our death.

"I'm sorry," he speaks. His voice conveys his words are sincere. Hermes has come here to carry our souls into the afterlife.

I can't die—*we* can't die. This isn't fair. We went into this knowing there was a chance we wouldn't make it out alive. But I still hoped . . . I feel tears leaking from my eyes and blink them away.

A glow lights up the sky behind Hermes, and he stands, turning.

"You shouldn't be here," he says to the newcomer.

"They are mine," the musical voice declares. *Althaea.*

"They are dying. There is nothing to be done," Hermes says, his tone soft as if he were a doctor giving a family member bad news.

Althaea's voice hardens. "There is always something to be done."

Hermes moves forward a step as if to intercept her, but Althaea's stern order floats through the air. "Move."

With a sigh, Hermes steps to the side and Althaea moves past him to kneel at my side. Her cool hands gently cup my cheeks, turning my face up to hers. Tears spring to her eyes as she takes me in. Her gaze shifts to Leila, a small crease forming between her brows.

"What's going to happen to us?" I try to whisper, the words sticking in my throat.

Althaea's eyes snap back to mine, a soft glow taking over the blue. They look like mine when I'm using my goddess magic.

"Nothing is going to happen to you, child. I will fix this. You and your sister will not die today."

Hermes steps forward, panic lining his boyish face. "Thea, you can't. You know what will happen."

Althaea's body lights up, her touch becoming warmer. "It is my decision."

I squeeze my eyes closed at the intensity of the glow. It's so bright. The flow of magic enters my body, its soft caress moving in wave after wave over my body. After a time, I feel I can breathe more easily.

I hear Hermes curse behind me, and I can just imagine him pacing, running a hand through that scruffy blonde hair. I can't suppress the smile that forms at the thought. Althaea's fingers stroke my cheeks, brushing away the tears I didn't realize were falling. I open my eyes and stare up at her. Her face is so gentle and serene.

"Take care of yourself and that little one. If you see my daughter again, could you tell her I love her?"

The warmth in my body is making me sleepy, but I nod. I struggle to keep my eyes open as everything blurs then fades. I seem stuck once more in the vast emptiness for what seems like an eternity. Floating on waves of air, I can still feel Althaea's presence somehow. Just knowing she's near allows me to rest easy.

The sounds of desperate voices begin to filter in, and I hear Lukas barking out orders. Then pull me into his chest. He strokes my hair, rocking me in his arms. Something wet hits my face, and I feel his body shudder.

'*Lukas?*'

Lukas freezes. "Nesrin?" his voice cracks on the one word.

I go to reply, but my lips won't move. I try opening my eyes, but I can't. My body is still healing. It's gone through a lot. I relax in my mate's arms. I am alive. That's all that matters.

Lukas

Primitive fear twists my insides. I have to get to her. Blood explodes in my mouth and bones snap as I jerk my head forcefully, ripping at the arm attached to a daemon.

My body locks up, everything in me fighting against what I see, what I feel. Shifting, I run over to her and fall to my knees beside her on the stone. Her long hair is scattered around her like a fiery halo on the white stone. Leila is lying lifeless next to her, Zee already lifting her into his arms. I reach out gently, brushing the hair from her face, and cupping her cheek in my palm. Her skin is paler than normal, and so cold. I feel something fracture inside of me; something I know will never heal. Grief strikes me hard in the chest and I shake violently with the force of it.

She wouldn't leave me. She can't leave me.

I dig my fingers into her and pull her body into my chest, everything in me sagging. I can't keep back the tears that fall as I try to hold back my emotions.

'Lukas?' her voice is soft and sweet in my mind, and I freeze. *Am I going crazy?*

"Nesrin?" Pain claws at my throat at the thought of losing her. I pull back, swiping my thumb over her cheek. Did I imagine her voice in my head? Grief sweeps through me again. But I feel it again, soft butterfly touches brushing against my mind and a small tug in my chest where our bond lies resting. I rest my trembling palm against her face and feel warmth. My heart stutters and I lean down, my ear resting over her chest, hearing the weak beat of her heart.

I jolt upright. "She's alive!" I roar.

Gabe and Finan are by my side in an instant. Gabe crouches down next to me. "She's gone, Lukas."

My growl is fierce. As I swivel my head his way, gripping his arm, I yank him down beside me and lay his hand over her mouth.

His wide eyes meet mine. "She's breathing," he whispers. Gabe shoots to his feet, frantically looking around. "Marcus! We need a healer!" he shouts.

"God dammit, sweetheart, open your eyes," I mutter around the emotions building in my throat.

'Lukas, I'm here.'

Her voice hits me like a punch to the chest, stealing the air from my lungs.

'Don't leave me, sweetheart. Help is coming.'

'I won't leave you.'

'You better fucking not. I'll never forgive you if you do.'

I feel a warmth in my chest blossoming into a strong sense of love and affection. I can feel her arms around me, as if protecting me from the world. When I lean down, her unique fragrance fills my senses. The sweet scent of roses, jasmine, and lilies, along with a subtle hint of coffee wraps around me, soothing the ache in my heart.

Marcus rushes over and looks down at Nesrin. Then Claudia comes, reaching for her. I growl, and her eyes fly to mine.

"Do you want me to help?" she snaps.

Reluctantly, I settle her down on the ground and watch as Claudia's hands roam over Nesrin. The witch falls back on her heels and sighs in relief.

"She will heal just fine. All the damage has been repaired. She's just weak, and needs rest."

Claudia's kind eyes meet mine and I let out a relieved breath, pulling Nesrin back into my arms. Finan's massive hand lands on my shoulder, squeezing.

Zee's startled voice sounds behind me, and I turn to see Leila stirring in his arms. It's a bloody miracle. One I don't want to begin to question right now.

CHAPTER FIFTY THREE

I can feel the warmth of his body around me, the steady beat of his heart under my ear as his chest rises and falls. I blink my eyes open, and slowly, carefully, take a deep breath. His scent surrounds me, filling my lungs. Sandalwood and rainforest.

"Lukas?"

His arms spasm and squeeze me a little tighter at the sound of my voice. I smile, burying my head deeper into his embrace, fingers curling around his shirt. I feel him draw one shuddering breath, and then another.

Pulling away, the brightest emerald green eyes are looking down at me, tears lining them. He closes his eyes briefly, a tear escaping. I reach up to swipe it away, and he captures my hand, turning it over and pressing a kiss to the inside of my wrist. I can still feel the tremble coursing through his body. I take hold of his face, my thumbs moving over his stubble. Leaning down, he captures my mouth in the sweetest kiss. One full of affection and tenderness. Our bond pulses between us; love and affection and relief flow back and forth along it. Lukas pulls back his hand, cupping the back of my head gently, as he stares down at me cradled in his arms.

"Never do that again. I swear to all the gods, I will tie you up, you'll never leave the house." Before I can plan a response, he buries his head in my neck, taking several deep, shaky inhales. I hold on to him and meet Leila's eyes across the courtyard.

We almost died—we were at the very cusp of death—and I think . . . Althaea gave her life force so that we would live.

Marcus brought two mages with him who could portal us out of here. Nero appears next, with Nikolas by his side.

"Ma reine," he breathes with so much affection I want to cry. Lukas stands, pulling me to my feet with him, but he doesn't let go.

"I'm sorry," I whisper, looking over Lukas, Nikolas, Nero, and Gabe. Leila hobbles over with Zee supporting her.

Nissa is suddenly right in front of me, thrusting her finger in my face, and I jerk back. "I can't believe you did this! How could you leave in the middle of the night?" The poor sprite is turning red, her wings fluttering wildly.

I smile affectionately. "I love you, too, Nissa." The sprite queen stops her rant and her mouth falls open, speechless. I grin. "Everything turned out fine. I'm here. Leila's here. Hera is gone."

The sprite looks affronted, crossing her tiny arms with a huff. Merve pushes through the crowd and wraps me in a tight hug, forcing Lukas to let go.

"My Nessy, what were you thinking?"

I wrap my arms around him. "Maybe I need to make a group announcement on how I'm sorry for making everyone worry, but not sorry we got this done without putting you all in danger."

A mixture of growls, grunts, and huffs fills the area. I glance over to Leila and hold out my hand to her. She takes it and falls into my arms. Lukas's arms are the only thing keeping us from hitting the ground. "I love you."

Leila sniffs. "I love you, too."

"Is it over?" Nikolas asks.

I glance at him over Leila's shoulder and nod. "Yes, she's gone."

Nikolas relaxes, and Nero rests his arm over his shoulders. Clearly, the two must have made up.

We pull apart and turn to face the group, Zee moving in quickly to hold Leila. The mixture of love and worry on his face makes my heart sing.

'I'm going to be so much more annoying now that you'll be my brother-in-law.'

Zee's eyes whip to mine. *'Two can play that game.'*

I chuckle lightly, and Lukas looks down at me. *'Care to share?'*

I reach up, stroking his face. *'Just teasing Zee.'*

Lukas's hand reaches up, grabbing my palm and gently laying a kiss to the inside of my wrist before his lips swipe over mine with the barest of touches. *'You scared the shit out of me, freckles.'*

'I scared myself,' I confess.

Lukas's arms wrap around me, lifting me off my feet. My legs go around his waist and the world fades as his hand sinks into my messy hair, bringing my mouth to his in a searing kiss. Hot fire whips through my body, setting my nerves on edge.

'Guys, maybe wait for the bedroom,' Gabe's amused voice filters through my lust-filled haze. Our breathing is labored as we separate, and his eyes are a kaleidoscope of greens and yellows. His emotions are high. He carefully lowers me back to the ground, his hands lingering on my waist. I hear a crunch under my feet and glance down. Pieces of the shattered pendant glint in the light as they lay beneath my feet.

I breathe in sharply as my fingertips brush against the jagged edges of the shattered stone. I raise my head to meet Nikolas's gaze.

"I'm sorry," I whisper.

Nikolas shrugs. "It did what it was meant to," he says, giving me a gentle smile. His response warms my chest, and I smile back. I still feel bad.

Nero turns and I look past him as Hermes, Hades, and Athena appear. Hades's eyes take in Leila, relief clear on his face. It looks like he wants nothing more than to go to her, but hesitates, unsure of her reaction.

In the end, Leila makes the choice for him, walking over and into her father's open arms. I smile as Hades's eyes meet mine over her head, the gold shining brightly.

"Well done. I can't say Hera deserved any less than she got. Still, Zeus will want answers," Athena says, coming to a stop next to Hermes.

Beth bounds over in her leopard form, letting out a long growl at the goddess.

I look to Lukas. "How is she here?" but it's Marcus who answers my question.

"She found the high priest as he fled. Her pack captured him for me. You were right . . . my father is gone. All that's left is the demon. The possession killed my father." Marcus's eyes ignite, his voice going gravelly. This is affecting him more than he'll ever voice. "She wanted to help, and who was I to say no? She owed you a debt."

Lukas kisses the top of my head. *'Astraea gave her the tick of approval.'*

The snow leopard sits between us and the gods. Taking a step toward her, I run a gentle hand over her head. "You don't owe me anything. But thank you for coming."

Beth pushes to her great paws and winds around my legs, then shifts. She stands in front of me, her brown bob sitting straight and sleek, and her kind brown eyes regarding me. "I wasn't sure how you would react. But when I caught wind of the awful thing moving through our territory, I couldn't allow him to escape."

"Thank you."

She bows her head and risks a glance at Lukas as he moves to my side, his arm wrapping around my shoulders, drawing me into his chest.

We look around the group. Leila and Hades are speaking softly between each other, with Zee watching closely, no doubt hearing every word.

Nero and Nikolas stand with Athena and Hermes, and Gabe is helping Jameson and Marcus, along with a few other witches, tend to the injured. I frown, not feeling a flicker of magic. My pulse kicks up.

'What's wrong?' Lukas and Zee ask at the same time.

'My magic. I can't feel it.' I step from Lukas, arms shaking my hands as if that would somehow kick start the magic.

'Sweetheart, calm down.'

'No!' I snap.

I stalk over to Leila, fear trembling through me at the thought of no longer having my magic. Not being able to heal my friends.

"Leila, your magic. Is it there?" I ask, interrupting her conversation with Hades.

"I–" Leila pauses. She flexes her fingers before looking to me in alarm. "No," she breathes.

I spin around, frantic and ready to call Marcus, when Athena steps over. "It's okay. You're just recovering. You both died," she explains with a gentle smile. "Your magic will take time to replenish. You haven't lost your gifts."

We both slump. The immediate relief that washes over the both of us is palpable. The very prospect of never again feeling the warmth of my magic in my hands sends a shiver down my spine.

"Well, daughter, I must leave. I plan to be there when Hermes delivers the news to Zeus."

Hermes whips his head to Hades. "What! Me?"

"Well, you are the messenger of the gods, are you not?"

"But–"

Athena rests her hand on Hermes's arm, silencing him. "We will all go."

Hermes regards the two of them and sighs in defeat. "Fine."

Hades turns to us. "You should all leave. No doubt Zeus will want to see for himself." Hades straightens his suit jacket and sends a charming smile our way. The three gods disappear before our eyes.

"Let's get out of here," Marcus says, walking over.

"How?" I ask, looking around. "Wait. How did you get here?"

Lukas chimes in. "Well, it seems Astraea may have had a hand in that. After Beth delivered the high priest to Marcus, he called. We couldn't find you or Leila and assumed the worst. Astraea had her sprites scouting, and they found Athena, who told us where you were. She transported Zee and I here. The rest followed her signature using portals created by two of Marcus's mages."

Leila and I share a look of gratitude. We've had so many people on our side. So many who would have done anything to see us win this fight and come out alive.

We still have a long way to go, but we accomplished our first task. We have removed the head from the snake. Hera is gone. The Order of Tartarus will be scrambling. And with Marcus's help, we can remove their claws from the covens, starting with the Shadow Lake coven. Marcus is now high priest, and he will have a certain pull over other covens. Then we will move into the council and petition for the rights of interspecies relationships and coexistence.

After gathering everyone around, Marcus's two mages, Peter and Nick, open two portals, allowing us through. Nissa and her entourage are the first to go. Nero has already transported Merve and Nikolas back to Nikolas's house, in a rush to get back to Suzy who has been left alone for too long.

Lukas's hand is firmly in mine as we step through the portal. Gabe and Jameson are right on our heels. I have a feeling these guys will not let me go pee without a shadow from now on. Once my feet hit the familiar ground, I sigh in relief.

I turn, facing Marcus and Beth. "Thank you both for everything. Marcus . . . I'm so sorry about your father. Maybe I could try healing–"

"No, it's too late for that," he interrupts me, shaking his head. There's nothing I can say that will take away his pain, so I remain silent as he steps forward, hugging me tightly. "I'm just glad she's gone."

I sink into his embrace. "Me, too. And thank you again."

"Anytime," he replies, squeezing me once more.

I'm about to pull away when a vision flashes behind my eyes. This one is different from the others. I'm only getting glimpses of the picture, like it's poor reception . . . *Dark hair, red lips, a dagger glinting in the moonlight. Then a sleeping Marcus in what I assume is his bed.*

I blink, stepping away. "Take care of yourself," I say, tucking my hair behind my ear as I look up, regarding Marcus curiously. Lukas's arms wrap firmly around my waist, and I lean into him.

'What did you see?' Lukas asks.

'I don't know.'

Marcus smiles and turns making his way to the other mages, Beth following him.

"Bye, Nesrin. I hope to see you soon," Beth says, sending me a cheeky wink, reminding me of our first encounter.

Marcus chuckles and waves. As he's now the high priest of the Shadow Lake coven, together Marcus and I are going to work toward changing the council laws forbidding hybrids. All should be free to love whomever we wish. We watch them as they open portals and step through.

My arms wrap around Lukas, and I groan, pushing up onto my toes so I can put my nose in his neck. I breathe in the smell of my mate, my husband, my forever. It's so good to have this over with. No more shadow hanging over our lives.

Turning, our small group makes its way to the house, the front door flying open as a head of blonde curls races out the door, a blue baby dragon right alongside her. Malachite lets out a tiny roar, his nostrils flaring and puffing with icy mist.

Astraea runs straight to me, and I pick her up mid leap, hugging her firmly against me. Kyra, Sander, and the boys push through the front door next, followed closely by Alex, Kate, and Roan. Gabe and Merve go past us and make their way up to the porch.

I stay where I am, soaking in my girl. I brace myself just before claws dig into my leg as Malachite scrambles up, and mentally thank Silver for the suit, otherwise I'd surely have scratches everywhere. He nudges the side of my face, resting his on my shoulder, his tail wrapping around my waist for support.

I know we haven't seen the last of the fae. There's still something they seem to want from us. Only time will tell what. Though I feel a little easier about it with Nero and Nissa with us. And Silver. We aren't friends, but we aren't enemies either. I'm holding out hope that she'll prove to be a good ally.

Lukas's hand lands on the small of my back, the warmth soaking through the leather. "Let's get you inside," he murmurs. I tilt my head back and smile at him. "It's good to be home."

Lukas grunts and I chuckle. I knew before we left that everyone would be furious over the decision Leila and I made, but I just can't muster any guilt. We made it back to them. Hera is gone, and those she cursed over the millennia have been freed.

There is a loud shriek from above, and a shadow passes over us. Talon lands in front of me, shaking his body and flaring his wings out. An excited squeak leaves my mouth as I hand Astraea to Lukas before dropping to my knees, embracing the creature. "Talon!"

Talon nuzzles the side of my head, almost shoving me on my back. I laugh, pushing my face into his neck. I soak in the warmth of my friend and laugh at the content sound he lets out.

I turn to my mate, my husband, and smile, "Look what followed me home. Can we keep him?"

Lukas's eyes are warm and I hear Zee snort behind me.

Smiling, Lukas replies, "I think we have to."

ACKNOWLEDGMENTS

When I sat down to write Nesrin's story, I was immediately drawn in and captivated by it. It consumed me day and night. Nesrin's story is a enchanting mix of Greek mythology and the beloved fairytale of Little Red Riding Hood.

I've always loved the story of Little Red Riding Hood, and I wanted to create my own version. I'm hoping one day to write where it all began, with Blanchette's adventure of finding love with the Big Bad Wolf- Leopold.

This story wouldn't have gotten this far without the help of my support circle. I have been able to accomplish more than I ever dreamed because of them, for that I'm forever thankful.

I wanted to convey my gratitude to Sanela and Catherine for responding to my countless messages, reading over chapters and brainstorming with me. My lovely cover artist Natasha, thank you for putting up with me. Bring on the next 5 covers!! Wink. Wink.

My editor, Marica, is an absolute blessing, and I can't express how grateful I am for her help and support.

I am eternally grateful for my supportive family and my loving husband, who listens to my aspirations and puts up with my endless chatter and stress.

I can't thank those who supported me enough. It fills me with joy that you had the confidence in me. Your kind and encouraging words that gave me the courage to keep going when I was feeling doubts.

Also a shout out to caffeine for giving me the motivation I needed to keep going, even when I felt like I had reached my limit.

ABOUT AUTHOR

Natasha is a new author based in Perth, Western Australia. She has had a lifelong love of reading, beginning in her childhood, where she would often immerse herself in the pages of fantastical worlds. Natasha's imagination would often take her on journeys of adventure, where she would dream of being a female knight, rescuing princes, running with wolves, and flying with dragons.

As she grew older, Natasha's passion for reading turned into a love of writing. She would spend hours crafting her own stories, drawing inspiration from the books that she had read as a child. Her writing reflects her fascination with the fantastical and her desire to create rich and immersive worlds that readers can get lost in.

Also by Natasha Madden

Finding Sanctuary Series.

Chosen by Destiny
Marked by the Gods
Night of Shadow and Death
Wicked Cravings
Fractured Souls

Crescent Moon Series

His Light in the Dark
A Spark of Madness

Fae Court Series

The Last Druid
Rise of the Druid Queen

Standalones

Savage Hero
To Kill a Nightmare